FIFTH GOSPEL

A NOVEL

ADRIANA KOULIAS

To Rudolf Steiner,
Who gave the world The Fifth Gospel,
And to the Good Men and Women of Montségur,
May we help you to keep your promises

First published 2012 by Zuriel Press Pty Ltd.

National Library of Australia
Cataloguing-in-Publication Entry:
Koulias, Adriana.
Fifth Gospel/Adriana Koulias
ISBN 978-0994611734
Cover design: Adriana Koulias, Adam Kenteroglou
Image: Nick Keevil
License: Arcangel Images

ABOUT THE AUTHOR

Adriana Koulias was born in Brazil and moved to Australia with her family when she was nine years old. She has a passion for Philosophy, History and Esoteric Science, and lectures internationally on these topics. Adriana has written three other books, all Best Sellers:

Temple of the Grail

The Seal

The Sixth Key

For more information

www.adrianakoulias.com

LIST OF CHARACTERS

MONTSÉGUR

Bertrand Marty - Bishop of the Cathar Church
Guilhabert des Castres - Bishop of the Cathar Church
Lea - Mysterious messenger
Marquésia de Lantar - Wealthy 'perfecta'
Matteu the Troubadour - Templar emissary
Pierre Roger of Mirepoix - *Seigneur* of Montségur
Raimon de Aguilhar - *Socio* of Bertrand Marty
Raimon de Parella - *Seigneur* of Montségur

PALESTINE

Yeshua's Family
Jacob the Nazarite - Brother of Yeshua
Jose - Brother of Yeshua
Joseph of Bethlehem - Husband of Mariam
Jude - Brother of Yeshua & member of the Sicarri
Simon Zealotes - Brother of Yeshua & member of the Sicarri

Mariam - Daughter of Anne, and mother of Yeshua
Yeshua - First son of Joseph and Mariam

Jesus' Family

Cleophas - Brother of Joseph
James the younger - Son of Cleophas and Mary
Jesus - Son of Mary and Joseph
Joseph of Nazareth - The Carpenter
Mary - Mother of Jesus
Mary Cleophas - Wife of Cleophas
Salome - Servant of Mary

Male Disciples of Christ Jesus

Andrew - Son of Jonah
James the Elder - Son of Zebedee
James the Younger - Son of Cleophas
John - Son of Zebedee
Judas of Cariot - Known as Judas Iscariot
Jude - Stepbrother of Jesus
Lazarus - Brother of Mary Magdalene
Matthew - The tax collector
Nathanael bar Tolomei - Otherwise known as Bartholomew
Philip, a fisherman
Simon-Peter - Son of Jonah
Simon Zealotes - Brother of Yeshua, and stepbrother of Jesus
Thomas the Twin - Cross-eyed merchant

Female Disciples of Jesus Christ

Joana Chuiza - Wife of a Captain of Herod
Leah - A widow
Magdalena - Otherwise known as Mary Magdalene
Mariam - Mother of Yeshua
Mary - Wife of Cleophas
Salome - Midwife and servant

Suzanna - Servant of Claudia Procula

Hebrews

Ananias - Father-in-law of Caiaphas

Caiaphas - Head priest of the Sanhedrin

Herod the Great - King of Israel

Herod Antipas - Son of Herod the Great

Herodias - Wife of Herod Antipas

John the Baptist - Nazarite, son of Elisabeth and Zachariah

Joseph of Arimathea - Israelite Pharisee, member of the Sanhedrin

Nicodemus - Israelite Pharisee, member of the Sanhedrin

Salome - Daughter of Herodias

Romans

Abenader - Roman Centurion in charge of Crucifixions

Anius Rufus - Roman Procurator

Claudia Procula - Wife of Pontius Pilate

Gaius Cassius Longinus - Roman Centurion, Initiate of Mithras

Pontius Pilate - Roman Procurator

Septimus - Roman Sergeant

AUTHOR'S NOTE

In German the word Minne comes from the Gothic word Munni, and means a remembrance or memory of love. Minnesingers, Troubadours and Bards were the keepers and finders of the memories of love, of the mysteries of the soul and spirit, those eternal truths that have always existed even before the world was capable of understanding them. Their 'songs' disseminated these truths in a way that was acceptable, in preparation for the future. This book longs to be such a 'song' and to disseminate such truths. The vessel may be a fictional one but the content is a mystical fact given to the world by the great philosopher Rudolf Steiner.

Having said this, I leave the reader entirely free to test this song's veracity by turning the page, for as Novalis tells us:

The empire of love is open,
The fable starts to unfold.

CHAPTER 1

MEETING LEA

Montségur, France, 1244

I am not a troubadour and yet I sing. I am a bishop and yet I do not belong to any church. I have come by what I know by way of ignorance, and what I possess is mine because I am dispossessed. That is how I have arrived at who I am – by sacrificing certainty.

But who am I?

I am old. I do not imagine myself old, no, but when I look at my hands I see they are veined, when I feel my face I know it is full of creases, and when I walk I am reminded that my joints are not always prepared to follow. Alas! I have lived long enough, near fifty years, without mishap, and I dare say I should have lived many more had destiny allowed it, but it has not. It has set me upon this difficult journey and will lead me on until I reach that place which you shall know in the end, if my tongue does not betray me before then.

But what was I saying? Oh, yes…I am old, and growing old means that I have watched my friends die, and the foremost of them was my *socio*, Guilhabert de Castres. Oh … I miss him like I would miss a leg or an arm! I can still see him so vividly: short, squat, with small hands and feet, a rounded face that wrinkles when he smiles, close, sharp eyes that see only the goodness in everything, and a jaw that juts out as if it were made of steel, a signal of his strong will. In fact his will was so determined that he never tired. Even in his later years, when we travelled all over Languedoc on our nocturnal rides to secret meetings, or on journeys from one village to another, he walked always with a certain rhythm, his back as straight as a rod and his head pointing the way.

In those days I was tall and muscular, and yet I was always amazed to see him climb the steep and arduous path to the pog, our mountain of Montségur, with ease, smiling and joyful to arrive at the top, while I puffed and grumbled with every step and trailed behind him, red faced and fatigued.

As I descend this same path now, keeping my mortal appointment with God, I think how fitting it is that Guilhabert has missed this end of ends! When I think of it tears fall from my eyes. They are falling now, and I wipe them with a hand as I pause to look up. The sky is yet dark and I am looking for the sign. It should come from the summit of Bidorta if all goes well. Ah! I feel a pang in my heart to think on the alternative, but the bee, this little creature, which has been buzzing around me for some days, has come again to cheer my spirit. The little sun being leads the way that descends and winds over these frost-covered stones. It reminds me of my promise and helps me to sow into my soul the happenings of those days and to weave everything into a song.

Those who walk with me have their own songs to sing, their own memories to store away: songs of children and husbands and lovers and life. I sing to remember the Gospel, and my song begins on the night Guilhabert died.

The week we were due to return to the fortress of Montségur, Guilhabert fell sick with a fever. I had some knowledge of herbs and berries and roots and tried to affect a cure, but, alas, I was not successful. For three days Guilhabert lay on his death pallet covered in a sweat. I sat by him, dozing now and again, waking up to wipe his brow or to pull more blankets over his shivering form, while outside our cave the wind whistled and moaned its dire omens. On the fourth night Guilhabert seemed better and I told him that if the worst should happen I would suffer the Endura, the sacred fast of our faith, in order to follow him into death desire-less and full of joy. But Guilhabert was not pleased by this, and gathered what strength he had to reprimand me.

'What madness you speak, boy!' He looked very hard at me, with those clouded eyes stabbing at my soul. 'Come closer and listen to me ... stop thinking about the Endura, you have something yet to do ... I know this because I have seen the future and I am returned from it to tell you something of great importance.'

Out of respect for his venerable person I tried not to betray my disbelief. 'When did you see the future, master?' I asked.

'When I was gone, when I thought I was finally finished with this carcass! Come closer ... why do you sit so far? I lose my breath! That's it! Lean in so that I can whisper. I will talk plainly ... I am dying, and dying men must speak plain.' He waved an impatient hand to forestall any words of hope. 'Come now! There is no time to skirt around the truth!' He gestured for me to sit him up and I did so, holding him in my arms as he spoke, his voice so low I had to bend my ear close to hear it.

'Firstly, we have been together ... what?' he rolled his eyes into his head, calculating. 'Twenty years? Yes, twenty years! And in all that time you have served me well, and I have never knowingly hurt you, I hope. But I must ask you now for your forgiveness, ahead of time, for what I am about to ask.'

I could not imagine why he should ask me for forgiveness and I told him so, but this occasioned a tempest of annoyance.

'You were always a querulous one, Bertrand! Always wanting explanations! Well then, I will tell you why. What I am about to ask will lead you into peril! It will cause you much heartache, there is no getting away from it. And though it is God's will, I ask your forgiveness for it ... since I do not wish to leave this carcass with a bad conscience.'

This was more a command than a request, and yet I would have forgiven him anything. I told him this and he said,

'That is good … that is good. Oh, Bertrand, just an ordinary man you look to others but not to me. To me there is more about you than appears on the surface of that face. That is why you were chosen, you see? And why I must now ask this next thing of you! Listen … when I die, you must go to Montségur as we planned. When you get there, look in the library until you find the Apocalypse of John … look for chapter twelve, where John speaks of the woman with the moon at her feet, the sun in her belly, and the stars crowning her head. That is what you must do … after that, let the light of wisdom guide you to love, like a bee is guided to a rose. For only love will open your eyes, and when it does, God-willing, you will know who you are and what you have to remember … that is the important thing – you must remember!' His old eyes grew wide. 'Tell me you will do it, dear Bertrand, tell me so that I can die in peace! Come, quickly!'

In that moment between question and answer, I hastily considered two things: I had seen how a fever could stupefy the mind of a sick man and cause him to speak nonsense, in which case I would be promising to do something that had no sure footing in truth; but, on the other hand, some men returned from the portals of death with a species of knowledge, and to fail to heed them was known to be a sin. As I looked into those loosening eyes, trying to decide which of the two seemed more likely, I realised that it did not matter one way or the other, for the promise seemed of so great an importance to Guilhabert, that my failure to agree might cause him to die of grief.

I made a nod and he sank back into my arms, calmer now. His eyes grew distant. 'There, there Bertrand, dear boy … don't be sad. There is a moment between sleeping and waking, between dying and living, when there is no sadness … it is a moment of becoming … I am sore-glad to return to it …'

I smiled a weak smile and he matched it.

'You do not understand, Bertrand, I know. How could you?' he said. 'Soon … soon.'

He turned his head slightly and his body shuddered and, like that, he gave up the ghost, dying in my arms.

I sing now how I mourned my friend, how my heart ached when I buried him and how lost I felt when I packed my meagre belongings and set off with my little mule for Montségur, alone now for the first time in twenty years.

Along the way, as I dissolved into melancholy, my mind returned, over and over again, to the promise I had made. However, the more I thought on it, the less I understood it. I was to go to the mountain to look for John's Apocalypse, in which I would find the part that speaks of the woman crowned with stars, with the sun in her belly and the moon at her feet. I would then let the light of wisdom guide me like a bee seeking a rose, and somehow my eyes would open thereby to who I was, and to what I had to remember – whatever it was!

Oh my.

That was four years ago, and since then I have lived in a rough lean-to constructed of wood, located on the outer walls of the fortress of Montségur.

In many ways these intervening years have been fruitful. I was made a bishop in my own right and was given many responsibilities to attend to. This new position not only demanded that I visit nearby villages in order to see to the spiritual wellbeing of the perfects who lived there, I also had to see to all the celebrations of the rituals of our faith in the fortress, as well as keep an eye on the instruction of the many children brought there by believers.

In all my doings I tried to resemble a bee that seeks here and there for its rose.

One year passed, then another, with so little harassment from the inquisition that even I began to grow a hope that the war was over, that soon we would see the shimmering light of the heavenly Jerusalem descending upon us. But that was before spring came and those feelings of foreboding washed over me as I stood upon the edge of the pog, looking out at the great expanses. But I would not understand my presentiments until Ascension Day, for that was the day that

Pierre Roger of Mirepoix, one of the *seigneurs* of Montségur, arrived at the fortress looking pleased with himself.

Flushed with excitement, and light in his step, Pierre Roger came directly to my hut to tell me of the great news. It seemed that he and his men had carried out a task on behalf of the Count of Toulouse, a task so grand that the people would celebrate it for a long time to come. But when he told me what it was I was fell into numbness. They had crushed in the skulls of several inquisitors at Avignonet and had stolen all their inquisitorial records!

'I would have drunk the wine from those skulls,' Pierre Roger boasted, 'had they not been smashed to pieces!'

Oh, I was very fearful for the people of our faith! Not only for those who lived here at the pog, but also for those on the outside who would bear the coming wrath of the Catholics and their Pope. Gone was the heavenly Jerusalem and come again was a vision of the beast rising up out of the waters.

I told him I could not sanction his bloody actions. 'One should suffer for one's beliefs, Pierre Roger, not kill for them!' I reminded him.

But he did not listen. He waved a hand at me and said, 'That is why I am not a perfect, *pairé*, but as imperfect as any man might be, so that I can do the bloody deeds that are necessary! Besides, the young count has promised to come to our aid with the help of Aragon, and soon we will take back our *paratge* ... Think on it, *pairé*! How free were our people before these troubles!'

Yes, our *paratge*! Our way of life, our right to worship and live as we pleased! I did not share his hopefulness. I had seen the ire of the Roman Church before, and the pyres that had blackened the skies for near forty years. I also knew the temper of our vacillating Count of Toulouse, who, like his father before him, could not decide which side to take. And so that evening, when there was great rejoicing in the fortress, food and wine and merry-making, I was alone with my prayers in the room at the top of the keep.

But the merriment did not last, for soon a shiver ran over the spine of the mountains warning of the coming of the French army. Not long after that the army itself arrived: ten thousand men singing crusading songs were pitching their tents and bivouacs, and assembling their catapults and mangonels on the *Col du Tremblement* below us.

That, you see, was the beginning of the siege of Montségur, of which you may know something in your time, and the end of our *paratge*.

The protracted siege continued through the summer and the dry season, but we southern people have grown used to hardship, and so we managed to survive cooped up in our small fortress. Each day when I walked about the inner court it seemed more crowded with knights and noble ladies and men at arms. Three hundred were now living on this little patch of rock, blown by the wind and battered by rain. Many had come by way of the secret eastern path to offer their skills to the garrison, or to help defend their friends, and if necessary, to die with them. I wondered how long our food would last and more than once mentioned it to Pierre Roger. He took it lightly and said the siege would soon be over. The French were weak and not used to discomfort. He was certain they would not countenance one of our winters, lying frozen to the bone under flea-ridden blankets!

Even so, whenever I went to the ramparts to take a look at the encampment below, I saw more soldiers and tents and siege engines. No, I told myself, the French had not come for a season. They had come for as long as it would take to bring down this fortress, the last bastion of our faith, a faith that the Roman Church had declared heretical.

Autumn had not passed quickly and those messages of support that came now and again from the Count of Toulouse were a welcome diversion. I kept my uncertainty to myself. I feared that these messages falsely raised the hopes of the people of the fortress, and waited to see what would happen. The messages came to Raimon de Parella by way of his brother, the Templar Preceptor of Montsaunes, whose preceptory formed part of a network of secret messengers created during the early years of the war. Through these, news came and went by way of troubadours, and ours was a man called Matteu.

I owe much to Matteu, a man I have known for a long time. If I am honest, I must say I have always envied him a little, God forgive me, because for him it was possible to live life to the full while possessing a willingness to die without a fear in the heart. This has lent a certain poignant tenor to his songs; songs of journeys to far off places, and of unimagined adventures, which greatly entertained the old people, brought a blush to the faces of the young girls, and fired up the courage of the lads, who for days afterwards repeated his tales, acting out those parts which amused them.

Sometimes he sang of something called the Grail – a stone struck from Lucifer's crown, a stone of the greatest beauty and purity, that had the power to bestow eternal life. At other times he sang of the bleeding Spear of Longinus, the spear that had pierced the side of Christ and was said to make any man who held it a king. I considered songs that spoke of eternal life and kingship contrary to our faith, and often told Matteu so.

But what is our faith?

Looking back now I realise that we are no better than our enemies. Like them we have only known one half of the truth, though we have defended it differently: we have been willing to die for ours while they have been willing to kill for theirs.

In truth, in that far off future in which you live, our faith will not be understood, since only the interpretations of our enemies will have survived and so, I beg your indulgence, for I will sing to you a little of the tenets of our beliefs, and how at Pamiers, in civilised debates, we explained our doctrine to the representatives of the Roman Church.

In those days, sitting beside Esclarmonde de Foix (that great lady perfecta) I listened as Guilhabert told the Catholics how Satan had created the world and all its creatures, including man. I smiled to myself to see their faces as he explained, with unequalled equanimity, that a Son of God could not, therefore, have entered such a world to live in the corruptible body of Jesus. I held my head high as he pointed out to them that this meant three things: that Christ, a God, could not have died on the cross; that Jesus' body of corruption could not have been resurrected; and that his mother, being only a woman, could not be called the Mother of God.

The Romans were aghast and incensed, for these tenets formed the very foundation of their faith!

As far as I could then see, the entire argument revolved around the difference between two words – similar and same. We Cathars believed Jesus was only similar to Christ – while the Romans believed Jesus was the same as Christ.

That is one reason why the Romans feared the Cathar Church and persecuted it, but there is yet another, a ritual called *Consolamentum.*

The Romans believe this ritual to be evil, because alongside the arguments of *similar* and *same,* came the arguments of *through* and *from* – which began in the 3rd century, and concerned the origins of the Holy Spirit, whom we call the *Consoler.* I will not dwell on these arguments, for they were many and varied, but I will tell only as much as can help you to understand how they have led to our present troubles.

Some time ago the Roman Church decreed that a man could not have a spirit at all – despite the assertion that the man Jesus had become one with the spirit of Christ! Since then, any man who dares speak of a *human spirit* is threatened with excommunication, and is pronounced to be 'anathema' which means, cursed by God. Our faith, on the other hand, argued that the spirit can be conferred on any man by way of the laying on of hands – this, despite *our* assertion that Christ's spirit could not have entered into a man's corruptible body!

Do you see how subtly, imperceptibly, each side has fallen into error? Each forming from out of the small and intricate contradictions of the past an erroneous foundation for new and more confusing contradictions in the present, until no man in the future will know if the ground he stands upon will collapse into an abyss!

Oh my! The foolishness of knowledgeable men! And I should know, for the Lord God has given us each a weakness and the foremost of my many weaknesses is that I have always considered myself a man of learning! Yes ... I may have sacrificed the love of a woman, marriage and children, meat and eggs and milk, and a wondrous life singing songs like my friend Matteu, but until recently I had not, God forgive me, sacrificed my thirst for knowledge. In truth, night after night I had dreamt of a great library that expanded to infinity and in which there were not a thousand manuscripts but one great book; a book that held the answers to all questions of religion – a book that could prove to the world the veracity of the one true faith: ours, of course!

What a pleasant dream! But I was speaking of the debates and how the years passed. Yes, each side could not convince the other and this eternal round of argument continued until one fateful night, near forty years ago, when a papal legate was murdered. That is how ill begets ill, for such a crime gave Pope Innocent, a cannon lawyer before he took up the keys of Peter, the pretext he needed to convince the French King of the lawfulness of a Crusade against us.

Fight the heretics and rob them of their lands and their goods! Those who take up arms against these plague-ridden un-believers will be granted heaven by God!

Ah, but the men of the south are proud! They would not be cowed and took our part, and have defended us ever since, paying for their loyalty with the slaughter of their citizens, the sieges of their castles and the burning of their friends and relatives – God bless them. That is why a small part of me cannot blame the vassals of Pierre Roger for killing those inquisitors at Avignonet, even though it has set me upon this path, which you shall soon know, for you see, now that I have an understanding of everything, I realise that it could have been no different, and to illustrate this, I will sing of the night I met Lea.

It was midnight and all was quiet after a day where nothing was heard save the pounding of shots from below and the shouts of the soldiers from the parapets. Seeking solace, I came again to the meeting room situated at the top of a long set of circular stairs in the keep. It was my custom to come here on sleepless nights so as to read from the contents of our sizeable library. Here, I could read not only the precious writings of the fathers of our church, but also a number of ancient texts brought over from Syria and other far off places. This night, mindful of Guilhabert's request, I was engaged in copying the Apocalypse (that part which speaks of the woman standing on the moon with the sun in her belly and the stars crowning her head) onto some parchments that I had prepared, when I heard a noise, no more than a whisper of a sound.

There was a small fire in the hearth and only a meagre light from my candle and so when I looked up I saw only a shadow standing outside the threshold of the room. When the shadow stepped into the lighted space I realised that it was a young woman. As far as I could tell she had azure eyes, wide-set and shining beneath fine curving brows, in a face that was moulded into a serious expression, as if she were a pure child, bruised by a cruel world. I dismissed this fancy and set down my quill and rubbed my eyes, for surely I had fallen asleep and was dreaming.

'What is it, my child?' I asked her.

'I would speak with you, *pairé,*' the dream answered, in a quiet voice, 'if that is permissible to you.'

I gestured to a place near the fire and her eyes flickered past me to an ample bench. As she walked to it, I had a moment to observe her better.

She was small of frame but the slender neck carried her head well, and this gave her an air of nobility. Her hair was the colour of wheat and tumbled in curls from beneath a clean napkin, framing a face fine boned and fair. She seemed neither young nor old, like every woman and yet not like a woman at all. Perhaps, I mused, she was a goddess trapped in the body of a woman, or an angel of mercy come to take me to my death! Whoever or whatever she was, she seemed to be touched by a recollection of the divine, by a memory of the soul before it fell to earth and entered into a corruptible body. And so, when her gaze returned to me, my old heart gave a leap.

Quite irrationally, I thought:

Here stands the very limits of blessedness!

Well, that was something new to me. How such an illogical thought had found its way into my dream I did not know, but I tried to dispel it by turning practical. I would treat the dream as if it were real and perhaps this would entice it to disclose its message.

'Who are you, my child, the daughter of one of our perfects … or a believer?'

The shaking of her head was almost imperceptible but her eyes were steady, each perfectly matched in the spirit of a disconcerting purpose.

'Who in this world can truly call themselves perfect, *pairé*? And what good is belief if one does not have eyes to see?'

These words confused me. My back was stiff and I rubbed it, my thin legs had gone all pins and needles, and my head, for its part, felt like a feather blown by the wind. By these incontrovertible signs I discerned that I was not asleep but very much awake and this made me full of vexation. For how could this girl think herself capable of speaking to a venerable bishop as if he were a simple minded man in need of instruction?

I cleared my throat. 'If you do not trust in perfection,' I said, sniffily, 'nor set much store in belief, why have you come to speak with a *perfect,* a believer?'

'To show you something ... if you wish to see it.'

She waited with an exaggerated patience for me to say something in response, but I did not know what to say, so I leant on the staff of procrastination,

'Can it wait till morning, my dear? My head is light and I shall soon faint from exhaustion.'

'Secrets are best shown in the night,' she said, emphatically. 'Both Orpheus and Virgil knew this.'

Secrets? Orpheus? Virgil?

'What sort of secrets do you mean, my child?'

'Have you heard, *pairé,* of such a thing as a *Libro Secretum?*'

I sighed. Secrets and books were nothing new. There were books locked away in the repositories of many monasteries, hidden from the eyes of the inquisition, such as those kept in our library; books that did not agree with the dogmas of the Catholics and so were deemed heretical. But what could such an elfin girl know about books in any case? Books were precious and not easy to come by, moreover they rarely fell into the hands of women, as few women could read.

'Is your secret that you know this book exists?' I said, peering at her.

'No ... there are many who know that it exists, though it remains unseen.'

'But you said ... didn't you just say that you have seen it yourself?'

'I see it always, *pairé*. In truth, anyone may see it.'

My faculties were bewildered. I changed my mind again – this was no woman, this was a dream apparition, and a curious one at that!

'If anyone can see this book, then it cannot be a secret,' I pointed out quite logically, knowing that this would surely wake me up, since logic had no place in dreams.

'This reasoning is reserved for ordinary secrets,' she said, with a polite smile, as if she had read my mind and would put it to rights. 'But this is not an ordinary book which I shall show you. Reason cannot explain it, only philosophy.'

Philosophy! A love of wisdom! I was pricked in my heart! This word recalled to mind my promise and I sat forward with attention. 'So, when you say it is not an ordinary book ... what do you mean?'

'It is a book ... and no book at all. It is invisible ... and yet it is visible to any man, for it is everywhere and nowhere at once. It lives in the very skies, in the cloud libraries of God, but it also lives in the memory of the heart. The question is, do you want to see it, *pairé*?'

What strange riddle was this? A sudden terrifying thought assailed me. Perhaps she was a sphinx? Would she kill me if I gave her the wrong answer? No, soon I would wake up, I told myself, with my mouth dry and my back aching, for I had fallen asleep thinking again of that infinite library and that book which encompassed all the knowledge of the world.

Having read in some place (who knows where?) that one must ask an apparition its name if one wishes to dissolve it, I did so.

She answered, 'Who I am is of as little importance to what I will tell, as the wind is to the perfumes that it carries. But you can call me Lea.'

What a singular dream creature was this that sat before me, with her face so poignant and wise, her voice so perfect, her mien so calm, and her answers so infuriating!

Realising that the stubborn spirit would not be put off, I acquiesced. 'Well then, Lea … why would the wind choose to carry its scent to me this night, in *this* of all places, with war all about?'

'Because you have willed it so … for you have called me here, *pairé*.'

I was confounded. 'How on earth, my dear, did I call you?'

'You are awake while others are sleeping.'

Perhaps I was awake in my dream but surely not in real life! I resolved that there was nothing more I could do except go along with the dream and see where it would lead until I finally woke up.

'What does the book show?' I asked.

'Many things, things that are in the past and those that are also in the future ... but the part which I will show you, could be called a Gospel …'

A Gospel no less!

'Why do we need another Gospel, child, when there are so many? Poor Eusebius was driven mad trying to decide which ones to include in the Bible!' I peered at her. 'Do you know he nearly didn't add John's Gospel … the only eyewitness of the sacrifice of our Lord? The truth is, after he had made his choice of gospels he spent the rest of his life trying to reconcile their differences! No, my dear, we don't need more gospels, only more faith!'

'But what are differences?' the apparition said, serenely. 'The back of your head is different from the front, and yet both back and front belong to you and are needed … is this not true?'

I had to agree that she had a point!

Weary and outwitted, I conceded. 'Well then child, if the Gospels of Luke and Matthew tell us about Jesus, and the Gospels of Mark and John tell us about Christ … what is there left to tell?'

'Have you forgotten John's words? that if all that could be said about the Lord were to be written down, even the world itself could not contain all the books that would be written.'

I nodded for this was so, and yet my poor old head was confounded by so many allusions to libraries and books and gospels, that all I could say was, 'Go on … go on …' and wave a hand.

'It begins with two children, not one.'

'What? What do you mean, two children?'

'There is a kingly child and a priestly one. The kingly child is the reason the centurion is sat upon his horse.'

'A centurion ... a Roman centurion?' I said.

'He rides into Bethlehem to kill the child ...'

'Oh, I see! On behalf of Herod.'

'Yes.'

'You are speaking of Jesus, then.'

'Not Jesus.'

I started. 'What do you mean, not Jesus?'

'This child's name is Yeshua ...'

'Oh my!' I felt my eyes popping, 'I am confounded in my mind already!'

'Then listen with your heart, *pairé*, and take up your quill and write it down, for I will speak ... are you listening with your heart?'

I took up my quill and dipped it in ink and took up those parchments and said, 'Yes, yes, my dear, go on.'

And that is how it began.

Before I knew it I was lost in a rosary of words. Words that followed one another, each dying away into the next, melting in her mouth like that green honey, which they say induces visions.

CHAPTER 2

MASSACRE

Into Bethlehem there entered, with a clattering of hoofs and a thunder of dust, a company of legionaries headed by a Roman Centurion.

A moment earlier, the man who wore the silvered breastplate, the greaves and crested helmet of Rome, was sat upon his horse the colour of obsidian, observing the mountain's rim-rock and the wheeling of the heavenly spheres towards the west.

The god of the sun, Mithras, was soon to awaken from his sleep and the centurion felt two things: an ache behind his eyes and something more – the restless souls of his men. Only a moment of worship, and soon the sun would light a path to their duty.

Only a moment.

Behind him and yet ahead of the others sat his *optio* Septimus, upon his own fine animal. The young man had brought his horse up and now made a whisper into the air between them, 'You wait, Cassius?'

The Centurion did not look at his junior, for the youth was not an initiate of Mithras and did not understand the moment's divinity. Instead he stared ahead to where the light worried the shadows.

'We wait,' he told him, cold and significant. 'The stars and planets have been on fire these nights. You see the combination of Gods? It is rarely seen … and now the Sun rises in the sphere of the Virgin.' He gave the boy a speck of a glance. 'I am no Magi, but I sense a portent in it!'

Septimus observed the sky and grumbled happily, 'Well, I hear Herod too has men watching the skies. It is said men from the east have come to whisper something in his ear that has caused us to have this charge. Why Roman soldiers must dance to that madman's tune, when he has his own dogs snarling at his feet, is not reckoned in my mind.'

The centurion looked at the boy full in the eye as he spoke, 'The Legions of Rome do not dance to Herod's tune, but to the tune of the Governor of Syria. This day, it seems, he is of the mind to stroke the madness of the Jew king by allaying his fears … and we are his instruments – that is all.'

'You were born in this place, Cassius,' the boy said merrily, ignoring his vexation. 'Is it the habit of Jew kings to fear children?'

Gaius Cassius Longinus quelled his vexation. 'I was not born in Judea, but in Syria … and Herod is not a Jew but half-Jew, half-Idumean.'

The optio shrugged his shoulders and shook his head. 'And there is a difference?'

The centurion drew in a breath. The boy was ignorant and too big for his skin. 'It makes him despised,' he explained to him, 'and men who are despised look at their children, at their wives and servants, with suspicion and with hate. They fear auguries and portents, conspiracies and wicked designs. The Idumean part of Herod doubts the prophecy – that a child will come to topple him from his throne – but he knows his people believe it, so he must do something.' He looked again to the horizon, 'On the other hand the Jew part believes the portent and will not allow him to use his own dogs, but asks the governor for his legionaries – so that it may never be said in future times, that Herod killed the Messiah of his people.'

Septimus grinned at these contradictions and Cassius suspected the smile was also for the contradiction that must live in Cassius, who was of both Syrian and Roman blood.

'Well then,' Septimus said, making light of it. 'We shall be the butchers of Quintilius Varus if it pleases him.'

Cassius told him plainly, so that there might be no misunderstanding on the matter, 'Only because it pleases the Governor.'

The *optio's* stare gave way then and he nodded and smiled and nodded again, the very picture of deference. 'It is as you say.' But the smile continued to play at his mouth, and there was no respect in it.

Cassius ignored him and his contrivances to concentrate on the sun, now edging the mountain. The air was full with the impending thrill of the regal splendour of dawn. This was the moment he longed for, before the first rays, when all of nature lay in a cool green sleep ready to be awakened.

As the fat round orb crept over the rise, these words escaped his lips in a gasp, 'It is!'

By degrees the sun began to lean its body low over the world then, pouring out one luminous beam after another. Divine and pure, its light entered into Cassius' soul and he yielded to its force, letting it mingle with the elements astir in his heart, in his organs, his muscles and sinews, his marrow and his blood, so that all of him fell to adoration of the one god, all-powerful and remote: the god that commanded water and fire, air and earth.

Sol Invictus!

The god arced a dagger of luminance, cutting a path over the dying stars, breaking over the back of the mountains, tearing the fabric of the world in half and dividing the shadow from its opposite, good from evil.

All plants and herbs, animals large and small, those that crawled over the earth, and those that swam or flew, all that was contained in an ear of corn, and all that was in the grain of wheat made bread by human hands, all that was from the vine to the cup – all of it was made and unmade for the glory of Mithras!

In the midst of this splendour of splendours, Cassius felt himself a small soul among many; a man descended from the empyrean heaven to the body that had been prepared from out of the noble qualities of the seven planets. In this body he would live out his years, his days, this very hour, a Lion of the Sun.

He closed his eyes and recited in his mind the words of the poet Horace.

Polvere e ombra. All is dust and shadow.

When he opened them again, the day was brighter.

He did not turn to his *optio* but took an in-breath of fire into his lungs and said, 'This day the God devours his children …' He took the Spanish Gladius from the belt over his left shoulder and raised it in imitation of the god, and with the words, 'We go!' arced it over the world and down to his side again.

The company, barely half a century on foot, saw the sign and moved in unison behind him, ascending the rise towards the settlement and through the village gates.

Some of the citizens of the township had already risen and were beginning the day's labours when the sound of earth thrumming to horses hoofs and the stamping of feet caught them by surprise. Cassius arrived first on his sure-footed horse and so he had a moment to sense the odour of clinker and coal, and the pleasant aroma of baking bread. A town bathed in a dream soon to end, he thought.

Septimus came up behind him and directed the company, made up of Samaritans and Syrians, to form a line before the rows of houses.

A moment passed.

Cassius waited. When he could wait no longer he gave the second sign: it told the soldiers to begin forcing their way into the mud brick houses. In a moment, there followed a concord of shrieks and a chorus of desperate howls, which moved through Bethlehem like an evil wind. But Cassius did not come off his horse. He watched the scene from above with his mouth a thin, tight line and his thoughts quiet inside his skull. He held the reins of his animal with one hand and smoothed its nape with the other. In the meantime, his soldiers dragged every boy-child from its crib and from its mother's breast out to the street, to be slaughtered before the horror-struck inhabitants. His face changed not. He moved not a muscle. His breath made clouds in the frigid dawn and signalled no stirring in his heart.

But something caught his eye. Looking south he could see dark figures, shadowed by the soft light, moving slow and steady in the penumbral distance. It occurred to him to send a soldier to those pleasant pastures, and his mind was bent upon this duty, when a piercing light entered into his skull to blind his eyes. It was not Mithras, this light, and yet he discerned in it something of the majesty of the sun! In its brilliance he saw the formless image of a child, and in his mind's fancy the child turned into a man, and when their eyes met the intensity of that gaze bored a hole into his soul.

He lost his breath and had to grasp onto the reins so as not to fall from the horse. When he had gathered in his wits he looked to the pasture again but the vision was gone. Instead he heard the revenant screams and wails of the people, rising in pitch and extremity in his ears.

He cast his vision-laden glance at the ground where a growing pile of little bodies lay before his horse. The image of that child conjured by his mind had fixed itself to those children that lay dead. Of a sudden he felt bewildered and surprised for it. These bloodied things, the pitiful sight of the women pulling out their hair, and the sound of the men dashing their heads against mud walls, all of it looked different now to him. The lamentation grew woeful and loud and the smell of blood was thick in his nostrils. He blinked and blinked again and when the feeling loosened he realised that his *optio* was paused watching him.

Blood spattered and smiling, the boy held a woman by the neck, almost choking her. In her arms a plump, pink child squirmed.

He is too fond of this, Cassius thought.

'She says the child is over two springs.' Septimus said, and let go of the woman to pull the infant from her grasping arms. It began a cry of horror that made the woman faint to the ground as though dead. A man then, whom Cassius guessed must be the father, tried to make a way to the child but the flat of Septimus' sword over his back prevented it. He too fell over his wife and from that position turned a red-streaked, tormented face upwards, saying in the Aramaic tongue of his people that the child had turned two only days before.

Cassius gathered up the metal in his sinews and looked at the screaming infant dangling by one arm. He wished it were true. The child was large enough in size, but it seemed young to him.

If he could spare one life ...

'Put the child down,' he told the sergeant on a whim.

Septimus hesitated.

'Put it down!' he shouted at him. The spit in his mouth was sour and his greaves chaffed his legs. 'If it walks it lives, if it crawls it dies!'

Once on the cobbled path the crying bundle sat a moment. It made as if to stand but its legs, unsure upon those tiny feet, gave way.

Cassius stared at the creature and willed it to walk; he willed it with all the force in his limbs.

The child, for its part, was paused in its crying to look at its father and the father, realising what would come, looked away, but it was too late – the child made a smile and began a crawl.

The man wailed and pleaded to Cassius but Cassius was resigned to it. He made a nod to Septimus and the young man took the child by one arm and held it up as if it were his prize. In that one instant a lifetime seemed to pass between the father glancing upwards, muttering prayers, and the pink child's terror-full stare. An instant, an aeon, and after that a sweep of the Gladius across the throat followed by the falling to white of the eyes and the gushing of child-blood over the father and mother below.

All is dust and shadow, thought Cassius.

Septimus dropped the carcass without ceremony into the pile of dead things, wiped the blood from his face, and left to see to his men.

The Centurion's head was a vacant, vast adamantine wilderness. He did not try to recognise the geography of its landscape, instead he turned his horse away from the slaughter and took a moment to notice the silence that had descended over everything; a silence so deep that he could hear the moment's heart pounding in the crib of the world; a silence that suspended the odour of bread and the scent of spices in the air, an imitation of a former peace now banished for always.

It was Septimus who broke it, warning the population of Bethlehem that should they speak of the slaughter, further reprisals from Rome would befall them. By then Cassius had directed his horse through the gates of the city and was on his way to the valley below.

When the young sergeant caught up with him to ask what he should do with the dead things, Cassius told him, with his mind full of scraps of thoughts:

'Send them to Herod … the man who calls himself King of the Jews!'

CHAPTER 3

KING OF THE JEWS

King Herod was dying. Beneath the cover of his vestments, the skin below his navel was black and his member was shrivelled and withered; that member, which had once enjoyed the flames of fleshly desires, had turned inwards to feed upon its master, and was now a putrid corpse that hung loose and impotent in the folds of his robes.

He was full of rage this night, full of hatred and suspicion. The pain in his groin, having fallen victim to this mood, would have caused him to cry out, if not for the special brew made from the roots of ancient herbs. This brew made his pain less big and opened his mind to visions. And so, he waited expectantly, looking into the flames, to the light that reflected, flickered and danced. He observed the altar, awash with congealed child-blood and encircled by priestesses chanting to the sound of the drums. He observed and waited and remembered how he had trembled with anticipation at the arrival of the Magi.

They had seen the star and had come, seeking to know more of the child destined to be the King of Israel. When they left to look for him, Herod summoned the priests of the Temple: the Sadducees, whose hunger for power made them grovel for crumbs at his feet; and the Pharisees, led by Hillel and Shamai, who looked upon him as a half-breed usurper, a puppet of Caesar and a thief of the crown of Judah.

The useless creatures told him of the prophecies of Balaam and two portents: a star destined to descend into the house of Jacob; and a sceptre presaged to rise up pointing to Bethlehem of Judea, the home of David. They said these portents meant the child-Messiah would be both a king and a priest.

Herod had shouted at them, 'Fools! How can a man be two things?'

But the priests, in their ignorance, had not known how to answer.

These portents and interpretations were nothing new to him - every Jew knew them. Why else had he built his Herodium between four seas if not to keep his eye upon that silent little town called Bethlehem?

But the Romans had slaughtered every creature less than two springs and still they had not found the child! He knew this because his ailment was not healed, and without the blood of that child he would continue to be a miserable man whose breath stank, whose bowels dripped, and whose feet were enlarged and oozing with fluid. Without that blood, he would die with no friends to mourn him, a man hated by the Romans and despised by his own people.

He let the dervish, the song, and the smell of incense enter into him and he asked the devil a question:

What now?

Immediately he received a vision. His eyes stared into the smoke-full air between the naked bodies that moved around the blooded altar lit by fire and candle, and in that space he saw all that was in store for him. A surge of terror clawed its way from Herod's colon to his eyelids and he gave out a yell that was drowned by the lament of dancers, the playing of instruments and the rhythm of drums. Something gripped his throat. He struggled for breath and tried to run out of the grotto but fell. Above him, dark shapes came, some with flapping wings, others with tentacles.

'I am afraid!' he said to them, but they did not heed him. They enveloped him in their delicate shadows and pulled him down into the dismal depths of his madness.

It took him long to die, and when the people heard of his agonising death these words rang out across the land:

'He is dead, he is dead! The Idumean who stole to the throne like a fox, who ruled like a tiger and who died like a dog!'

CHAPTER 4

MARY

Forty generations after Abraham, and some months after the birth of that first child, a young woman called Mary accompanied her husband on a journey from Nazareth. It was the era of Caesar Augustus. Herod the Great had died and his cruel, sadistic son and successor, Archelaus, had been deposed, leaving Syria a Governorship of the Roman Senator Quirenius.

Under his rule, a census was announced for the purpose of taxation and the people of Judea were required by law to travel to the seat of their ancestors to be counted. Mary's husband, Joseph, was of the lineage of David and so he and Mary had to make the journey to Bethlehem, the town of his forebears, even at this difficult time.

For Mary of Nazareth was long with child.

Nine months earlier the seed had been sown in her belly on a fateful night when the Essene priests had called her and her betrothed, Joseph, to the veiled place. There they had been given a cordial that made their minds fall into nothingness. So it was with surprise and anxiety that Mary herself greeted the news of her conception, for she could remember nothing of her union with Joseph. Only the warmth and protection of that radiant angel of God had calmed her worried heart. For the angel's soft whispers had announced the birth of her child in these words:

Ave Maria! Blessed are you among women! To you will be born a child, and you will name him Jesus, and he will be called the Son of God.

This was the same voice that had compelled her to travel to her older cousin's house, to help her with the imminent birth of her own child.

Since her youth, the world had seemed a recent thing to Mary, and she had felt like nothing more than a dust mote drawn upwards by the breezes and the winds of heaven. A dust mote that rarely falls down-to-earth. But on her journey to see her cousin Elisabeth, she had found that an awakening was taking place in her soul. She had walked through the cold southlands, among the sadness of the mountains and the misery of the desolate trees, among the mocking face of the unforgiving brown coloured sky of Judea, until she had found herself, not only at the threshold of Elisabeth's house, but also at the threshold of her own life.

It had been made clear to her then, that she was coming down to earth, and she had understood what she must give up.

That had been six months ago and now, as she cast a glance at her husband, the young carpenter with the soft brown eyes and hair like charcoal from the fires, she knew her descent was near complete and she put her trust in Joseph. He saw to all her needs and pulled the animal gently on the road, so as not to cause her unnecessary discomfort. He toiled over the frozen hills and mountains with his feet blue and blistered and his hands callused and frigid and made no complaint, as others did, of the Romans and the census.

For Joseph did not squander his words.

She remembered his face upon her return from Elisabeth's house, when he saw how she was grown with child. No memory lived in his heart of the union brought about by the ministering of the priests and yet, in his dream-full eyes, she had seen no recrimination; from his mouth no harsh words had come. When the township gathered to call her to account and she feared the people would stone her, Joseph remained steadfast in his love for her, refusing to shun her, making it possible for the priests to keep to themselves their workings.

She looked out of her thoughts now, and realised they were nearing Bethlehem. Darkness was fast descending over the highland wilderness of Judea and only a red outline remained in the west where the road to Hebron made a thread through the valleys and hills that separated Bethlehem from Jerusalem. The last of the sun was touching the pinnacles of a mighty palace. She looked to the east, to where a star-like moon was rising behind purpling clouds; a strange moon, a moon unlike any moon she had ever seen. At that moment, the dusk was pierced by the howling of a wolf. It filled her with dread, and she was glad they had arrived at the outskirts of the town.

It was cold, but the fields that continued upwards to the heights along which the city stretched, were rich with terraced vineyards and gardens well tended. Lights flickered in the houses, full with guests. The sound of merry talk and laughter reached them even here and it cheered her heart, which until now had been heavy with the bitter knowledge that she was homeless and may not have a warm place to bring forth her child.

She bent over to hold her belly for the pain that came then, and she told her child – *not yet*!

Her husband, having heard this, grew concerned. He hastened through the ruined gates of the city, going from house to house in search of accommodation, but no one had room. Joseph asked those on the crowded streets if they knew of any small space wherein they might spend the night, since his wife, he showed them, was great with child and her hour was at hand. They told him the little town was much burdened by visitors who had come from near and far to be counted. Every house was full. Perhaps they should try the Inn?

The Inn was also full to the brim, but the innkeeper took pity on them and told Joseph of a rocky grotto outside the city walls. He warned Joseph that it had once been a place of sinful ritual. Part of it was used as a stable, because Bethlehem was so full that even those places usually reserved for animals had been taken by lodgers.

The young couple, having no other choice, made their way there.

And thus it was that Mary entered into that grotto where, two years before, Herod had performed a black ritual with the blood of the children of Bethlehem. And in that dark space surrounded by animals, fragrant with dung and straw, she sat. Above her, a cleft in the rock allowed a little of that sun-like moonlight to enter. It brought her peace. Here she could make herself comfortable. Here she could wait for the onset of the more painful contractions that would soon come. In the meantime, her young husband would go and find help.

When he returned he was accompanied by two women – a midwife and her young attendant Salome, whose dark round face and clear eyes made a gladness in Mary's heart. The midwife told her the girl had a withered hand from birth, but this deformity would not prevent her from collecting the water and folding the cloths and cleaning the knife with wine.

It was many hours later, as Mary lay exhausted, with her child suckling, that the old midwife sent Salome to fetch more water. When she returned, Mary noticed that the girl's malformed hand was now made well and Salome, following her gaze, noticed it also.

Salome dropped the water vase and fell to the ground and gave thanks.

By and by Mary fell asleep, and the midwife, seeking her own rest, sought to leave and called for Salome to follow. The girl refused to go.

And thus it was that Salome remained with Mary until her dying day.

‡

'But Lea, what happens to the other child, the child sought by Herod who escaped the Romans?' I asked her when she had paused.

'That is what I shall speak of next...when I tell you of Mariam.'

CHAPTER 5

MARIAM

Lea told how Mariam woke with a start.

'The dream had come again, and as always she could not remember it very well. In it, she woke to the howling of a wolf, and found herself not in her husband's tent but in a house among a number of sleeping women. In her heart there was always a feeling of despair and horror for something that had not yet come to pass, and a longing to be with someone – someone she did not yet know.'

‡

Awake now, Mariam searched the darkness for her child and found him sleeping soundly on his rush mat in their tent. On their journey to Egypt three years ago, fleeing from Herod and his madness, she had taken to dreaming such a dream, but upon coming to Heliopolis – that island of green calm in the middle of the barren desert – the dreams had made a pause. They had only come again upon this return journey to her homeland, and she did not know what it meant, though it seemed to her to be a portent of peril.

She lay in the darkness listening to her husband's soft breathing and recalled her years in Egypt with a fond eye. She saw Yeshua walking in the ruins of the fallen temples, his skin browned by the sun; she saw him bathing in the cool waters of the oasis for the holy ablutions, or sitting in the shade of the sycamores eating dates. She longed for the peace and safety she had felt then.

The priests had sequestered them for some years and at the appropriate time had begun to instruct Yeshua in the cool, dark, depths of their sacred places. He was taught many things: how to listen to what wafts on the warm breezes; what resounds in the songs of birds; what lives in the harmony of growing grass; he was taught how to see behind the shapes of twigs and branches; and what lay behind cloud, sky and storm: the thoughts of God!

She knew this because she was always with him, and she was with him again on the day the priests took him to see an old anchorite.

The anchorite lived on a limestone hill not far from the great city of Alexandria. He had retired to a contemplative life and now spent his days in a holy room, a sanctuary wherein he celebrated all the mysteries of the holy life. He never admitted anyone to his house, and yet he had wanted to see Yeshua.

On the appointed day Mariam sat with her son before him. Mariam felt anxious for what the anchorite would say. But the old man said nothing for a long time. Instead, he inspected Yeshua from below his wrinkled brow, making soft noises to himself. When it seemed that he would never speak, he smiled suddenly and began to laugh with merriment, as if relieved of some great burden.

Surprised, Mariam said nothing, but watched and waited for it to stop, knowing that old sages were known for having a peculiar wisdom. When he addressed her finally, his face was as unwrinkled as a child's might be and his eyes were as clear as a stream.

'Long ago,' he told her, 'there was a teacher whose name was Melchizedek. Old Melchizedek had a favourite pupil to whom he taught all the mysteries of the Sun. This pupil, my dear, was destined to incarnate many times, and a long line of ancestors had to be prepared to make a body suitable for him. So Melchizedek tutored another pupil, Abraham, and he taught him all the secrets of the

Moon, the secrets of the blood and the creation of the perfect body. His task was to prepare the forty-two generations of your ancestors for the birth of that favourite pupil, that first pupil. And it is due to Abraham's faithfulness that you are here today with the fruit of your loins. My favourite pupil is come again, and I am rejoicing! For my task is near done, and I must now remind him of his past and bring to him all that he has left behind, in order that he might perform a special task.'

He reached out and passed both hands over Yeshua's eyes and immediately her son fell asleep in her arms. The old man closed his own eyes and uttered many prayers over her boy. When it was over and her son was returned to his senses, the old man looked at her with kindness and familiarity.

'Soon you will give birth to another child,' he told her.

Instinctively she moved a hand over her flat belly. Not even Joseph knew that her blood was late.

'Herod is dead; soon you will be too big with child to travel. You must go. Take your child and husband and journey by way of the Sinai desert in the direction of your homeland, but do not go to your Temple in Jerusalem, for the hope of your priests will nurture your boy towards earthly and not heavenly ends. There is a safe place to which you can go, called Nazareth. The people who live there are not so different from us; they are called Essenes, and you may live among them untroubled, until the time comes.'

She wanted to ask him when that time would be, and what Yeshua was destined to do, but could not bring herself to say anything.

He told her, 'A mother must love her son, but you must love the Son of God, even as you love your own son...for the love of a mother can make all things taste sweet.'

Now as she lay upon the rush mat, she wondered what he had meant, and scolded herself for not asking the questions that continued to plague her. What was to be her son's task? When would it come? And how must she love the Son of God as her own? Her vexation with herself made the child in her belly give a kick, which took away her breath. This reminded her that by the time they reached Nazareth she would be a mother twice over.

She did not know what she would find in Nazareth among the Essenes, the *pure ones*. She only knew what she remembered of her Temple days, that these ascetics were more strict than the *Therapeutae* of Egypt, more strict than the Nazarites, for they wore only white and sequestered themselves in their Mother Houses for fear of defilement. What would become of Yeshua's task in such a place as Nazareth? Could the heir of David be made a king of Israel in such a place, among men whose faces were turned away from Jerusalem? Nothing good had ever come out of Nazareth – that was the saying, and she worried that it was true.

She turned to hug her husband, who seemed to be older by the day. In truth, the memory of her former life at the Temple in Jerusalem had become more and more distant to her eye and the details had lost their clarity and distinction. She remembered how she had been taken to the Temple as a child, and how the miracle of the greening staff had proved the eligibility of an ageing Joseph as a choice of husband. She had not wanted to marry, but the priests reminded her that it was the duty of every person of sovereign lineage to further their ancestral lineage. She had consented only as a service to her people, and yet in time she had grown to love her husband, and if the love she felt was not a young love such as she had seen in others, it was weighty and costly and she was glad of it. She only hoped Joseph would live long enough to see his son's task accomplished.

Outside, the night deepened. Tomorrow would be another long day's march and she put away her thoughts and fears and resolved to sleep.

She closed her eyes and sleep did come, but it was not peaceful.

CHAPTER 6

YESHUA AND JESUS

Two boys sat on the grass. The priestly child, Jesus, was only twelve springs and fair, for he was a Galilean of mixed blood. The older boy, Yeshua, was fourteen springs and from the lineage of kings. As a Judean of pure blood he was of darker of complexion.

Yeshua watched Jesus play a plaintive song on his flute. One moment, the song wafted downwards over the ridge of the mountain, floating over the Nazirite township below with its rows and rows of houses scattered among figs and pomegranates and grape vines, and another moment, the song soared upwards to the sun's jewel, whose gleaming fell over the world and came to rest on the squat fig tree beneath which they sat.

Before them plump, white sheep stood silent and obedient in the grass. From the wide spaces there came a sharp breeze, herb-scented and cool, carrying the sound of a flock of doves flapping their wings in time to the dying and becoming of the soulful tune.

Yeshua was restless.

He held a stick in his hand. He made figures with it among the cyclamen and the anemones and in a moment he threw the stick away and fell to watching the rustling leaves of the small tree.

He told himself,

I see all created things because they are; and they are because God sees them, and because God sees them I see them in the world, and because they are perfect, I see them in my heart.

But this thought did not content him.

He looked beyond the sky, to where the clouds melted into the heavens. The flute's song should have calmed him enough to make him sleep, except that a dream in the night still lingered in his heart and filled him with puzzlement and concern. Jesus would know its meaning but he was taken with his flute and so Yeshua would have to wait, for he did not wish to interrupt him.

Years ago, when Yeshua and his parents had arrived in Nazareth, Jesus' family had been the first to befriend them. Discovering a shared lineage had added to their kinship, and soon the two households seemed to have no distinction between them. This meant that he and Jesus passed season after season in each other's company and thereby had developed a particular understanding between them.

From the beginning the Essene teachers had singled them out from the other village boys, and had sent for the Chazzan, the officer from the synagogue, to instruct them on the Torah, the Mishnah, and the unity of the Law and the Faith. But the teacher soon discovered that a great gulf divided the two boys.

Yeshua loved reading, singing and praying. The rituals of the festivals and all that could be learnt from papyrus and from the word resounded in his soul and gave clarity to his mind. In truth, the older he became the more he felt one with the destiny and the trials of his people upon whom he knew lay the destiny of all peoples of the world.

Jesus was different.

He was not one for things of the world. His mind could not take up the teachings that the rabbis prized so highly, for it was flown away with the song of a bird or the flight of a butterfly or the angle of the sun as it fell on a leaf. There seemed to be no space in his memory for knowledge, and his vision of the world seemed, to Yeshua, like a soft-spoken dream, dusted with the pollen of heaven.

The rabbis were knowledgeable but they were not wise, for they could not fathom Jesus' soul. They could not see his capacity for love with their hardened minds. They did not realise, therefore, how with one touch of his hand, one look from his far-seeing eyes, one word spoken tender and rounded from his lips he could awaken truth and undo all manner of harm, illness and worry. They could not see it, and so they thought him 'addled', a child that could not be taught, and concentrated on Yeshua instead, letting go their training of Jesus and allowing him to spend his days as he would spend them, with his sheep and the playing of his flute song.

Now the flute-song came to its end and the silence of afternoon invaded the empty spaces of the day. Yeshua looked at Jesus, and Jesus in turn let his eyes – not blue nor green nor brown, but all three in equal measure – meet Yeshua's dark ones.

Feeling like a boy and forgetting for a moment that he was more knowledgeable than the priests in their synagogues, he said,

'I wonder what the sheep are thinking?'

Jesus wiped the spit from his flute and glanced at the sheep.

'Sheep do not have thoughts, Yeshua,' he said, all matter of fact.

'*Maze*!' Yeshua said, surprised. 'No thoughts?'

'None.'

'What do they *do*?'

'They feel … they long for warmer days and greener grass … also,' His face lit up in a smile, 'they do not have sympathy for the goats …'

Yeshua smiled himself. 'They do not like the goats?'

'The goats annoy them and they smell bad.'

Yeshua nodded. 'Yes, they smell bad and they are stupid!' He raised a brow. 'So, what am I thinking then, what do you see in my head?'

Jesus' gaze fell on Yeshua's face. 'Your thoughts are too complicated for my reckoning,' he told him. 'They are knotted up, one with the other, and made of sharp corners.'

'Well … if they are made of sharp corners …' Yeshua threw a clump of grass at Jesus. 'How can they be knotted? Knots are rounded!'

More grass was thrown, and soon the two boys were covered in dirt and laughing like anything.

They fell on their backs then, and Jesus turned over on his belly, contented, cupping his chin with his hands.

Yeshua, for his part, observed the leaves on the tree, chewing on a blade of grass. 'Last night,' he ventured, 'I dreamt I was an eagle.'

Jesus gave him a sideways glance, 'How high did you fly?'

'I flew so high I reached the sun, that's how high! Then, something strange happened. The sun turned into a beautiful woman, who stood on the moon and wore a crown of stars. She told me her name was wisdom, and she showed me things in a deep well: strange things, terrible wars, and fearful sights! She told me it was the future, and that it would be grave but that I would perform a task that would save the world, but first I had to remember something that I had to forget again! But I can't remember what it was!'

'That is because you have already forgotten it!'

'That is true!' he said, with a sigh.

'What happened after that?'

'The woman moved her hand over the well and showed me something more ... she showed me an image of you.'

'Me?' Jesus was all smiles and frowns at him. 'What was *I* doing?'

'You were climbing steps, carrying something on your back ... when I looked closer, I could see that it was me you were carrying, and that I was heavy. And you told me that I would be light if I let go of my treasures ... that I would find them again one day. When finally I threw off all that I possessed I was light, like dust in the wind! I knew that from that time onwards, there would be no need for words between us.' He looked at Jesus, 'I do not know what it means, this dream!'

Jesus nodded, thoughtful. 'This is a difficult dream.'

Yeshua sat up to look at the heart-form of his friend's face and the wide set eyes full of colours, 'Not for you! You always know!'

Jesus shrugged his shoulders. 'Not this time.'

'I don't believe you.'

'Perhaps you know too much already?' Jesus teased.

Yeshua let his gaze roam over the sheep and the long view of the world, grinding his teeth. 'I always tell you what *I* know!'

'Yes.' Jesus frowned. 'You know many things.'

'Brothers tell one another everything!'

'We are not brothers, Yeshua,' Jesus corrected him, resting his head on the crook of his arm.

Yeshua scowled, feeling querulous. 'Why not?'

'Jacob and Simon and Jude and Jose ... they hide behind corners to throw stones at me, they do this because they love you, because *they* are your brothers, not I.'

Yeshua felt the blood rise to his face. His brothers were mean spirited and ignorant. 'If I could swap them for you, I would a thousand times over!' he said.

'That is why they throw stones,' Jesus pointed out, with a simple clarity that cut at the roots of Yeshua's anger.

There was a long thoughtful moment and something occurred to Yeshua. 'Where is your knife ... the one you carry for cutting rope? Come ... give it to me.'

Jesus hesitated. 'It is sharp; I am told never to take it from its sheath unless I have to.'

'The sharper the better ... come on ... I'll show you,' he gestured full of impatience.

Jesus complied, but with caution. Yeshua took it and in a moment had made a cut in the palm of his right hand.

Jesus grew alarmed to see blood, but Yeshua ignored it, and said to him, 'Do you remember how the rabbis taught us that the body of a man, his flesh is *Tzelem,* the image of God, and that his blood is *Demut,* the likeness of God. Do you remember? This blood is the likeness of God because in it flows the soul. Look at it! Don't be afraid!' He showed him his bloodied palm. 'This is my soul you are looking at ... now give me your hand.'

Jesus sat up and gave him a weak smile.

'Don't you trust me?'

There was a reluctant nod.

'Then give me your hand!'

Jesus put out his palm and winced.

'The knife is sharp, it will not hurt.'

Yeshua made a swift cut and the boy stared at the blood now flowing from the wound in his hand with appreciation.

'It did not hurt!' he said, amazed.

'Your blood,' Yeshua told him with a serious voice, 'is also *Demut,* the likeness of God ... Now, when I bring my blood, my soul, together with your blood, your soul, like this ...' he joined his hand to Jesus' hand in a clasp and held it firmly, 'it means that we are the same. Do you understand? We share the same *likeness* of God in our bodies. This means more than just brothers in the blood of Abraham, Jesus! Even though I share in the same blood with my brothers, my spirit is not in Jacob, nor is it in Jude, or Simon or Jose, and theirs is not in me. But you and I, we are one now, and this means they can never come between us. Do you know what else, Jesus?'

'What else?'

'It means that if I die, my spirit will still live in you ... because we now share the same likeness of God, the same soul.'

They let go.

Jesus' eyes grew soft and distant, and he seemed to be fitting this idea to his mind as he nursed his wound.

Yeshua wiped the blood away from his hand and watched it ooze from the cut and spread into every crevice and line. He sucked the wound and said, 'Now you must tell me the meaning of my dream, because we are brothers.'

'I would tell you, because we are brothers, Yeshua, but in becoming brothers the meaning has winged away from my mind!'

Yeshua sighed and rolled over on his back again. 'You goose! You have lost too much blood!'

The freshening breeze came and Yeshua felt a strangeness creep over him. He turned his eyes to the old road, and saw a caravan making its slow way in the valley. 'I feel something will soon change, Jesus. Perhaps this is the meaning of the dream? It may happen when we go to Jerusalem, to celebrate our coming of age ceremonies ... Do you know the first thing that I shall do in Jerusalem?'

Jesus took up his flute again. 'What will you do in Jerusalem?'

'I will go to the priests to ask them why they shed the blood of sheep and goats and doves, and why they burn them for sacrifices, when Isaiah and David tell us we must not bring burnt offerings to God ...'

Jesus began to play and Yeshua was not surprised, for talk of cruel things, of temples and kings, never entered into his knowing. They were like the breezes that moved over this ridge on which they sat. They did not go deep, but brushed past and moved on towards other mountains, and other boys sitting with their sheep.

Yeshua watched the shivering leaves. 'I think we shall be awakened at the Temple to something new, you and I.'

Jesus paused then. 'When our eyes open, because we are one, shall you see through mine and I through yours?'

These words made an impression on Yeshua. All day his dream had made him feel something in his heart, and now that *something* sat on the lip of his mind, perched just so - near enough for him to taste, but too far from his reach to be grasped. It was tantalising and frustrating, this remembering, and he was so taken with it that he barely noticed Jesus begin to play another tune. And in this way they remained for a time, listening to God in the wind that carried the spring-song, God in the bleating of the sheep and in the chewing of the goats, until the sun began to fall towards the mountains and from below there came the sound of a woman's voice, calling them for dinner.

They stood together then, as one, and descended the hill to their homes, arms over shoulders.

They spoke no more of their newly won brotherhood, or of the future that awaited them.

CHAPTER 7

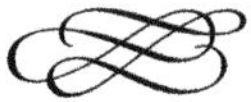

THE PROCURATOR

Annius Rufus sat stiffly in his litter. He looked beyond the handful of centurions that made up his retinue, scrutinising the small army that preceded him into the gardens and villas of the new suburb of Bethesda, outside Jerusalem, and sighed, feeling the rising of an evil humour.

He was a procurator, a representative of Rome and so his soldiers carried the standard of power augmented by the sword, signifying to all and sundry that he had the authority not only to imprison and to torture but also to put to death any man, be that his will.

He burped and reached for a bowl of dates and chewed them, tasting nothing, watching with a disdainful eye as his litter emerged through Jerusalem's northern gate, and the bulk of his soldiery proceeded to the Fortress of Antonia. His back ached and his head was heavy from the heat, and so his mind turned to the comforts he had left behind at Caesarea. But he was also reminded then of his wife, a dry twig of a woman from the upper classes of Roman Society, and to think on her mollified his torment, for if nothing else, this journey would give him some respite from her endless petty rasping, and her ignoble concerns.

His personal guard now steered his litter in the direction of the northwest-most corner of the upper city and headed for the Palace of Herod Antipas, where was situated his pr*ae*torium in the city of Jerusalem. The thought of seeing Herod brought him back to the other reason he had come to this infested place, to quell another one of those uprisings that had become a way of life since the death of Herod the Great, and the rise of his violent and wicked son, Archelaus.

Over the years, uprisings against Archelaus had caused Rome to crucify thousands, and to send just as many into slavery. Finally, sick of the killing spree, Archelaus' own subjects had begged Caesar to intervene on their behalf. Caesar then, quite wisely, had Archelaus thrown into exile, creating a new province called Judea and appointing a governor to rule it. But these measures did not put a halt to the unrest, which continued below the surface, and not long ago his own spies had warned Rufus of a renewal of discontent, this time against Roman taxes.

When Rufus heard of this uprising predicted for the sacred holiday of Passover, being the ambitious man he was, he had seized it as a perfect opportunity to make his mark and had petitioned Quirenius for a Legion. Quirenius, however, had responded by sending him only two cohorts – barely enough to prevent a skirmish – and had wished him a good journey into the bargain. Thus had he forced Rufus to see the entire matter to the end, despite the indignity shown to his person.

To think on it now filled him with an evil humour, a humour that grew more evil the closer he came to Herod's palace.

The palace was almost a city, flanked by three great towers whose walls enclosed spacious grounds, and terrace upon terrace of stately mansions and gardens. To his mind, it cascaded like an overgrown weed towards the crowded streets of the lower suburbs of Jerusalem. Now the noise coming from those suburbs invaded his sheltered carriage and reminded him of how much he despised this place, with its bazaars and spice markets, its shops and its hawkers. In truth, he hated people in general, and Jews in particular, despising their language and their dress, their peculiar religious fervour, their superior mien, their exaggerated piety, their exotic customs and their frequent and cumbersome rituals. He loathed the priests and scholars and students who congregated near the Temple to chew on the ears of those who would listen to their endless diatribes. Moreover, he found the discordant strain of the Levite chant distasteful, and the reek of their sacrifices nauseating. It seemed to him as if his people had swallowed up the entire known world, and were now suffering indigestion for it.

After all, into Rome's belly had gone countless races and their cities, their vineyards, farms, villages and provinces; their produce, their merchandise, their culture, their art and their religion. For Rome did not believe in any one god but rather chose to impregnate herself with the seed of all the gods of the world, changing only their names and giving birth to them anew. Was it any wonder that Rome found she had too many gods to feed? Mithras, Isis, Adonis, Attis, Astarte … all the gods and demons of Greece were hers and all the devils and angels of Asia and Africa were hers. Yet Rome had never once sought the loving attentions of that hard-hearted god of the Jews, the god whose arrogance would have no other god before him, the god who was so devastating to behold that no image could be made of him. From this god, Rome cringed and snarled, since he dared to call Rome a whore!

Rufus looked around him. What arrogance from a world soiled, noise-some, disordered and decadent! What haughtiness from a backward-gazing spawn-hole of insurgents and dissenters, from an uncivilized rabble of mongrel races and tongues! He was wondering, with distaste, what good could come from travelling to this end of the world, when his litter came to a stop and he was forced to turn his mind to the moment.

Herod Antipas was waiting for him in a luxurious room, sitting upon a dining sofa strewn with soft cushions of gold and burnished red damask. In truth, the man's silken dress was dyed in similar hues and contrived to make of him an oversized cushion, were it not for his raven hair, curled and braided and dotted here and there with precious stones, and his thick neck and arms adorned with gold and silver. To Rufus, he looked more like an Arab than a Jew, and less like a man than a woman. And although he had never met the man before, he loathed him immediately.

Herod clapped his plump hands and music sounded from some unseen place. A breeze made sheer curtains shimmer between columns and carried the heady smell of incense, which made Rufus cough and sneeze.

Herod Antipas, friend of Augustus, King of Galilee and the whole land east of the Jordan, did not stand to greet him. He pulled a half smile, lank and thinly made, at him and said,

'Welcome, welcome, procurator! I hope your journey was not too unpleasant? Come, sit at my table and take some refreshment before retiring to your pr*ae*torium ….' He turned to a smooth faced boy standing in the shadows and waved a ring crowded hand at him. 'Wine and fruit!' he said. After that he turned to Rufus, and in a loud whisper full of intimacy, said, 'As promised, I have a number of nubile servants awaiting your attentions. I hope they will satisfy your appetite … though to look at you I am reminded of a Roman saying – that hunger makes all things taste pleasurable!' He laughed a little, and let it fade to nothing.

Rufus, for his part, took to grinding his teeth.

'You may thank me tomorrow,' Herod said serenely, when no word from Rufus was forthcoming. He paused, no doubt turning the wheels of his mind to some base mischief and added, 'There is another matter … I hope you do not find me presumptuous, but when I heard of your imminent arrival, I took the liberty of calling for the captain of your Roman guard in Jerusalem to meet you here in my apartment. I thought you would want to be informed at once of the state of affairs … that way your mind, freed from any unpleasant business, can incline upon the pleasures that await you … I was *certain* you would agree.'

The fox had contrived his own presence at a discussion between him and his Commander in Jerusalem! Rufus scratched absently at his cheeks and fashioned his voice to be cold and laconic, 'You are too kind.'

The other man's head made the slight nod of a thoughtful uncle. 'Yes of course! Many people say it.'

The wine and sweetmeats arrived, lavish, fresh and inviting, but even before the servant had poured Rufus a draught of wine a Roman Centurion was announced.

The man's name was Gaius Cassius Longinus. He was tall and carried the burden of his armour over well-muscled shoulders. A man of no more than thirty-five springs, at a guess, though his eyes bespoke the weariness of older years, a weariness that Rufus determined must come from living in a nest of vipers.

The centurion took one look at Herod, made his salute to the procurator, and inclined his head in the appropriate fashion.

Rufus waited for his cup to be filled and took a sip of the Galilean wine. He let it sit in his mouth. It was dry and tasted of ashes and made his tongue stick to the roof of his mouth. It was a moment before he could say, 'What have you to report?'

The Centurion looked his superior in the eye. 'All seems peaceful.'

'And our spies?'

'They report nothing out of the ordinary. There are madmen on every street corner announcing the coming of a Messiah. They speak of a miraculous deliverance that will soon come from heaven, to rid them of the rule of Rome ... but this is nothing new. These men come in from the hills, dishevelled in appearance and dress. The Jews call them Nazarites.'

Rufus took another thoughtful sip of the foul-tasting wine and said, 'So in your estimation these Nazarites are harmless … they will not incite the people?'

Cassius shook his head slightly. 'In my experience they are not like the zealots. They are nothing more than soothsayers who presage the future, and call not for violence but for repentance and wakefulness.'

Rufus did not like it. 'Repentance and wakefulness, you say?' He sat back, feeling Herod's eye upon him. 'Well then, what measures are we implementing to wakefulness so that we do not repent our stupidity?'

The centurion's discomfort was also plain to his eye. He looked askance at Herod, and only continued after a nod from Rufus, 'From the Census we know all who live within the walls of the city. In the next day or two the larger masses will arrive for the holiday. I will have men posted at all the gates taking names, ages and birthplaces. They will check all goods brought in and out of the city.'

Rufus was dissatisfied with everything. 'How do you suppose you will find dissidents this way?'

'During the holiday we are outnumbered. Once the dissidents are assembled they will move like a wildfire through the city, and there is no way we can stop them. But if we can put out small fires, one by one, before the holiday begins, then we may have a chance of preventing a conflagration.'

'You must search every house then, every street!'

Herod Antipas made a noise, a clearing of the debris at the back of his throat. 'Forgive me, procurator, but might I interject with a word of advice? Before your soldiers start breaking into the houses of the people of Israel … perhaps you should take a moment to cogitate …'

Irritated, Rufus cast a sharp eye over Herod. 'What do you mean?'

'Contact with a gentile,' Herod said, with a look of apology, 'a … heathen, especially as it nears the great feast, may render a Jew levitically and *inconveniently* unclean, and so disqualify him for a day from participating in the rituals, for he shall be … defiled.'

Rufus dismissed it, 'Nonsense!'

Herod was not to be put off, 'Also, the houses of Gentiles are considered defiled, procurator. So you may not bring any suspects to your *Praetorium*.'

Rufus scowled. 'This is an outrage!'

'Romans are idolaters.'

'Idolaters?' he said, at the peak of irritation.

'You make idols.'

'What does that have to do with anything?'

'These are contrary to our laws.'

'Damn your ridiculous laws!'

Herod took hold of some grapes and popped them into his mouth. 'They may be damned, and yet … they are what they are. A procurator must know them in detail,' he continued, chewing, 'if he is to keep peace in his province. Peace is good for business, don't you agree? After all, dead men are not usually disposed to paying taxes.' He flashed him a grape-stained smile. 'And, as you have paid an inordinate sum for the revenues of this province, procurator, I trust you would not want to see future handsome dividends lost to your purse through rashness. No ... all in all, it will be far wiser to have any suspects brought before the Sanhedrin, for questioning by the priests.'

Rufus grew weary with the cynicism in Herod's voice, but he knew his orders were to remain, at all times, sensitive to the volcanic temper of these bedlamites.

'You say my prisoners should be at the disposal of the priests, but the priests themselves have defended the rebels.'

A paternal smile lit Herod's face. 'You need not fear for the High Priest, Ananias. He was given his position by the Governor himself and relishes the comforts that Rome provides. Besides, I have just come from my astrologers ... they see only peaceful times ahead.' He leant forward. 'And the stars never lie.'

Rufus huffed. 'Well, the stars may never lie, Herod, but astrologers have been known to lie about the stars!' Then, to his commander, 'Be vigilant, captain, watch and wait, do your searches discretely and let me know what you find. I want good soldiery everywhere. I myself will not leave the pr*ae*torium again until after Passover. But at the first sign of trouble, I wish to know it ...' He waved a half-hearted salute and dismissed the centurion.

When they were alone Herod clapped for more wine, but the procurator raised a hand to prevent it, saying he wanted better wine, perhaps that fruity wine from Cyprus, brought to his praetorium, where Herod's pleasures awaited his eager attention.

Herod sighed, seemingly pleased with himself. 'You must not give way to nervousness, procurator; nervousness has been known to turn a man to madness.'

'You mean to say, as it did your father before you?'

There was a long, odious moment between them. Rufus thought he could see shadows, wings, flapping over the Jew but his reverie was broken by Herod himself, who spoke now with a strained voice,

'You are weary … go to your rest … remember … soon you will return to the cool airs of Caesarea and Judea will be a distant speck in your mind. This night you need not concern yourself with anything more than the pleasures awaiting your attention!'

Rufus did not know how true these words would come to be, for Herod had made certain that he would be taken to new heights of carnal ecstasy, surpassing all others in the quality of flesh prepared for Rufus' amusement.

Three days and nights were spent without a thought for insurrections and dissidents. Fear had no moment among those orgies of naked flesh, wine and gluttony. At the zenith of his sexual raptures, an ecstatic vision of his wife, in her death throws, struck Rufus such a note of joy that he consummated his lust with a power he had never before known, and it caused him to fall into a satiated unconsciousness that lasted the rest of the Paschal Festival.

For this reason, he did not hear of the strange goings on at the gates of the city … though it is unlikely he would have, even if he had been sober and awake, for his Captain, Gaius Cassius, would not have reported it.

CHAPTER 8

PASSOVER

Mariam was among the pilgrims from Nazareth who travelled the Jordan valley to Jerusalem. In a solemn ceremonial mood they had come to the other side of Jericho, having left its palm groves, gardens of roses and balsam plantations behind them.

This was the last leg of the journey, and many thought they could almost smell the Temple incense wafting in the breezes. The anticipation of it made all minds and hearts full of gladness, all except Mariam.

For her husband Joseph had died some months ago, leaving her a widow with seven children to raise, gardens to tend, flour to mill, and sheep to graze. With so much to do, she never found the time to cultivate her love of reading and learning, and began to neglect even her prayers. If her friends had not offered to look after her animals and garden, she would have let another year pass before Yeshua's youth ceremony.

As she followed the others, with her dress wrapped around her legs to make walking easier, she told herself that she should accept her destiny with equanimity and look on all the vicissitudes of her life as opportunities for mastering her stubbornness. Still, her destiny had been a difficult one, and it would have been even more difficult had she not befriended Mary, the young mother of Jesus.

Mary, walking beside her, was of mixed blood like many Galileans, and some years her junior. It was true that she lacked learning and sophistication, but this lack was compensated for by an abundance of love, a child-like spirit and a fresh, youthful innocence. Mary seemed to her like a sun trapped in a house of flesh, whose rays, falling daily over the icy landscape of Mariam's soul, made it come awake again. Mariam had not known such innocent and loving company since her youth.

She had been joyous when she discovered that Yeshua and Jesus had also found friendship in one another. For although dissimilar in temperament and learning, the boys too sensed, like their mothers, that a thread of destiny was spun between them.

This brought her now to the primary reason for her concern. She looked about the group for Yeshua, and found him walking vacantly beside Jesus. Since their journey to Jerusalem she had sensed a change in Yeshua. The closer they came to the Holy city, the more markedly did she observe a strangeness overtake him: Yeshua, once so wise, alert and questioning, had grown long in his silences and dream-like stares and there were moments when she felt him taken by a great oppression of the heart. In truth, when she looked directly at her son she saw only an emptiness, as if his spirit had grown loose in the cavity of his body and would wing away at any moment and leave her grasping at the shadows of his ghost.

She did not know what to think. She hoped that Yeshua might awaken from this spirit-illness upon seeing the great city, for who could be unmoved by the sight of Jerusalem? Sparkling as if snow-covered and gold dusted it rose now from out of the clefts of the valleys like a jewel, with its great walls, its palaces and criss-crossed streets clotted with houses of every shape and kind. Her companions fell to their knees in a prayer of thanks to see it, for soon they would walk through the gates and find their way along those bustling streets to the Temple, and they could even now hear the chanting of the Levites and the blowing of the horns. This was surely a dream experienced in the day! A gleaming heaven-made manifestation of the fulfilment of God's commandment!

Everywhere there was joy.

Mariam took Yeshua aside and pointed out the sacred girdle of walls within which stood the splendid Temple, with its magnificent courts and its holy sanctuary. She reminded him that Jerusalem was the seat of the Sanhedrin, the greatest place of learning and piety in the world. The place where he could finally feel at home, for one day his destiny would lead him there again so that he might accomplish a great task.

But this did not seem to stir a fire in the boy's heart. Instead, the eyes that stared at her appeared removed from life.

'My task is near at hand, mother,' he said.

These words struck her as a blow, and she found she could not move. What did he mean, *near at hand*? The others had already walked beyond them and were melting with those crowds at the gates to the city – all except her friend Mary who waited, quiet and patient, with Jesus.

Mariam did not wish to draw attention to them, so she walked on and told her son, 'Come.'

At the city gates Roman soldiers took stock of the names and ages and the birthplaces of all who had come, and now her concern for Yeshua was traded for a palpable, terror-filled knowledge of peril. She stood back in the line, away from the others, letting them pass. She must think. What should she say? That her son was born in Bethlehem at the time of Herod? On their return from Egypt she had heard of the terrible massacre of the children and she had long grieved for her friends and relatives who had lost their sons. Yeshua was the right age to have been one of those children and the Romans would know it. Within her a force compelled her lips to form a lie to save her son's life and she searched in her mind for support from the scriptures but found only admonitions:

'A false witness shall not go unpunished; and he that speaketh a lie shall perish!'

A great crowd came from behind and pressed her forward. She

realised that she had lost sight of Yeshua again. This added to her mounting anxiety, so that her voice came out shrill when she called his name into the bevy of pilgrims.

She found him standing before a Roman soldier, whose face bespoke a cruel heart, and prayed for two things: for the strength to tell the man the truth, and for the man's ignorance of its importance. She thought she might faint to the ground on saying it, but she did not. She stood perfectly poised and still.

'Cassius!' the Roman said to a centurion who stood not far off, inspecting some bundles tied to a mule.

When this man looked in her direction Mariam saw that he was possessed of a young man's body, but that his eyes went deep into his skull and were shadowed like those of an old man. He left the mule and came to see.

Her heart moved in a lump to her throat.

'Come, hear what this woman tells ... her son was born in Bethlehem, at the time of Herod!'

The centurion's face was all a-frown, his voice a sting in her ears, 'Bethlehem of Judea?' he said to her.

She nodded.

'She says he is fourteen springs!' the other man said, with a smile playing at his mouth.

She felt demons of fear un-spooling a thread of misery into her bowels. She said another silent prayer and caught Yeshua in a protective grasp. A desperate desire to flee fired up her legs, and yet, where could she go?

'Is this true?' The centurion pressed.

'It is,' she told him squarely. 'My son's name is Yeshua bar Joseph, of the house of David.'

The centurion was fiercely attentive as she spoke, and she noted that it seemed as if a number of pictures were flitting past his eyes as he looked from her to Yeshua and back again.

'Bethlehem of Judea?' he asked again, 'In the time of Herod the Great?'

She nodded.

An expression of relief now surfaced on his face and made it soft, as if all cares were of a sudden taken from it and put away. The moment was suspended, while the world moved in loops around them. She thought that he would soon call for his guards. But he said nothing. He allowed his teeth to worry his lips and his eyes to narrow.

She waited.

There was an imperceptible nod of the head and with it the scrap of a moment passed, taking the softness from the man's face and replacing it with a rigid shield of flesh.

She shuddered and closed her eyes.

'Mind your son, woman,' she heard him say, stern of voice. 'This is a great crowd, and the city is large. You have come so far it would not do to lose him now!' He drove his eyes down into hers to make the significance of his words more clear and turned away.

'Let them through, Septimus!' he called out over his shoulder.

The other man hesitated.

There was a look full of danger in that young man's eye. He let loose a seductive whisper between them, 'See these hands, Jewess?' he showed them to her, 'These were bloodied from killing all the children of your township … one by one I cut their little throats and stacked their pitiful Jew bodies in piles, and milked the blood from their veins for your mad king to drink … what do you think of that?' He watched her, waiting for a response. When none came, he made a cold, perilous laugh at the back of his throat. 'You were clever to have saved him, I'll give you that! But you can't change his fate,' he leaned in, so that she could smell his wine-sour breath. 'Fate is a hard mistress, Jewess … she always comes to take her earnings, believe me, and when she does …' he smiled, 'I hope I am there to see it!'

Mariam kept her eyes steady on his and her face calm. Meanwhile, the line of pilgrims swelled behind her and the people complained, so that the soldier, now drawn from his reverie, was made to shift an eye to the hordes. He straightened and a look of frustration passed over his face for a menial task that has no end, and with a wave of a hand dismissed her and shouted to a place behind her,

'Next!'

CHAPTER 9

THE KISS

It was in the Temple that what had begun three days before came to fruition. Before that there had been three days of endless marches and toiling over rough roads, while around him there had been the constant noise from prayers and songs and psalms, the ever-movement of the people onwards, the laughter of the children and their games and his mother's concern in his ear.

In the night, dreams shadowed his soul. He had seen an abyss, a dark, fiery furnace molten hot in which he glimpsed many things of darkness, dreadful to behold, waiting to ensnare him. On a far shore stood his friend Jesus, adorned in light, with his heart-face radiating love. In the dream, he had gestured for Yeshua to cast into the abyss all his hard-won treasures, but Yeshua's heart had been weighed down with sorrow for the loss.

His friend's voice had told him, 'Remember, we are brothers, Yeshua. All that you lose will one day return to you, and all that dies will live again through me.'

On the last day he fell ill; faces came and went, but his soul was awake only to the process that was mysteriously and cautiously working its way through him.

And his question to it was:

Am I?

And the answer was:

Not yet.

He did not understand this voluntary leaving of his body but he was not afraid - his concern was for his mother.

When she had shown him Jerusalem she had spoken of the Sanhedrin, of its Temple and palaces, of its gardens and of its people. She had expected that it would quicken his heart with excitement. But his heart was grown too big in his body to be excited and it could only strike a slow rhythm.

When they entered the city, all around him he heard the clamour of the pilgrims, the calls of the merchants in the bazaars, the noise of the camels and horses and entertainers, the chanting of the priests and the clanging of bells – all these sounds were seeking to bring him back to life and to entice him from his task, but the will of God was set. Death, he knew, lay at the end of the way, and he walked this long road with Jesus to his Father's house, where it would be accomplished.

Once over the twelve steps of the Temple, he followed Jesus through the Beautiful Gate whose massive double doors were made of brass. Now in the courts of the Temple, the world was left behind them, and amid the dissonant cacophony of sounds his mind began its unravelling, so that his soul rose up from his bones and his muscles, and his eyes grew blind, little by little.

He turned to Jesus but could not see his friend. Tears flowed over his cheeks. He bowed low and fell upon his knees. What had sustained him until now was spent, burnt up and consumed.

'Am I?' he asked his friend.

No answer came.

He took in a breath, allowing it to enter deep into his lungs, so that it filled every corner of his being, right down to his very finger tips, until he could hold onto it no more and his heart felt as if it would burst. How could he let go? And yet he must! He must let go. But in a moment between one breath and the next, a memory came; a memory of himself as a great king standing on a ziggurat observing the sun. Something told him that what had been prepared for aeons could now come to pass. A sense of peace came over him. He remembered!

Now he could forget.

He breathed out.

All of his learning, his wisdom and his selfhood, moved completely out of him then – his treasures. They stood before him a moment and made a descent into that other self, into the soul and body of Jesus.

And, as Jesus looked down upon his dearest friend with concern, he felt his heart torn open and he breathed in, and by way of this breath something entered into him, and he knew. He knew that somehow he and Yeshua were truly united, like two sparks meeting in a gentle flame, pellucid and brotherly. From now on Yeshua would see the world through his eyes, and there would be no need for words between them.

Am I you?

Jesus asked Yeshua now, his gaze full of the familiar and unfamiliar.

And the answer came from within his heart:

We are Tzelem and Demut ... image and likeness.

‡

'And so it was a metaphysical conception.' Lea said to me, 'What had been foretold in the Testament of the Twelve Patriarchs of Jerusalem came to pass: a priest came from Levi and a King from Judah, and they became one for the salvation of Israel.'

'The Testament of the Twelve Patriarchs ...' I said, pausing in my writing and extracting my eyes from the images she had conjured before them. 'I do believe I know it!' Now my mind was on something else. 'What you have just told me makes sense! I realise why the Gospels of Luke and Matthew differ. I realise why the Magi visited one child, while only the Shepherds knew the other! Poor old Eusebius would laugh now to hear it, since this had caused him so much pain.'

'Matthew has Yeshua born at the time of Herod, *pairé*, while Luke has Jesus born two years after that, at the time of Quirenius, and the census.'

'Yes … that's it! That's it, my child.' I thought it over. 'Even their genealogies are different, yes ...! Matthew has it beginning with Abraham, while Luke begins it with Adam. I always thought it a curious thing, but now I think it must signify that Jesus is related to the first man. That he is angelic.' I shook my head with astonishment. 'There have always been men who believed that Jesus was not a man at all, you know, that he was a phantom … others have thought that he was nothing more than a man … now all is reconciled … they were only seeing different sides of the one face. That is, two persons in one body, image and likeness combined!'

The elegance of this solution caused me to feel a cautious elation. Still, I had to find proofs and so, in the days that followed, I resolved to search through our library of scrolls and parchments and rats and rat dung to find the Twelve Testaments. In my search the first thing I found was a forgotten gospel, called the Gospel of Thomas, and it occupied me for some hours. When I found that it also spoke of how two must become one, I hit the side of my head with such force that I saw stars! Again, on searching further, I found the Testament which Lea had spoken of, written by the Twelve Patriarchs of Jerusalem, and she was right, it foretold the coming of a king and a priest – one from the line of Levi, and the other from the line of Judah!

All day I pored over scrolls written by the forefathers of our faith, by the Essenes and others whose tenets had mixed with those of our founder, Mani. I realised that they all spoke of the same thing – of two Messiahs. Parchment after parchment described two children! I was astonished. There it was for anyone who cared to see! Why no one had understood it in all these years I could not guess! But you see, I was conveniently forgetting that I had not seen it myself!

The next night, when Lea came again, I told her of my discoveries and my thoughts. She listened with quiet interest.

'Do you know what this means?' I told her, 'It means that our two sides, Cathars and Romans, have each held one part of the truth!'

'Yes, *pairé* … together you would have the whole truth,' her eyes regarded the fire, 'and yet you are not together - one side sits here upon this mountain, while the other is below throwing shots from their catapults and mangonels.'

I frowned; she had thrown the calm waters of her wisdom over the fire of my enthusiasm and I was now forlorn, when before I had been so elated.

'What is there to do then?' I said, in dismay.

'Men must come to know the contents of the Fifth Gospel, that is all,' she said.

'That is all! You say that is all, but that is impossible! Because it is not written down!'

'Not until now.'

'But no man will believe what I write, since I am not one of the apostles!'

'But *pairé,* no man would believe it even if you were an apostle,' she said, evenly. 'Look at those parchments and proofs you hold in your library, they would not last in the hands of the inquisitors even a wink, for they would burn them as heretical lies.'

My head and my heart ached with these contradictions. 'Yes, yes ... quite right, quite right ... so why am I bothering to stain my hands if there is no hope that anyone will believe what I am writing?'

'There is hope ... in wisdom.'

Wisdom? I looked at her with annoyance. 'All my life I have desired knowledge, but wisdom, well, that is something else ... so far it eludes me, and look at how old I am!'

'Wisdom does not come by thinking about things, *pairé,* it comes when you become ripe for true judgement; when you can allow the truth to meet you from out of the things themselves. But you must be desire-less, for the more you desire wisdom, the less you will find it,' she said. 'When you no longer desire it for your own sake, it will find you. That is when wisdom becomes revelation. Men will need to see it for themselves, it will be revealed to them.'

'Well,' I said, put out, 'I do not see much good in such a thing that is revealed only when you don't want it and a book that no man will believe!'

'The desire for knowledge feeds the self ... but one must love wisdom not for the self, but for the sake of wisdom itself, *pairé* – that is what it means to be a philosopher, and only a true philosopher can see the Fifth Gospel.'

A sudden understanding came then, and with it an uncomfortable feeling of shame. She was talking to me, yes, that learned man that I thought I was! She was telling me that I must let go of this learned man (who loved learning for his own sake) if I ever wished to become wise, or to see these things she recounted for myself. I was chided, yes, bewildered certainly, but at the same time I was struck by a sudden desire to let go of all I thought I knew in order to become a philosopher.

CHAPTER 10

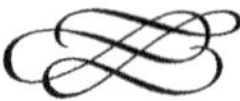

JESUS OF NAZARETH

She often reproached me and instructed me like a child. And yet every night I looked forward to her coming and I grieved when dawn came, always sooner than I wished.

In the day, when amongst my many duties I thought on all that Lea had told me, I felt both fear and joy. Fear that I was losing my sanity, and joy for what I was gaining because of it. Unable to reconcile these two disparate emotions, I kept myself busy.

Countless days passed devoted to our survival. Sometimes I was so exhausted I could hardly walk and yet each night, by some miracle, I came awake when I heard her say,

'Shall I continue?'

My heart would give a leap then and I would answer, 'By all means, my dear!' My ears would fall receptive to her words and I would pick up my quill again with anticipation.

One such night, she continued to tell how Mary could not find her son, Jesus, upon their journey home from Jerusalem,

'She did not know that Jesus was missing,' she said, 'until they had reached Sichem. It was the eighth day after the great Feast of Passover and the company from Nazareth had lawfully left the city to make their way home by way of Jericho, to avoid passing through Samaria – a land defiled.'

‡

The children often followed behind in the daytime, mingling freely, seeking out companionship, singing, telling stories, throwing stones and sticks in the air, or at shrubs. But it was in the evening, when the camp was formed and the tents were pitched and the members of each family came together, that Mary looked for Jesus and realised that he was missing.

Immediately she went to Mariam's family tent, thinking he would be with Yeshua, who had taken ill in Jerusalem, but she found Mariam alone, sitting beside her son's listless body muttering prayers.

Worried, Mary set off with Salome to walk among the tents calling out her son's name, but none had seen him. Ordinarily, this would not concern her, for Jesus did not disdain his own company and would often take himself to some quiet corner to play his flute. It was the onset of darkness that concerned her. Where could he be?

As dusk fell over the desert she clutched the woollen shawl over her shivering shoulders and bit her lip to prevent herself from fainting. She had not felt well since their arrival in Jerusalem and now her heart seemed to be loosening its rhythms.

When she returned to her family tent Joseph resolved that they must not wait for sunrise. They must return in haste to Jerusalem to look for their son, knowing Mariam would go on with the caravan to Nazareth, for the sake of Yeshua.

The journey was difficult in the night, with only the waning moon to guide them. When she and her husband arrived, weary, thirsty and hungry, the sun was already high and a great wind was sweeping the city.

Fear bit into Mary's heart when she entered through the gates, but she did not give it a voice. She kept her face calm and serene as she walked, glancing this way and that, calling out her son's name. The bazaars that occupied the ever-rising rows of streets thronged with noisy Hellenists, Galileans, Judeans and Jerusalemites competing for the best ironware, the most practical clothes, good wood, fresh bread, fruit, vegetables, fish and spices. No man had seen her son. In the upper city markets they asked if anyone had seen her boy, but it was the same.

They looked until nightfall. Exhausted, they found lodgings and rested, but Mary's sickness had increased with her sorrow and concern. In her feverish sleep, she heard the song of a night bird and it was woven into her dreams with an Arab tale that she had often told Jesus. It was the tale of a Nightingale that loved a white rose. The bird sang the most beautiful songs to it each night, but only from afar for fear of its thorns. One night, beneath the swollen moon, having drunk her fill of song and emboldened by love the Nightingale resolved to embrace the rose. She clasped it to her breast, which was pierced through by a thorn. Thus she sang the most beautiful song she had ever sung, pressing the thorn closer and closer to her heart, a song of sacrifice and true love found. In the end, having stained the rose with her own heart's blood, she died, and the rose, in mourning, forever after bloomed red.

Mary had woken from this dream crying out.

'No! Not my son! Not yet! Not Yet!'

In the morning of the third day, gathering what strength was left to her, she resolved to join her husband and his relatives in their search for Jesus. They made their way beyond Herod's palace and crossed the bridge that spanned the valley of the Cheesemongers, which connected the eastern and western hills. Staring down at the lower city they called out his name. Dust flew up into Mary's face, since the wind was born anew and wove around her dress and made it come to life with movement.

The wind said, *Go to the temple.*

She had heard this wind-voice before and it had never failed her, so she directed the others to climb terrace upon terrace towards that great edifice of marble. When she neared the royal porch where the priests and their families mingled, she did not pause to show courtesy but hurried instead towards the Temple itself. Once through the porch to the court of the gentiles she swept them with her gaze, her heart hammering out its paces without rhythm and her forehead wet with perspiration.

A silent crowd had gathered here to listen to the members of the Sanhedrin, for it was the custom of the elders to come out to the terrace of the Temple on Sabbaths and feast days to teach the people and to listen to their questions. She made her way through the knotted crowds and a sudden and great relief entered into her heart when she saw her son, but it was mixed with amazement because Jesus was among the priests and scribes, discoursing with them!

When her husband and Salome caught up with her they were equally astounded. Mary near fainted then and would have fallen if they had not caught her.

'Wife!' Joseph voiced into her ear, 'Can you not see how he is safe?'

But she trembled all over, for she knew he was not safe. She looked at him closely. Her son held his head erect, and his fair eyes, clouded with dreams since birth, now darted sharply to this man and to that, flecked with fire. He was altered! It was as if a different spirit now lived inside him and was moving the mechanism of his thinking. For how else could she explain to herself the sight of him questioning the rabbis, when only a week before he could barely recall the most basic teaching?

'Why do you sacrifice the beasts?' Jesus was saying to them, as sharp as a nail.

An old man dressed in the garment of a scribe answered with paternal irritation, 'It is God's command, for the sins of the people.'

'But David tells us it is a sin itself to bring before God's face burnt offerings,' Jesus returned. 'Isaiah tells the same. The last lawful sacrifice was for the sake of the people of Israel, when a ram was killed in place of Abraham's son, Isaac!'

The scribe laughed, and looked down with condescension, 'Child! Do you presume to know more than the wise men and the priests of the Temple of Israel?'

Jesus looked at him. 'Wisdom does not live only in the souls of priests, and a Temple is not always made from marble and gold.'

A young rabbi asked the boy, 'Tell us, child, what is the greatest commandment in the law?'

Jesus turned to him and said, 'There are two: love the Lord with all your heart; and love your neighbour as you love yourself. On these two commandments hangs every law.'

A man in the crowds said, 'He is smarter than you, Gamaliel!'

There was a round of laughter.

Mary did not look to see Gamaliel, for her eyes were guided to another man, the high priest Ananias. He stood some way from the others, dressed in resplendent fine linen over which he wore the breastplate studded with gold and gemstones. His eyes met hers and what they reflected did not come from a heart dwelling in goodness. In that gaze she saw an old serpent coil itself, green and oily and smooth, and it spoke to her thus:

Heavenly Eve! You may have escaped me in Paradise, but your heavenly child shall suffer all the tortures an earthly man can bear, and you shall not be there to comfort him!

The force of this communication pierced her heart and she made a shout, 'Jesus!' She broke through the crowds to go to him and to take him by the hand. 'We have worried three days for you and looked for you, come with us now ... let us go home!'

But in her son's eyes glared a powerful spirit, wise in years. These were not the soft-spoken eyes of her son.

'It is time for me to be in my father's house, mother, and to be about my Father's business.'

And it was so.

‡

'But how do the two families become one, Lea? I asked her now. 'There have been great disputes over whether Jesus had brothers or not. Some have said yes, while others have argued that the brothers mentioned in the bible were only his cousins.'

'Well, *pairé,* it is like this: Mary did not recover from her illness and died soon after their return from Jerusalem, but not before she whispered her dying wish into her husband's ears: that he take Mariam into his house, to be a mother for their child and a good wife in his bed. And that is why, after an appropriate time passed, Joseph the Carpenter married Mariam and the two families became one. The brothers mentioned in the bible are actually only step-brothers, while James, the young son of Cleophas, the one who goes on to become a disciple, was a cousin. You see how natural it is?'

I saw it and I did not know what to say. I wrote instead.

CHAPTER 11

THE RABBI

Gamaliel was so impressed with Jesus of Nazareth that he asked the child's father to permit the boy to stay in Jerusalem, and to come from time to time for instruction in his Academy.

But the boy had only been with him for some days when his mother died suddenly and he had to return home. In truth two Passovers would pass before he could come again to Jerusalem, and by then he had grown into a young man of fifteen springs, tall for his age and upright of bones, with fair hair and eyes shining intelligently from out of that heart-shaped face.

Gamaliel was the son of Simon and the grandson of the famous Rabbi Hillel. Like his father and grandfather before him, he was a Pharisee – a doctor of the law – and although he was not yet thirty springs he had been marked for greatness. He liked to indulge his imagination by classifying his many pupils in the same way that fishermen classified their fish, and it had worked well for him, that is, until Jesus came to him for instruction. For Jesus defied categorisation.

Yes, Jesus was well educated and could apply his knowledge to answer the most puzzling questions with eloquent perspicacity, but he did not wish to answer questions, his desire was always to ask them! Never before had Gamaliel found a pupil with knowledge and understanding who had no wish to proclaim them!

Jesus always came in autumn and remained with Gamaliel throughout the winter, learning the deeper truths and laws of the tradition of Israel. But as soon as spring announced itself, he would leave again for his home in Nazareth to help his father with his carpentry. He came and went, and the short months they spent together grew precious to Gamaliel.

During his stays, when he was not being taught at the academy, Jesus would go for long walks on his own. Gamaliel knew this because the boy would later take him to the lower city, or else to those places outside the city walls to show him what he had found: the poor and the wretched, the beggars, the lepers and the insane. Afterwards he would ask Gamaliel, in the cool and quiet of the Temple court,

'What do the priests and scholars and scribes do for those poor souls, rabbi? What good are all their sacrifices and hymns and rituals, all their learning and commentary, all their scrolls and parchments and laws – if they do nothing for the suffering of their people?'

The sadness and anguish in Jesus' voice seemed to go deep into his heart, and Gamaliel could think of nothing to ease his pain or to answer the questions that plagued him. In truth, Gamaliel soon realised that he could teach Jesus nothing more, for the young man's soul seemed to be nourished from a source far beyond Gamaliel's comprehension; a secret fount of wisdom, which Gamaliel could kindle, but to which he had no access.

Now, as Gamaliel and Jesus sat together on the terrace of the Temple court, he observed the sky, milk-blue and cloudless with only a hint of spring in the air, and he was certain that the time for the youth's final leave-taking was at hand. He felt such a sadness for it that he resolved to ask Jesus to remain at the Temple permanently and be proven worthy of an elevated position. Prudently, he broached the question by asking Jesus how he passed his time in Nazareth, when he was far from the Temple and his teachings.

'I work with my father,' he answered, simply.

Gamaliel nodded with a knowing smile, 'All work is profitable, Jesus, but do you think such work is worthy of your understandings and talents?'

Jesus looked at him with a bland eye. 'You have taught me many things, rabbi, but my father also teaches me.'

'Of course he does. Can you tell me this: what have you found to be the most important teaching of all?'

A long time passed in quiet but Gamaliel was patient, sensing the birth of a new intimacy. Would he finally know what truly lived in the soul of this remarkable youth?

When Jesus spoke, however, his voice was different, weighty and burdened, so that even his face seemed cast in darker tones.

'I have learnt that whatever is made by a man will one day turn to dust, like the tables my father builds; that all that begins in the world must have an end. But I also know that there exists something that has no beginning, and no end.'

'What is that, Jesus?'

'Truth, master Gamaliel. That is what lies behind all that is made. And it does not change from person to person, from aeon to aeon, but lives above all things and exists even before a man can know it … this truth belongs only to God.'

Gamaliel was pleased. 'And what is man, among these truths?'

'Man is truth and falsehood combined. In a man's heart there is wisdom, which is his feminine part, and in his head there is the possibility of intelligence, which is the masculine; to bring both together in the body and the soul, is to birth the spirit in a man.'

Gamaliel was astounded at the wholeness of his answer. It made sense of that Hermetic riddle, which had plagued him since his time with the Therapeutae: the riddle of a stone that is no stone at all but is derived from three and two and one. Now Gamaliel knew what it was!

Body, soul and spirit; male and female; in one human being!

His heart soared with enthusiasm! How simple and graceful! How elegant it was! He sat forward, stumbling over his words, asking in an excited fashion if Jesus would remain in his academy, telling him of the many things they could explore together, and the possibility of his advancement. Forgetting he was a rabbi, he laughed with joy and let all his feelings come out. But when he was finished he noticed that Jesus had said nothing, and that his head was bent downwards. He admonished himself then, for being too hasty, too forward, too brash and forceful, and wondered if he had trampled on the sapling in search of the water jug.

'I thank you,' Jesus said, raising his head again, 'but I will not stay, I must leave here and go in search of knowledge.'

Gamaliel's heart sank. Perhaps he had not known how much he loved his friend until that very moment. 'Leave here? But Jesus, the Sanhedrin is the greatest centre of knowledge in the world!'

'That may be … but it does teach the knowledge I seek.'

'What knowledge are you after?'

'Forgive me, master Gamaliel,' he said. 'but you have always told me to be frank with you and so I will be frank. I will tell you that your logic and codes are fine and beautiful, your laws and regulations shimmer and glitter, and yet … they die away to nothing in my ears. They die away because behind them there is no experience. They are,' he searched for the words a moment, 'only shadows of the truth … forgeries.'

Gamaliel was slighted – *forgeries*! He felt the blood rise to his face. 'Listen to me, Jesus! Do not mock the tradition of Israel, which was given to us so that we, the chosen people, might prepare for the Messiah!'

'I am not mocking it,' Jesus explained. 'I am only telling you the truth as I know it.' His coloured eyes held Gamaliel's as he spoke, 'Tell me, what hinders the coming of the Messiah?'

Gamaliel was flustered by his directness and looked away. 'You know as well as I that there must first come repentance and good works …'

'Repentance and good works?' Jesus asked with raised brows, while beneath them those previously tranquil eyes were a-fire. He stood and walked to the porches. 'Is that what Elijah tells?'

Gamaliel was annoyed that his friend was in so querulous a mood, and he answered harshly, 'No … Elijah tells that He will come when His voice is heard!'

Jesus began to pace the terrace, his body full of nervous activity. 'Yes! He will come when his voice is heard ... but where are the ears that can hear it over the rabbis quoting their quotes?' He paused in his pacing to give Gamaliel a sideways glance. 'Your teachings have dulled your ears and have fashioned eyes that are trained only on kings, and priests arrayed in resplendent robes, only on those who sit on thrones, or in the cool shades of the Temple courts. How will your ears hear Him and your eyes recognise Him if He comes among the poor and the lowly, or if He is seen speaking to gentiles and idol worshippers?'

Gamaliel watched him a moment before making his voice cool and laconic, 'When He comes to us we will know Him because we have the words of the prophets in our ears; those who tell us how to recognise Him!'

Jesus took this into consideration. 'Then you will not know him in your heart, is that what you say? You will only know him if he fits the image you have made of him in your mind?'

Gamaliel, confounded, replied, 'It is in the way of young men that they desire to know everything for themselves, in their hearts. But you must be satisfied with what those who came before you have left you, those who could still hear the voice of God. You will travel the world and you will not find a man who can teach you to be a prophet.'

Jesus stopped his pacing to look at the sky now. 'For that I need no teacher …' he said, 'what I need is someone who can help me understand what I already see and hear!'

Gamaliel raised his brow. 'What did you say? Are you telling me that you can hear the voice of the Bath Kol? That you think you are a prophet?'

Jesus closed his eyes and allowed the meagre sun to wash over his face a moment. 'It speaks to me, and there are times I near understand it … times when I think I know what it says …'

'What does it say?' Gamaliel was breathless for his answer.

Jesus turned to him sadly. 'It tells me that we have forgotten our Fathers in the heavens.'

Gamaliel took this in. He searched in his repertoire of answers for something that would make him seem wise and helpful, but found nothing. After a moment, he settled for this,

'If what you say is true, you should stay! You can teach others to hear the voice … in time, your teaching itself will make you wise, wiser than me, wiser even than my grandfather before me, for you will teach from experience!'

Jesus shook his head, wincing as if Gamaliel's words were hurtful. 'No! Stop! Don't you see? I will be no greater and no wiser! I will become a dead man like you are becoming! Dead …' He pointed to the Hall of Polished Stones, 'like those men in the Sanhedrin who use cheap tricks and enchantments, incense, sacrifice and song to deceive the people and themselves!'

The boy reined in his temper and his face grew soft. The man who spoke now was so different that even his face appeared to have lost its dark shadows. 'Forgive me, master,' he said. 'I don't mean to insult you. Just the opposite, I am grateful to you for helping me to understand that mine is a different destiny and that I must find a place where I can live it.'

Gamaliel was slighted and wounded … perhaps also a little envious. 'I have listened to you throw in my face everything that I hold dear, everything that sustains our people! I hope your soul is not falling into heresy, for if you speak like this to others there is no telling what the priests will do. They can unmake a man with just one word!'

Jesus considered this and blinked and nodded, as if he were fixing these words to the nub of his heart. 'The priests may unmake me and perhaps they will, that is true, but they can never unmake the truth. That, rabbi, is imperishable!'

He turned to go, and Gamaliel stood, for he realised, despite his anger and hurt that he was losing his friend. 'Our paths may be different ones,' he called after him, 'I grant you that, Jesus! But must our friendship be over? I would like it to be renewed one day ... if, by then, you still love your teacher.'

Jesus paused, and his voice was gentle over his shoulder when he said, 'I do love you, rabbi, but I love truth more.'

With that he was gone, leaving the young rabbi looking after him, dazzled and puzzled, full of wonder and woe and confusion, as if he had seen the sun at midnight, or the stars poking out of a midday sky. What should he think of such strange and shocking words, spoken so mightily by the young Jesus of Nazareth? If they were true then all his life, that which had so far come to pass, and even that which was yet to come, had been, and would be, founded on an untruth, on a falsehood. Such a thought could have made Gamaliel sink to his knees, had the marble floor not been taken from under him!

He consoled himself with the thought that Jesus might be of the lineage of David and a fine student, but in the final analysis, he was only a youth full of notions. He was not a teacher or a prophet – he was not a priest or a king. Still, such words, such words ...

This uneasiness lingered in Gamaliel's heart for many years before he would understand it. In that far off time he would be standing upon the same spot, but he would not be puzzling over the student full of despair who was walking away into the spring afternoon, he would be marvelling in recognition of a man who was not a student, or a teacher, not a prophet, a king or a priest, but the hope of all Jews and the consolation of all Israel.

CHAPTER 12

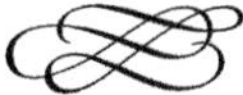

SALOME

The house was clean swept, the bread was made, the lamps were filled and burning, the bowls were laid out for the modest repast that simmered aromatically in the hearth and Salome, having a rare moment to herself, went out of the house to watch the sun sink into its bed.

From behind her came the comforting sounds of the young men washing for the evening meal, the bustling of Mariam and her daughters, and Mariam's sister-in law, the wife of Joseph's brother, Cleophas. But for now, Salome was alone with the long view of the hills and dales of Galilee and the stars poking out of the sky, speaking their silent language, one to the other. And she was so taken by this celestial spectacle of twilight that she did not hear Jesus come to the low stonewall and sit beside her.

So well known to her was the sound of his voice that Salome did not flinch or jump or feel startled when he said, 'You are gazing at the kingdom of heaven, Salome. Do you feel it descending into your heart?'

Salome's name meant peace and it was peace she felt when she looked to her favourite – the reason why she had followed her beloved Mary, who was now dead, to Nazareth those many years before. She put a hand to his face and he did not mind it, for she had long been his nurse and that hand, once so malformed, had nurtured him through illness and health and raised him through the various stages of his youth.

She narrowed her eyes to look at him and made her voice practical, 'You like to see into the hearts of others, Jesus, which is a fine gift … but you hold your own thoughts close to you … so that even I cannot see them.'

He acknowledged this with a nod of the head. 'Yes, and it is a strange thing to me also, Salome. Strange and yet familiar! When I am working with my father and my hands are busy …' He looked at them. 'I feel like I am one man and I think I know who that man is, this son of a carpenter … but when I am with myself, when I gaze at my thoughts, I find that I am a different man. I find myself full of memories of things that I have not seen or heard or felt! At those times, I am a stranger … even to myself.'

Salome had a gift of second sight which ran in all the women of her family, and so years ago, after the death of Yeshua, she had seen the reason for the change in him, which even Jesus himself did not seem to understand. She had waited for him to find a quiet space in which to speak with her.

'You are full of restlessness, Jesus, I sense it, and I also sense that you will soon leave because of it … the question is, where will you go?'

Jesus looked at her with surprise. 'Well … you have surely read my mind! As you know, this village is small and has never supported us. And father is too unwell to travel in search of work … so I am of the mind to go alone this year.'

Salome passed a hand over her face. 'You see? I had guessed it! Promise me you won't venture *outside the land,* where my forefathers once dwelt … you know that in those places you will find only darkness. Even the dust under your feet will be unclean on your return and all will think you defiled. The dirt of those places is like death and putrid things to a Jew. Will you seek to bring death home, so that men will have no traffic with you?' She looked at him, to make sure he had taken it in, and he matched her gaze with his own steady eyes.

'How should I concern myself with men whose view of the world is narrowed?'

This was his other self, the one full of defiance!

'What do you hope to find in that wider world beyond your homeland?'

'A teaching that is true, that can help me to understand why everything is falling into ruin. This, I shall not find here in Nazareth.'

'You know,' Salome said, 'my mother once told me a story about a mule who wandered the world looking for the source of a wonderful perfume. One day the poor thing realised that the perfume came from a twig of jasmine caught behind its ear.'

'When did the mule realise it?'

'Not until the jasmine was already dead and withered, and had fallen to the ground.'

Jesus nodded. 'And the meaning of the story is that I will go in search of something I already have, something right behind my ear, is that it?'

'That is it, for certain,' she said.

'Even so … I must go,' he told her cheerily. 'I am as stubborn as a mule!'

She paused a moment, listening to the ring left behind by his voice. 'Yes … yes,' she confirmed it, 'so you are … I know … and that is what I told my mother, and if I hadn't wandered the world I wouldn't be here with you this night. You see … all is as it should be.' She glanced up at him. 'Have you told your stepmother?'

He gave her a sideways glance. 'Not yet.'

'Oh, Jesus!' she chided. 'You mustn't be unkind to Mariam. Her life has been a puzzle. Take a moment to think on it. First she loses a husband, then she loses her son, not long after that her other son moves into the Nazarite order to live a solitary life. Of the two youngest children, one has fallen into the lap of the zealots and the other is too young to help her. All of them have disdained their stepfather's trade as something beneath them. Since your father's illness, you have been her handhold in the world … how must she lose you too?'

'I do not see how I am her handhold,' he said.

'Well, let me tell you that over the years, in all that time you were coming and going from Jerusalem, I observed her sadness each time you left.'

He looked at her. 'She never seemed full of joy each time I returned. I appear to cause her pain no matter what I do, if I go, or if I stay ... it is all the same,' he said, with a shrug.

'That is because she is troubled, Jesus. The love that grows in her heart for you, does not sit well with the memory of her dead son, and so she stows it away like a seed awaiting its season ...'

Jesus was long quiet, until it seemed his breath near stopped. 'Then I shall let it germinate while I am searching for wisdom,' he said.

'For how long will you search?'

'As long as it takes to find it, or else to realise there is none to be found. In the meantime, perhaps her heart will mend if she sees me less.'

Salome held back her tears, for she remembered how she had missed him herself when he was away at the Temple. 'And mine will break ... for I fear I will not live to see you come over that rise again, my heart's child!'

He laughed in the purpling light. This was Jesus now, the one who could laugh.

'But you will, Salome! You will see many things yet, even before others see them, you will see them!'

She nodded her head with resignation. 'Yes, yes ... I suppose you are right ... in my family women live long years ... I will be alive to see many things ... that is what I am afraid of,' she said to him, and fell to watching the sky.

'Don't be afraid,' he said to her, 'Things will be what they will be, despite your worry.'

She smiled to herself. 'Yes, I know they will, and still, it does not prevent me from worry.'

He put an arm around her shoulders and she felt his warmth. Thus they remained together, united in fellowship, until noises reached them from the house and the spell was broken.

CHAPTER 13

SUN HERO

Gaius Cassius was blindfolded and cold, holding a dagger in his mouth. In the stillness, he sensed the movement of his blood, the intake of his breath and the turning of his heart. He did not know where he was or how long he had been here, only that his stomach gnawed with hunger and the dagger was making cuts on his lips and tongue.

He told himself,

Harness your mind! Soon you will rise, not Gaius Cassius the Roman, but Gaius Cassius the Sun Hero, a representative of Mithras. You will taste honey on your tongue and feel the warmth of the sun on your shoulders and you will be given to eat of the bread and given to drink of the blood.

First, however, he had to pass the test.

This was the sixth degree. Men had died in the attempt.

'Roman!' The voice rang like a bell, coming from all directions. 'Ascend the ladder!'

He knew there were seven rungs. Each represented a stage achieved. In years past, he had climbed to five rungs, now he must climb them again, and add a further rung.

He climbed the first and second rungs. He had swum across a fast moving river for the first and had jumped blindfolded over a burning fire for the second. For the third, he had climbed a steep mountain and had become a member of the sacred militia of the Invisible God Mithras.

He put a foot now, tentatively, on the fourth, and it was not where it should be. His head spun and he felt the pull of the abyss below. He slowed down his breath, for that was how he had achieved the fourth degree, by harnessing the air in his lungs. He pulled himself up to the fifth rung, by bringing rhythm into his blood and heart; this ability had once earned him the title of *Roman.*

He was aware now, that he had come to the sixth rung and the trial he must undergo to achieve the sixth degree. He must recognise the bull, and kill it with the ancient weapon he carried.

Hunger, pain, darkness, all seemed immense to him. That great yawning hole below beckoned him to fall into its waiting mouth. But death, he told himself, only frightened weak minds. Worse than death was to lose all rank and honour.

Suspended, he heard a beast. It would be an ugly creature, full of instincts and passions, and it would topple him from his ladder. The beast snorted in the darkness. Slow and careful, Cassius took the dagger from his mouth and grasped the hilt of the weapon, while holding tight to the ladder. He brought it to his chest and felt the cold tip sharp against his skin. He felt his heart, beating against the steel in rhythmic strokes. The muscles of his hand and arm strained against the bones, strained to hold the knife still, strained not to let it go. His jaw clenched and unclenched. He took an in-sweep of breath and let it out and took it in again and held it, listening for the animal that would soon come. When the earth began to tremble he only had a moment. Then, as he lifted the weapon, between the upward arc and the downward thrust, a doubt tore through him.

There is no bull! You are not holding a dagger. This is a test of your discernment; good from evil, truth from untruth ... and this is an untruth!

The world shook beneath him and disclosed a crack in the matrix of the ritual and into it he fell, into the cavity, into the abyss of his body.

When the blindfold was removed from his eyes he saw that he was on the stone floor of the cave, kneeling before a statue of Mithras killing the bull, in a room lit by torches and candles. Someone had come to pour wine, the source of ritual ecstasy, into his throat, and to stuff his mouth full of bread, the flesh and substance of Mithras. A purple cloak was placed over his shoulders and he was crowned and told to rise.

'You have ascended the ladder without falling; you have killed the bull; you have reached the Sun and become one with Mithras! You are a Sun Hero!'

There was a loud battery of noise, now, the clashing of cymbals and the beating of drums. Figures wearing animal masks, invokers and worshippers chanted hymns describing Mithras' journey across the sky. But Cassius was confused. He tried to bring sense to his thoughts. He looked to the chanting priests and wondered why they did not know that he had not climbed the sixth rung.

It was a moment before he understood, a moment before it was clear. The trial had occurred in his heart, in his soul. The bull had been his lower self, and he himself had taken the place of Mithras. The priests had not seen it because they had lost the ability to see into the heart of a man! They could not go beyond the fifth degree themselves!

This realisation brought with it a sense of dread, followed by a deep woe. He felt like a man who wakes up from his sleep to find that his entire family has been butchered while he slept and that he is alone. Outwardly he might be a Hero of the Sun, but inwardly he had lost all rank and honour. He had lost his brotherhood, for he would never again consider himself an initiate of Mithras. And so he grieved, because to lose this was more painful than death; it was like losing the very flooring and purpose of his life.

‡

'Oh Lea!' I said now. 'I feel for this man, Cassius Gaius Longinus, he has lost everything he has ever believed in!'

'And he will lose much more before his meeting with Christ,

because he has to let go of what he is, in order to become what he might be.'

CHAPTER 14

BATH KOL

At the appropriate time, Jesus left his ailing father and his stepmother and took up his mind's resolve to find work in far off places, not only as a means of supporting his family, but also to learn something of the world beyond what could be known in Jerusalem and Nazareth.

In his younger years he had accompanied his father in the pursuit of his trade and now he used those same routes, following in the skirt-tails of the caravans that passed through Nazareth and journeyed to the new city of Tiberias.

Tiberias lay on the shores of the Sea of Galilee and was the thought-child of Herod Antipas. Many Jews considered it to be the waste-hole of the world, because Herod had built it over an old burial ground. For this reason, the grand unfinished city was in need of men who were good with their hands; stonemasons, carpenters and engineers, and so Jesus had found work, not only in the construction of Herod's new palace, but also on the many stately dwellings that were being built for the upper classes of Roman society.

It was his habit to speak little, to listen, and to observe, as he worked, the temper and customs of the people around him. In Tiberias Jesus had seen the worship of Caesar and the cult of madness that the man inspired in those wealthy Romans who came to the city for the wonder benefits of its hot sulphuric springs. The worship of the ordinary people of Tiberias also interested him, and one day, when he heard celebrations in the streets for the god Attis, he went to see what it could teach him.

The procession consisted of men and women dancing to the sound of tambourines and flutes. The women wore amulets and flowing robes and painted faces, and the men cut their bodies with knives to let their blood flow - an act which the people said inspired visions of the future. Intrigued by it, he allowed himself to be led to the Temple of Attis. Here, while his everyday eyes observed the offering service performed by a priest at his altar, his other eyes saw a monstrous vision: the sacrifice offered by the priest was taken up by evil spirits! The idols of the pagan gods had become the likenesses of depraved beings and these were responsible for the frenzy and agitation of the people. The sight of it made him sick to the stomach and he had to take himself out of the Temple for air, his spirit crestfallen and deeply troubled.

After that he set off again, westwards to Syria, and to those great cities he had frequented with his father in his younger years, cities bordered by oceans: Tyre, Zerephath and Sidon, Byblos and Sarepta. Their ports were doorways to other lands and other races and their pagan religions. He studied their cults and spoke to their priests, seeking the grandeur of the ancient life of the gods. But again he found only ignorance and empty rituals, which called forth the attention of those same evil spirits of corruption. He also met many people at their work or during those quiet hours of rest in the evenings, when they sat listening to the murmur of fountains. He met others in the day, in those bazaars where they paused from their labours to exchange banter and thoughts. On the roads he spoke to merchants and itinerants, he listened to the woes of the pilgrims, to the gripes of the tax collectors, to the stories of the farmers and fishermen and the concerns of the labourers, publicans, priests, laymen and landholders. He befriended Gentiles, Jews, Samaritans, Greeks, Egyptians and Syrians, and wherever he went, whispers followed him:

A Nazarite of special qualities has arrived among us!

For this reason he often found himself surrounded by those who were in need of moral comfort, and he would tell them the stories and sayings he had gathered from here and there. The people listened to him for hours, and this listening seemed to comfort them. Even so, deep in their souls Jesus discerned an emptiness, which they did not know how to fill. He searched in his heart for a way to help them but realised he could not give them what they needed, for they needed more than stories. They needed their leaders to show them the way to God. And yet, how could they lead their people to God when the priests themselves were also lost?

Was he the only one who could see the world crumbling away?

He wandered long and travelled far and wide, and in his wanderings his concerns grew until an inner crisis of soul reached its apex on his return from the outer lands, at Caesarea Philippi.

He was nearing the city, built on the slope of Mount Hermon, some furlongs northeast of the Sea of Galilee. It was perched on a lofty terrace, overlooking fertile valleys and a road that meandered through temples and grottoes and places of pagan worship. Walking this road he observed the quality of the air. He could see the spirits of the trees, of rocks and soil, and he tasted the spirit in the water of the streams. He saw in nature the memory of the mighty power of the pagan priests, their wisdom and piety, but his spirit was directed also to the men who lived here and he saw that these people, more than any he had seen so far in his travels, had suffered a decline. Lepers, insane persons, lame and deformed children came out of hiding holes to regard him with their eyes as he passed. He could hear scuffles and arguments breaking out here and there, and lewd language and uncontrolled laughter coming from one place or another. It reminded him of his journeys to the outskirts of Jerusalem with Gamaliel, and he now realised that the pagan priests, like the Temple priests in Jerusalem, had deserted their people. They had left them to die a living death.

A leprous child stood some distance from him stretching out a skinless hand for a morsel of food. Jesus went to the child with pity and love in his heart and held the child's hand in his to comfort him. He gave the child some nuts and soon he ran away and returned with others, the afflicted and the desperate, the forlorn and the hopeless. They lamented and pulled at their hair and cried into their hands.

Someone called out, 'Are you a priest come to save us from this disease that has taken us? Will you offer up a sacrifice to the gods on our behalf?'

'A priest! A priest has come!' more voices joined in.

A groundswell of joy and praise broke out around him and the people began to press him towards the threshold of their temple. It was with anxiety that he entered the ruined place, full of cobwebs and brick-dust and broken effigies and idols.

The crowd, moved by longing and hope, pushed him towards the altar and he could not stop them. From this vantage point Jesus looked about him and saw something emerge from the shadowed corners, a red-winged being. It peered at him and said:

'Well, well ... you've come in and made yourself comfortable, have you? Look at you, poor fellow, pale as a ghost! You can see that the world is perishing ... the end of the world is near and you cannot stop it! So why not enjoy what time is left? You can lead this rabble and make something of yourself ... go ahead ... stand up on that altar and shout 'repent, repent!' This mongrel lot will follow anyone who says those words!'

Jesus noted the expectation on the faces of the men and women and children. He was no priest; how could he give them what they desired? Looking at them he saw all the pagan peoples that he had met in his travels gathered together into one great corpse made from unwashed bodies and wild faces; a corpse of human suffering overflowing with wickedness and with desperation and disease. He sensed the smell of rotted flesh, of darkness, stagnant, dank – the odour of human degradation. The world whirled around him, and in that moment he felt the universal suffering of humanity as if it were his own. It streamed into him like a rush of white fire from all the faces that looked up to him for comfort and he could not take a breath for the immensity of its weight.

'What's the matter? Don't you like my handiwork?' said the being.

Jesus shouted at it, 'Who are you? Why do you do this?'

When the people heard his words they seemed to grow afraid, for they sensed an open traffic with evil and began to push and shove to flee from the temple.

But Jesus felt a pain, a dart of poisoned ice burst into a thousand lighted candles, each shimmering in the air ahead of his eyes. He was removed then, from that place and the people and the evil being.

In this realm of nothingness, he heard these words:

'Listen, Jesus ...'

Aum

Evils hold sway

The I-hood of man struggles free

And guilt is incurred at the expense of others,

Which is experienced in the daily bread

Wherein the will of the heavens does not rule

Because man has separated himself from our realms,

And forgot the names

Of our fathers in the heavens!

Jesus recognised this voice. He shouted into the open vaults of the deserted temple, 'Yes ... evil holds sway because men have wanted freedom from the gods but now everything falls into ruin, the world is old, how can the people rise up to remember the gods again?'

The voice said,

'Watch and wait Jesus, soon comes my Son and He will make the old new again!'

'Who are you?' he asked.

A warm, love-giving radiance entered into his heart.

'I am knowledge and ignorance, I am shame and boldness, I am shameless, I am ashamed, I am strength and I am fear and I am war and peace, I am the truth and the speech that cannot be grasped. I am the name of the sound and the sound of the name; I am the sign of the letter and the designation of the division ...I am Bath Kol, I am Sophia, the voice of the Wisdom that is All.'

CHAPTER 15

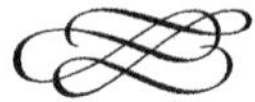

REMEMBERING

When Jesus returned home he was twenty-four springs, though in his heart he felt himself as ancient as Mount Tabor.

His father had long awaited his homecoming and they were graced with some quiet weeks together, before Joseph fell deeper into his illness and succumbed to it peacefully in his bed. Afterwards, custom dictated that he wait a year with his family, and he passed this time at work, reflecting upon his travels, allowing his experiences to enter deeply into him.

The Essenes of Nazareth had time and again attempted to recruit him for their order, but Jesus had always said no. Now, on his return from the outlands, they came again, having heard of his travels, and he welcomed them, for he was interested in their warm conversation and the lively exchange of ideas which they offered.

Throughout the winter months, fulsome in long shadows and cool winds and resplendent skies, the Essenes came each day and sat with him in the garden. He knew they were gleaning from him the measure and nature of his knowledge and the dimensions of his experience, and soon they made Jesus an offer. The knowledge he had gained all these years was similar to that knowledge attained through initiation, and so if he chose to enter the order, he would not need to undergo the trials of the lower grades. They assured him they could teach him more than he already knew.

'Do not judge us too hastily, Son of Mary, for what you see around you in Nazareth and other cities is not a reflection of our order's true nature. It is in the monasteries that you will find our saints, our seers, men who live by the pure rule. Only they can teach you the deepest and most profound secrets of our order.'

They left to await his answer.

Over seven nights Jesus pondered his decision.

While reviewing his life since his twelfth year he came to an understanding. The Essenes, among whom he had lived all his life, had separated themselves from the ecstasy of the pagan people, and also from the calculated inward brooding of the Hebrew priests. Perhaps in their inner sanctum they held that living knowledge which he was seeking? Perhaps wise Salome had been right: he had been like a mule in search of a scent that had always been behind his ear. There was only one way for him to know, and so he made up his mind to say yes. He would follow them to their sanctuary at Engaddi to learn their ways and laws, on the provision that he would be permitted to remain aloof from those same laws, if he so wished.

They agreed.

Jesus was aware that Mariam did not ask him why the *quiet ones* came and went from her home, or what they asked of him, but he knew the question lived in her soul as she busied herself with everyday matters. These days she was surrounded by people: his aunt Mary and his uncle Cleophas, who had come to help since his father's death; her daughters and her other sons; and her servant, Salome.

There was rarely a moment of quiet to tell her of his decision.

On the anniversary of his father's death, when the winds announced the coming of warmer days, there came the opportunity.

She was alone, kneading bread.

He took a long time to come to the point, for he always sensed in himself a hesitation and awkwardness in her company. When he finally told her he would soon leave, she took a long moment to answer, so that it seemed almost as if she had not heard him at all.

'Why so soon?' She blurted out, without looking at him, her attention on her fists pounding the dough, 'You have barely returned from your wanderings, now you want to go again! What makes you so restless?'

Looking at her, Jesus pondered their peculiar friendship. In many ways they were strangers and yet he had known her near all his life. It was true that her blood did not run in his veins, but there were moments when her heart, in its slow measures, opened up to his, and he felt the warmth of recognition and love. When those moments came, her face, framed by the black mourning mantle, with its nose and the angle of the jaw and the bones of the cheeks, seemed etched in his memory, as if each detail had been carved there with a knife.

But there were other times when, along with this feeling of the deeply familial, they held each other aloof, as they were doing now, as if they were seeing each other for the first time.

He could not explain this strangeness to himself, and now when her eyes met his, the expression in them was so close and natural, yet so distant and strained, that it was unbearable to look upon it. Something told him that they were sharing an unspoken act; that they were each seeking to remember something through the other, but whatever it was they sensed sorrow in it and so they swung like a pendulum, from closeness to distance, seeking out one another one moment, and pulling away from one another the next. Forestalling the moment of recognition, again and again.

He realised that he had not answered her question. 'What makes me restless? I suppose it is that I haven't found what I'm looking for.'

'And do you know what that is?' she asked.

'I will know it when I find it.'

She considered it a moment and returned to her pounding.

'You need not worry for money,' he told her. 'You have all the earnings of my journey and you must use it as you see fit.'

She paused. 'That's not my worry, Jesus.' She took up the dough and slammed it on the table to make her point. 'My worry is not for money, it is for the tongues of the people ... they don't know what to make of you ... they say you're lifted up too high for yourself. Mind what I say … such talk can lead to suffering.'

He felt her concern and he gentled her, 'Doesn't Isaiah tells us that we must not hide from suffering?'

She made a gaze into his eyes and poured out all the strength of her Temple education and intelligence into it to convince him of her words, 'Isaiah was speaking of the Messiah, Jesus, the Messiah, whom Israel awaits … we, ordinary people, should not run towards suffering like a thirsty camel runs towards a water hole!' When she said this, a sudden remorse moved over her brow and she squared her shoulders and bent to her work to hide it.

'The world thirsts,' he told her.

'Yes … yes … and you thirst also …' she said, without looking up.

'What if I said that I am the thirst and also the water that quenches it?'

She paused in her work again and into her unhappy face there entered a trace of a smile. 'Oh! So now you are two things?' She gave a sigh of resignation. 'Where will you go to this time?'

He broached it gently, 'To Engaddi.'

She stared down at her dough – Jesus could see that it was sticky. She nodded to herself as if she now knew two things: she had not added enough flour, and she had guessed at Engaddi – neither appeared to sit well with her.

'To the Essenes … well!' she said, 'Now I know why they have been at our door like bees hovering over a bush in flower! Engaddi is a desolate place, Jesus!' She looked up at him. 'Why must you go there? With all your learning you would be welcomed any time at the Temple as a rabbi. Must I lose two sons to the ascetics and have nothing to show for my life?'

Jesus was reaching into the great earthenware pot wherein was kept the flour. He took up a cupful and brought it to the dough. 'This camel must quench his thirst,' he said, and sprinkled the flour.

She turned her dough over and over to take up it up. 'That's your mother in you talking! She always knew how much flour was enough, and yet she did not seem to live with her feet on the ground! For my part, I have always felt the ground keenly beneath my feet and that is why I treasured your mother.' She sighed. 'You may not know it, but my comfort has always been that I see her in you, in the fairness of your skin and the love of your heart. But Jesus, I also see something else in you! Yes ... something more than joy and calmness. There are times when a flame rises up in you that seems not your own. I worry then for you ... and when it comes, the moment I recognize that fire, I look away!' She halted, searching for additional words, 'What overcomes me? I don't know! Sometimes I fear that if I were to look too deep into your eyes ... I would not meet Jesus bar Joseph at all ... but some other man!' She made a nervous laugh and said, 'Is this not a remarkable madness?'

His response came to him without a thought, 'What is an eye, mother? Is God not capable of fashioning an eye in place of an eye and a hand in place of a hand?'

This surprised her and she didn't seem to know what to say. 'God is capable of anything, Jesus. That is what we are told ...'

But Jesus did not hear her, for he was taken by his own words. His heart grew wide with recollections that were half forgotten and half remembered - of two boys sitting in a field, or walking arm in arm, two boys sharing meals or laughing together. He had not thought *on* Yeshua in some time but he had always felt him *in* his thoughts. Yeshua was the one who would have said such words. A realisation came to him then, an understanding of why his stepmother loved him and yet held him remotely from her; why she seemed close to him one moment and distant the next.

What lived within him, that part of him that was like Yeshua, said to her, 'God can make two into one if it serves his design. He can make the inside like the outside, and the outside like the inside, and the above like the below, and the male like a female and the female like a male, one and the same ...'

She stopped kneading her bread, to look at this with a frown. 'How can he do this?'

'Perhaps it is like a woman who conceals leaven in her dough, and though she can make two loaves from it makes only one. Perhaps if you were to recognise the son in front of you, the Lord would make the son hidden from you plain to you!'

She gasped. 'Praise the Lord our God!' Tears welled up and she opened her mouth to say something else, but her lips would not utter the words.

‡

'It was only a moment, *pairé*, spent this way, while the afternoon crept through the shadows of other rooms. Afterwards, having acknowledged it, they both returned to their duties – he to his workshop and she to her dough.'

'What was she going to say, Lea?' I asked.

'She was going to say that she could see Yeshua, her son, in Jesus. But these feelings could not rise up into her thoughts.'

'Why not?'

'The time was not yet come, pairé, don't be impatient! First she must let her feelings sit in the warm silence of her heart, like 'leaven', until they can rise up to become words.'

'Oh my!'

CHAPTER 16

THE ENLIGHTENED ONE

Jesus travelled with the pure ones to the valley of Engaddi, an oasis of fresh water springs and palm trees thrust up out of a stark, apocalyptic landscape. Here, atop a sheer windblown hill overlooking the abundant desert skies and those salt-laden waters of the Dead Sea, he was taken to the motherhouse of the Order of the Essenes, where its members lived in complete and silent seclusion.

On his arrival he was welcomed with respect, and over time he was given instruction and shown the library of scrolls preserved in clay pots, wherein the elders and guardians of the community had sealed the memory of their founder, the ordinances of their people and the prophecies of the holy ones. Jesus had lingered many an hour in this repository of wisdom, reading by the light of an oil lamp.

Below the motherhouse, in a modest convent, there lived the celibate educators of the children of outsiders. Beyond this could be found the dwellings of the married Essenes, the weavers, carpenters, vine growers and tillers of the soil, the life-blood of the order. He saw that this community was not unlike the community at Nazareth, where the lay people supported the priests and the teachers, and so it had not been difficult for him to grow accustomed to its ways.

At Engaddi, however, the community not only provided for the priests, it also provided for the many penitents who came here from every place, and the ascetics who lived in the desert gorges and hillside caves of the neighbouring areas. Jesus wandered through these desolate places with his teachers, garnering their knowledge. At other times, he went alone into the village to talk to the simple folk. When he was feeling the need for quiet, he would take himself to where the trees shaded the coolness of a waterhole not far from the settlement. Here, he could sit and ponder the purity, or impurity, of the teachings he was receiving.

One day, when he came to the waterhole, he found one of his teachers waiting for him. The old man's head was roughened by the sun, and his white beard flowed like a shiver from his chin. He greeted Jesus with a nod, and asked him if he knew what he had come for.

'You wish to speak with me.'

'That is so.'

His time at Engaddi was nearing an end and the old man had come to seek from him his decision: to go or to stay.

'Much time has passed since your arrival in our community and I am sent by the elders not to convince you to remain with us, since a man must decide freely to enter into our cloister, but rather to speak of the grave and solemn responsibility you shall undertake if you decide to join us in our doings.

'You know that Nazarites are reverenced by all as holy men. They are holier even than the Levites born into the priesthood! When they go to the Temple in Jerusalem, they are given every convenience and are permitted at any time to enter the court of the Nazarites, where they can gather up their hair and cook their peace offerings.

'What I have come to tell you is this … if you become an Essene you will not be respected or given conveniences. You will not be understood by any man! For we Essenes walk like shadows …' he whispered, 'silent, quiet … and none know that we prepare the world for the coming of the Messiah through fasting and penitence and deep prayer. We live a grave life, Jesus, as you know, because it is only through purification that we gain knowledge, it is only by shunning the world and its un-cleanliness that we shall rise higher than other men. Listen to me, Jesus,' he sat forward, 'the world has stained the soul and the soul has tainted the breath, which was given as a gift to man by God, so that when we breathe out ... we kill the world. Once you enter into our cloister all that exists outside its gates, all that lives in the kingdom of the world must be forgotten. That is why there are no images at our portals, Jesus, because our eyes must be kept pure for the images that are true. Have you seen the pagan idols in your travels? Are they not like the beings we meet in the world? How can we presume to be the creators of the likeness of God? All images must be left behind at those gates, for only in seclusion can the mind make images of higher things, and only these higher images can change the heart, and only a change of heart can cleanse the breath ... so that a man becomes like a plant, life giving.'

But as the man spoke, before Jesus' eyes the image of the Essene softened into the green foliage, and in its place came the image of another being.

The figure wore a smile that conveyed a likeness of all the love in the world, all that was valued as worthy and holy. He spoke even as the other man did, but his words were heard in the heart and not the ear.

'I was born on the night of a full moon in far distant lands, long before this time, Jesus. I was the son of a wealthy king and queen. When I was your age, full of thirst to know the world, I too left my home, just as you have done, and what I saw was full with ills. Yes, I saw the pain of disease and the ravages of old age. I saw poverty and hunger and pain. I saw women crying for their lovers and mothers crying for their children and drunkards crying for their drink. I saw the cold, the weary, the beaten, the helpless and the hopeless. I saw these things as you have seen them and I too mourned for those I could not help. The truth is, Jesus, I would have returned home to the palace of my father, feeling despondent, had Vishva Karman, the artist of the gods, not appeared to me. After that, I sought enlightenment as you have done. I sat beneath the Bodhi tree where I was transfigured and it was through this illumination that a light was shed upon the ultimate truth:

'Birth is suffering. Illness, thirst and hunger are suffering. Old age and death are suffering. Separation from loved ones and unification with those we do not like is suffering. Pain is suffering and the absence of pleasure is suffering. Attaining what is desired is suffering, and attaining what is not desired is suffering. Ignorance is suffering and knowledge is suffering, craving and grasping and consciousness are suffering. To end suffering, to release the soul from the eternal chain of incarnations, to find salvation, I realised that one had to extinguish the self, and blot out the thirst for existence.

'And so this is what I, the Enlightened One, went on to teach men.

'But now, Jesus, the time for such a teaching is ended. For just as there are those who follow the path willingly, relinquishing all earthly things, walking with their white robes carrying their bowls in their hands, not labouring for their meals but living only from the alms that others deign to give them, so there must also be those who cannot follow the path, those who cannot relinquish earthly things. The world needs labourers and street vendors and women who can bear children and cook meals. There must always be those who do not wish to escape the endless wheel, for without them who would support those who walk the path? The priests could not collect alms if all men were to relinquish the world for enlightenment!

'The fulfilment of these doctrines would force all people to be like the elders of this order, but this is no longer lawful. Something new is entering into the world, Jesus, and I have prepared for it. The most excellent of spirits will soon come. He was known in ages past as Vishva Karman and Rama and Krishna, and when he descends into the body of a man, He will be called Christ. He will bring with Him this understanding: that it is by way of death that man is born again; it is by way of suffering that compassion arises; and that it is by way of compassion that conscience can come into being. You see, conscience comes when we feel the pain of another. This voice of conscience now asks: how pure is enlightenment, if it is selfish and leads to the exaltation of a few through the suffering of many? He is near at hand, Jesus, and only conscience will recognise Him.'

Jesus felt the majestic truth of these words and asked, full of wonder, 'Who are you?'

'I am called Buddha, because I have sat under the Bodhi tree and I have been enlightened, and so I have escaped the endless round of incarnations. Long ago, it was I who made smooth the way for Christ! He will not escape the world but He will unite Himself with it for all times, not to save a few, but to save all.'

The vision melted away then, and the image of the Essene was returned to Jesus. The man was sitting as before and Jesus realised that only a moment had passed.

The elder was waiting patiently for a response, and he gave it: he could no longer remain with the Essenes.

Afterwards, he returned to the motherhouse with his mind crowded with thoughts, and as he reached the gates, upon which no graven images were seen, his now enlightened spirit eyes were directed to the creatures that were sat upon them. Had he seen these creatures before? Were these the same as those creatures he had seen among the Temple priests and on the pagan altars?

As he entered the compound the spirits fled in haste, and on seeing this a question arose in his heart:

Where do you go, spirits, when you flee from here?

For a long time this thought plagued him. This thought and the words of the Enlightened One.

CHAPTER 17

WATERMAN

John, son of Elisabeth and Zacharias, neared his thirtieth year.

In fulfilment of his father's vow to God he had been taken as a child to the Nazarites to be instructed. Thereafter he had lived in the desert among the peoples of the caves and the peoples of the gorges, and for this reason he now remembered little of his mother and father, and his youth in Hebron. Instead, he remembered other things: the surface of the salty sea, the scorched winds that fanned the palms, the taste of cool waters flowing from natural springs, and the endless round of fasting and deprivation, which formed a part of the life of every Nazarite. John had never taken a razor to his head, he had abstained always from any fermented drink, ate no animal flesh and had never come near a dead body. Moreover, the exercises he had endured since childhood and continued to endure had been harsh, the maceration and mortification of the flesh had hardened his body and loosened his soul in readiness for the coming of the Messiah.

Towards this end he spent long days and even longer nights in meditation and fasting, sitting before the mouth of his cave with his throat parched and his hunger gnawing and biting him like a ravenous animal. The cave was located in the walls of a steep gorge. From its lip he could look over the mountainous wilderness of Judea, over the death-imbued waters of the Dead Sea and the rigid bareness of the low-lying deserts. This landscape recalled to him the impoverishment of the human soul, the soul that chose only a striving for earthly things. In the distance he could also see that other place, which had once been cursed by God – Gomorrah. This was now the colony of the Essenes, who came to call it *Qumran*.

He would sometimes go to Qumran, and on the way he would pause to visit those little colonies that here and there dotted the wilderness. He spoke to the people of these hamlets of his hopes for the coming of the Messiah. But they did not hear his words with open ears, for they possessed lame spirits.

At Qumran he acknowledged the struggle for purity of the Essenes, and they, in turn, seemed to approve of his pious life, and allowed him to enter their cloisters from time to time, disclosing some of their ways to him. He knew they only did so, however, in the hope that he might incline his heart towards them. But he had always sensed something misshapen in their teaching, and for this reason he never remained long with them, preferring the solitude of his cell, his own rules, and his own ways.

It was on such a visit to Qumran that John met the man whom they called Jesus of Nazareth.

The day of the meeting he sat on the highest pinnacle of the Essene house, feeling particularly troubled. A deep gloom had settled over the expanses, making the desert's pillars and domes seem to him like sinister beings. The entire world was cast in murky tones by the grey-green clouds of an oncoming storm; a storm, which loomed above and made his bones and sinews creak; a storm, sure enough, caused by the devil.

He was torn from his thoughts by a voice.

'You are the prophet?' the voice said, and when John turned to look, he saw that it came from a man no older than he, a man who was tall, brown of skin, fair of hair, with eyes that were neither brown nor green nor blue: the eyes of a Galilean, a stranger of mixed heritage.

He did not like strangers.

'If I am a prophet …' he said, turning around again. '… then I am a solitary one.'

The Galilean did not seem put-off by him, which in itself was enough to make him curious.

'All prophets are solitary,' the other man pointed out, sitting next to him. 'Elijah was a voice in the wilderness, unknown by a world that did whatsoever it wished with him.'

John made a huff. 'What good did Elijah do? The souls of men have not changed, the world remains the same.'

'Did you hope you would find it otherwise?' the other man said.

What was this question that did not seek an answer, but seemed to be the answer itself?

He took a closer look at the silhouette of the stranger sitting beside him. He was gazing out at the desert as if it were a pleasure garden!

On the one hand, this man seemed as old as Abraham and on the other, there was something fresh and youthful that played about his eyes. The perception of these opposing natures made John fall into bewilderment and he did not know what to make of it, so he did something rare – he smiled, and asked,

'What is your name? It seems to me that we have met before.'

'I am Jesus. I was born in Bethlehem, but I come from Nazareth.'

'Nazareth?' John said, 'Nothing good ever came out of Nazareth, isn't that what they say?'

'Yes … that is what they say.' Jesus looked at him with a wide smile in his colourful eyes.

There was something in that smile. 'I have heard tell of you, I think …' John frowned, trying to put a finger on it. 'Are you one with this Order?'

Jesus shook his head slightly.

'What are you doing here, then?'

'I am the same as you.'

John nodded, reflecting on it. 'I am a solitary wanderer … a seeker …'

Jesus said, 'And that is what I am.'

John threw him a hard stare. 'What are you seeking?'

Jesus returned it, measure for measure. 'The truth.'

John shrugged. 'That is what every man seeks.'

'Is that not also … what you seek?' Jesus asked.

'Yes …' John said, disconcerted. 'But have you found it? That is the question.'

Jesus was tranquil and courteous, 'I had hoped to find it among the *good men*, but I didn't.'

'And where else have you looked for it?'

'Among the pagans,' Jesus said, 'and the priests at Jerusalem before that.'

'And you didn't find it?'

'I found temptation, but I also discovered that when a man flees from temptation, that is when he falls all the more into its pit.'

John smiled again to himself. This was a day full of rarities. 'Yes … that is so,' he agreed.

'I had to ask myself,' Jesus continued, 'why must salvation come only to those who have the blood of Abraham? Why could it not come to all men?'

John thought it a novel idea – salvation for all men!

'In this seclusion …' Jesus looked about him. '… the Essenes strive for purity. They touch no money and don't stain their hands with labour, and yet, a man has to eat bread and drink water, he has to have clothes to ward off the cold and a shelter to ward off the sun, don't you agree?'

John nodded. 'So he must, and the Essenes, who need these things, lay the burden of sin on those who support them, those who are willing to taint themselves with worldly things for their part, and do what the Essenes will not do.'

Jesus looked out to the desert. 'I have seen what happens to what they turn away from their gates … it goes out into the world to taunt ordinary people.'

John was attentive. 'What have you seen?'

'I have seen Satan, and the Devil.' Jesus said, gravely. 'And when they flee from here, they tempt those that live outside all the harder.'

John was dumbstruck. His own concerns and intuitions were, through this man, made more understandable to him. He peered into the landscape, torn and abandoned. Yes, he had seen the Devil and Satan: one a hot creature that made men fall into frenzy, the other a cold creature that lived in hard thoughts and hard hearts. He had known them in his meditations, and they had tempted him. It was difficult for him to speak of these things, which defied the tongue and words, except with this man.

'Yes … as you speak I realise that a time for seclusion is passed!' He looked at Jesus. 'And a time must come, when blood is of no importance … it is so near I can taste it on my tongue! Surely redemption cannot come by selfishly casting off burdens, but by shouldering the burdens of others!'

'That means,' Jesus told him, 'that if we are to find redemption we cannot escape suffering.'

John looked at Jesus squarely in the eyes. 'For men like you and me, men who spend a long time looking at the same desert and wondering when He will come, this suffering cannot come soon enough!'

'For whom do you wait?'

'The Messiah,' John said, 'whom else? I tell myself that Daniel's prophecies are all fulfilled! Lions and beasts, war and famine, degradation and enslavement have come to us. A great supply of calamities! How much suffering will convince God that we are ready for the consolation of Israel? How much suffering before the liberator comes to relieve us?'

'You sound angry with God.' Jesus of Nazareth said, pointing out the obvious.

'I have a bone to pick with him, it's true!' John said. 'All my life I have fasted and waited and fasted, and denied the flesh and fasted again – does God not hear the anguish of the soul that is alone and weary and waiting for the day of the Lord to come?'

The Galilean looked thoughtful, 'Perhaps the Lord is waiting for *you* to fulfil Elijah's task.'

John measured his guile. Finding none, he said, 'Tell me once more who you are.'

'We are kin, I think. My mother was Mary, your mother's cousin.'

'My mother's cousin …' he said. Amazement again washed over him and a sense of destiny signalled his soul to attention.

Jesus stood.

'Wait!' John moved to stop him. 'What do you mean … God is waiting for me to fulfil Elijah's task?'

'That is not for me to say …' Jesus answered, 'that is something between you and your angel.'

Jesus left and John remained, pondering his words.

By the time afternoon had gathered up the day to its bosom, John had gathered up his things to return to the seclusion of his cave to ask the question.

'How must I fulfil Elijah's task?'

There he sat, over twelve days and nights, until his longing for understanding had reached a feverish pitch and his devotion was poured out towards the planets and stars, when, in the darkness, he heard a mysterious tone – louder, gentler, louder again, resounding harmoniously in the night. He saw his soul as a dark disc around which bloomed an effulgence of light. Ring upon ring of rainbow colours appeared to form a radiant iris around it. The colours gathered in strength and began to eclipse the darkness, revealing the violet-red orb of his inner sun.

This sun spoke thus:

'John! Come closer, straighten your ears, lean them on my heart and listen. Yes … I am your angel; before I was your angel I was the angel of Buddha, but he no longer needs me since he is now transfigured so I am come to you, to tell you how you must fulfil Elijah's task. Come, my dishevelled one … you must prepare the way for the Being of the Sun who descends to the earth. You must make the path straight for his descent. Go forth and preach the gospel of repentance. It will be like Buddha's Sermon at Benares, for I will inspire you as I inspired him! You will tell all men that the 'kingdom' of God is at hand. After that you will plunge their dirty souls into water to loosen them from their bodies and cause them to see that they belong not only to bones and flesh, but also to the spirit. That is how they will be reborn, in the water of life, like fish.'

'Will I also baptise the coming one?'

'Yes ... but the Son of God is only once born! That is the secret.'

'Oh, angel!' John anguished, leaning on that angelic being with all his might. 'Tell me, how shall I know Him when he comes?'

'Leave that to me! I will prise open your eyes and you will see the spirit descend. Then you will be a witness that He is the Son of God. For you are the last of the prophets ... my little baptiser ... and the constellation from which you have seen the sun at midnight shall remain a memory of your deed and be known forever as Aquarius.

Men will call it the region of The Waterman.'

CHAPTER 18

BROTHERS

Yeshua's brother Jacob was a Nazarite. After his brother's death, those years ago, he left his home and offered himself to the Essene elders. They had welcomed him, because they nourished a hope that one day he might take his brother's place as the Messiah's chosen instrument. This, however, could only be known with certainty on his thirtieth year. Until then, he was expected to enter into the strictest branch of the order of Nazarites and become an Essene.

Over the years he passed every trial and all was well, but when time came for him to ascend to the highest grade – that grade which leads the son of darkness towards 'enlightenment', he failed, and the elders were forced to turn him away from the sanctuary doors at Engaddi. He could remain in the outer circle and live his life in the Essene communities, but he would never partake of the ceremonial meals with the elders.

When he left Engaddi, he did not return to Nazareth, but instead journeyed through the land; a man without a reason to sustain him, like a bird without a sky.

The world was a tense, dangerous place; everywhere prophets

shook their fists at the heavens, the Sicarri plotted against the Romans, and the Romans taxed the people, crucified them and caused blood to flow through the streets. The Levites, priests and rabbis were powerless and watched from their high places as if the trials of their people were none of their business. In the meantime, every faithful Jew waited for the Redeemer of Israel to come. But he did not come!

The sun pressed its fingers into Jacob's head now and told him of the suffering and anguish of his people and he shouted back to it:

If I was meant to take Yeshua's place, why did you let me fail?

Yeshua would not have failed. In Yeshua's eyes there had always lived the seal of his ministry; the testament of his kingship had always throbbed in his heart. Did Jacob recognise such a kingship in his own mind, such a ministry in his own heart?

He did not know.

But to think on Yeshua was to recall a resentment, which had long ago settled into the soil of his soul for the son of the carpenter, Jesus, the addled shepherd who could only play the flute and stare at the clouds. His brother's affection had been reserved for Jesus alone and after his death, Jacob's resentment had combined with his grief and had grown in him a suspicious, childish obsession, and it was this:

Years ago a bewildering change had come over his stepbrother, Jesus, in Jerusalem; a change that could not be explained. Suddenly, the backward boy was speaking eloquently, thinking unclouded thoughts and even arguing the law with the rabbis! How had he come by such cleverness? Even Jesus' coloured eyes had flecked with his brother's intelligence, and Jacob grew certain that Jesus had stolen Yeshua's soul and taken it for his own by some strange magic.

This had lived in him as a child, but as an adult he had buried these suspicions, jealousies and hatreds deep below his thoughts, concentrating on his destiny and his work with the Essenes. But now, on his journeys, when he took refuge at inns and khans, these feelings began to surface again. For in these places Jacob found himself taken for another man, a man from Nazareth who had sat with the innkeepers and with the poor and the lowly – a man who had made such an impression on them that at times, when the firelight was soft and the conversation turned mellow, he seemed to be among them. Jacob had been full of misery to learn the man's name – Jesus.

To add to his woes, when he finally returned to his home, he learned that the Essene elders had begun to train their eyes on his stepbrother, and had invited him to Engaddi on his own terms! And so his deep-seated spite drove him to visit his stepbrother, to have it out with him.

The home of Jesus was simple but skilfully built. It was set away from other houses, amongst a grove of olive trees, with a small garden and a place for the animals and for work. This day, Jesus was in the carpenter's workshop and Jacob stood a long time watching him from behind a tree, trying to find the courage to confront him.

Watching Jesus busy with his work reminded Jacob of a life grown distant to his mind. And as he watched, the angle of Jesus' head, half-turned to the light of the morning sun, began to play a trick on his eyes. Jesus' face began to grow about it the likeness of Davidic descent, and Jacob was taken aback by it – for was this not a reflection of his dead brother? His mind told him it could not be so, he was falling once again into the delusions of his childhood, and yet … and yet … his heart could not deny what his eyes were seeing!

A pain tore his soul from its hiding hole and it now stood before him, perfectly clear and visible to his eyes. He saw himself as a despised creature, full of snakes and vipers in his heart. He understood the reason for his failure at Engaddi – he had not managed to purify his diseased soul!

He left without a word to Jesus, and made his way to the Nazarite caves in Judea, where he hoped to burn away his earthly failings and self-loathing through a regime of fasting and solitude.

He spent long months living in these caves, grappling with himself, and yet he did not find himself altered. Finally, defeated and on his way to Jerusalem again, word reached him of a man who was baptising for the remission of sins. He was baptising in that place where an arm of the Jordan formed a bend in the river and created a clear, still pool. Crowds were gathered on the riverbank, men and women, even children stood listening to his words.

The baptiser was broad-made and tall. He wore a garment of camel hair over his chest and a girdle of skin about his loins and stood waist deep in the water. His eyes were dark and troubled, his hair was auburn, long and unkempt, but when he spoke his voice was full of authority, an authority beyond the world and its men. He told the people that the kingdom in the heavens was approaching the earth. He spoke of the Messiah who would soon come to redeem the errors of men. He said he would be able to recognise Him when he came, and so would all those who made pure their souls and repented their sins.

After that, men wearing only loincloths clambered towards the water to enter the cool depths of the river. They were completely immersed in the water and when they surfaced Jacob saw them gasp like newborns. And when they walked past him, he saw the edifying and majestic inner change apparent on their faces.

Jacob, loaded with a consciousness of his sins, heard the call of the river. He heard the murmur of pleasure and the cry of sorrow; the thunder of righteousness and the shame of wrongdoing. He heard the laments of mourning and the sighing for lost dreams. He heard stories of envy, murder, adultery and false witness. He heard of heresies, robberies and lusts. The river, for its part, chorused and harmonised these deaths and rebirths until all sin was turned to its opposite.

In his heart Jacob felt an urgent pull to join his voice to the river's voice, to immerse his failings in the healing waters and to surface again free from them; free from the festering and the spoilt deeps inside him. This was the redemption he had been seeking! Perhaps, free of his jealousy and covetousness he might find the path to his destiny?

He stood before the river's rim. The crowds were near gone. The sun, in its lowering path watched over the pastured lands, and the haze of afternoon began to fall over the trees. He removed his only garment and moved towards the water in his loincloth. The river was chilly. He stepped into its coolness and let it gather around his knees, then his thighs, until he was waist deep. It made him shiver. He felt alive.

He paused before John the Baptist, and trembling, asked, 'You say you can recognise the Messiah?'

The other man answered, 'I have put my soul at the disposal of an angel, and he has not opened my eyes yet … so He is not yet come.'

Jacob took this in. He was not the awaited one! He was surprised to find relief flooding his heart!

He crossed his hands over his chest as he had seen others do and the Baptiser immersed him into the water. He held his breath. An instant stretched to eternity, an eternity fashioned an instant. Full of fear, fear and panic and fear again he held to his heart, for harder tests had he withstood. Finally, he let go his dread of death and allowed the water to drown him.

He was dying, and in this dying something began to prise open the eyes of his soul, to reveal not the form-dwindling water, but something else – the weaving of his life in picture forms. Everything lay around him: his accomplishments and his many imperfections; his desires, his passions and his weaknesses; all of his vices and his transgressions; all the defilement of this life's journey and the dust of his misplaced hopes and dreams. All the content of his life was added to the river's many voices and, by way of the stream's sacrifice, these remnants floated away from him, leaving him clean. Now, a vision of profound beauty was granted him, so great and so mighty as to cause him to feel the very ground of his being shaken with love.

He saw, in his mind's eye, a man carrying a lamb on his shoulder.

Of a sudden he was lifted out of the water and he gasped for breath. He felt life enter into the dead parts of his soul. He heard a voice,

'Arise, you have seen the good shepherd!'

Jacob knew that his wound was healed and so his pain was eased. He had found harmony in the stream of his life, for in the river's stream he had found his salvation.

In this peace there was a species of loneliness. The world had grown alien to him and he would never again return to his former life. He would not remain a member of his family but would always be like a man in the wilderness, a solitary soul.

Such was the price of a new life, and a new name.

CHAPTER 19

PETITION

Herod Antipas travelled the road from Callirrhoe like a child in search of a new experience. He was on his way to meet the man hailed as a prophet, a new Elijah called John bar Zacharias, whom his people referred to as *the Baptiser*.

Yesterday, a courier had left his camp with a message for John – Herod Antipas would give him an audience. This morning came the ascetic's answer: *The Baptiser* would not see him at Ainon but at the place of baptism, some distance from it. So it was to this place that the small caravan now travelled.

Accompanying Herod on this journey was his soon-to-be bride, Herodias, and her daughter, Salome. Looking to Herodias now, sitting as she was beside him in their carriage, he felt a thrill at the base of his spine – she mesmerised him. She was a well of dark water, a soulless abyss and a bottomless chasm. She was spellbinding.

Some time ago, while in Jerusalem visiting his half-brother Philip, Herod had taken a fancy to Herodias, then Philip's wife. Herodias was not only his sister-in-law but also consanguineously, his niece, since she was the daughter of another half-brother, Aristobulus. Upon seeing her Herod had desired her, despite her being an ugly thing to behold, and this had quite amused him; it amused him still! He looked at her now. Her hair was black and thinly woven and her forehead was carved low over mud coloured eyes that were rounded and strangely askew. She seemed to be all head, all shoulders, all chest; as if the upper parts of her were put together with the lower from mismatched portions. And yet ... and yet ... what eyes! The first time he had seen those eyes they had seized him with their claws, and had thrust into his mind the content of an awesome knowledge, an elemental and infernal vigour, and an appetite that worked like a lightning strike into his apathetic limbs.

Thrilled and exhilarated, he convinced Herodias to divorce his brother, but his vacant mind had not foreseen the chagrin of his Arab wife, Phasaelis. In truth, before he could do away with her, the woman had escaped from his clutches and made for the bosom of her angry father, who now threatened war. To add to this unfortunate turn of events, he found the council of priests at Jerusalem obdurate on the subject of his intended divorce and marriage. How could they ratify a marriage of uncle and niece?

Not one for exerting himself unduly, he would have given up on the entire idea had he not become enamoured of a certain other advantage. He cast a glance at Herodias' daughter, Salome, a child of sixteen. All the characteristics that had assumed a misshapen proportion in the mother had combined differently in the daughter so that her black eyes were clear and deep and shaped like almonds, and her hair was the colour of a raven's neck, falling in thick looms over the fine curvature of her pale form, over the perfect proportion of her breasts, over the rounded belly shaped in a design to nourish the eye of desire.

While Herodias tantalised him with the wiles of her magic, just one look from Salome enticed the blood to his manhood in long painful throbs, whose intensity was wanton and incautious. He felt himself caught between the hammer and the anvil! Kept on a tight leash of hope one moment and craving the next - as compliant as a faithful dog that must-needs please its master's every wish and whim. For how could a man who thought himself mystical and sensuous resist a union that promised both the pleasures of the spirit and the flesh?

The Baptiser was well respected among the people of his province, even the Sanhedrin feared his power over them. If Herod could coax this man to ratify his marriage to Herodias, he would march into the Sanhedrin and demand the priests follow his example. But he had a secondary reason, which he did not like to think on.

At about the same time he met Herodias, he also made a visit to Caesar to contest his father's will. In Caesar's house he had a dream in which he ventured to a place, a gloom-laden blank expanse of nothingness, a naught of naughts, an eternal null and void, where all was disappointment and despair. In the midst of this dimness he could hear screams and he saw a man chained to a rock, with a bird-like shadow gnawing at his liver. When he looked more closely he realised that it was his father! The last thing he remembered was his father's laughter ringing in his ears and the words:

Now he is yours!

On waking, the memory of the creature had not diminished and in time it grew into a real thing, a great black bird that came and went, announcing its arrivals with a flapping of its dark and ominous wings and its departures with a foul stench of stagnant air.

In moments of despair he told himself,

It is my father's demon of madness, come to eat away my soul!

Herodias could not help him for although she was skilled in the magic of herbs and metals and the forces that can manipulate births, she did not yet possess the power to harness demons, or control the forces of death.

He hoped John bar Zacharias would help him.

But his thoughts were interrupted. His entourage was paused before a throng of people headed for the baptismal bend in the Jordan and his mind, like a weak flame in a breeze, was bent to those scores and scores of old and young, poor and rich alike that were walking the rough road. His guards shoved and pushed the crowds with their pikes to make them move out of the way. To his chagrin they only gave his royal person the slightest acknowledgement, causing a new emotion to battle lust and fear for chief position in his heart.

Envy.

His father had overlooked him! His brother Archelaus had stolen the throne from him! Now this upstart was taking what little he had left, if he had ever had it – the love of his people.

By the time Herod and his entourage arrived at the place of meeting, he had already calculated how he would get what he wanted from the man before doing away with him.

A short distance from Ainon, a number of crude, rush-covered huts encircled a small space, a natural court in the middle of which stood a rock. The cavalcade dismounted and rolled out an assortment of opulent carpets, food and wine for Herod and his women.

The royal group waited beneath the canopy of a tree near half a day. When John the Baptist finally appeared it was sun down. The man was tall and muscular and his face looked as ancient and dry as the dirt of Judea. He entered the enclosure surrounded by a swarm of students. He saw Herod but his face did not speak of it, it remained as it was. He whispered something to his pupils and they dispersed one by one, whereupon he took himself to the rock and sat down, as if he were a king and Herod a subject who must pay homage to him.

More vexation heated Herod's cheeks. Herodias rasped in his ear. She told him that John the Baptist was making a mockery of him. But Herod weighed his vexation and humiliation against his need to know the power of the man, and found, to his surprise, that his curiosity was greater than his pride. This was another strange realisation in a day full of portents and it did not bother him particularly. He took a sip of wine and waited for John to speak.

He waited, but the other man had a patience that was beyond his own.

'You are come, finally, John bar Zacharias,' Herod said, in Aramaic, using his friendship-making voice, 'we have waited long.'

John did not answer immediately but cast a glance about. Noting Herodias and her daughter sitting upon their fine cushions and carpets, he said, 'I have spent a long day baptising the citizens of your country who are morally sick and in want of guidance. Now, I see why it is that they are so.'

Herod bent a smile upwards. The man has a sense of humour. 'Yes,' he said, 'I saw the crowds on my way here. I too have come to meet the one whom they say is a great prophet to rival even Elijah ...!'

The voice was restrained, 'I am no prophet ... I am only a forerunner, a messenger of the One who will come after me. It is to Him that you should go.'

Herod made a little laugh at the back of his throat, a giggle, which sounded like a nervous cluck to his own ears. He cleared his throat. 'Then I have come to meet the messenger, to whom I wish to put a question. I seek to ask for your ratification of my forthcoming marriage to Herodias. The priests of the Sanhedrin state that my petition is unclean because Herodias is my niece ... but you and I both know such a marriage is not uncommon among our people. They say you are holy and wise and so I have brought the scrolls pertaining to the subject of my suit ... for your perusal.' From his half-sitting position on the grand carpet Herod gave two scrolls to a servant.

But as the man approached the baptiser shook his head. 'I will not soil my hands with your iniquity!' he thundered. 'What lives in you, Herod, seeks the gratification of two things: your lust for the pleasures of this world and your fear of the other world. But what lives in that viper ...' He pointed to Herodias. '... is a devil, and in her he burns his purposes like a fever. She lusts for power over the souls of men! She is Jezebel reborn!' he said.

Herod was full of excitement, for he was now certain the man was a seer, a prophet. Herodias, on the other hand, was snarling for him to act.

'Have him seized!' she rasped. 'How dare that animal say such things against your future wife! Have him arrested, you fool!'

Herod ignored her. He was thinking.

Salome, for her part, stood, and prowled her way to John. She was arrayed in the most resplendent silks bordered in the finest gold thread. Jewels crowded her neck, her ears, her wrists and fingers, and her veil - a last minute attempt at modesty - now fell from her hair to the ground as she walked. Her painted eyes darted at Herod as she encircled John upon his rock. She inspected him and sniffed him and paused a moment before saying,

'You are a stupid man!'

The Baptiser narrowed his eyes. 'Do not come near me, Lilith, daughter of evil!'

She smiled, her eyes wide and innocent. 'I would not stain my hands on a man who is simple and uneducated, and ... boring!'

When she laughed, it was like a ripple in water and her mother and their attendants laughed also and the entire entourage fell about in a flood of laughter as she returned to the comfort of her cushions to braid her hair. Herod was not laughing.

He directed himself to John, 'I have heard that you can make men lose their sins by immersing them in water ... is this true? Is it also true that you can cleanse the soul, perhaps even of madness? Shall we go to that place in the river so that you can baptise me?'

John fixed him with an eye. 'No. I cannot.'

Herod scoffed, 'You would refuse a king? I have guards at my disposal, ready to arrest you should I but give the sign.'

'You cannot arrest me,' John pointed out, 'I am not in Galilee, but in Judea, which is not your country.'

'Then I'll have to return to Jerusalem and petition the Sanhedrin for your arrest,' Herod said, angry and put out.

'Be careful, Herod,' John the Baptist said. 'At any moment, the curses of hell are ready to pour into you ... I see their wings touching your head.'

Herod lost his temper and his voice was shrill when he said, 'Is it not your task to ready the souls of men, Baptiser? Why will you not ready mine?'

'My task is to prepare souls to see the One Who will soon come. Some souls are not destined for seeing Him ... These are vipers destined for what is prepared for the iniquitous, in this life and the next! Look to Him who comes after me. He is the saviour, not I! He will have the power to redeem the shadow of evil that pursues you, if you believe in Him.'

'Order him killed!' Herodias shrieked. 'Do it now!'

But in Herod the creature of fear overtook the creature of anger and lust and envy, for he knew the shadow was back, flapping its wings and causing that moribund wind to fan his face. He shouted to his attendants and servants and guards to take up the rugs and the food and wine and to prepare the animals. Herodias and Salome scurried behind him to the chariot and they were soon away.

On their return to Callirrhoe Herod heard of the riots inspired by John the Baptist's sermons against the pagans in Dothain, and instantly he knew what pretext he would use to have him arrested. He would go with his captain and take stock of the situation and report back to the Sanhedrin.

He was confident that soon he would have it all, a sorceress for a wife, a nubile lover, and a cure for that shadow of madness! For the dungeons of Machareus were good for making even the most disobedient man acquiescent.

CHAPTER 20

SCORPION

The sun entered Scorpio on the night of his birth and in a dream his mother saw that her boy child would be the agent of three betrayals: he would kill his father, he would marry his mother and he would bring about a disaster so great that it would taint his name and stain the blood of his people for all ages to come.

On hearing of the dream the father wanted to kill the child, but the woman feared committing a sin and convinced her husband to have the boy taken from Cariot in Judea to a distant land - to avert his maleficent destiny.

And that is how it came to be that the child was spirited away in the night, and taken by merchants to a community of Diaspora Jews on the Tigris, near Seleucia in Parthia.

This was a quiet, hidden community, peopled by Mandeans - those who had brought together the mysteries of the Persians and combined them with the religion of the Hebrews.

In this community there lived a wealthy childless couple known to the Jew merchants, who, upon seeing the tiny innocent creature, grew warm with love, exclaiming to one another that here at last was a son delivered to them by God!

Gladly they paid the merchants thirty pieces of silver for him and raised him as their own.

They named him Judas.

As the years passed, Judas grew into a bright youth with a sharp mind who excelled beyond all others at his instructions on the laws and the prophets. But in truth, what he loved most were those Hebrew stories of the great Jewish Heroes, the seven sons of the widow and the five sons of Matthatias: warriors who had struggled against the enemies of Judaism. He was drawn, in particular, to one of the five sons of the priest Matthatias - his namesake, Judas Maccabeus. Judas Maccabeus was described as a lion from the house of Judah, and many a night did young Judas spend pondering the hero's alliance with Rome against the Greeks, and his underestimation of Rome's powers, which had caused so much sorrow for his people.

This pondering affected him in two ways: on the one hand, he dreamt of leaving his village to return to Jerusalem and join the fight against the Romans like a Maccabean hero; on the other he longed for a life of piety and simplicity as a Mandean priest.

In his heart he could not decide which of the two he was destined to be, the fearless warrior or pious priest.

In time he grew into a strong man with a dark face framed by unruly black hair, whose curls hung loose above eyes the colour of grey stones. His beard was as red as clay and from its deeps there would come a smile that spread over the geography of his face like a snake moving through grass.

His brooding nature and his heart's wild-hearted lean attracted the young girls of the small colony to him and they pursued him with their shy eyes. But the warrior in his soul struggled with the postulant in his spirit. The warrior was red-blooded and desirous for these attentions, while the postulant was full with disdain and looked away from these displays of sexual promise with a superior eye.

The villagers and his teachers could see that Judas' soul was made of two opposites, for his face was like a dial created to measure that running quarrel, which never ceased, and could find no shared purpose in the wilderness of his soul. In time, however, he proved to his superiors that he was a good scholar, hard working, devoted and pious. Moreover, his mystical abilities grew beyond even those of the priests, so that they found themselves unable to prevent him from entering through the portals of the mysteries. For he had passed every test they set him, and, almost without their noticing it, he had begun to steal into their hearts.

And so it was that after much deliberation, the priests agreed to allow him entrance to the House of Creation.

The House of Creation stood not far from the Mandean settlement. In it the secrets of light and darkness were revealed to those who risked life and madness and were capable of overcoming the abyss of death to find daylight. The successful ones were baptised with water and anointed with fire. The unsuccessful ones who survived were exiled.

One fateful night, in the inner sanctuary, Judas was given the lighted lamp and told of the original causes of things. He was given a cordial to drink and told to lie down and after a time the high priest came to guide him to the underworld. Here he would have to pass those strenuous tests meant to measure his endurance and his courage, his revulsion and his steadfastness.

He was taken to a black place without light. Alone, and only guided by a voice, he endured test after test, each more gruelling than the last. Finally, exhausted and near broken in his spirit, he heard the resounding voice of the priest and saw the lighted torches come to meet him.

Weak and fatigued he was led to a room where he was dried, dressed in fine linen, and told to rest. Overcome by lassitude he stretched out on the soft couch provided and soon fell asleep. A languorous music entered his dreams, the sound of harp and flute and sighs reached his ears, and when he opened his eyes he saw a woman, clothed in a dress of iridescent gauze hung loose and limpid over her oiled Nubian body. On her face he observed a mocking smile, full-berried and white of teeth. It pulled upwards to high-boned cheeks. Around her neck, precious necklaces gleamed in the dim light and around her wrists bracelets of different coloured metals shimmered. In her hand she held a cup filled with aromatic wine. She told him it was the Soma juice of bliss, the sacred ceremonial wine of remembrance. She told him to drink it, for he was in the Temple of the highest wisdom and she was his prize, the ceremonial meal.

He paused a moment, uncertain. But the woman held the wine closer to him, and he was taken with the vigour of his victory, and so his manhood became heated with ardour.

As his pride swelled so did his body swell, for he had outwitted the priests and could now collect his reward! He took the woman to him and pulled her to the bed, bending his lips to that mouth, to that long neck, to that perfumed breast, to that bronzed shoulder and bejewelled ear. He took the cup from her hand and let its contents fall down his throat and held her then, beneath him. He commenced to pull away the silken dress and would have taken her with the wild insatiate desire of a beast had he not been plunged, at that moment, not into the depths of desire, but into the deeps of nothingness.

When he woke again he was alone in that first dark chamber where the priests had given him the cordial of forgetfulness. Disoriented he tried to bring reason to his mind and in a moment realised that he had been fooled. He had been duped! The priests had deceived him! His trials had been illusions, his triumphs dreams!

The smell of failure hung in the air. He fell into a rage, and called out with an angered voice to the priests. The hierophant came to him. Awesome was his expression and grave were his words:

'You were victorious over the darkness, over fire and water, and because of this you are alive and are not dead. But the earth has conquered you, you have killed your father, your body, to marry wisdom, but you have wedded your soul to lust and darkness instead, killing your soul, the mother in you. For this reason you are like a scorpion, which must sting itself and die to avoid the light of the sun. And you shall ever more be named *scorpizein.*'

He was taken then, by the broad-bodied servants of the House of Creation, and sent into exile.

A deep, violent hatred moved inside the mechanisms of his thinking, it moved into his will and drove him to Seleucia, where he announced to its leaders the whereabouts of the order's hidden house. Artaban, King of Parthia, despised the practices of the Mandeans as aberrations, and he took no time in ordering his generals to send forth soldiers to the community to slaughter every woman and child, to hang the priests from the trees and to topple the House of Creation.

Full of hatred and dissatisfaction Judas travelled to Judea with a sting in his tail in search of the restitution of his other hopes. If he could not be a priest he would be a warrior, another Judas Maccabeus. He would lead his people towards the creation of a great empire.

In Jerusalem he found a group of like-minded men who called themselves *Sicarri*, or dagger carriers. It was their custom to slip, sleek and unseen, into the crowds to assassinate enemies or to inspire bloody revolts. He met one of their leaders, a man called Bar Abbas, and three other men, Simon of Nazareth, Dismas and Gesmas. His charm seduced them and they allowed him gradually into their confidence, telling him their secrets and of their every conspiracy and plan. One such plan was near ready for implementation.

Pontius Pilate was a new Roman Governor and he had no care for Jewish custom and religion. Time and again he had transgressed the laws of the Jews and recently had misappropriated Temple funds to build an aqueduct for Jerusalem. The *Sicarri*, seeking everything to their advantage, planned to use this sacrilege as an excuse for inciting a riot.

Judas thought long on it. A week before the Easter festival, disguised *Sicarri* would enter the city of Jerusalem via a series of ancient passages and tunnels built to carry water from the Gihon Spring into the Ophel quarter. These were large enough to hide a number of men until the city was overfull with pilgrims from near and from far. When the festival was at its height and the crowds began to throng to the Temple for the services, no one would notice the *Sicarri* merge with them and begin to incite them with speeches. Pilate's sacrilegious tampering with Temple funds would feature prominently in their rhetoric, and it would take but one strike of the flint stone at a time when sensibilities were heightened by religious fervour to ignite a conflagration of passion against the Romans.

It was Pontius Pilate's custom to come from Caesarea for the festivals and to spend his time ensconced in the pr*ae*torium, where, from a distance, he could keep an eye on the festivities. He was always heavily guarded but the *Sicarri* figured that an uprising would cause him to send all available men to the streets, and in the ensuing chaos a number of them could force their way into his palace and sink a dagger into his heart.

With Pilate dead, Rome would need to send a new prefect to Jerusalem, and in the meantime there would be disorder and confusion - the food of revolution.

Such was the grand and auspicious plan.

Judas was disturbed by it.

It was fraught with traps but more importantly it did not fit with Judas' own ideal. In his mind there still lived an image of the Messiah, which had become entangled with the likeness of Judas Maccabeus. This Messiah would be a great king and he would unite the glory of Rome with the wisdom of the Jews. Rome might even be persuaded to become the benefactor of such a transformation if it were to her benefit. Moreover, Pilate seemed to be a man of principles. He may have used Temple funds to build an aqueduct, but was Jerusalem not arid and dry? Did its population not cry out for water? Was there not a practical logic to using these funds - which often fell into the pockets of the corrupt priests - to quench the thirst of the people? Perhaps there was a way of preparing for the Messiah by stroking Roman pride?

He resolved that he would start by warning Pilate of the insurrection. The Roman would look favourably upon such a warning and consider its messenger a man he could trust. Trust, Judas reasoned, led to favour, and favour led to outcomes.

And so, in his mind he calculated his next move. He would take himself to the Procurator of Judea and beg an audience. He could not know that such an action was destined to bring about the realisation of his mother's dream.

CHAPTER 21

PONTIUS PILATE

The moon filtered through the silk curtains and Pontius Pilate lay sleepless in his bed, watching it and listening to Claudia's soft breathing in the oppressive airs of the night.

In the day she was calm and in the night she slept untroubled. The heat and disorder of this place did not bother her. Pilate, on the other hand, found that the climate of Jerusalem made his mind seek to stand still in the day and his thoughts to run leagues in the night.

But this night, something more prevented his sleep.

Some time ago, on his arrival in Jerusalem and following Caesar's orders, he had his men erect standards bearing Caesar's image on the walls of all prominent places, including the Hebrew Temple. Immediately a great uprising broke out, with thousands of people clamouring into the streets and into the Temple. Inspired by the Zealots and their speeches they had climbed the walls of the Temple to take down the standards, and when his soldiers tried to stop them the priests stood in their way and offered their throats.

Pilate sighed now. His orders on his appointment had been clear – maintain peace in the province and do all that is necessary in this regard or else find yourself answering to a Caesar who likes to throw those who displease him from cliffs into the sea!

To prevent an escalation of violence he had ordered the images taken down. Ah! These were a difficult people, beyond reason and common sense. In no other province had the Romans encountered such obstinacy, such militancy and extremity.

Afterwards, wishing to better know their minds, he had invited the tetrarch of Galilee and the priests of the Sanhedrin to a feast. But his guests did not come; the high priests were afraid of defilement, and Herod feigned illness. The message could not have been clearer: the conquered people of Judea thought Rome beneath them and would always see themselves her enemies.

His administration had since passed through bloody times, ending in the latest incident, which on such a night, with the swollen moon and the smell of death for company, weighed heavily on his mind.

Before coming to his bedchamber he had taken a lamp to his library to consult his favourite philosopher Cicero. Cicero expounded that some men were only guided by what provides comfort and happiness in life. Pilate had seen it in Rome, where those things that were good for the self were sought at the expense of what was moral and good. But his doings had never been dictated by his own needs, only by the needs of the state, and these needs he had always regarded as good! However, since arriving in Palestine a change had worked its way into his thinking like a worm into an apple. Roman law was becoming more and more distasteful to him and he was beginning to think of it as something expedient and immoral. Such were the thoughts of the man in him.

The smell of his wife's hair was comforting. He touched her bare shoulder lightly and thought how lucky he was. Claudia Procula was beautiful and he loved her despite their union being an arranged one. Everything in his life had been arranged, since it was customary for the future of a man born to the equestrian class to be laid out like a map divided into the provinces of youth, middle years and old age. His only hope was to live long enough to follow these signposts to that final destination.

Born the son of a woman from Gaul, and Ponti, a Samnite general in the service of Rome, he had been inducted into the Roman Cavalry as a youth and had performed military duties in Gaul and other places by the time he reached maturity. His services were rewarded in the giving of three gifts: a spear, the name Pilatus, and a province to govern.

He thought it a grand thing then, to move so easily from soldier to statesman, from Pontius to Pilate. Now, in his middle years, his mind turned differently. These days he found himself not thinking on a senator-ship in Rome, but rather on a quiet house in the hills of Gaul, where, surrounded by vineyards and pastures, his time might be divided between horses, children and the pleasures of his books. But destiny had not marked such a path before him. His only son was a sickly child and he could see himself lodged in this godforsaken land for all time, forgotten by Rome and hated by the Jews.

His wife curved towards him in her sleep. She smelt of roses. He knew she used the unguent to dampen the stench of blood, which, ever since her childhood, made her faint to see it. This made his thoughts take a turn to what was troubling him.

Some days ago, a Jew by the name of Judas had come to him with word of a conspiracy. The man had told him of plans hatched by the treacherous *Sicarri* with the support of Herod Antipas; plans for an insurrection that would plunge the province of Judea into an abyss of revolution not seen since the times of Quirenius.

Pilate had not known whether to believe the Jew, for the man had a fiery eye and the heart of a traitor. Moreover, Judas' seeming betrayal of his own countrymen had the scent of a trap and he almost clapped the man in irons before another thought occurred to him.

There was only one legion at his disposal in Jerusalem, a little over five thousand men. Syria was stretched thin from Roman wars and would not provide him with further soldiery. Tens of thousands came each year to the city for the festival and a Roman Legion would be no more than a shout in a tempest of revolt. He had no choice but to take the man at his word and to set about his own plans.

He decided that his men would not search the underground tunnels and passages. These were many and various and well known to the insurrectionists who may have prepared a trap for his legionaries. Moreover, it was not his wish to scare the plotters off and to drive them further into the bowels of the city, but rather to ensnare them. So, on the day of the proposed revolt, he left the exits out of these tunnels free and had a portion of his legionaries lying in wait, ready to prevent the Sicarri, once they were exposed, from retreating into their hiding holes. A further portion of his men were dressed as pilgrims and set to mingle among the crowds, while another portion, led by Gaius Cassius, would strengthen the guards along the walls and all the entrances to the Temple. His own personal guard would lie in wait at his pr*ae*torium to seize those seeking to assassinate him.

On the day of the Passover Feast, the appointed day of the revolt, he and his men were among those crowds that made their way to the Temple to purchase the Passover lambs. When dissenting voices were heard in the streets he gave the signal to his legionaries, who acted immediately. Throwing off their cloaks, they descended like a storm of well-honed swords upon the rebels. They thrust their weapons into the bellies and limbs of the insurgents but they also killed and maimed those who came between them, so that in the end the streets were littered with carcasses. The blood of old men, women and children, of youths and men in their prime, all who were caught in the fighting, mingled with the blood of the Sicarri zealots, and ran together in a stream over the stones, making puddles like spring rain.

Pilate ordered the blood of those killed collected in a clay vessel and took himself through the mourning crowds to the Temple. Flanked by the insignia of Rome, he climbed the steps to the inner sanctuary, and in a show of Roman defiance, pushed aside the old priests, who were horrified at his desecration of their sacred place.

Those who were gathered in the court began a lamentation. The paschal festival was despoiled! The presence of a gentile in the courts and the smell and sight of death had defiled the celebration of the sacrifices!

Pilate ignored the cacophony of howling and weeping and stood looking down upon the throngs with no pity in his heart. He ordered the priests to bring forth the sacred scrolls kept in the sanctuary so that he could throw them into the sacrificial fires.

Terrified, the priests fell on their knees and began to tear at their vestments and to offer up their necks to his guards.

'I will kill you all!' Pilate warned them, 'Before your own people!'

Still they did not move.

Overcome with exhaustion and frustrated by the quarrelsome nature of these people, he called for the blood collected in the clay vessel, and said to them:

'Rome will have peace in this province, and she does not care how much blood is shed to obtain it! Behold, what Rome thinks of Jew blood!'

With these words, he took the vessel, and poured its contents into the sacrificial fires where the blood of the Hebrew people, the sacred blood of Abraham, encountered the blood of the animals.

The symbolism of this act threw the crowd into a strange and immense silence.

For his part, Pilate asked for a pitcher of water to wash his hands. He took himself from the Temple then and had those zealots who had been captured by his guards scourged and taken to Calvary to be crucified.

That had been yesterday. The sound of wailing had continued all day and only at sundown had the people been allowed by their religion to bury their dead. This meant that the smell of decay, warmed by sun and visited by flies, still lingered as a reminder of Roman vengeance on defiance.

But what else could he have done? These were a treacherous people! Leniency would have encouraged future riots and revolts; only harshness and severity could control them. This was the soldier speaking in him now.

He wondered which he truly was, the soldier or the man?

He did not know.

And in this unknowing he lay, with the sickly aroma in the breezes. He brushed a wisp of hair from Claudia's face and she stirred from the cloudy airs of sleep to open her eyes.

She reached out to draw him near. 'All is well?' she asked. 'You do not sleep … something troubles you … come … hold me.'

He took her in his arms and whispered in her ear, 'How must a watchdog of Rome sleep while there are devils at the door?'

She yawned. 'Oh Pontius! Do you speak of those devils you dispatched to the realm of shades, or to the thoughts that trouble your heart for the innocent that were killed?'

He bristled at this rebuke and turned on his back. 'If you were a soldier you would know that sometimes it is necessary to shed blood.'

She turned on her side to look at him. 'You are a soldier and you say it, but you do not relish it.'

He sighed, resigned. She knew him too well. 'I marvel at how clear things are to you.' he said to her.

She laughed softly. 'Your mind is not clear because you read Cicero!'

He turned to her. 'How do you know?'

'I have been your wife for fifteen years … you always seek his counsel when something worries you. Does he give you comfort this night?' she asked.

He took to looking at the darkness and away from her probing. 'Nothing in this strange country – not our laws, not even Cicero's words – give me comfort.'

'No … but perhaps that is because laws and reason cannot determine for you what is right and what is wrong, husband. This,' she said to him, 'you must do for yourself.'

He looked at her again and felt a gratitude to the gods that she had not remained in Rome like the wives of other Roman officials, for she alone had the courage to speak her mind and he esteemed her for her honesty. Even so, she could be a stubborn woman, full of her own opinions. Now and again he needed to put her in her place.

'Without laws and reason, there is only anarchy and disorder,' he told her.

She lay on her back now and stretched her long, supple limbs. 'I think some day men will know something higher than the laws they spin from their heads with their reason, something women already know.'

'So …' he said, making his voice soft, 'there is something that women know before men?'

'Yes, does that seem so strange to you?'

'What is it then, this something you know?'

'Women *feel* right from wrong.'

'How do you mean, *feel*?'

'It comes to us naturally, this feeling for truth,' she said. 'But it isn't found in your books, Pontius, nor is it dictated by what you esteem so highly, your reason. Reason, my dear, is a child of convenience … I speak of a truth that is true, absolutely.'

'Yes, but such truths can only be known by the gods … this you say *you* know? Tell me, how do you know it?'

She hoisted herself on her elbows to look at him. 'A woman knows it, by listening.'

He dismissed it with a hand. 'Nonsense!'

'You may laugh, but I say to you that if more men heard this voice there would be no more war!'

'There will never be peace,' he told her.

'Not while men rule the world,' she pointed out.

'Now you have me intrigued … what do you hear, where do you hear it?'

'In the heart speaks the voice that tells what is right, and what is wrong! What is true!' She took his hand, and placed it between her breasts. 'Here …' she said. 'Here speaks a truth that is beyond law and reason.'

The frankness of her words and the nearness of her womanhood stirred him. She knew how to remind him that he was something more than a soldier of Rome. He gentled her body over his and her fine legs straddled him.

He told her, 'Is the world of men ready for this heart's truth then, in your estimation?'

She smiled down at him, playful and wise. 'To imagine that it is, is a pleasant dream …'

There was the warmth of love between them. She bent to kiss him.

'Your dream awakens me,' he whispered in her ear.

'But Philosophers must sleep, if they are to dream.'

'Philosophers are lovers of wisdom,' he gave back, 'They dream while awake.'

And so she moved his soul from Pilate to Pontius, from statesman to man, and he forgot the melancholic rounds of his speculations and instead drank the living air of her soft Elysian fields. She was Persephone and he was her Pluto.

Very well.

Perhaps this was truth enough.

CHAPTER 22

ISCARIOT

Judas lay in hiding for hours. When he came out all was quiet and it was near dark. He wanted to see what his work had realised.

He found a massacre.

His mind was taken by panic. He had not intended that it should end this way! He ran then, from himself, from the tempest of blood, from the vomit, the urine and excrement that covered the cobbled streets. He left the city with his heart pounding and with voices crying in his head.

Along the way, upon the road that led to the north, he came across his friend Simon Zealotes, who was fleeing with his brother Jude. He fell in with them and they gave him consolation, assuming that, like them, he had fought valiantly and escaped death. They saw his anguish and took it to be sorrow for his friends, having no suspicion in their hearts of the enormous betrayal that was carving him hollow.

Only Judas knew it, and the further he was from Jerusalem the more terrifying was the clarity in his head. He had shed the blood of Abraham, which to a Jew was the same as killing the father of his people. He had slain his father and succumbed to the seduction of Rome – a harlot who would never be his mother!

As they travelled the road that followed the river Jordan their party came to a bend in the river. Here, they saw a great crowd gathered around a large man dressed in skins. This man spoke of repentance and of the imminent coming of the Messiah; he told the crowds that only by being immersed in water could they be cleansed of their sins before His coming. He also said that he would know those who were ready, just by looking at them. These he called the lambs. The others, the vipers, he would turn away, for they were not ready for what was new.

Judas turned his mind to his words and considered his situation in a different light. He had done a terrible thing, but his intentions had not been evil ones – he had only desired to prepare the way for the Messiah! If he were cleansed of his sins he could start again, as this man professed was possible. A clean slate! But there was the risk, he reasoned, that such a prophet would recognise his crime just by looking at him. Would he not then pronounce him to be a viper and denounce him before the world?

Uncertain, he stood on the river's lip. The others, inspired by the Baptist's words, had already taken off their cloaks and were entering the water. Judas considered that it might be his destiny to die here and now, and to have it over with. For how could he live with the terrible weight of his crime on his shoulders? A burden, he knew, that would grow more weighty by the day. Then again, in the depths of his heart, in his sinews, his muscles, his bones, a voice spoke to him of his grand place in God's design. If this were so, well, the baptiser would cleanse him of his sins and mention not a word of his misdeeds. He would take this as a sign that God yet favoured him.

When at last he stood before the man, he felt himself stripped naked and observed. He waited long, while those eyes probed him with a fierce intensity. It seemed like hours, but it was only a moment.

John the Baptist said nothing.

A great enthusiasm replaced his woes. God had not forsaken him! His ideal had not been misguided. Misguided had been his means, but not his ends!

The baptiser put a hand behind Judas' back, and soon he was

entering into the nullity of the water. Fear gripped him and he struggled, but soon there came a sense of peace and abandon, a loosening of the burden. He had never felt so light! When he came out of the water the world looked different, as if he were looking through another man's eyes.

Afterwards it was possible for Judas to join the others as one of John's disciples, without guilt or concern. Day after day he was among them. He ate his meals with them, and listened to the words of the teacher. In the night he slept with them in huts made of rushes and felt that finally he had found a home and a family, for he sensed he belonged among these men, who were so unlike him in their experience and education – the simple fishermen from Galilee. It was as if he were rediscovering something long lost to him, as if in their midst he were reliving the miracle of the age of the Maccabees who had fought and died side by side.

In the reflection of their eyes he did not see himself Judas Iscariot, the unwanted child; he did not see Judas Scorpizein, the betrayer of his village; or Judas the Sicarri traitor to his nation. He saw a newborn Judas Maccabeus, that great warrior who had once fought to restore the Kingdom of Abraham.

CHAPTER 23

EAGLE

On the day of his birth the sun rose in the constellation of the Eagle, signifying that destiny had chosen the boy's kinship with all that exists above in the rarefied airs of the world.

Lazarus had two sisters, Martha and Mary, and theirs was a family of wealth and position, for their father had rendered a lifetime of service to the Roman Caesar in Syria, and in return he had earned riches, and property in Magdala and in Bethany. In Magdala stood the family's principle home, a house, steadfast and stout, set among a lush oasis of walled gardens and waterfalls. This was by far the grandest house in the region. Bethany, on the other hand, was a modest castle but well situated near Jerusalem.

Lazarus loved Magdala for its tower, and Bethany for its serenity and silence. For as well as a love of heights and wide spaces, he also possessed a deep sensitivity and inwardness of soul, which had fashioned for him ears more acute than other ears and a heart more perceptive than other hearts. And they were to remain so, even after learning began to stimulate his intellect.

His mother, a Jewess from the lineage of Pharisees, had made certain that Lazarus was given a good Hebrew education. His father, an Egyptian noble who had been broadly educated himself, ensured that his schooling was supplemented with tutoring from the best Roman and Greek teachers.

His Greek tutor, Photismos, was a wiry old man with clear blue eyes and a quick mind. He had developed in Lazarus such a love for the Greek language that some said the boy resembled a Greek, even in his manners and outward appearance.

Lazarus and his tutor also shared a love for high places, and Lazarus rejoiced whenever he was taken, as he was this day, to the Migdal tower, to observe the plains and mountains.

The tower had been built to observe and to defend the ancient trade routes connecting Nazareth to Damascus, and so its walls were mighty and steep. From them Lazarus could follow the caravans carving their way through the fertile plains of Gennesaret. Now, standing upon its ramparts, Lazarus demonstrated his oratory skills by calling out his name, which echoed in the distance. He told Photismos that he liked to hear this call and that sometimes he imagined that it came from another boy answering him from the ramparts of another tower.

Photismos nodded, and as was his custom to use any opportunity for instruction, said, 'Does the sound of your name express your inner self?'

Lazarus considered it and answered, 'It must, since it is my name.'

'Ah …' The old man smiled. 'But Lazarus is not so strange a name, is it? There are many boys called Lazarus. Tell me, what is the name that only *you* can use?'

'I do not know.'

'You have just said 'I'. Can you give this name "I" to any other being?'

Lazarus paused. 'You are right! I alone can say 'I' to myself. But are we not also given a name, according to the quality in our souls?'

'Yes … this is true,' his teacher conceded. 'Names are not given without rhyme or reason. Your name means *helped by the Lord*, but I do not believe that you alone in the world are helped by the Lord. The word "I" however, you alone can say. It is yours even if you do not have a name.'

'But who has named me, I?'

'God has named you, of course ... who else? You see, you are a word that was once spoken forth by God! Just as you have spoken your name forth a moment ago, and it has created a sound that manifests your inner soul. This means that by uttering your name, you have also created something!'

'And so, I am a God?'

'Do the Hebrews not say that all men were made in His image and likeness, child?'

'Yes … but I have never understood how that can be.'

'Let us see if I can explain it. Do you know the meaning of the word, Logos?'

Lazarus shook his head.

'It is the word of God, my son. In the beginning, the warm word of God was spoken out into the world and it created life.'

'But the sun creates life.'

'Yes, but what quality does the Sun possess that enables it to create life?'

'Light?'

'Bravo!' Photismos clapped him on the back. 'Yes … in this world nothing can grow in the dark, except for evil things, and no man can see on a moonless night, except for sorcerers … am I right?'

Lazarus agreed, for this was well known.

'In the same way that the sun shines over the world, a spirit light shines over your soul, did you know that? This divine light is the word of God, and it has made you divine. This is why you can say "I", because this word shines into you! A plant cannot say *I am,* nor can a camel. The *I am,* the divine light-word of the universe, has entered only into man so he can say I.'

'But why do my teachers at the synagogue not teach this marvellous truth?' Lazarus asked.

Photismos looked out to the valleys and hills and mountains. 'A long time ago, the great prophets and teachers could still see the light-word, but as time passed they grew blind and saw only the physical light of the sun, and it damaged their eyes to look upon it.'

'Do you say that men have grown blind to the word of God?' Lazarus asked.

'Yes ... and it is for this reason that a god descended to the moon in order that from it he might reflect the wisdom and the love of the sun; for this reflected light caused men no harm.'

'Who is this god?'

'He reflects the light-word, and so he is called ... Jehova! *I am that I am.*'

Lazarus grew fearful; this was the forbidden name, which was never to be spoken out loud. Men were stoned to death for saying it.

'Do not be afraid, child ... soon a man will come who will see the fullness of the word, and he will speak of it without fear. This man will look at the God of the Sun directly in the day, because His light will not harm his eyes.'

'Who is this man who will see this God, and why will His light not harm his eyes?'

'He will be the forerunner, child,' he said to Lazarus, 'and he will see this Sun God, the true light of the *I am,* because He will enter into a body of flesh, to dwell among men.'

'Will I ever see Him, the bearer of this light?'

Photismos looked at the boy with a serious face. 'You? You most of all, child! Why do you think I spend so much time on you?'

'But how will I find him?'

'Many years from now, you will hear the voice of His forerunner, crying out in the wilderness. He will direct you to the Man who will be the bearer of the light-word. You must listen to that call.'

‡

'And did he hear it Lea?' I asked setting down my quill, full of amazement.

'As the years passed, *pairé,* Lazarus waited for the call of the one whom Isaiah prophesied; the one who would bear witness to the incarnation of the Word of words. But it was not until he was a man, some months after he and his sisters had moved from their Galilean home to Bethany, that Lazarus had a waking dream. He dreamt that he was standing on the parapets of that great tower of Magdala again, but now it was not his own voice calling out his name, but another voice from afar, in the distant wilderness of Judea. The sound of it entered into his ears, and moved his heart to make it skip beats, it made him flush with warmth and it directed him to the wilderness, to a man called John.'

CHAPTER 24

ISIS

She finished her words, and I realised that it was morning again and another night had passed. That is how it was during those nights with Lea, sitting in the upper room by the fire. The hours went by in a dream, but a dream more awake than life itself, for it was a life that took me to the heights of knowledge. When day came then, and life in the fortress resumed its dismal rhythm, I was forced to fall back to earth, forced to face the siege with its moments of frenzied fighting, followed by long hours of inactivity.

In the daily hours I received those who wished to see me, I bandaged wounds and applied compresses and saw to men and women who were dying from injury or from disease. It was an endless round of waiting and prayer, of hope and despair for the injured and the dying.

The night was my solace.

But when some nights had passed without a visit from Lea it made me full of concern and I resolved to go in search of her. Perhaps she was not an apparition but a woman after all? If so, she may have fallen sick like so many, from lack of food and clean water, from the cold and the crowded conditions. I imagined her in some corner of the fortress, coughing, with a fever on that brow as pale as a pearl, and felt my heart quickening with devotion. I could not tell if this devotion was simply an illusion sent by the devil to try me, and so I put it out of my mind and searched, looking for her in the pentagonal courts and where people gathered for the sermons.

Sometimes I thought I saw her, or at least something of her. But what I saw was the warm smile of a mother, the peculiar turn of the head of a lover, the wisdom in the eyes of a grandmother – evidence of the soul that is shared by all women, that which a man can only aspire to love from afar. I was thinking this as I looked for Saissa de Congost, that wonderful woman whose castle at Puivert had once been the home of music and troubadours before the French seized it.

Saissa had taken it upon herself to keep the young girls of the fortress busy, and I reasoned that she might know something of Lea if she was, indeed, a real woman. But along the way I was diverted from my task by a tearful boy wandering among the crowds of people without aim. A beautiful child with delicate features and far reaching eyes. I asked him his name but he did not answer and those around me did not know who he was. I took him by the hand to Saissa, who was teaching embroidery to a group of young girls.

She recognised the boy as the charge of the Marquésia de Lantar. The boy, she said, was a special child and needed care. He could not yet speak despite being near seven years of age. She asked one of the girls to take him back to the Marquésia, and as he was being led away the boy turned to look at me. What hovered in the space between us at this point was a glimpse of something rare, as old as eternity, and as new as a moment. When I blinked the child was gone and the revelation faded from my heart.

I became aware of Saissa regarding me with a curious eye, and I was struck by the realisation that my nightly dreams were turning into daydreams! Surely, if I did not soon harness my thoughts I might never again wake up!

There was one way to clarify the mystery that was occupying my every waking hour and driving me from sanity. I asked Saissa if she knew a woman called Lea. I told her that she might be a *credente* or believer or perhaps the child of a perfect. I said I was worried that she was unwell, for I had not seen her for some time. Saissa shrugged her shoulders and shook her head. She did not recognise the name, but she would ask among the other women and would let me know.

More nights passed in silence, and I felt deserted and abandoned by my dream vision, that is, until the seventh night.

I had fallen asleep at my parchments and woke with a start. The wind had picked up and was fanning the flames in the hearth to a bright glow. When I adjusted my eyes I saw her, sitting on the bench, as was her custom. And oh, how it pierced my heart's deep chambers to see her! Tears veiled my eyes and I had to speak to forestall them.

'You were gone long …' I said. 'I went looking for you. No one seems to know you. I am thinking that perhaps you are just a dream.'

She found this amusing. 'What is a dream? When men are awake, that is when they are truly dreaming. Besides, have you never been with people who do not know you though you are always with them? They do not know you because they are asleep. To be awake to what others cannot see – this is love.'

I do not say that I always understood her. She was a strange creature, full of wisdoms and secrets and riddles, and I did not press her lest she melt away and leave me with an unfinished dream. I decided to ask no more. From now on, I would think of her as an angel … as the evening star!

'Of what will you speak this night?' I said, holding my quill tightly, lest she see my hand tremble.

'I will show you Mary Magdalene, *pairé* ...'

'That makes sense ... since you last spoke of her brother, Lazarus. It is said that she came to France with him on a boat, that she married Jesus and bore him children.'

Her nod was faint, her azure eyes narrowed a little, and I felt deeply scrutinised. 'That would mean that Jesus did not die on the cross … is that what you believe?'

I told her the truth. I told her that I did not know, but that the tale came from the troubadours, who sang of such things.

'There are hidden truths buried deep in these tales, *pairé,* but one must know how to decipher them. Did you know that the name

Magdalene is connected to the word Magda? Magda is a high tower that unites the soul with God. In Egypt, too, there were such women, but they were called brides of Osiris, or Priestesses of Isis.'

I was aghast. 'Are you implying that Mary Magdalene was a bride of Osiris, the Egyptian god?'

Lea's smile was wide now, and her teeth were like a flock of sheep, each one whiter than the next.

'Why is this so strange to you, *pairé*? In a previous life Mary Magdalene had been a priestess, yes, but she came again to be the first bride of Christ. Not in a physical sense – in a spiritual one. You see how misunderstandings arise?'

'That may be … but what of her travelling to France on a boat? What do you make of that?'

'Once again, *pairé,* you must look for the hidden truth; the soul is the woman in every man. In this tale, the soul is not just a woman, however, it is also a vessel, a boat, and it travels upon an ocean of time. In this boat there is a child, the spirit, waiting to be born. These understandings came to France and inspired your troubadours, who sing of a love for a lady, though she is not a woman at all. She is their soul, seeking the spirit.'

I was confused. 'Oh, Lea … I am a feeble-minded man; all this talk of souls and boats and children and spirits – all of it confounds me!'

'Do not be too impatient, *pairé,* soon you will understand, just listen to me again …'

She began to tell how Mary Magdalene had to suffer many things before she could find her way to Christ.

And I wrote it down, as best I could.

‡

From the day she was born, all could see the child was blessed. For not only was she quick of mind and full of mischief, she was also possessed of physical attributes rarely seen wholly together in one parcel.

'One day,' they said, 'her beauty will be her undoing!'

In time, her hair grew to a deep auburn shade that trapped the sun's light and fell long over her shoulders. Her face, unblemished and smooth, was made more pale by the redness of her lips and the darkness of her almond shaped eyes. To her parents the child was a jewel in their crown and they turned a deaf ear to all who suggested that they not dote on the girl; that they not dress her in resplendent clothes, and sit her upon fine cushions and expensive carpets, to display her to all who came by.

But her parents died, one after the other, and she became the responsibility of her sister Martha, who was five years older. Martha was pale and sickly, and prone to a nervous temper, the result of an issue of blood, a disease that defiled her and prevented her from ordinary social intercourse, from attending the synagogue, and even from marriage. This meant that Martha lavished all her love on Mary, and appeased her mothering urges by nurturing her as if she were the centre of her world. Martha dressed her in only the finest garments under embroidered silk girdles studded with precious stones and dusted her hair with gold and adorned it with the sheerest Arabian veils. Her arms she garlanded with the finest bracelets and wherever Mary walked all heads turned, not only for her unparalleled beauty and the fineries of her toilette, but also because around her ankles Martha had wrapped numerous lengths of silver chain, specially wrought to make little sounds!

This attire, far from being unusual in young Galilean women, composed the dress of the distinguished and the fashionable, but when such richness was wedded to a girl of Mary's exceptional beauty it created a vision that attracted both the attention of men and also the derision and jealousy of women.

Mary herself did not think much of these luxuries, and Martha would scold her when she returned from the markets bare of purse and jewellery, having left rings and bracelets and money in the hands of some unfortunate beggar.

In truth, Mary felt smothered by her sister's incessant fussing, and preferred her own company and would often wander out far beyond the scrutiny of the people to sit alone in the valley, or on the green hillsides or in the cool shade of a sheltering tree where she could think her deep thoughts.

She did not know when it was that a second sight began to unfold in her soul, for this transformation was a quiet creature whose footsteps were soft and left no trace. She only knew that at one moment she was gazing at the sky, and at another she was noticing how the sun dreams the world, how it shines over the minerals and stones, and penetrates even into the plants, unfolding the work of nature spirits. But such visions were not meant to last, for soon something changed these ecstasies into agonies.

It was autumn and she was sat, as was her custom, beneath a low hanging tree. The crops were off the meadow, and the wind that came now from the north brought a chill. Not far from her a bee was making traffic with a flower that grew wild in this valley. When she reached out to touch the creature she felt a sting.

A strange lightness in her head made her swoon.

The world fell away and she saw herself in a dream.

In this dream she sees a long river, cast silver in moonlight, striking a snake's path through a dark valley that lay between the clefts of a black-faced mountain. She is in this river, on a boat, among other women who wear their hair braided, their breasts oiled and their eyes painted. When they arrive at the shores of a great dark Temple they adore the moon, they intone auguries and they make sacrifices. She is taken to the Temple where she is admitted into the torch-lit antechamber.

In the warm half-light they dress her and adorn her in fine white robes and costly veils. They sprinkle the essence of roses on her hair and they braid its lengths with copper and gold. The women attendants point to the layers of the heavens, to the realms above the open roof where lives her bridegroom. She sees the starry cluster from which He shall descend. She is the virgin priestess.

She waits.

When he comes into the womb of her heart, she is overcome with ecstasy, for she is the keeper of the light, she is the Wife of the Sun, His mother, His sister, His servant and handmaiden.

She is the image of Isis...the tower that unites heaven with earth.

Awakened by cold, the pain in her hand was returned to her. She realised that night had already descended over the valley, and shaking, she gathered her wits about her and ran home with tears in her eyes and the palm of her hand to her mouth.

Amid the pain and the cold of her run, she recalled her mother's jar of Alabaster, full of the fragrances of Egypt. It had been left to her, and she had always imagined that her mother's very essence lived in it. For this reason she had thought it deeply holy and had never once used it on herself, and had long forgotten about it.

Now she understood the thread of destiny that wove her soul with Egypt.

After that day, she began to see other visions, and she realised that the world was not only populated by beauty-bearing, life-begetting beings, but also beings of darkness, beings of death and foulness. Everywhere she turned her eye she saw legions of demons lying in wait for any error or failing in men and women. Lies, jealousy and gossip were food to them, nourishing their growth, and they attached themselves, like parasites, to those who would feed them according to their nature.

For this reason, she avoided places where groups of people met, the bazaars where the merchants called out the virtues of their wares, or where people bargained for silks and baskets and gold and trinkets. She did not venture to those places where tradesmen, their minds intent on money, worked with tin and gold, silver and iron. She shunned the squares where musicians played their music; she did not even wish to go to the synagogue where men and women, crowded with devils, sought redemption and purification. Her dress became confused, her hair untended, unperfumed and uncombed, and she wandered about, speaking to herself.

Those men who, in the past, had never cherished even a hope that she might look in their direction, now jeered at her and spat at her feet. The women who had coveted her position and privileges, her beauty and noble bearing, whispered behind their veils, gloating with self-satisfaction.

'There goes the fine, rich, harlot! There goes the mad one!'

Her sister, worried for her health, took her to doctors, one after the other. All of them agreed that hers was not a physical malady. Beside herself with worry, Martha called a rabbi to the house to perform an ancient ritual of banishment.

It was a fine day when the rabbi arrived.

Dressed in the wide fringed garments of the order of the Pharisees, he sat beneath a tree in the walled garden of the house at Magdala, chewing on the dates and nuts that her sister had served him, while frowning over an assortment of parchments. Mary, full of sorrow and guilt for her condition, sat opposite him, waiting for his diagnosis.

For a long time, the rabbi said nothing. When he spoke, finally, his voice was bitter,

'It is the way of demons...' he said to Mary with a contemptuous slur, 'that they like to enter into the backbone of girls who are not reverent ... have you been bowing low to worship God, my child?'

'Of course I have, rabbi.'

He observed this with a sceptical turn of the lip, 'Have you borrowed drinking water?'

'No, rabbi.'

'Or walked over water that has been poured out?'

'No, rabbi.'

'And the water you wash your hands in, and the oils which you use to anoint them ... do they come from a known vessel?' He looked at Martha. 'Never leave a vessel unattended outside the house! It can be cursed by the evil eye of a neighbour, or a jealous suitor, or a demon of the morning intent on causing havoc.'

Martha answered from her corner, 'All our water comes from our own wells and is drawn just before we need it. The oil is our own and kept in sealed pots.'

He gave this some moment of sour consideration and bent his head again to study his parchment. 'Here it says ... that women who go about with their hair uncovered are prone to enticing evil spirits ... that those who walk between two palm trees in the moonlight, especially when the space between them is wider than four cubits, are in danger of becoming possessed by demons. Have you been walking about in moonlight, child, between palm trees?'

'No …' Mary hesitated. 'Well, not exactly … but I have dreamt of moonlight, of rivers and temples.'

He stared at her, watchful, eager, and his lips ran a constant activity. She knew he was inspecting the air around her for demons and devils and spectres. But she also knew he must be blind to them, since about him there hovered so many that he did not seem to see. They pressed into him and squeezed him from without and made him slap his own head with a hand, which occasioned a great,

'Oof!'

After it, a general silence fell.

Astounded by this unbidden action on the part of his hand, the rabbi said quickly, as if the foregoing were a prelude to this one word, which he knew would sum it all up:

'Danger!'

He looked to Martha then, and gathering vehemence to his heart, said it again, only louder, 'DANGER! Dreams of moonlight! Dreams of temples and rivers, more danger! Demons love moonlight! For they live in the shadows of temples, in the shadows that move in the waters of rivers and streams. In the shadows of shadows!'

Meanwhile, Mary watched his own shadows whisper into his ears and scratch under his chin, but the rabbi, not cognisant of them, reined himself in, wiped his lips and consulted his parchments again for a cure.

'Perhaps these dreams are caused by a chill of the head?' he suggested. 'If we cure the chill, the dreams might stop and the demons, not having a place in them, might leave!' But he did not consult the women, for he was lost in the clever paths of his thoughts. 'The remedy is to pour a quart of goat milk – mind that it is a white goat – to pour a quart of goat milk over three cabbage stalks in a pot, and to boil this together, stirring with a piece of Marmehon wood. It should be drunk during the full moon. And just to make certain you must wear an amulet of plants and herbs containing a verse from the Pentateuch.' He looked up. 'This has been tried?'

Mary nodded, losing all hope in her heart.

'To no avail?' he looked to Martha.

Martha affirmed it, from her safe position.

He put away his parchments and was taken with the devil of a thought. He shook his head like a dog with canker and scratched his nose at the place where sat numerous little devils and then, of a sudden, made a pause. He looked this way and that, full of concentration. 'Do you know … I think I can smell them …' he said. 'Yes ...' He was cautious. 'Indeed ... I smell demons!' he exclaimed. 'They are here!' he shrieked. 'Among us!' he shouted. 'What shall we do?'

The black creatures disappeared into his nose and into his ears, and a sudden thought occurred to him. He dug into a great woven bag to retrieve from it some herbs and a large bone. He brandished these items like weapons that are to be used with extreme caution. 'These,' he said, significantly, 'will exorcise the demons!'

'Cress and a bone?' Martha was sceptical, and sat forward to look at them.

'Yes, woman! Cress and a bone! Ancient are the ways of the learned ones!' he said, with mystical authority. 'Besides, we have no other recourse!'

He stood and made a gesture in the air, an ancient, dust-laden sign, and cried out with such boldness and unexpected vehemence that it startled Mary and caused Martha to make a little shriek in her corner of the garden.

'Burst! Curst! Dashed! Banned! *Bar-Tit, Bar-Tema, Bar-Tena, Chashmagoz, Merigoz, and Isteham, Ruach Raaah, Ruach Tumeah, Seirim, Shedim, Sheyda, Mazzikin, Geber Shediyin!*'

He struck Mary on the head with the herbs then and shouted, 'I cast you out and I enchant you into this cress!' He flung it to the ground. 'And I beat you, with the jawbone of an ass!'

When it seemed he had punished the herb sufficiently, he surveyed his work and found that it was good. He straightened, coughing, wheezing, and coughing again he said to Martha, 'Bury it in the garden, dear woman, far from the house, and spread the ashes of a dead bird over it. That should do the trick!'

Throughout this dismal ritual Mary had her eyes closed, and when she opened them again she saw that for all his magic, the rabbi had not cured her. For she could still see demons all about him, slipping in and out, crawling over his face and tickling his chin. She closed her eyes again.

'Open your eyes, child,' he said gently, paternally.

When she did as she was told, she saw that he was peering at her, so close that his nose near touched hers.

'Look, child ...' he said sourly, with his own look of pleased complacency. 'What do you see? Well? Are they still there, the demons and the visions?'

She hesitated. 'I ...'

'Come ... come child, we haven't all day!'

'Yes ... rabbi.'

'Yes ... yes ... what?'

'Yes, I still see them ... my visions are not flown away.'

Frowning, he said, 'Describe them to me, my child!'

'They are foolish, hideous, bashful things!' Tears fell from her eyes. 'Horrible to behold!

'Oh!' he said, 'Where do you see them?'

'All around you ... rabbi,' she answered, 'inside your mouth and in your ears, on your back and crawling through your hair and beard! They come out when you speak and enter when you cough!'

'By the beard of Abraham!' he gasped, shot up, and stepped back so abruptly that it caused a mishap to his back. Holding it he shouted, 'What do you mean around me? Inside me? When I cough or speak!'

'The banishment you made was not successful on them, rabbi!' Mary said.

Panicked, he stepped on the hems of his robes and they became entangled with his legs, and he dropped his parchments to the ground. 'I was not banishing them from me, evil, evil, girl!' he cried, taking up his documents. 'I was banishing them from you!'

He hastened to the gate and paused, whereupon he pulled his

features into a distorted terrain of wrinkles and pointed at her. 'She is *Hêrem*. She is cursed!'

He left then.

Word of Mary's demonic possession and the priest's failed exorcism soon reached the ears of the people. When the rabbi died not long after, the townsfolk accused her of having cursed him. After that life became an unbearable round of humiliation and disgrace and, having no other recourse, the family moved from Magdala to Bethany, where no one knew them, and where Mary, Lazarus and Martha, could live without shame.

Here they were to remain, and such would have been Mary's life had Lazarus not set out after a spiritual calling, in search of a man called ... John the Baptist.

CHAPTER 25

RECOGNITION

Mariam, stepmother of Jesus, had been sorrowful on the day Jesus had journeyed away from their home for Engaddi. Wearing her mourning mantle and veil, she had watched him from the dry stonewall with her back straight as a rod, waiting for him to turn, but he had not turned. He had walked onward without looking back, and was soon over the hill, carrying the food she had made for him in a bundle.

Recalling that day she grieved, for she had not told him what she had seen in his eyes when they had spoken of Engaddi. She did not know why her voice had fled from her.

Since then, the years had moved in a noiseless chain of days woven together by unspoken words.

The time waiting for him was long. Now and again, she would take a moment to observe the road, hoping to see his form coming over the rise. But he did not come.

Sometimes, when the others were busy and she had a moment to herself, she would go to Joseph's deserted workroom, where Jesus had often fashioned tables and doors, and chairs, and other useful things. She would touch the hammers and nails and hold up the saws, she would let her hand roam over the cool anvil or take up a piece of wood to smell its fragrance. In all these trivial things she sensed the soul of Jesus. Jesus, who had always seemed so troubled in his heart.

Her sons and daughters and relatives had never understood him and thought his behaviour more and more strange and incomprehensible. 'Why does he speak so little?' they asked. 'Why does he stare at walls? He behaves like one who is above the ordinary, for he does not do ordinary things: he leaves his home and his family to live the life of a vagabond; he refuses to continue his father's trade, and he will not take a wife and maintain the lineage of his fathers. If he thinks himself a sage, why did he not remain in Jerusalem? Now this further arrogance! What man went to Engaddi to live at the Motherhouse without taking vows? What man imagined himself so high as to impose conditions on the perfect ones?'

She wished that she had defended him from their unkind words and mocking smiles; she wished that she had sat with him more, listened to his part, and consoled him.

But she had not. What had prevented it? She did not know.

One day, pondering these things while sitting on a stool in the workshop, she fell to observing the sun coming through the slats in the roof. Rays of light had stolen into the dark corners, and in them dust motes floated like warm snow. These began to form themselves into a shape, which came to stand before her, as bright as day.

Was this Jesus? Jesus, with his soft-spoken eyes and his mother's smile, made from sunlight and air?

She felt his spirit incline towards hers, desiring to draw out all the worldly dross of her life.

As in a dream, she poured herself out, all her weaknesses, her fears, her longings and hopes. She asked him to forgive her for not being a better mother, for letting the others speak ill of him. She told him then of all the disappointments of her life, and in so doing a feeling of strength began its slow descent into her spine to make her steadfast.

Now she felt she could say what she had failed to say out loud to him before he left.

'In my heart you are my son, Jesus!'

From that moment in the workshop her soul became full of calm acceptance. Peace replaced the never tiring round of thoughts that had previously tortured her, and she grew to be as still as the moon, as steady as the sky, as sure as the rhythm of day and night. She did not seek to understand this joyful feeling, since it was a thing more suspected than seen, and had come from a singular meeting of souls – far removed from the comprehension of an ordinary mortal. And so she did not speak of it to anyone. She decided to make him a robe, and into it she would pour all of her wisdom transformed to love.

The afternoon she saw his silhouette come over the hill as if rising upwards from out of the deepening sky itself, she could not believe it; her breath was near taken away with happiness.

She came to him shyly and took his load from him, and led him to the house. He was older, weary and thin, and her heart was troubled by the look in his eye. She had Salome prepare him a bath and lay out the robe she had made for him during his absence. In the meantime, she would prepare him a meal of bread and olives and goat cheese.

He ate sparsely and afterwards did not wish to sleep, but told her he wanted to speak with her.

In the cool of the inner court of the house, she sat beside him and waited for his questing soul to open its doors to her, as she had opened her soul to him. When finally he spoke, however, it was not of intimate things, but of the destiny of men.

He told her that in the beginning, humanity was like a child, it crawled and walked and learnt and came of age. Now it was grown old and entering into decline. He had seen it clearly from his twelfth birthday.

'Before that, I remember only dreams … grass and sky and rain and the smell of sheep …' he said to her, 'I remember my mother's heart too, in my ear, and the whispers of angels …'

She nodded, remembering that many had shunned him for being addled.

'But on the steps of the Temple a bewildering happening took place which I didn't understand at first. Afterwards, I lost my mother and my life changed. My eyes lost their ability to see the dream-full spaces of heaven, since everything became sharp-shaped and clear to them. I began to forget all that was spontaneous and pure, and from that moment, in forgetting, I began to remember other things and to accustom myself to looking with different eyes … with the eyes of wisdom … eyes that were not mine.' He looked at her sorrowfully. 'What I saw caused such loneliness in me! Ah, my mother! If only you knew! That is why I fell into silence, and could barely speak for the pain of it! During my stays with my teachers in Jerusalem, I saw and heard the decadence of their teaching, how it had lost its life, how it was no longer given out of direct knowledge. I realised with sorrow that if the prophets came again, no man would understand them!'

'Oh, Jesus!' a sob was caught in her throat for his words. 'How your sensitive soul has struggled! But think of Hillel, my son! He was a great teacher of the law! In my time he spoke with a voice so sure and powerful. Could such a man not recognise the voice of the prophets if they were to return again?'

Jesus' face, lit meagrely by the penumbral light, was gravely cast. He said, 'Hillel was wise, it is true … but there are no more Hillels!'

With these words, a coldness settled over her and she pulled her shawl close and hugged herself to keep from shaking. 'How can this be true?'

He recounted his journey to the pagan lands, and spoke to her for the first time of the downfall of their temples. He told her of his experience at the altar, where he had fallen as though dead, and where he had heard the Bath-Kol in all its terrible splendour. After that, he recounted his experiences with the Essenes and his disappointment with their ways, and he told her of his meeting with the being called Buddha.

'I am alone!' he said to her, 'There is nowhere left to turn! This has been my last realisation. All has fallen into decadence and there is no truth left in the world. No light of hope can brighten the darkness that lies ahead! I have seen the portent of humanity's future suffering and the destruction of the world!'

She stifled a sob with her hand, for the entire burden of Jesus' sorrow had moved into her on the wings of his words, and they had formed in her mind a vision of what he had seen with his eyes - an entire panorama of calumny and misfortune. Mariam's hands and arms lost their strength and she felt faint.

'What will you do?' she asked him.

'There is a man in Judea who baptises with water for the remission of sins. He announces the coming of the Messiah, who will bring youth to the soul of the world. This Messiah will speak forth the voice of God and reverse the words of the Bath-Kol, to unite us with what we have lost.'

'What are these words that you speak of, my son?' she asked.

'Aum, the evils hold sway ...'

When he finished the ancient prayer, Mariam sat in stillness, allowing the words to resound in her soul.

Jesus' eyes grew distant. 'It is time.'

This brought her back to the moment. 'Time for what, Jesus?'

'God can make two into one, if it serves his design.'

His words to her those years ago, now made sense to her ... for as he said them she did not see only Jesus, no! She also saw Yeshua! Now were the eyes of her soul opened to what she had always sensed with her heart! She understood finally! Yeshua had accomplished his task after all! Long ago, on those Temple steps he had become one with Jesus! That is why Jesus had begun to see with different eyes, why he could argue with the rabbis, why he seemed like two men, one serious and wise, the other playful and loving. That is why she had loved him with a love she could not voice!

So this had been Yeshua's task - to weave his wisdom into Jesus' loving soul!

What now?

Jesus stood.

His face was framed by the dark sky full of stars one moment before he turned to go.

She remembered two boys now, sitting beneath a fig tree, arm in arm. Two boys who many years ago had left their mothers to ascend the Temple steps in the broad light of a sun-full day.

They gave this mother one last glance over their shoulder, and left to make their way into the night.

And, with her heart near breaking, she watched them go for the third time.

CHAPTER 26

FISH AND FISHERMEN

Simon was a fisherman, and he lived in a city on an ancient trade route called *The Via Maris*. Here, on the north-western shore of the Sea of Galilee, stood a city called Beth-saida, meaning *House of the Fishes.* It was so called because seven springs flowed into the waters of Galilee at this point, attracting fish and creating a lucrative trade for those who did not mind hard work.

The Sea of Galilee was little affected by tide, so its waters were profoundly clear, and for this reason the best fishing was not conducted in the day, but after sunset.

Each night Simon and his brother Andrew would rise from their beds, take a meal, and walk the dark path from their modest home near the eucalyptus forest to the shores of the inland sea, where waited those who worked with them in the cooperative: Philip, old Zebedee and his two sons, James and John.

In conditions favourable or unfavourable the fishermen would set off on their boats, travelling by the light of flares made from oily rags, which were kept in iron cages suspended from their bows. They journeyed forth into the sea's wide expanse with the air in their lateen sails, heading for the deeps where the weighted trammel nets were thrown between the boats to encircle the fish. A great number of fish of every size and quality could be ensnared this way, and when the nets were full the men would drag them to the shore and pull them onto the sand to sort the clean fish from those that were deemed unclean.

Backwards and forwards from the sea to the shore, the boats came and went through the night until the full-bodied baskets were brimming with fresh catch and the sun's pink herald stained the margins of the mountains.

At sunrise came the townsfolk and merchants to buy fish. When all was sold and the crowds were gone, the daily work truly began, for the men had many tasks yet: picking off the weed and dead creatures of the sea that had become entangled in the nets, repairing any tears, sorting the hooks and lines, liming the hulls of the boats and mending the sails.

These moments made ample time for conversation and companionship and the men spoke as they worked.

Simon was slow to speak, but in his mind he thought much. While the others talked he listened to their words and thought his own thoughts, for when they spoke of fish, and sky, and lake, they spoke as any man might. But Simon saw other things.

He saw the interplay of the sun's gold-shimmer with the lake's smooth surface; he saw the dance of the dark water with the moon's lustre, and the interaction of mountain and plain, lightning and earth. He saw the sea transform itself before his eyes into a celestial womb that was fertilised by the light of the sun. For what is a fish if not a drop of sun gleaming beneath the surface of the water? And what is a man, if not a drop of the eternal, a collection of sunbeams gathered up and born into the passing moment of life's stream?

These, he knew, were strange thoughts and philosophies and so he did not speak them out loud but only thought them, and he was thinking them this day as he knotted a rope, when James tore him from his ruminations.

'In the market this morning the people spoke of the pascha and their journey to Judea with such excitement,' he said, 'I wish that I could go!'

Andrew, Simon's brother, looked up from his work and said, 'Don't waste your wishes! They say the airs of Judea are full of death and that the rocks have a magic in them that can send a man mad.'

Of those gathered together on the sandy beach, Philip was the only one to have been to Jerusalem, and he raised his dark head now from his work with an air of wisdom. 'Nonsense! I have been there, and I am not dead or mad! But it is true, the land is like stale hard bread … the people are hard also … and when the rabbis speak, their voices are like a cold wind.'

'How do they speak?' said young John, leaving his liming to listen.

'With words like pointed arrows that pierce the head!' Philip said, sourly.

'Ah, but your head is soft, Philip!' Andrew quipped, merrily. 'It wouldn't take much to pierce it!'

All around there were smiles and soft chuckles.

James did not laugh or smile, he spoke almost to himself, 'We should not speak disapprovingly of the priests!' He cut a length of rope with his teeth. 'They are closer to heaven you know … closer at least than we are, it stands to reason that we don't understand them.'

Andrew cocked his head to one side. He had not heard well in one ear from childhood, having sustained a beating from his father for his impertinence. Now he shook his head and said to his brother, 'What did he say?'

Simon, whose task was to always repeat everything, sighed with impatience. 'He says we should mind the priests, for they are closer to God.'

Andrew nodded gravely. 'And James is right, they are closer to heaven … but only because you are too down to earth, Philip!'

They laughed like anything.

Little John of Zebedee said, between giggles, 'And Phillip is down to earth because he is so short!'

Phillip was put out. Feeling himself abused he continued his work of liming the hull of the boat in a bruised silence.

'Still,' Andrew put in, 'when the rabbi at our synagogue speaks, and his cold words gush out about the Messiah, my eyes almost see them like slippery fish, dropping from his lips!'

More laughs made Simon, who had listened to all of it, scratch at his greying beard. He decided to add wisdom to this foolishness,

'It seems to me,' he said, 'that when the Messiah comes he won't pass his days in Jerusalem among the proud priests and the law-abiding Pharisees … he won't answer to the rabbis, even in our synagogues. Perhaps he will come to sit here among us, where the sun marries the lake!' He looked about him, at the incredulous faces. 'Why not, you fools? Why would he not come to speak to those of ordinary expression and vocation, who are more likely to hear him and to love him?'

James threw him a sceptical eye. 'What? You think he'll come to stinking fishermen, to spend his time among fish guts and scales, and turn away a life among the rich, with fine wines and good food?' He shook his head. 'Your head has seen too much sun, Simon! No … it is my guess, he shall do as all kings do!'

Simon tilted his head up, until it seemed as if his beard would near touch the sky. 'Who can tell?' he said, 'Why should he be a king? Are we not told to expect a king and a priest, like two fish that move in different directions? One swims upwards to the heavens, while the other swims downwards to the earth? Don't we have two eyes, two ears, two arms and two legs? With only one of each we should not see our fish, or make many steps on the ground, or steady ourselves on our boats, or pull up our nets!'

Phillip nodded, considering it. 'Think of it, James! You are elevated to spiritual thoughts when you are in the synagogue on the Sabbath, but the next day your mind turns only upon how much money you can make for your old father! You are also two men!'

These words made them all laugh again, even James, who recognised their truth.

Simon was made full of confidence by this support. 'We are like fish ourselves! But we are also fishermen! Why should the Messiah not be like a fish, and also a fisherman?' he ended with a slap on the knee, pleased with himself.

All could see that this was a fine comparison.

James sat forward with a certain fear in his eye. 'Lads! Lower your voices! What if this is blasphemy, to speak of fish and men?'

Simon dismissed it with a wave of a hand. 'Glory be to God, James! Do the prophets not always speak of fish, and draw a line from them to men? Ezra and Habakkuk speak of fish. No one accuses the prophets of blasphemy!' he cried, having lost his temper with himself for speaking out his philosophy and inviting ridicule. He put his head down and continued with knotting his rope, now in a dark mood.

Philip, having recovered from laughter, said to him, 'Oh Simon, son of Jonah! One would think your father that same prophet who was spat out by a whale! You think too much of fish! And you think too much of fishermen!'

'The Essenes spare fish,' young John put in, 'for they revere them.'

'What did he say?' Andrew asked.

'He said the Essenes don't eat fish!' Simon answered.

Andrew nodded, 'Yes, the boy is right, they don't, and it's a good thing there aren't many of them, or else we would have no trade.'

Philip was not listening. His hand was raised high in the air, while the rest of him was stock-still. 'Wait!' he said, 'I remember something ... a short time ago I overheard a customer speak of a man who is not an Essene but who speaks with their words. He baptises in the Jordan for the remission of sins. I remember it only now!' He looked at them with wide eyes. 'This man says that because fish do not breathe air they are pure. He says that men must change their breathing, they must repent their sins and become like fish. And they must rise up out of the water and ready their hearts for the coming of the Messiah!'

The men traded astonished looks, and it seemed to Simon that their eyes were shaking off a sluggish indolence.

'There, you see?' Simon said, vindicated. He put down his rope and stood. 'What's his name?'

'John the Baptiser.' Phillip told him.

'John the Baptiser, eh?' Simon said, rubbing his speckled beard. '*John the Baptiser*!' he said it again, as if contriving to make the name fit a shape held in his mind. 'This is a sign!' he told them finally. 'We must go and hear this man speak, this *John the Baptiser,* for it seems that he speaks true.'

Young John paused his liming. 'I will come!'

Andrew frowned his annoyance at the boy, 'That is because you do not like liming boats, that you will go!'

John smiled in answer.

'But what of your precious fish, Simon?' James said, half in jest and half in seriousness. 'Will we leave them uncaught in the sea? What of my father's livelihood?'

'Yes … old Zebedee will curse us! After all, who will take care of the nets and the boats?' Phillip added.

'What of the customers and the merchants that come from every place?' Andrew threw in.

Simon paused to look out at the sea's glimmer skipping over the calm lapping of the waves and made his resolve.

'These things shall take care of themselves.'

'But shall we leave our homes, our wives and families and the sea, to become homeless men?' James was astonished.

'Why should we not become homeless men for a time, James? Look at us, we do this stinking work, day in and day out; is there not more to be known in the world than the beauty of this sea and the smell of fish? Are we always to remain like children who are three years old and lulled by a song?'

Phillip thought this through. 'For my part lads, I have always been of the mind to trust Simon. He has a good sense for things, but this … I don't know. This is something new.'

Andrew made a sigh. 'We have always listened to your good counsel, Simon.'

'Yes,' added young John, 'he always knows where to cast the nets, so that we do not go hungry like other fishermen.'

James got up. 'And all of you suppose that we should go then and leave everything behind?'

The men looked at one another, as if contemplating a lunacy that confounded human explanation, and yet a lunacy full of logic to their minds.

James nodded, smiled and rubbed his beard. 'Well, I am outnumbered it seems, perhaps all will be well for a day or two.'

The five men now looked to Simon.

Simon frowned. 'We go then.'

And they resolved to make their preparations.

CHAPTER 27

THE ISRAELITE

At the same moment that Simon in Galilee was making his resolve to go in search of John the Baptist, in Jerusalem a Pharisee called Nicodemus sat in the judgement hall of the Temple, among those who were gathered to judge the Baptiser.

While the priests of the Sanhedrin conducted the various opening formulas, Nicodemus looked about the vast hall. It had been constructed in a long rectangle out of great slabs of stone, with round stone pillars supporting a lofty ceiling. In between these pillars, upon stone benches, were seated the Levites, scribes and shorthand note takers. At the front of the great hall upon a dais sat a sem-circle of judges. They faced the middle of the hall and the laity, which on this day could not be contained and was spilling out of the oaken doors to the terrace beyond.

The Great Sanhedrin was indeed the highest tribunal of the land and was made up of seventy-one members. Nicodemus had always felt very fortunate to be counted among them and to be called an Israelite, a representative of Israel. In truth, every Jew was united by a common memory through the blood of Abraham. In this blood was imprinted all the abilities and disabilities of their people, all the laws and transgressions, even the air, the sky, and the soil of the Promised Land! Because of this, all Jews could say 'we'.

But an Israelite could do more. His blood was like an open book, in which the archangels glanced to make their decisions about the future of the people. For this reason, an Israelite considered himself not only one with those of the blood of Abraham, but also, and more importantly, one with the God of Abraham himself.

A voice tore him away from his thoughts now, and he realised how long he had been daydreaming. In the centre of the hall one of Herod's captains, not long returned from troubles in Dothain, was recounting something about a man called John the Baptist.

'He tells the people to repent, to change their hearts, for The Kingdom of Heaven is at hand. He tells them this, but then the people do not suffer the heathens that dwell among them and they burn their idols and cause havoc, and this has made the prince of Sidon send his armies to protect the idolaters from John's disciples.'

Nicodemus looked to Caiaphas the High Priest - a Sadducee and so naturally, corrupt. The weak-willed priest, who leant on his father-in-law, Ananias, like a dizzy man holds to a wall, was short and squat, and sat ensnared among vestments glistening with gold thread and studded with gemstones. He stared out from a face full of creases gathered together around a moist nose and two bead-shaped eyes. Upon his head a mitre of great proportions hid the source of thick braids that fell on either side of his face, and met in a neatly oiled beard. Caiaphas stroked this beard fondly with one hand, while the other held a crosier, which every now and again he used to scratch his back.

'But how many followers could this man have?' Caiaphas asked his captain.

The man answered, 'There are thousands and thousands ...'

The hall buzzed with conversation and the shaking of mitred heads.

Herod Antipas, sitting on Caiaphas's other side, nodded in agreement. 'We have just returned from Callirrhoe, where I was forced to send my troops to quell the disorder.'

There was another swell of whisperings among the judges and those on the flanking benches.

The soldier spoke directly to Caiaphas, 'We come to ask if we should be baptised by this man, so that the people may take notice of us, and do as we say.'

Herod made a smile. 'I have already told my men that I see no need for baptism! Particularly since this John the Baptist is an impostor. I met him myself at Ainon! He does not produce miracles nor does he work wonders. He is a hands-breath from being an animal from what I could see, for he wears a camel garment that barely covers him and his hair is unkempt, and his beard is a tempest of knots! The only thing we can account for is his cleanliness, for he is in the river all day long!'

A round of restrained laughter echoed in the hall.

Nicodemus did not laugh. He looked about and saw that his friends and fellow members of the Sanhedrin, Joseph of Arimathea and Gamaliel, were also serious.

Herod said, 'He tells all who will hear him that the blood of Abraham is polluted, and must be cleansed!'

There was a chorus of gasps.

Satisfied, he continued, 'He teaches that priests and Levites are further from God than even a Samaritan!'

A confusion of voices and exclamations broke out, but in the great space where stood the laity there was quiet.

The captain spoke now through this marriage of silence and sound, 'John the Baptiser was meaning that the goodness of a man does not rely on his station or on his birth, but on his own efforts! That any man can change his heart and see the Messiah!'

But derision and mockery drowned out his words. The judges called out, 'Blasphemy! Blasphemy! Blasphemy!'

Herod widened his smile from ear to ear. 'This John the Baptist also says that he is the forerunner of the Kingdom of God, that he is the forerunner of the Son of Man!'

A quiet descended at the sound of those words. Nicodemus knew why. The Kingdom of God was something that was awaited with fear.

The Pharisees feared the Messiah, for they saw him as a priest destined to usher in the end of days and bring about the destruction of the world. Conversely the Sadducees saw him as a mighty king who was set to take over the Sanhedrin and strip them of their power.

To Nicodemus they were both in error. He believed the Son of Man did not have the task of ushering in the judgement of God, nor would his kingdom come to change the world. It would come to change the soul of a man, so that he could judge for himself. For this reason the Baptiser's words now rang true in his ears.

His friend's voice interrupted his thoughts. The usually shy and prudent Joseph of Arimathea was standing among his peers and speaking. Nicodemus sat forward to look at him.

'I have heard that this man has come from the wilderness of Judea like Elijah once came from the wilds of Gilead, and that he bears the same appearance and speaks a similar prophetic message! Should we not hear him before we condemn him?'

'Our colleague is correct ...' Caiaphas said then. 'We must send a deputation to find out who this man is, and what is his aim; a deputation of priests and Levites will bring back their findings to this court, which will decide on a judgement.'

'Splendid!' Herod said brightly. 'I will offer the delegation the convenience and protection of my own personal guard. My own captain shall guide them.'

Nicodemus was suddenly filled with enthusiasm. Perhaps this man John the Baptist was a true prophet? If so, the Son of Man was near at hand! Could he do less than find out for himself? He stood and all eyes turned to him.

'I too, will go!' he said.

CHAPTER 28

WISE MEN, RICH MEN AND LEPERS

Jesus walked the road that led from Nazareth to Judea with his feet moving of their own accord and his thoughts vacant in his head.

During his conversation with his stepmother, what had lived embedded in him like a seal on wax had begun its leave-taking. This had made him feel bewildered and abandoned, and unable to think coherent thoughts. His movements too followed only a predetermined design, towards the man who would take his destiny further.

At daybreak, a windstorm announced itself in the anger of a red sky. Soon the air had picked up the sand around him to sting his eyes. He stumbled and fell. Two men dressed in white garments with hoods over their heads and scarves over their faces came from the road ahead. They were leading an overburdened mule.

The taller man helped him up, and said loudly over the din, 'What's this? Jesus of Nazareth, is that you? Where are you going alone, my son?'

Jesus looked up at him, trying to understand words that no longer made sense. When his voice came from his mouth it sounded hollow, as if it came not from him but from the wind, 'I am going to where people like you do not wish to direct your vision, where human pain can find the consolation that comes from what you have forgotten!'

'Jesus of Nazareth!' the other man shouted. 'Do you not remember us from Engaddi?' The man took the scarf from his face momentarily. 'Do you see who I am?'

The shorter man did likewise, and said, 'I once sat with you in the grotto … do you remember?'

Jesus did not see them clearly. He saw however, what they represented.

'Come away from this scorching wind!' the taller one said, 'The Lord is a storm come to sweep away the world.'

'You are lost lambs!' Jesus coughed, walking away.

'We are all lost, Jesus!' the shorter one cried, 'It does not matter how many psalms we sing, or how many temples we build, God continues to deny us our Messiah!'

Jesus stood in the tempest of elements and looked at them. 'And when I become your shepherd,' he said, 'when you realise who I am, you will run away again and become lost, just as you ran away from me long ago.'

The men put scarves to their mouths to ward off the dust and debris.

The shorter man said, 'You must come with us … you are not well. Not far from here there is a house of the order where you can rest.'

'Leave me be!' he said to them. 'I won't go to your secluded house! You wear white and you pretend to be pure, but you are not pious men in your hearts, because in you burns a fire that has not been kindled by God but by your own ambitions. You bear the mark of the tempter! It is the tempter that has made you arrogant, so that your wool glitters with his fire!' He put his fingers to his face. 'But the hair of this wool you try to pull over me pricks my eyes.'

The taller man shouted, 'Rest assured, Jesus, it is the dust that pricks your eyes! You know we have shown the tempter the door, he has no part in what we do … you should've stayed with us, now look at what the world has made of you! Let us help you!'

'Oh, what arrogance and pride! But you are only greater than others because you stand on their backs!'

They did not know how to respond to this, and he left them standing in the desert. Behind him the mule made its loud complaints, shaking its head, as the breath of Jehova carried the world away to blot out the sun.

The storm abated, and days passed without beginning and without end.

It was night.

Fatigued and cold, Jesus wandered towards a light in the distance. When he drew near to it, he saw a man sitting by a fire preparing to eat a meal. When the man looked up, he stood in a hurry, afraid, and called out to Jesus with a mustered boldness,

'Who are you? I am alone but I have a knife, and I shall not be afraid to use it!'

Jesus showed him his empty hands. 'I thirst,' he said, knowing he must pause, for his legs would soon give out from under him.

The man came to Jesus and helped him to a place beside the fire.

'Forgive me … I am constantly afraid of being robbed by thieves or killed by bandits! I see you are no thief and no bandit … come, be my guest, eat at my table. I have made soup,' he said, showing Jesus the watery stew which he was pouring into a bowl. 'There's crow in it, and wild mushrooms,' he pointed out those meagre morsels with an approving eye, 'and some other wild things I have no name for. Once, you know, I would have spat at the thought of such a meal, but now I shake with anticipation. Look at my hands, how they shake. Because of the crow, I have made it boil a good long while, to kill the poison. That is what it has come to; still, thanks be to God, I have something!' He sighed, 'Israel mourns, Israel hungers, its people cry out in pain for deliverance, but first I must cry out for something to put into my belly! After that, a man can turn his mind to the hunger of the soul. In the meantime we are all animals …' He looked at Jesus. 'You need something in your belly too, I'll wager. You look like you have eaten nothing in days. Come, it's good you'll see, I have let it boil long to kill the poison …'

Jesus shook his head. 'I want only water.'

'Only water …!' the man said, peering at him with more intensity. 'Are you a prophet? Yesterday I heard tell from a holy man of a prophet in these parts. So help me God! He was described to seem just like you! Many don't trust prophets, they think them mad people, one foot in heaven and the other in hell … but I believe it a good thing to know a prophet who can speak to God.'

The man gave him some water, which Jesus drank with gratitude. After that he looked at the man and said, 'I thank you for the water … but I am not a prophet.'

'What a shame!' The man's spirit drooped. He took a thoughtful gulp of his soup. 'If you were a prophet,' he continued, 'I would ask you to speak to God on my behalf … on account of the paths my soul has taken.'

Jesus was directed to an apparition that loomed large and red over the man. 'What are these paths? I have seen you before, a thousand years ago. You were different then!'

The man grew fearful. 'What do you see? Oh, dear God of Abraham, what do you see? Is it the Devil sitting on my shoulders? Is it?' He shuddered and moaned, and shuddered again. 'Would you send it away? It hounds me. I have given up everything, and yet it follows me! I admit that I was never a pious man. My heart was always bent on acquiring riches and high honours and I thought that I was of greater value than others. One day I had a terrible dream. I saw what had made me rich. It was not I, myself, it was a black angel with huge red wings, and I was terrified because I knew that it was the devil! I took to my heels to escape him, abandoning everything, and I have been going about for a long time, fleeing from what sits on my own shoulders.' When he said this, his eyes clouded with tears and he seemed to be lost in a vision of his own wretchedness.

'I have seen this spirit that hounds you before,' Jesus said to him, 'at the pagan altars … it is the spirit of pride and arrogance!'

'Yes … yes …!' the man said with eyes wide. 'Pride and arrogance! Exactly! These are my weaknesses!'

Jesus could not help him, he could not help anyone, not yet …

something was waiting for him in the river and he had to go. He stood then and with a heart full of sorrow, left the man in his misery.

He walked day after day with the sun's fingers on his brow, and spent the nights huddled, trembling from cold, with his teeth chattering and only the robe his stepmother had made for him wrapped around him. On the morning of the twelfth day, when the fire-ball came out of its rocky bed he was up again, walking, and came upon the disfigured shape of a man sitting beneath a solitary tree.

Already the world was a furnace and he knew he must have shade, but as he neared the tree the man sitting there raised his head and Jesus saw that his skin was covered in pustules leaking with suppurations, that his nose was a hole in his face and that the lids over his eyes were missing, giving him the look of a living cadaver. The leper tried in vain to cover his malignancies with a hand eaten and ravaged.

'Go away!' he said to Jesus. 'I am foul! Hurry! Don't come near, for the path I walk is not your path, my son. I beg you to leave while you can …!'

Jesus sat near the man and wiped his brow with a sleeve. 'It is hot,' he said.

'Yes, yes, it is hot, but please, save yourself! Must I take upon my soul your death on top of everything else I have to bear?'

Jesus heard snakes hissing behind rocks and when he looked at the leper he saw blue wings and a cold eye. He had seen this eye before in the faces of those Temple priests. The eye looked at him while its wings enfolded the man.

'Tell me,' Jesus said to him, 'where has the path your soul has taken, led you? I know you, I saw you thousands of years ago, but you are now changed, you are come down to earth!'

The leper was terrified. He sucked in a breath through the purple edged crater that was his mouth, and from within this cavern he emitted a strangled voice, 'Do you see it? Oh, the misery! Where is the Messiah? When will he come to release me from this dreadful thing that claws into my flesh? He came so gradually, you know. At first I thought he was the Archangel Gabriel and I adored him, but I soon realised that he was another … I realised he was the angel of death!

Death itself gnaws at my bones and feeds on my flesh … look at me! Me, a learned rabbi, a powerful man in the synagogue! Now I am defiled and no one will have me near them, and I have to walk alone in desolate places like this, scarcely able to beg for what scraps people will give me at their doors.

'When you came I was waiting for death to tear me to pieces with his jaws … I have waited! But he wants to torture me more.' He began weeping then into his ulcerated hands.

'I have seen it,' Jesus told him, putting a hand on the man's shoulders, 'It is the sharpness of your dead thoughts, rabbi ... these are like corpses and rotting carcasses.'

The man was so frightened that he put both hands over his face to ward off the picture of it.

Jesus pointed his head to the sun and bellowed an, 'Ah!' into that white light that blinded his eyes. 'I am a grain of sand in the desert! What can a grain of sand do?' he said to it.

He got up, hot tears falling on the dirt at his feet, and went on his way.

And like the wise men and the rich man, this leper did not see him go until he was a speck on the horizon.

CHAPTER 29

A NEW SEASON

It was in the fifteenth year of the rule of Tiberias, on a day when Venus stood in Aquarius, that John the Baptiser awoke feeling his muscles and sinews taut, his mind awake and alert and his heart calm.

The sun had popped up out of its desert crib to cast its fiery eye over Israel and to beat upon the brows of men and the backs of beasts. Each day he faced this sun, standing waist deep in that freezing river, observing with an unfaltering eye the whirling tumult of dead thoughts and sins that were discharged into the river from the souls of those whom he baptised. Each day he wondered where the strength would come for his work and each day he was given the forces necessary. But this day something was altered. In himself he felt it, the nearness of the fulfilment of his task, accompanied by a strange bewilderment, since he found himself desiring to forestall it!

In this mood he left his hut of rushes to say his prayers to the God of Israel and to perform his ablutions, before taking himself to that little bend in the river near Bethany, situated in the lower Jordan.

Large crowds came to be baptised and he worked for hours without pause, looking into each soul to determine its measure and value, dividing the lambs from the vipers. Near the midpoint of the day the leaders of these vipers arrived at the river, a deputation of priests and Levites upon asses, preceded by a retinue of guards whose swords caught the bold sunlight and reflected their sharp sting into John's eyes. They pushed aside the crowds to allow the priests to come to the shore.

Well … well … his words had moved across the land, so that even the Temple in Jerusalem had heard of him! He was pleased for the sake of his task.

He said to them, 'The Masters of the ancient wisdom of the snake, the brood of vipers, the initiates of Lucifer, have come!'

One Pharisee said from his high position, 'We are here on behalf of the Sanhedrin, to ask you some questions.'

'Questions?' the baptiser said, looking about with mockery in his eye. 'If you come asking questions concerning laws that are written in books, you will not find anything here to satisfy you. I do not answer to laws that indicate this or that to be right or wrong. I answer only to the power that exists in every man to know right from wrong in his own heart!'

'Heresy!' the Pharisee said, 'A son of Abraham must follow the laws of Moses!'

The Baptist looked at him with flares for eyes. 'You make much of having Abraham for a father, but this alone does not make you worthy! Your body of flesh is like the stones at your feet; in the same way that you can pick up any of these stones and make it yours, God can make any man a child of Abraham.'

Gasps came from the priests. Rants and raves and astonishment filled the air. 'You dare to say that any man can be a child of Abraham? Any man can enter the lineage of the blood tree of your forebears, which is sanctified by God?'

The Baptist roared like a lion at them, 'Why do you call on this dying tree! God has given me the axe and I will cut it down!' He pointed to the people and cried, 'Israel! This tree no longer bears good fruit!'

The delegation was turned over into a rumble of voices. The guards stood at the ready with their weapons.

'Jerusalem!' He pointed at the delegation. 'Your laws and your knowledge were brought to you by way of Moses, but the time of these laws is finished now! Soon, grace and truth will come into the world by way of the anointed one. He will descend to earth so that the blind sons of Israel may see Him! But only those who can hear the voice of conscience in their hearts will recognise him!'

The rabbis, priests, and Levites talked in an excited fashion among themselves, shaking their heads and distorting their countenances. They could not agree. Meanwhile, in the crowds, a man called out to John,

'But how shall we become good men? What is this voice you speak of that is in the heart?'

John the Baptiser answered, 'Do you not shrink to see others cold or hungry? Do you, who have much, not hear a voice that tells you to help those who have little? This voice speaks tenderly in the wilderness of your soul, and it will say to you - he who has two coats, let him share with him who has none, and he who has meat, let him do likewise.'

Then a publican called out, 'But what of our livelihood? We have to earn a living from the sale of shelter and food! What will you have us do? Give men a bed, and a bowl of soup for free, to be good?'

'Listen to the voice. It will say: *Do not ask for more than is rightfully yours.*'

The soldiers, who were Herod's men and had come with the priests and Levites, asked him, 'How can we soldiers be good men if we must use a sword and accuse others for our wages?'

John the Baptist told them, 'The voice will say: do not do violence to any man and do not accuse another falsely. What you do must be good and right, if you are to take to yourself your wages and be content.'

'Who are you?' Another Pharisee called out, 'Are you the Messiah?'

John knew these questions needed to be asked, to prevent confusion in the people's minds, and so he answered, 'Listen to me ... all of you. Know that I am *not* the Christ. He shall come after me!'

'Do you say that you are Elijah, then?' Another priest said.

John shook his head, 'I am sent in the *spirit* of Elijah.'

'But it is said that a prophet will come before the Messiah comes. Are you not that prophet?'

'I have told you ... do not look at me, look for that other who will come!'

'Who do you say that you are? We must return to tell those who have sent us, the council of great men at the Sanhedrin,' that same Pharisee said.

'Tell them that I am the voice of the soul, crying in solitude, cut off from the likes of those who hold fast to the blood of Abraham. I am the free voice without a folk, who seeks Him who comes to sustain me!'

'Why do you preach repentance and baptise, and make pure men, if you are not a prophet, or Elijah, or the Messiah?' a Levite gave back.

'I baptise with water, but there stands one among you that you do not recognise. He has the forces derived from a higher source than mine! He is mightier than me for I am not worthy to stoop down to unloosen even the laces of his sandals. I baptise you with water. I do this in preparation for Him who will baptise men not with water, but with the Holy Spirit fire!'

'Is he here?'

John's heart was full with joy, 'I feel he is among us!'

The priests looked about them.

Each man searched his neighbour.

'Where is he?' they asked.

'You shall not see Him until He makes himself known to you.'

The priests mocked him and said he was a madman. They told the crowds that no man should believe such lies and, with their dispositions proud, gathered to them the reins of their animals and took themselves and their soldiers from the shores of the river. But two members of the Sanhedrin remained behind and sat among the crowds. John sensed that these men had been touched by his words.

After that, he continued with his work until the sun reached its zenith, and the crowds began, as was their custom, to disperse for the midday meal. Now standing alone in the chilling water, he saw a man step forward and come to the edge of the river.

He put a hand up over his eyes to see, for the sun's rays were shimmering on the surface of the river, blinding him.

He recognised the man's form and the contours of his face. How bright did the sun shine at that moment! As if its body were leaning over to touch the river! John squinted, and still he could not see, and yet he did see. This was a man he knew, and yet it was not simply that he saw a man he knew, for this man, whom he had met at Qumran, seemed not to be there at all, but in his place was a soul that he recognised in its essential foundations. It was as if he were looking at his own reflection, a part of himself, long lost and forgotten. Did this soul that came towards him not seem like the youngest and purest soul in the world? And was this not the opposite of his own soul, which felt to him ancient, cracked, and used up, like an old jug emptied of its contents?

His heart near burst with the mighty impression this thought created, and his eyes filled with tears. He let go his staff into the water, for he knew that the day he had longed for had arrived, and it had brought to him the reason for his very existence.

CHAPTER 30

THE BAPTISM

The day was nearing its apex. Talons of light fractured the water and made short shadows of men. From the crowds, Jesus saw the priests of the Sanhedrin leave the river, and he waited for a time, until the voices of the people had died down and many left, seeking their midday meal.

He then laid aside his garments and took himself to the river in his loincloth. The man in the river was aglow with light. Colour spilt over him like fluid fire. Jesus saw him put a hand over his brow to see him. Jesus did not pause but entered the silvered water. First his feet, then his ankles, his knees, until the cold came over his thighs, until he stood before the man whose height was greater than his and whose face was, of a sudden, full with awe.

John let go his staff into the water. His knees seemed to buckle and he stumbled. He cried, 'I should be baptised by you! I cannot endure to do it!'

Jesus said to him, 'In the same way that once my presence awoke your limbs in your mother's womb, I shall awaken your thoughts to your duty!'

The man called John looked up and Jesus' shadow fell over him. Jesus could now see, unclouded and undisturbed by the light, a reflected mirror image of himself in the other man's face. An image of something he had misplaced. He was given the knowledge at Qumran that this man was the same as Elijah, and now he recognised in him the oldest soul of humanity, Adam, and he realised that some part of him belonged to this man and was conjoined by a remembrance of times lost in a dream.

When the baptiser stood, it was a signal to Jesus.

He crossed his arms over his chest and felt a support behind the small of his back. It seemed to him then, that although Yeshua was leaving him, little by little, the soul of the baptiser was uniting with him in order to sure up the pathway to the God whom he sensed descending. And he was comforted by it.

John guided him into the water and he was submerged into light and colour and sound. His soul was wedded to the element of the river. All the pictures of his life rushed past his eyes until he heard a flute song, and he could smell sheep, earth and grass. All of it was married to the warmth of friendship, the lulling breezes, the glow of the sun, the fingers of the wind, the soothing feel of his mother's hand and the cry of a child in the wilderness.

Now, there was nothing more.

He did not breathe. He was lost. He was alone. A flame hovered over him. A sparkling, ever-tranquil, lilting radiance issued from the encircling round, and above him the spirit of Yeshua gathered up to form the shape of a bird. It lingered a moment over him, as if in a final farewell, and was given up, with light in its wings and life in its breast.

Surrendered!

The majestic and wise spirit of Yeshua, which had fashioned his soul and body over eighteen years, was severed from him. Within him was left a hollow place, unopened yet to the spirit, like a spring bud that trembles in a cold wind.

How could he open it, when he had no forces left to him? A great lassitude overwhelmed him and threatened to extinguish him. He was alone. And yet … and yet … Jesus sensed the soul of his dead mother draw near. His mother, whose purity was the likeness of his own, came to his aid. She plucked tenderly at his heart, to unfold him in readiness for the descent of grace, for the pulse of heaven's glory. When the clouds parted and rent was the veil that separates above and below, the God fell downwards, from the heart of the Father, like a brand of light moving through the spirit's fluid stream. Jesus inhaled the breath of the God into his lungs, and the spirit, orphaned from heaven, innocent of evil, immortal, blameless, without guilt and eternal, began its descent into the soul of Jesus.

Now, when Jesus opened his eyes, he saw the world differently for the second time in his life, and in his ears the thunder call came:

'Thou art my beloved Son, in whom I behold my very own Self, in whom my own Self confronts me! Now you are begotten in Jesus!'

CHAPTER 31

TEMPTATION

The man Jesus walked through the crowds on the shore swaying and stumbling, while the God in him saw the world as foreign and unknown, a distortion of faces and loud noises, of heat and sun and overwhelming smells. In the body, the muscles strained, air rushed in and out of the lungs and the heart pounded in the chest, while in the mind thoughts flitted past like shadows. How painful it was to cram his mighty power into that mind and that body! A power that could now harness nature and cause miracles, so that his mere presence would seem to men like a world of marvels, a tempest of splendours. It was not his purpose to enrapture and bewilder, to dazzle and astonish, so he directed Jesus into the wilderness in search of a quiet place wherein he could guard the birthing of his new forces.

That is how he came to be in the old cave situated high above the vast mountainous wasteland of Judea. From its lip he could observe the sun falling into the night, and partake for the first time in the splendour of colours that are separate from the self. Above, Christ looked to the home of his heart, now distant and detached from him. From beyond those stars he had come, descending downwards aeon after aeon. Men had seen him in their mysteries and had worshipped him in their rituals and given him many different names, and now he would walk among them – a God extracted, separated out from heaven and born into the body of a man.

This conception on earth was to his Fathers in the heavens, like a death.

He heard a lamentation. He listened. It came not from heaven but from the sleeping souls of the world. They were reaching out to him in their supplication as they had always done. This was why he had come, to make this earth his heaven and rescue it from the maws of hell.

Jackals called as the moon made a rise. He had never seen such a moon nor heard such a sound and an intuition drew his attention to the shadows of the night. From them came the vision of a red-winged angel, falling from the sky and landing at the lip of his cave.

It thrust one sad, melancholic eye at him, and said, 'If it isn't the favourite come down from his high perch to visit his poor relations!'

'What are you?' Christ asked it.

'Where are your manners, brother? Did no one tell you that this is my kingdom? Come, before you step across my threshold you must first recognise the master of the house! Bend low before me and our little quarrel shall be forgiven. Perhaps I'll even share some of the riches and power I have gained from this wretched world with you? You have to concede this is more than you did for me!'

A vision came then of Jesus standing before a man who was running from the Devil on his shoulders. This was that Devil, he realised. This was Lucifer, his brother who was cast down from heaven.

'Lucifer,' he said to it now. 'Look into my face! I see you haven't changed ... You think you can lure me with power because this is your weakness, but listen carefully to me ... I have not come into this world to rule it, nor have I come to serve you, I have come to serve the rightful gods!'

Lucifer's gloomy eye turned to white and a shiver passed over his wings. 'The rightful gods ... yes ... what do they know of the world? Do they know anything about thirst? Well? Do they know that human thirst is unquenchable? You are a God, you need not thirst for puny human knowledge, when you can be an angel, like me, an angel is wisdom itself! Throw yourself from the lip of this cave and you will see, as the Psalms say, God will give his angels charge of you, and you will be among them, and they will bear you up with their own hands so that your foot will not even strike one stone!'

But there was something more in the cave with them. From out of the shadowed corners came a blur of blue wings, desiccated and clawing, and the world stirred to make way for them.

Another voice came into his ear:

'Son of God! Do as your brother says and let us see? Jump! What can happen to you? Fear is something only mortals feel, angels are above such feelings!'

What was this thing called fear? He felt it now, when he thought of jumping from the cave to that great distance below. He was not an angel. If he jumped, Jesus would die, and his task would die with him.

'Listen to me, Lucifer, your arrogance is made weak by your companion, who has just pointed out that fear is perfectly right for a mortal man! I *am* a mortal man and fear has given me wisdom! Again, it is written – do not tempt the Lord thy God, to whom *you* should surrender yourself!'

Lucifer cried an anguished cry, and flew off towards the moon, defeated. But that crawling malignant thing had entered into Jesus. He could feel its blue wings furl and unfurl inside his soul, and he plunged in after it.

'Son of God!' the creature breathed. 'Let me tell you something of hunger. Hunger is a terrible torment for a man; capable of driving even the most pious to sinful acts. But you need not suffer hunger, for you can so easily turn stones to bread by merely saying a word! Say it to impress us!'

Christ tasted ashes and felt the thickness of the bones under his skin, and the mind, imprisoned by a skull, found a memory of the leper … this spirit had tempted that poor man, and had eaten him alive. This was an archangel, and he was far mightier and more dangerous than Lucifer, his brother.

He knew his name.

He cried out to the ancient creature, 'Satan, you father of lies! Leave me alone. It is written: man should not live by bread alone, but by every word that proceeds from out of the mouth of God!'

'That is what they say,' whispered the creature, 'those gods who know nothing of men. But men have turned a deaf ear to them, naturally, since they know that the belly must be fed, or the body dies! You see how I love men more than you? When you made life and death a law and left them to their own devices I showed them how to turn stones to coins, and coins to bread so that they might live. And so, as there are stupid men and cunning ones, there are also the rich and the poor. One man can feed his hunger while the other cannot and each trespasses against the other, grasping for the daily bread. If you have come to preach love and eternal life to these animals called men, you might as well go back to that starry home from which you came, Son of God! Brotherly love is impossible while there is death! Over this mystery the will of the heavens cannot rule!'

Christ understood. These backward angels, Lucifer and Satan, had caused men to swing from one extreme to the other. But he had come to show how it was possible to live between extremes, to overcome pride and arrogance through wisdom, and death through love. And here in Jesus' soul now he discerned a dual nature, a weaving of wisdom and love so endearing that it worked like a great power of attraction for him, and he united his forces with it, and became one with Jesus.

He felt a sting, a sudden gnawing in his bowels!

The blue archangel Satan gave a mocking laugh.

'Now you've done it! Feel the tearing of hunger in Jesus? That is why men must live by the rule of the daily bread, and walk side by side with me ... the archangel of death!' The whisper came closer, 'Listen to me, I am like you, I am stubborn and full of longing, I am eternal, so I shall not be inspired by haste. When the time comes, I shall return for what is mine!

And he was gone.

Christ Jesus let out a gasp and fell to the earthen floor of the cave.

Above him he sensed warmth; the love-radiant thoughts of the stars were making a way into his heart to comfort him.

And so it was, the orphan from heaven closed his eyes then, and slept his first earthly sleep.

‡

'So that's how it was!' I sat back so astounded that I could hardly take a breath, my fingers black with ink and my back aching. 'Yeshua and Jesus had been two persons in one, but when Yeshua lifted up to make way for Christ, the Son of God then entered into the Son of Man and the two natures, human and divine, were united!'

Illuminated and reconciled were all the arguments of same and similar, image and likeness, persons and natures! So many disagreements, misunderstandings and half-truths! So much blood had been shed when it had all been so simple!

But my elation was followed by a sudden fear, a fear that there might not be any mysteries left to tell. For what mystery could be greater than a God permeating a man? When I told Lea, she smiled quietly.

'Oh ... *pairé!* Now it really begins; now we see how a man becomes a God!

I hit the side of my head, for I realised that she was right!

CHAPTER 32

THE FIRST CALL

So it is that I continue this path to that field below Montségur, with the sound of priestly chants in my ears and the bee guiding my descent; I sing to remember how life in the fortress had, by that time, grown more and more unbearable.

Storms and sleet and bitter cold came to keep the women and children indoors. In the keep it was crowded, and the stench of animals and bodies was high. To this was added the boredom of days spent waiting, and the hunger, which drove even the most affable to arguments and sometimes to blows. So terrible were the aimless days that whenever there was fighting with the French it seemed almost a respite.

The *seigneurs* of the fortress had hoped to wear out the patience of the army, expecting that when bad weather came, the French would pack up and go home to sit before their fires. But as winter approached the army grew in number and in boldness, while we began to dwindle and to grow weak.

One night, the noise of shouts and screams reached the room at the end of the spiral stairs and when I came to the court below, I found the fortress in chaos.

Basque mercenaries had taken a narrow ledge on the eastern face of the pog, some way below the fortress. We all knew what this meant: it gave our enemies a foothold from which to assault us. I told the people that we were not yet desperate, for that ledge was perilous and difficult to reach from below, and that even if a siege engine could be built in such a place the French would have to guard it day and night, and they would suffer bitterly from the cold winds and the snow. On the other hand, I told them, we still controlled the barbican and our secret path had not yet been discovered. This was a blessing, for it meant we could continue to communicate with the world below and have soldiery and fresh supplies brought to us. Secretly, however, I knew it was only a matter of time before the French found our secret path, a path that would lead them to the Barbican, and to the sealing of our fate.

When I saw Lea again my heart was filled with a mixture of joy for being with her and apprehension for what would come. She said nothing about our troubles and I tried to put the gloom and foreboding from my mind. I asked her what she would tell next.

'Well, *pairé*,' Lea said, 'after the baptism, those who saw it with their own eyes could not agree, for each had his own understanding. They were like men standing around a tree; each man only sees one side and believes he can know the entire tree from it.'

I pondered this. 'But Lea, if those who saw it with their own eyes couldn't agree, what hope is there that we, centuries later and with only meagre documents and word of mouth to guide us, will find agreement?'

'But *pairé*, it was important that there be very little evidence of Jesus Christ.'

'Why do you say that?'

'It was important that his life not be a historical fact, but a mystical one, for how else could faith be born?'

'But look at the suffering it has caused, Lea!' I said, aghast.

'The angels are not concerned for the suffering of men, *pairé*, they are only concerned with learning.'

'If that is so why are we told that our angels weep for us?'

'They weep when men do not learn from their suffering! You see, *pairé*, only men can transform the wisdom they gain from suffering into love, and only love can save all of creation.'

All of creation – now there was a hefty weight!

'But is love not happiness, Lea?'

'Love does not always make us happy, for happiness should not be preferred over goodness.'

'Then what good is love, if it makes one unhappy? Oh, I am confounded!'

'Love helps us to endure our suffering, it makes us steadfast in our sorrow.'

I was unable to suppress a faint moan, which escaped my lips in reply, for now I thought of the love that kept those in the fortress from despair, the love that enabled so many to endure hardship and suffering, and I knew deep down that she was right.

She began again, without waiting for another comment from me, to conjure before my eyes a picture of John the Baptist sitting upon his rock, watching over his flock like a faithful dog awaiting its master.

'A kind wind from the north had come to tame the heat, and his followers were taking advantage of it, since they could do no work,' she said.

And as she spoke, I could see it myself, with my inner eye.

‡

Into John's communion with God there entered the words of the red-bearded, hawk-eyed Judas. John opened an eye. The man was standing among the fishermen and he was saying,

'Well, for my part, I'll only believe he's the Messiah if I hear that he'll make Israel great again. I want to hear him say that he'll avenge our enemies, that he'll kick out the Romans and the priests, and release us from the bondage and the curse that we have suffered! I am after the joy and the glory that was promised by the prophets! And, *I shall not let that fish off the hook*!'

John had discerned darkness in that man's heart at his baptism and would have turned him away if his angel had not told him Judas' destiny was sealed in the circle of those who would recognise the coming one.

The fisherman Andrew spoke next.

'Stop, zealot! Stop, for heaven's sake!' he said. 'Your words are daggers in my ears! You speak of hooks … but you should spend some time on the sea! That would settle you down. Out there you have no charge over anything … you are always at the mercy of God and what he will do for you! Not the other way around!'

'I only require what has been promised,' Judas gave back. 'Why else do our people eat and breathe and breed if not to make a body for the Messiah who will come to save us? Why have we come to this river to be soaked in its icy waters if not to prepare for when he comes?'

'Wait a moment, Judas!' Simon, the brother of Andrew said, with an officious air. 'He *has* come! Did you not see the lighted wings that flew over his head yesterday? I saw the whole world stop from adoration of it. Even those devils that live in the plants and in the river, in the trees and stones, were gathered together to see it before scurrying from the place in fright! He is come, Judas! Now we can all rest easy, for all men will be brothers.'

'Yes, yes,' Judas said, with a snake for a mouth inside that red beard, 'and the cow will sleep with the lion, and the chickens shall play with the fox! Fairy tales! Only through blood and war shall anything be accomplished, my brothers. Believe me! Only through blood and war! Love is not the way of our God! He is a hard God. We know our God, don't we? He bares our backs and roasts our carcasses, and milks our veins! He is that same God that swallowed up Sodom and Gomorrah into His belly! The same God Who sent plagues and flood and famine to those who did not mind Him! If this God is born into a man, as the baptiser would have us believe, then He will also be a hard-hearted God – a God of war! What else could he be? I will wait … I will watch and see.'

Simon regarded him with a frown. 'It looks like you have not seen anything at all, Judas! These two eyes saw it. I saw no hardness, only a gentle glow and a tender light. Whether an angel or a spirit, who can say? But it was divine, of that I'm sure! It came and I saw it. Andrew saw it too didn't you, my brother? And what about you, James, did you not also see it, and you, little John? Did you not see how the lighted wings, silent and tender, fell over the chosen one whom our master baptised? Philip, what do you say?' he trawled their hearts for an answer. 'And you, Nathanael, surely you if no one else?'

'I saw something,' Nathanael affirmed, 'but I can't tell what it was for certain! Besides, the man Jesus is from Nazareth … I told Philip before, nothing good comes out of Nazareth!'

James said, 'I don't know that it was wings I saw … but I'm certain there was something in the air above him.' He shook his head. 'No, I didn't see it fall.'

'Wait!' said little John, 'I saw it come down like a dove, and land on his head … and do a little dance … well, maybe it wasn't a dance … I don't know what it did but it landed, that's for sure!'

Andrew looked around with a red face. 'I'm ashamed lads, I didn't see anything, I was afraid and looked away, and by the time I looked again, it was over!'

'Well then, it's all the same, going up or coming down … all the same!' Simon summed it up: 'We saw the spirit of God, that's what it was and no mistake! Just as the Baptiser said, the spirit of God descended into Jesus!'

Judas made little imperceptible nods of the head, and looked at the fishermen with hooded eyes. 'I think you see what you want to see!'

'You may not believe us, red beard,' Andrew spat, 'but you had best believe John the Baptist, a prophet of God!'

'Prophets are unreliable people.' Judas dismissed. 'They've been shouting about the end of days and calling for fasting and prayer since Moses! And where has it got us? We're still in the wilderness, still under the yoke of our enemies! Still licking their hems! Prayer and fasting are not the answer. Sometimes a man must rely on his knife.'

The Baptist came down from his rock.

He wondered why men were plagued by obstinacy. Why they were so preoccupied with trivialities, so spiritually dull that only moments after they had seen the most significant event in the world, the vision of it was faded away into the hollowness of petty concerns. He scanned the grounds and his eyes found the rich youth from Bethany, sitting alone some distance away. Lazarus was his name. On the boy's arrival some days before, John's angel had torn open his eyes to show him the workings of the boy's soul. For this reason, he had not baptised him, but had spent long moments alone with him, moments of quiet conversation, preparing him for what was to come.

He nodded to himself. At least him, if no one else!

He looked up to the tormenting sun and, full of frustration and disappointment, he cried a long, wounded howl.

All men regarded him with fear and awe.

'How many have I baptised?' he asked the startled people. 'How many are prepared for His coming? How many? Woe!' he said, pointing his finger at his followers. 'Woe unto you, spawn of Israel, if you fail to recognise your Messiah! Be not concerned what he will do for you, but rather be mindful of what you can do for him! Then offer up your souls ... leave everything behind you ... follow his shadow! Do you not see that my only purpose has been to prepare you for Him? Do not fail me!'

But as John had finished his words, an intuition made a pass over his heart and he stood paused, listening. When he looked, he near lost his bearings. He fell to his knees and pointed to a man who was moving among those who were resting by the water.

'Look!' John said sucking air into his lungs, 'There is the Lamb of God! Do you see Him? I bear record to you ... He is the Son of God! He is greater than I, and you must prefer Him above me!'

Those most prepared by John, and even those who had not yet experienced the loosening of baptism turned to look. Those who could see it were stricken by palsy. Only two men were able to overcome their shock enough to make their way to Him – Andrew, and John of Zebedee.

The Baptiser watched them go. It was done, nothing to do now but wait.

He climbed his rock and sat down again and as the slight chill announced to him the waning of his days he continued his meditation.

CHAPTER 33

WATER AND WINE

Mariam saw the form of a man come over the rise. At first, she thought him a shepherd walking ahead of his flock, until she saw that his flock was not so many sheep but so many men.

She saw Jesus shield his eyes to look at her, and in that moment she too shielded her eyes, but not from the sun, which was behind her, but from what seemed to overflow from him. She did not know yet what it was, but she was full of comfort to see it.

Now came a shy greeting, full with intimate expectation. Jesus had brought home her other sons, Jude and Simon and Jose, and she was also glad to see them. After meeting those others who had followed him, her daughters set off to prepare the water for their ablutions while she and Salome went to the house to prepare a simple repast.

Later, while they shared the meal in the cool of the evening, she heard of Jesus' doings, of his baptism by John the Baptist and of his travels with his followers in the wilderness of distant lands. The fishermen took turns in telling how in every place, men, women, and even children had recognised Jesus and had sought him out for a blessing or a healing.

When the guests, weary from their long travels, retired to sleep, she looked for Jesus, desirous to speak with him alone, and to learn what lay in his heart. She found him in Joseph's workshop tinkering with an old chair. From the shadows she observed him working in the half-light of the oil lamp and recalled the many times she had come here seeking solace. A desire swelled to go to him and to hold him like a mother holds a son, but he seemed so different. Much had passed since that night long ago when he had left to seek out the Baptist. The time in between seemed to her like a vast ocean and she only a weary boat looking for a shore. And so she hesitated.

Sensing her presence, he looked up. 'This chair needs mending.'

'Chairs break from too much sitting down. I allow those who sit to mend the chairs.'

Jesus made a smile at her playfulness, and a smile grew on her face to see his. She had brought a pitcher of water with her and now poured him a cup. 'Are you thirsty?'

'Like a camel!' he said. 'You see, I haven't forgotten your words.'

'No ... I see that you haven't.'

He drank a little and paused to observe her, and in that pause she saw him change before her eyes. In a flicker, both a tempest of pain and the most expanded lightness of being became apparent. He seemed like those Nazarites who returned from their caves having battled with the devils in their souls. He must have fought and overcome something, and now this overcoming had generated that great effulgence she could see spilling out from him.

'It seems I am always seeing something in you!' she said.

'What do you see?' His eyes held hers.

To look at him near blinded her and so she looked away. 'I don't know what to tell you ... I see a dazzling glory!' she looked again, 'Praise be God! I see ...'

'What?'

'I see the *Son of God!*' Immediately she put a hand to her mouth as if she had blasphemed.

'Don't be afraid, you have committed no wrong ...' he said, 'trust in your heart.'

Tears came into her eyes. 'I feel joy!' She lost her balance then, and she was shaking. He steadied her and held her face close to his.

'This is heaven expressing itself through you, for this is the first time my mother in heaven sees the Son who long ago departed from her … she sees me through your eyes!'

Again she felt she would faint.

Seeing it, he held her with one hand and took the cup of water and brought it to her lips.

'Drink this,' he said, 'it will sustain you.'

When she took a sip she was full of confusion. She looked into the cup, trying to decide whether she believed it.

She stared at him, 'How does this taste of wine, Jesus?'

Jesus nodded. 'It is only water … but what lives between you and me can make even water taste of wine.'

She had heard these words before; they echoed the words spoken by the Anchorite in Egypt so many years ago.

'This is a mother's love for her son,' she marvelled.

'And his love for his mother,' he replied.

Before she could say more the storm of light that had surrounded Jesus ebbed away. So swiftly did it go that she wondered if she'd seen it at all.

Returned to those eyes was the calm expression she knew. 'You look tired …' he said to her, 'Tomorrow is another busy day.'

She hesitated. 'I have been saying fare-thee-well to you all your life, Jesus, and now I find myself not wanting to leave you, lest you disappear into thin air!'

Jesus whispered, 'I know. But this is a new season, and we must not say fare-thee-well, we must say, *Shalom.*' Fixing her with his eyes he let his face open in a smile. 'Shalom, mother … shalom!'

He hugged her and she hugged him and, embarrassed and happy, she closed her eyes, settling this word into her heart.

Shalom.

When the moment was over she took the pitcher and cup from Jesus and turned around to walk out of the workshop, feeling the swelling of a love so great in her heart that she could neither contain it, nor properly express it.

‡

'But it was only days later,' Lea explained to me, 'at a wedding of a relative that she realised how destiny had fashioned that moment with Jesus for her understanding.'

'You are speaking of the Wedding at Cana, aren't you? Where the water tastes of wine,' I said to her. 'This has always bewildered me.'

'You see, *pairé*,' she said, 'the love of a heavenly mother for her heavenly son is a love beyond earth and blood ties. Such a love can inspire a feeling of *good will* that is so strong that it can make water taste of wine; that is, that it can make all men, even those who are not related, feel like kin!'

'But this love, Lea … is it magic?'

'It is wisdom, a wisdom that works like magic in the soul. To one, this wisdom is as sweet as honey, *pairé*, while to another, it is bitter. This *good will* enabled those at the wedding to see what lived in Mariam, and they never again called her the stepmother of Jesus. They called her … the Mother of God.'

Now, as I walk in this darkness, those words ring in my ears and I remember how a rush of understanding had washed over me.

'Oh my! This is the Mother of God!' I said to Lea, 'This is how the Sophia of our faith, the Sophia of the Greeks and the Gnostics, is one with the Mary of the Catholics!'

'Yes, *pairé*,' she said simply. In her eye there was a look I had seen before, the look of a mother observing a child experiencing the simple joy of discovery.

CHAPTER 34

A GOOD WIFE

As Claudia Procula entered the large court on her husband's arm she sensed his muscles tense.

This night he wore a red cloak over the insignia of his military office, and it did much to temper the paleness of his face, held in check to appear calm and relaxed. She watched him scan the open court of the pr*ae*torium, decorated with plump cushions and silks, lighted candles and flowers. Beyond it the sun was setting and a hint of coolness had come to rescue the heat of the day. All seemed harmonious. Only Claudia knew the reason for her husband's discomfiture and, perhaps because of it, she walked beside him with calm and poise, her back straight, her chin raised so as to accentuate the length of her neck, the curvature of her cheeks and the groomed hair that cascaded in browns over gold combs.

She had chosen a regal dress that moved in long volumes of white and yellow silk around her legs. There was no jewellery to accompany it, save a necklace of gold, a present from her grandfather, Caesar Augustus. Yes, Claudia was a creature of politics, accustomed to intrigues and machinations, and she knew she must not seem grand, she must exude a simple grace and charm, and her smile must make even the most difficult person melt to the soles of his sandals.

For this was an important night.

The previous week, after a disturbance at the Temple, her husband had cancelled his family's return to Caesarea. He wasted no time in dispatching messages to Herod Antipas and the High Priests, requiring them to attend a banquet, over which they would discuss the disturbance. This would not only redress the imbalance of power which had existed since his posting to Judea, but it would also give him the opportunity he had long sought, to see what friendship and alliance, if any, existed between priests and king.

Claudia had made it her personal task to see to all the practical arrangements, and had spent the entire week before the banquet attending to the smallest detail. She had the pr*ae*torium appropriately cleansed of idols and representations of the gods of Rome. In her kitchen, Roman cooks and servants were traded for Jew counterparts, and all utensils, dishes and trays, everything down to the smallest knife, was discarded and bought anew to ensure no unintentional contamination by forbidden substances. She allowed a handful of priests to come then, to inspect every corner of her home for anything that might be seen as unclean – anything that might contradict Hebrew law. In truth, it had been a monumental task, for even their son's playthings had to be removed from the house, lest they injure the priest's sensibilities. But she understood the reason for these measures. She did not wish to give any opportunity to those who would cast her husband in the mould of a man insensitive and dishonourable, a desecrator of Hebrew law, and a hater of the people of Israel.

Now, as her husband led her to the tables where sat their guests, she greeted them cordially and gave a command for the servants to bring in the food: the best fish cooked in garlic and spices, fried locusts, fresh vegetables and fruits, pastries and sweetmeats. One servant after another came and went, serving food and pouring Galilean and Judean wine, while from the galleries wafted the sounds of drums and flutes.

The high priest Caiaphas sat at the table on her right. The short, portly man was too small for his garments and his towering mitre, which threatened to topple from his head. He sat scratching his back and looking discomforted, as if he had left something of himself behind at the Temple and would now need to return for it. Beside him sat another priest, a taller and thinner man, who appeared to be the senior of the two. His sour-eyes were those of a man who is dragged to a place foul and suspicious, fraught with hidden desecrations.

Conversely, on the table to Claudia's left, the family of Herod were to the priests like night is to day. Herodias, entirely dressed in red, seemed comfortable and confident, and nodded with an air of amusement in Claudia's direction. Claudia returned the nod with cool urbanity and acknowledged Herod Antipas, who wore robes of Murex purple threaded with gold. He sat between his wife and his stepdaughter Salome, who was adorned in a silken dress of azure blue embroidered with silver. She appeared the opposite of her name, for there was nothing tranquil about her. When her eyes touched on Claudia the impression they made was of stagnant ponds full of insects. Her mouth was curled in scorn, as if Claudia had been a promise of entertainment, which had failed to meet her expectations. Claudia, for her part, ignored it.

A Roman citizen in the provinces had to endure the contempt and hidden hatred of the conquered peoples. However, nowhere was it seen more openly and plain to the eye than in Judea, where the Jews considered themselves the chosen ones, while all other men they deemed heretics, heathens and idolaters. Against this, she reminded herself that Herod was disdained by his own people for not being a pure Jew, that his marriage to Herodias was unlawful, and that rumours abounded of his lust for his stepdaughter.

She turned her eyes to the priests. They also despised Rome but on principle only, for they had grown fat and wealthy on power and indulgences which had come to them through peace and the quelling of revolt. Having measured disdain against advantage, they had found it wanting.

This group might be displeased at being forced to come to the house of an idolater, but neither Herod nor his priests would risk insulting a prefect of Caesar, at least not to his face.

To her mind, these were not real Jews; those she had, time and again, encountered in the streets of Jerusalem. For it was her habit to revel in the colour, the noise, and the smells of the places she lived whenever it pleased her, and she thought nothing of speaking with the local women in their own language, eating their food, and delighting in their children. After all, were women and children not the same in every place? Differences existed only in a man's world. This was her first philosophy.

Her husband did not understand her adventurous nature, and often scolded her for her foolhardiness. She always listened and promised to be more cautious, and yet the world, again and again, enticed her. In the end, her husband had ordered a man to follow her every move, which would have annoyed her had the centurion not provided her with entertainment. Having sensed that his eyes worked poorly, she toyed with him, hiding in the crowds, or in dark corners, deriving an unusual pleasure from the frustration and bewilderment of a hardened soldier over so small a thing as a woman's whim. No, she did not take danger seriously, for she did not wish ill on any person, and it did not seem possible that ill would come to one who wished only good.

Ill attracts ill. This was her second philosophy.

During the meal, a mood of introspection descended over the group, and it was only some way into it that the conversation turned to the matter at hand, the occurrence during the Paschal week, which had so raised the ire of the priests and caused a stir among the Jews.

'I want to know something of this man, Jesus. How can he so easily create havoc in my city?' her husband asked.

Caiaphas' face turned quizzical. 'Why do you bother with an insignificant man like him? He is only a follower, not a leader …'

Her husband kept his tone polite, but she could tell that impatience lay beneath his words, 'Insignificant? So insignificant that he can enter the Temple and threaten its priests and moneychangers? This would not happen in Rome, I assure you. Who is his leader?'

'John the Baptist, the blasphemer!' Ananias said, 'But don't be fooled, it is my estimation that this man from Nazareth may yet cause havoc for us.'

Her husband moved a cold eye to the other priest. 'I repeat my question therefore, who is he?'

A shiver seemed to whisk through Caiaphas. Claudia realised the two priests were joined but in conflict, for beneath their common purpose there ran a longstanding quarrel of opinion.

'He is insignificant,' Caiaphas said, 'because he is a descendant of David's son, Nathan, and not of his other son, Solomon.'

Pontius paused, awaiting elucidation. When it did not come, he leaned forward and said, 'Well? What does this mean, not from Solomon?'

Caiaphas was the model of paternal indulgence. 'I beg your pardon, Governor,' he said, 'of course … how could you know? King David had two notable sons, Solomon and Nathan. You see, to Solomon he gave the kingdom, to Nathan, the priesthood.'

'So?' her husband said, looking from one priest to the other. 'What of it?'

'If Jesus of Nazareth had been born in Bethlehem, of the lineage of Solomon,' Ananias said, 'well, procurator, Caesar would have much to worry from such a man … for he might be the expected king ... the Son of Man, destined to bring the Kingdom of God to Israel, and to resurrect its power!'

Her husband seemed puzzled. 'So … this is your Messiah, the man from the line of Solomon?'

Herod turned from his task of enticing Salome with fruits, since something in the conversation had caught his attention. 'Solomon … Nathan … The sun that falls on Israel breeds prophets like weeds, procurator! They spring up all over the place, telling of a Messiah who will come to put the poor in the place of rich, and the rich in place of poor; to topple kings and to bring about a consolation of all of Israel's troubles. And if the *Sicarri* are to be believed, he will do it by taking for himself Caesar's crown. But, as it is said that he will come from Bethlehem, you have nothing to fear from this man, Jesus of Nazareth. It is well known, no good has ever come out of Nazareth! In my opinion he is only a harmless madman!' He flashed a condescending smile.

'Your father was a madman ...' Pontius pointed out. 'Would you have called *him* harmless ...?'

Herod's smile grew less big.

Caiaphas seemed amused by this exchange, or perhaps it was the terrible Galilean wine, which had begun to work its wonders on him, for when he spoke now his voice was indulgent and calm. 'Let us not waste time on the Messiah ... but rather, direct our faculties to what we are to do about the troublemaker, John the Baptist ... already he has aroused people to burn idols, and to ransack the houses of the pagans. Who knows what they will do next? Jesus of Nazareth is only one, out of thousands of followers!'

Ananias' temper was grimly cast by the light of his fellow's merriness. 'Yes, Caiaphas, but don't forget, Jesus of Nazareth has Zealots ... members of the *Sicarri* who travel in his train ... men who may be using him to incite sedition against Rome!'

Pilate leant back, seemingly mining his cup for wisdom. When he looked up, there was a fire in his eyes. 'I do not need to look far to see conspirators; one fool tells me he is harmless, and the other fool tells me he is a danger!' He set his wine cup down loudly and made them bend before the wind of his anger. 'I do not know whom or what to believe, in this cursed place!' He gathered to himself a measure of restraint before adding, 'What is the name of the man who inspires Jesus of Nazareth, again?'

Ananias, having weathered the storm better than his younger counterpart, said, 'John the Baptist, procurator.'

Herodias would add her own part to this and sat forward. Her entire mien was autocratic and impatient. 'I was insulted by that man! He is an animal, a degenerate and an insurrectionist. Someone should arrest him and have him executed!' She threw her husband a significant eye.

Her daughter laughed and said, 'Poor stepfather! Your people hate you and so you are jealous of this man who is loved. In truth, you would kill the man for this alone, were it not for the hope that he could cure you of your father's curse!'

'Salome!' Herod said to her, in vacuous astonishment.

She ignored him and continued, 'But in my opinion, you should be more afraid of my mother ... who is a witch, and can turn a man into a toad!'

'Shut up, Salome! Have you no shame?' Herodias barked.

Claudia saw a spark move from daughter to mother, mother to husband and back again, in a triumvirate of disdain, dislike and discomfiture.

Herod took to being cheerful and clapped his hands. 'Salome, my dear, why don't you delight us with a dance!'

Salome narrowed her eyes and shook her head. 'No, I should think not.'

Unabashed, he enticed her further, 'Our hosts have not seen your marvellous dances! Your twists and turns that defy the eye! Music!' he shouted, 'Music!'

The Jew musicians paused their present song, and after a momentary hesitation, began a hurried tune with cymbals and drums.

Salome's face moved in a snarl. 'I said, no!'

Herod shot fire from his eyes at his wife. 'Herodias, your daughter does not mind her father!'

'That, husband, is because you are not her father,' she reminded him.

There was an awkward silence, in which Herod's face bloomed, and he drank down a gulp of wine to flush down the sting of his wife's words.

In the meantime, an opportunity arose for the conversation to return to the subject at hand. Caiaphas was the first to take it and interpolated a clearing of the throat before saying, 'The Sanhedrin has decided that Herod should seize John the Baptist when he comes next to that part of the Jordan which falls under his jurisdiction. Rome need not stain her brow with concern.'

Pontius, still contemplating Herod's family squabble, took a moment to register these words. 'On what charge?'

'No charge ...' Herod gave his part. 'First the council will hear what the man has to say, it will consult the law and make its decision.'

Caiaphas oiled his sharp voice on the tip of his tongue, 'The point is,' he said, 'that you should not waste another moment on this matter.'

Pontius turned the wine in his cup around and around and around. 'If you seize him it will lead to unrest, perhaps even a revolt ... didn't you say he has thousands of followers?'

'The arrest will be carried out quietly,' Caiaphas assured him, 'without fuss or spectacle. Besides, what Jew would contest the power of the Sanhedrin and risk excommunication?'

Claudia's husband did not look convinced. He said, almost to himself, 'Well, for my part, I will send someone to follow this Jesus of Nazareth. I am of a mind to think him more important than this John the Baptiser, whom I consider not yet a matter for Rome. I will not interfere with what you do with him so long as it is quiet. But mark well what I say,' he looked at them with pointed eyes. 'If I smell the slightest whiff of zealotry or hear the smallest whisper of an uprising, I shall send a message to the Governor of Syria calling for a sea of Roman Legions, and Israel will again suffer the wrath of Rome. Who knows what reprisals shall then befall the likes of aberrant kings and suspect priests?'

These words quickened fear in the hearts of the ignoble guests and soon they were thanking their hosts and making their hasty exits.

Claudia was relieved, for they seemed to take a pall of evil with them.

For his part, her husband called for his *primus pilus*, Cassius Longinus, his senior centurion and adviser. This was that same man who followed her when she ventured into the streets. Now, from the shadows, Claudia heard Pontius tell Cassius to look for the man called Jesus of Nazareth, and to report back to him on the man's doings.

That night Claudia was troubled in her sleep. She dreamt strange dreams in which the faces of the priests and Herod and Salome came and went and in which the name Jesus of Nazareth was repeated over and over.

In the morning when she woke, she knew she had to do something. She took herself to the fortress of Antonia, to that centurion, and informed him that she wished to accompany him on his journeys to see the man, Jesus of Nazareth. The Centurion, dumbstruck by this request, did not know how to answer.

For her part Claudia considered this silence his affirmative reply.

CHAPTER 35

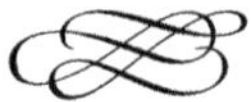

THE ARREST

It was midsummer, the sun would soon begin its diminishing days and John was not surprised to see Christ Jesus come again to Ainon with his disciples.

He remained a time with him and they kept a quiet company. Moon after moon passed, sun-full days, rain-full days, sitting in the huts or by the hearth. The two men had no need for words, since their hearts conversed in the silence. In those moments John basked in the heart-light that lived in Jesus, and let his own overgrown heart retreat little by little into the horizon of his soul.

Some of Christ Jesus' disciples had taken to baptising along the Jordan, and Christ Jesus had gone with them. John's followers approached him then, calling them upstarts who would take from him his doings. John explained that it was right and fitting that they should to do so, for soon he would not be among them.

When he said this out loud, however, a deep, inconsolable sadness struck him. It was true! He was not destined to walk side by side with the long awaited one! He would not hear His words, or share His meals or sleep under the stars with Him.

This is what it means to stay behind and to diminish! he told himself.

On a day when the sun-drenched land bore the last heat-throes before winter, a great portion of Herod's army arrived to take John by force. The multitudes that were gathered around him made to prevent it, but John admonished his followers not to defend his person but to go to Christ Jesus instead, for his time was over.

After that, John allowed himself to be seized by the guards, and gave his hands to be clapped into chains like an animal. He braced his heart, for they were headed across the river and over the old roads to Herod's country of Perea.

He knew this road. It was the way to the fortress called Machareus.

CHAPTER 36

THE LORD OF THE SABBATH

Jesus taught in the synagogues. He walked up and down the countryside speaking to those who lived in the areas outside the larger towns in Galilee. In the evenings, when the sun was blood red and a shiver of light stood on the horizon, he would heal those who came to him, and he would cast out the devils that lived in the souls of the weak.

Judas followed his every move, observing with one eye all his miracles and his healings, while the other eye measured the man, Jesus, for the pluck of a king.

He found him wanting.

Jesus was meek and spoke of meekness, he was mild and preached mildness; even his healings were made without majesty or regal authority. How could such a man lead a people to a renewal of the Jewish kingdom? He had envisaged a Messiah who would make fiery speeches, calling all men to arms. Not a man who spoke of turning the other cheek and of loving even those who hate you. In truth, his doings were few, dotted here and there among long intervals of silent, inward gazing. The others despaired whenever he retreated into his seclusions. For his part, Judas observed it with a growing feeling of disillusionment and impatience.

Nearing the Feast of the Trumpets, Judas followed in his train to Jerusalem. It was a long, painful march and on the way Jesus taught those who came to hear him. Some listened, some walked away waving their hands at his preaching of love and tolerance and at his parables, which they did not understand. Those who listened to him were mostly a mixture of defiled Jews, Samaritans, gentiles, publicans and tax collectors - a band of ragamuffins. Such a band would not do Jesus much good. They would ruin his reputation and make true Jews reticent to support him. This became all the more obvious the closer they came to Jerusalem.

In Jerusalem itself, Jesus led his band of followers to the Temple and here he spoke to the people on the steps, as was the custom in those days. His words found willing hearts in some quarters of the populace, but in others it did not. The Pharisees and scribes would not accept him; they remembered him from that puzzling incident at the Temple some months ago, when he overturned the tables and cursed the moneychangers. Now, they took the opportunity to rebuke him publicly and to cut him down to size before the people.

'We see that you teach those of mixed blood; that you eat and drink with publicans and sinners and lowly people. Why do you break the laws of Moses?'

Jesus took this in with a silent, calm serenity, and closed his eyes.

The pause lasted long. The people began to wonder if he would ever speak.

Judas had seen this strangeness before.

He had seen him keep a hundred people waiting while he bent to observe the details of some flower he found fascinating. When he caressed the trunks of trees or the long grass, or pressed soil between his fingers, it seemed to Judas that these were like gold or precious jewels to him, and yet, when he handled the parchments of the law at Nazareth, he treated those ancient and friable items as if they were so many poisonous weeds.

Judas could not understand why Jesus overlooked the rich and powerful to serve children and paupers as if they were kings. Or why, when the rabbis and men of learning came to fathom the depths of his knowledge, he spoke of simple things and sent them away thinking him addled. He spoke in parables concerning the most mundane things, and at other times, he spoke in a language that was clear as day, of the most complicated mysteries. When he met with zealous patriots, he said he had not come to rule. When the peaceful came to him for guidance, he said that his coming would not bring peace, but war. When the melancholic asked him for salvation from suffering, he told them there was joy in pain. When the proud and self-righteous spoke of the sins of the world, he told them that the persecuted would inherit the kingdom of heaven. When he observed the maltreatment of others, he spoke with a fiery zeal that made all men think the world would soon end. And yet, when he was abused, accused, or insulted, he stood silent, motionless, as if he had all eternity at his disposal, and did not need to answer to anyone.

This day was no different; faced with the protestations of the Pharisees, he remained with his eyes closed and his face upturned to the sun for a long time, long enough for the question to come at him again.

'Why do you teach those of mixed blood? Why do you eat and drink with publicans, and sinners and lowly people?

When he opened his eyes, he did not regard the Pharisees, but instead, turned his gaze to the simple people who had followed him, those of whom the priests spoke. He breathed in their fragrance, as if he were standing not before a group of defiled men, but before a landscape full of wild flowers. 'Tell me, my friends, do the righteous need repentance? Do those who are well need a physician?'

The crowds were pleased with this answer.

He considered the Pharisees now. 'My message needs new ears. For what I bring has to enter into souls not blemished by the old ways. To give what is new to souls infected with your old ways would be like sewing a new cloth onto an old garment, and that is why I choose those who do not belong to you, for my words would soon tear those who belong to you, apart!'

From the Pharisees came a rumble of voices, but only one was raised higher than the others.

'We have heard that you do not observe the fasts, and that you allow your men to eat and drink as they wish; is this true?'

Jesus nodded. 'Why not? Why should they fast? Is it not true that in your tradition the guests at a wedding feast never fast while the bridegroom is among them? I am the bridegroom, and while I am here it is a wedding celebration. My guests will eat and drink, for they are the children of the bridal chamber. But the day will come when the bridegroom shall be taken away from them by you and your old laws, and in those days, my followers will fast, since there will be a great sadness. While I am here, your old laws will not serve them.'

'What do you say, then, of John the Baptist!' one Pharisee shouted. 'What do you consider him? Old or new?'

He looked at this with a placid regard. 'Among those men who are born from a woman,' he said, 'none is greater than John, that is true, he is the best of what is old among you, and yet those whose hearts are made new by my teachings, they shall be *greater* even than John, that is also true.'

'Do you call yourself an initiate? Show us a sign, the sign of Jonah or the sign of Solomon, so that we may see and be contented!'

Jesus halted. Something in this had raised his ire. He looked at the Pharisees now with the fullness of his condescension. 'You old serpents! You ask for signs and wonders because you only see with the eyes of your body! But I shall not give you signs to make your eyes contented! I am not an initiate! I am greater than the man Jonah! I am greater than Solomon, for I am not a seer! I am the subject of seeing, the subject of initiation itself, and those who have spirit eyes and ears will see and will hear me and they will be contented!'

The rabbis could say nothing, they seemed confused by his words, and this had stilled their tongues. They made to leave.

Judas said to them, 'Wait!'

But they did not wait.

He went to Jesus and said to him, 'Why do you not reason with them? Surely it is good to have them on our side. Teach them of your greatness! Perform some miracle to convince them!'

Jesus turned to him with a look he had seen before. A look that was quizzical and serene, and yet it pierced the heart and winkled out the truth from its opposite. 'There are as many men who can perform miracles, Judas, as there are teachers in the world. My task is not to perform miracles or to teach, it is to live and to die.'

'But why not tell them of the mysterious things you have told us, the secrets of existence and of the Kingdom of God?'

'Would you give grass to a dog, Judas, or meat to a cow? I look at the condition of a man's soul and I give him what he can bear, according to whether I see in him an animal, or a man. Only to my brothers do I give the fullness of my teachings.'

He led Judas and the others away then, across the forum and through the Sheep Gate. They were headed for Olivet, where they would spend the night, and to do so they had to pass a place called Bethesda, the 'House of Healing'.

Bethesda consisted of five porches, which enclosed a pool made from the waters of an intermittent spring. The bubbling up, or 'troubling' of this pool, was said to foreshadow healings attributed to an angel. Around it, sick people congregated and when the spring began to swirl, the sick and afflicted scrambled to enter its waters to be healed, and for this reason every expectant eye was fixed on the pool.

Judas saw Jesus go to the most wretched man of all, a man who sat without an attendant or friend to help him to the pool. Jesus asked this man if he had the will to stand. The man said that he did. Jesus looked at him, full of love, and told him to take up his coverlet and to go since he was healed. When the man did as he said, all were amazed, not only because the man had been healed but also because this healing infringed upon rabbinic law, which forbade work on a Sabbath.

Judas did not know what to think.

The next day, when they came again to the Temple, the Rabbis and Pharisees were gathered waiting for him. They had heard of the healing.

'You healed a man on the Sabbath!' one Pharisee said, pointing a dry bone of a finger at him.

'It is true,' said Jesus, tranquilly.

'Did you tell him to take up his bed and to walk, knowing this to be unlawful?'

His voice was so quiet that the old men who had gathered around had to cup their ears to hear it, 'I am the Lord of the Sabbath; and if I wish to do good on a Sabbath, then I will do it. You, on the other hand, should be ashamed, for you do not care about the man's cure or the spirit that enabled it. You think only that he took up his bed on the Sabbath.' He looked at them and his face did not change but his voice became deeper. 'Your rigid laws need to be broken! You see God as a God of death, but I tell you He is a God of life! You see him as hateful and disdainful, a God Who longs for revenge, but I have come to show that He is a God of love and warmth and light. He comes to bring salvation and redemption of sin to mankind; to save it from the fear that you cultivate!'

Angered, the rabbis shouted, 'How can a man bring redemption? You cannot forgive sins! This is only for God to do!'

'I can forgive sins because what lives in me is above the laws of the Sabbath, the laws of the Sabbath are the laws of necessity, the laws of death. But I can free a man from necessity, I have come to free him from sin, for my power does not come from dark Saturn which names your Sabbath, my power comes from the Sun and my day is Sun-day, the day of light, and life!'

After that, there was heated discussion. The priests were displeased and left to confer amongst themselves. Judas followed them to the hall of justice where, after a further scrutiny of the blind man's evidence, they plotted against Jesus.

Backwards and forwards they disagreed on the finer points of the law. In the end, they resolved that Jesus was certainly more than a prophet, or perhaps even more than a priest, but they could not allow the people to know it. The people, that childish rabble full of lusts and desires and propensities to sin, had to be kept in their place, and such a man had a mind to set them free! Free from sin, free from the Sabbath rule! What would result, if they began to believe in a God of love? What consequences would befall Israel from evildoers if they were robbed of their fear of the pain, disease and death that God inflicted on the iniquitous? Healings and speeches were one thing, yes, but what next, the expulsion of the priests from their positions, the tearing down of the Temple, and the burning of the sacred writings of our forefathers?

Before their eyes lay the devastation of Israel and the ruination of the faith of generations, and it was too great a vision to be contemplated by so small a number. They resolved, therefore, to take the matter to the full gathering of the Sanhedrin.

At that moment, Judas realised that what Jesus had done, though dangerous and foolhardy, was acceptable. For it had revealed to all men not only the hypocrisy of the priests, but also that Jesus was indeed more than John the Baptist; that he was more than a prophet or a priest. For he had spoken with a Godly authority that even the priests could not deny, and which had made them fearful!

When Judas returned to the circle in the outer suburbs of Jerusalem he went directly to Jesus and spoke to him again.

He said, 'Jesus … you have shown me why you do not bother with the Pharisees, for they do not want the truth, and yet they will prevent any other from knowing it. You must prepare how and when you will take up your rule of the Kingdom of Israel from them. It is time for pruning and you must do it in a hurry, while you have many supporters who can help you cut down the dead stalks!'

Jesus penetrated him with eyes like rainbows. 'I am not come to prune the garden, Judas, but to make it lush. You have been with me long and still you do not understand me! The kingdom comes to this world through me. It is not of this world, but it comes to save the world, it comes to save even the weeds … I have not come to rule Israel, but to serve all of humanity!'

Judas' blood grew hot and gall was stuck like a rock in his throat. He walked away from Jesus with sparks flying from his muscles and sinews and marched full of fury and impatience into the streets of Akra.

He was thinking his wild thoughts when an old dog launched itself from an archway at him, growling and snarling for all it was worth. Before the animal could blink Judas had already felled it with a kick to the side of the head, and was leaning over to look at one eye, full of blood and surprise.

He whispered to it, 'I will speak plain, one beast to another, next time, don't growl before you bite!'

He looked to see if the animal had taken it in before walking off towards Jerusalem.

CHAPTER 37

MACHAREUS

Our aggressors had constructed a *gatta,* or siege tower, which day after day crawled a few feet closer to the summit. Now that the French were so close, our fortress was battered day and night without pause. Our walls were strongly built, but Hugh of Arcis was persistent and I knew it was only a matter of time before his shots found a breach.

Skirmish after skirmish had left many wounded, and these were taken to rooms set apart for them. My fellow perfects and I gave those who desired it the *convenenza,* which unlike the *consolamentum* could be administered even to those who could no longer speak. I worked long hours without rest, and yet I did not feel weary.

In truth, of late I had discovered in myself a boundless vigour. Even Raymon, my socio, God bless him, had seen it, and had been puzzled at the spring in my step, at the lilt in my voice, and my ability to climb to the end of the spiral stairs without being seized by breathlessness.

He told me he had seen the light in the room at the top of the keep, and asked, 'How can you be so full awake in the day, when you seem to spend night after night without sleep, *pairé*?'

I wanted to tell him I was becoming full to the brim with knowledge and that it surged through my blood. I wanted to tell him this knowledge caused me to feel a peculiar love and warmth for everything and everyone. I wanted to say that I might appear an old man in the autumn of my days, but that in my soul I was renewed - reborn and that it was all due to a beautiful apparition, or girl, or whatever she was!

But I did not tell him any of these things.

Christmas came and went without fighting on either side. We, like the Catholics, celebrated the rituals of our faith; we blessed the bread and sang our songs and joined together in a communal meal. But when I looked around at my fellow perfects, the bishops and deacons of our faith, I knew that not one of them had a true understanding of the birth of Jesus, nor of the man, Jesus of Nazareth. They likened him to a stone over which one steps to find the Christ.

It was a cheerless existence, to be so alone and yet surrounded by so many. I knew now what Lea had meant when she said that to know a person one must first love him. How many here truly knew me? I felt like a forgery, and so whenever the *credentes* fell to their knees to kiss my hand, I did not feel worthy of their veneration, and I told Lea how I felt when next I saw her.

She was looking at the fire and did not respond or even turn her face to me. I felt I should say something else, 'I know now what you meant that first night we met, when I told you I was a *perfect*. How I could have dared to call myself that, I do not know!'

She looked at me evenly. 'These men who stop you and fall at your feet, they do not see your soul, *pairé*, they see the spirit in your soul. The spirit is always perfect, do you see?'

I did not know what to say and she did not wait to for me to find my words; she began to tell her Gospel again. This time she spoke of the fortress of Machareus.

She said the name was Greek and that it meant sword. She said it was named thus by the Hasmonean King, Alexander Jannai, because it occupied a narrow, craggy ridge that had once been thrown upwards, like a sword of bile, from out of the belly of the Moabite mountain range.

I could see that fortress with my mind's eye, a giant of stone sitting upon the shoulders of cliffs and screes. It was situated, she told me, at the extreme southern end of Herod's tetrarchy of Perea, and defended his borders with his Arabian counterparts. I wondered if it might not have been a little like ours, with walls that reached dizzying heights. I asked her if its storehouses and arsenals were large enough to stockpile weaponry and food to outlast long, protracted sieges.

'Machareus was not a fortress like yours, *pairé*. To onlookers, it was an evil hound looking out over a devil's terrain: boulders and splintered rocks, ancient grottos and hot and cold sulphurous springs. From it one could see the cloud-topped summit where the Archangel Michael battled with Satan, and in the valleys below it, giant trees grew, whose fruits were used for casting spells, and whose roots, when powdered and drunk, were said to bestow power over the souls of men. Around about, caves penetrated deep, some to the centre of the earth itself, from whence had bubbled those terrible forces that so long ago caused the destruction of Sodom and Gomorrah. 'Such a place,' she said, 'was well suited as the primary home of Herod Antipas, and his demonic wife.'

‡

Herod had moved here after his illegal marriage, leaving his beloved palace at Tiberias for fear of war with his ex-wife's father, Aretas. But he did not much like Machareus, for it was cold and dry and subject to violent winds and storms. Herodias, on the other hand, thoroughly approved of the stronghold, inspiring the vapours of death, blown upwards by the restless winds, as if these were the freshest breezes.

It was now some time since Herod's return from Jerusalem and his meeting with the Roman procurator. Three days earlier a sizeable portion of his army had returned from the river Jordan with John the Baptiser in chains and irons. Since then Herodias would not come out from her chamber, angered that Herod would not execute the man immediately. But Herod was obstinate. He would not be bullied and browbeaten and intimidated by a woman, and summoned up a stubborn will over which even Herodias was powerless. No, he was not about to do anything on a whim, at least not until he could discern what was more to *his* advantage: to have this upstart put to death, once and for all, or to keep the man alive until he agreed to baptise him and cure him of the bondage of the wings of death. Even now, they hovered over him as he walked the halls of the fortress to his prisons. He could hear them flapping, suspended by the wind that rasped a song of lament over the edges of the mountains. He looked up and saw only the forlorn sky streaked with clouds, and he hurried his step.

The dungeons were meagrely lit and cavernous, and as he neared John's cell, he saw him only as a shadow. A shadow restrained by shackles. A harmless shadow, he assured himself.

He had a guard light a torch and place it on a bracket nearby and ordered him to unlock and open the rusted iron gates that barred the cell. The cell was illumined and the way into it unobstructed but he hesitated before the damp threshold. In this pause, occasioned by fear or excitement or both, he fell to observing the man.

He did not seem like a magician, he was sleeping in his filth like a dog, and yet, he was more than that, yes, more than that. The light played around him in a peculiar way, and Herod of a sudden sensed something unseen in it, but what? Not the shadow of a curse that made a man seem small, but rather, something uplifting that made him larger than he was!

There was certainly more to the man than met the eye, and this certainty frightened Herod, and he was close to turning on his heels when the Baptist groaned and changed position. The light, having fallen away from him, made all things seem different. No! Herod told himself with some relief, just a man after all – a trick of the torch. And yet the man was a prophet, he knew that much, at the very least.

He entered the cell.

The Baptiser raised his head; his beard and hair were matted and his skin was broken. In his eyes there was a flash of recognition.

'Husband of the devil! Why come you here?' his words flew out of his mouth like lashes from a whip and caused Herod to make a little backward jump to get away from them, and he nearly slipped on the oily grime at his feet. His more immediate impulse was to call for the guard, but his practical nature stepped in to prevent his anger from getting the better of his needs.

'Well, well, well … I see that there is fire left in you yet!' he said, pulling himself together.

There was no answer.

'I trust your stay has been unpleasant and damp, though I should think not as unpleasant and as damp as what you are used to!'

A moment of awkwardness passed. The stupid man had missed his sarcasm. 'Have you nothing to say to your judge and jailer?'

The man's eyes did not falter but were steady upon Herod. 'You are not my judge! You have no power over me, for only God is my judge. And as to my jailer, while my body touches the floor of this cell, my spirit soars to heights you shall never know!'

Herod felt a ripple, a little thrill of darkness swoop over his head, and he ducked from habit. When he straightened himself again his voice was rattled. 'John bar Zacharias, I demand that you cleanse my soul so that I, too, might see the Kingdom of God! I shall have my guards bring a little Jordan water that you can pour over my head, and we can get it over with.'

To the man on the floor, his need seemed of no moment. 'To loosen the soul a man must near drown, Herod. Besides, I cannot loosen what is bound to the earth like a snake. The Kingdom is too high; it cannot be reached by one so low as you. Leave me in my misery. You are set apart for wickedness, and to wickedness you shall bend to play your part.'

Herod did not allow this to vex him. He crossed his arms and dug his heels in. 'And you profess to know my part?'

The Baptiser's eyes were lustrous with righteous venom. 'To kill me … that is your part!' he shouted.

Herod stood stock-still, having come by a sudden perception. This man was no prophet! Otherwise he would have known that he feared the curse of madness too much to kill him … but wait! Killing him had indeed featured in his plan! No, no! He was now more certain than ever! He may not manage to bend him to his will by torturous means, but he would break his spirit by passing on the contagion of his madness – by giving this pompous upstart something to ponder while he sat rotting in his stinking cell!

'If I were to kill you, what should become of your followers? To whom shall they turn? To that simple man from Nazareth called Jesus?'

The caged ferocity was so immediate that Herod clutched himself for safety,

'You impudent man! He is a light brighter than mine! He has come to flood the darkness of the land. My followers shall go to Him and they shall leave you in your pit, for He is the Messiah!'

Ah! There it was! The sound of doubt sang in his ears. He had managed, finally, to throw a stone into the workings of that self-righteous mind! He sharpened his tongue. 'How do you know that this man you speak of *is* the Messiah? How do you know it for *certain*?'

'My angel has seen it!'

Herod laughed, marvellously pleased. 'Your angel? If your angel is so great as to recognise the Messiah, why does he not help you now? Why does he not remove your chains, and free you from this hell-hole and take you to your heaven?'

The man's eyes flared. 'Because, you spawn of iniquity, it is not my time!'

'Perhaps you cannot die yet, because you have not found the true Messiah!'

The man squinted and opened his mouth, but nothing came.

'Did you ask him, this man you say is the Messiah, if he is the one? Has he said so himself? Perhaps you were clouded in your judgement? If he is not the awaited one, you have lived a counterfeit life! All your efforts have come to nothing! What will the world tell of it, I wonder? Will they say you missed your boat? That you mistook a simple man, called Jesus, for the Messiah and died in a dungeon like a rat?'

He waited to hear the sound of a crack in the man's mettle.

'Well, you will never know I suppose. But if you baptise me, in return I can send a message to your followers with a question from you to this man. That way you can die in peace – or not, as the case may be!'

'I ask nothing of you!' the Baptist said. 'You only wish to know the answer yourself so that in your jealousy you can persecute him as you are persecuting me! But mark well, husband of the devil, he shall be even more loved than I am among the people! Even after you and I are food for worms, shall he be known throughout the world! Go to him, ask him for forgiveness. Throw your sorry soul at his feet. Only he can rid you of what is in you!'

Herod was caught short. 'What is *in* me? What do you mean?'

'It is perfectly visible – the Devil's wings and Satan's breath!'

Herod's composure collapsed. This revelation now made his mockery fade away to nothing and he looked up, hoping to see those wings over his head, but he did not see them. Oh dear! There were two creatures, not one? Had he swallowed the Devil, so that it was now living in his guts, flapping about in his heart and creeping through his veins? Could he feel it feasting on his bones? Could he smell the odour of Satan's decaying breath coming from his mouth? Yes ... perhaps he could!

He ran from the cell then, leaving the baptiser behind in his stinking misery. He hurried to his wife's chambers, seeking the comfort of her ministrations, but he found her obstinately antipathetic to his needs.

Alone and forlorn, with the night's howling sounds and his terrors for company, he called for a messenger and dispatched him to John's disciples in Judea with a question for Jesus, from John the Baptist:

Have I understood correctly? Are you the One long awaited, or are we to wait for another?

And he himself, waited for the answer.

CHAPTER 38

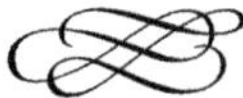

SERMON

In the meantime, James bar Zebedee followed his master to their home, Galilee, with a glad heart. For the world had changed to his eye, it was no longer a place of woe and sadness, but a place of joy! The Sabbath was no longer a day of wrath and deathly silence, but a day of life and merriment, a wedding day! He wondered what his old father would say to it when he saw how his son was no longer shadowed by sadness, but was full of hope for each new day!

Their journey was long, but who measured the time? Days and weeks and months and leagues passed in a moment, and then again, a moment could seem to last the span of a life, it could seem like the crossing of an ocean. One day, his master walked with no apparent aim, finding everything fascinating and lingering long in small insignificant places others might overlook. Another day he would go about with a feverish purpose as if he were looking for something that eluded him. In between he taught them as they journeyed or sat at meat under the great blue expanse strewn with cloud, or beneath the cold black dome crowded with stars.

One such evening when the sun was westering, his master chose twelve men from among the seventy followers. James, happy to be among them, followed him to a mountain, where he said he would teach them how to pray.

'Open your hearts, for I will tell you something …' he said, as night closed about them. 'Once I travelled through these lands and came nearby to Caesarea Philippi where, not far from the township, in a Temple, I heard a voice. The voice came from the Bath-Kol, the thunder of heaven, and I was taken up by it, and it spoke a prayer of lament into my soul for the downfall of man. Now I will give you a reversal of this prayer. A prayer of the hopeful soul, that rises up from the fall towards its spirit home.'

He began it, 'Our Father … who art in heaven, hallowed be thy name …'

And oh! What majestic choruses did James hear coming from his words! All of creation seemed at that moment consumed by light! Yes, praised be God! Reversed was the original darkness of sin and the fall into degradation, and begun was the ascent towards heavenly newborn life!

The moment passed and Jesus, now sitting among them beneath the cedars, said, 'This prayer tells that what lives in me is the kingdom, the power and the glory of heaven come down to the earth. I have come to bring the heavenly bread, the heavenly teachings that can feed you. Whoever is fed by these teachings in life will not suffer death, for death in the body is only the beginning of life in the spirit; suffering in one life becomes the seed of joy in the next.'

James puzzled over it and said to him, 'Can you tell us, master, what the kingdom of Heaven is like?'

Jesus sat back against the tree and it seemed to James that even the calm breeze was paused for his answer. 'To others I speak in parables, but I have chosen you and brought you here because I wish to speak plain with you. The kingdom is a light, a light that shines into the darkness of your souls,' he said to them.

There was quiet.

'How is it like a light?' James did not understand.

'When a seed falls on prepared ground it creates new life. When you prepare your souls, when the light of heaven enters you, it can grow your heart into an eye, which can see more than the world, it can see the spirit that lives behind the world.'

Judas, the red beard, huffed from his position, 'On earth we have the sun and we see with our eyes, but now you say we need an eye in the heart?'

'It was the light of the sun which created your eyes before you could see the world, Judas. And similarly, in your heart an eye must be created from the light of faith before you can see the world of spirit.'

'Where is this world?' James asked.

'It is here, behind these trees, and behind the clouds and the meadows, my brothers,' Jesus told them.

Andrew looked at Simon. 'What did he say?'

Simon sighed and scratched at his beard in irritation. 'The master said that the spirit is everywhere among us, but if we want to see it we have to make our own suns inside our hearts, so that it can illuminate it!'

Andrew frowned. 'Make our own sun? Right here, as we sit, you say? Right here, we are among heaven?' He shook his head. 'I do not know ...'

'Heaven is before you, Andrew!' the master affirmed. 'It is only that you can't see it until the spirit light fashions the eye of your soul.'

'What must we do to prepare our souls, master?' asked little John.

'Think good thoughts, feel for others, and do good deeds. That is how you prepare your souls. Such men can make themselves new again. This is what I mean when I say, *you must be born again*.' He looked at them, 'If you foster calmness and balance, all comfort and well-being on earth shall be your reward. When I am gone, you must teach others to do the same.'

'But if we were to tell people such things they would laugh at us! A man hungers and thirsts, and these must be satisfied,' said Thomas, a cross-eyed merchant who had joined them at Capernaum.

'Thomas, you must say to them, if you purify your souls, you will hunger and thirst only for what is good. Then, this goodness in you shall feel compassion for all men who hunger and thirst, even those who hate you, and revile you.'

'These are just words!' Judas dismissed. 'What you ask for is impossible! How can we feel compassion and mercy in our souls for an enemy that crucifies us and kills our children, our women and our old men? Sinners must burn in hell if God is just.'

'Judas, my friend, God is just but I have come to tell you about love. A soul full of hate has only hate for a harvest. Those men that you love in this life, though they do not merit your love, will love you in the next life. If you feel compassion and mercy for a man now, you will find it returned to you later ... this is preparing the soil of the soul for a harvest of love.'

Simon said, 'I have seen what lives and plays in the water and the air and the light, I have seen it! Is this then, the spirit world of which you speak, master?'

'Yes, Simon, but blessed are those that do not see it and yet still believe in it. But when faith becomes vision it will be as though you had stepped out of your body, as if it were nothing more than a garment. The soul will then shine out like a light over the world of spirit, that is what I mean when I say, *you must become naked before God* ... you see? To you I speak plain.'

Cross-eyed Thomas gave a dismal sigh. 'If we become seers master, then we are done for! Prophets are not only hated by powerful men who fear their judgements and admonitions but the ordinary people also hate them for they don't always agree with their opinions! Prophets even hate other prophets who do not foretell the same things! Nobody likes them. They are either stoned or run through with a blade, or else they are torn apart by the crowds, or thrown over the edges of cliffs! And afterwards, no man raises statues to them or truly honours them. All in all, master, they do not fare well!'

'One would think a merchant would be used to being hated!' said Matthew, the tax collector. 'Specially a cross-eyed one!'

Thomas took in a breath of indignation. 'Look who's throwing stones! A man who is hated even by his own mother!'

The master sighed, and quieted them with a hand. 'There is no doubting it. You will be persecuted and killed if you have the light in you, as I shall be persecuted and killed. This is because the blind don't understand light, you see? But when you are persecuted for the sake of your goodness by blind men, rejoice and be glad, for great shall be your reward in lives to come!'

Judas' eyes were like two sparks in the night. 'Well … you say these things to us, and you expect us to believe you, and yet we still do not know who you really are, the carpenter from Nazareth or the Son of God … which is it?'

'Forgive me, Judas, my brother,' Jesus said to him, 'but if you had the light in you, you would see me, and know me.'

Judas fell quiet.

After that James and the others, feeling badly for the way Judas had spoken, settled down to sleep.

The night encroached and James lay beneath the cedars thinking that he was so full of love for his master that he would die for his sake. And in that moment between sleep and wakefulness he looked up to the stars and heard a tender voice in his ear say that one day he would die a martyr's death in a far-off land in a place called 'The Field of Stars'. But he would not be forgotten. Centuries later a great French King called Charlemagne would follow those same stars to that field. He would call that route *The Way of St James*, and he would be the first pilgrim to his grave, not realising that the grave of James was really his own grave. In time, a great temple would be erected to house his grave and every year thousands of pilgrims would follow the stars for miles, just to see it.

James drifted off to sleep, thinking these things with a smile on his face. And he was still smiling for these rewards when he woke up, though he remembered nothing of the voice, or of its portents.

CHAPTER 39

NIGHT SUN

The night the French took the Eastern Barbican the fortress was thrown into a panic. There were perfects coming through the gates holding their belongings, followed by archers and knights who locked the gates behind them. The rest of the fortress came out into the starless night to see what all the fuss was about and found themselves gathering up what weapons were spare to help the knights on the ramparts.

The Barbican had been stormed by surprise. The French had come not by way of the well-defended path that separated the narrow ledge from the fortress, but by way of our trail cut out of the eastern rock face. The Basque shepherds had discovered our secret path and this meant two things – the French were only a few paces from our walls, and we were cut off from the outside world. Soon we would have to make a decision; starve or surrender.

Heavy was my heart when Lea came again to the room at the top of the spiral stairs. I told her things did not look good for us, and she looked at it with a nod and said,

'No, that is certain.'

'You say that lightly, but many will die!'

'For every action there is a compensation, *pairé*, as Jesus has said.'

A memory surfaced unbidden. 'At Beziers, the French came after the dirty work was done,' I told Lea. 'In the end, they burnt the church and all the people in it; thousands of them, both Catholics and Cathars, were kneeling at the altar praying! My mother and father and sisters perished with the others. I only survived because a dream woman like you took me from my bed and told me I must go into the woods. She saved my life. Many years later I heard that the Bishop of Citeaux had told the Crusaders to kill them all, for God would recognise his own in heaven. Tell me Lea ... how can a war of religion not care for its faithful?'

She gave this her patient attention. 'You should know that when an army enters into a city, faith soon leads to murder.'

'Should I? Why should it be so? I have no idea!'

'Think of it *pairé*; what you call faith is not really faith at all. It is only religion. Religion is only a short step from zeal, and zeal only a margin away from fervour, which is only a hair's breadth from frenzy – the cradle of hate and murder. The truth is, *pairé*, that evil and good share the same small space in the soul.'

'What makes one man evil and another good, then?'

'How close or distant one is to the good gods.'

'And what is the compensation for the atrocities committed against innocent people, against innocent children for God's sake!' I said with vehemence, for the memory of Bezier's had come unbidden and was stirring up an anger I had not let myself feel all these years.

She sighed. 'There is another way to look at it, *pairé*. It could be that destiny has brought these souls together, to a place where they can suffer, in order that in the future they can return again, together, for a good cause ...'

This did not ease my heart. 'I know we must suffer for our sins, but why has God turned away from the innocent?'

'God is just,' she said.

'But is that all he is? What of love?'

'God is Love, and His wrath is also His love.'

'How can wrath be love?'

'Do you remember what Buddha said to Jesus? Suffering leads to Compassion. When God spills out his wrath it causes suffering; this suffering not only leads to a cleansing of sin but it also gives us wisdom; it allows us to recognise the suffering of others. It is the memory of our own suffering that brings about the understanding that helps us to forgive those who have done some wrong to us ... this is true love, *pairé*. Wrath seen from the other side is true love; a Love that cancels out sin.'

I looked out of the window to the hard snow drifting over the crests and peaks and valleys and chasms of our mountains. I realised more than ever how far I was from perfection. If she saw my despondency, Lea did not show it. True to her nature she began to speak calmly of the road to Capernaum and I let myself fall into her words, for what good was there to dwell on bitterness?

Her pictures healed my heart; pictures of that woman I had grown so fond of, that highly spirited Roman woman, the wife of Pontius Pilate. I could see her sitting proudly in her chariot and I could hear the thoughts of that near blind Centurion, who rode ahead of the small retinue ...

‡

Gaius Cassius was gladdened to leave the confines and tedium of Jerusalem, to travel the wide-open spaces of the land. He was happy to feel the chaffing of his greaves and to suffer the aches in his spine, legs and buttocks from being in the saddle. For it made him feel less like an old man, which he was, nearing sixty springs, and more like a soldier.

He looked about him. His eyes had turned bad since his failed initiation those years ago and had grown worse each year, so that now he saw the world through a brown haze. This loss, though debilitating, had not prevented him from doing his duty, for he had grown skilful at finding ways around it. And yet, as his outer eyes had begun to see less and less of the content of the world around him, in the same measure did his inner eyes begin to see more and more of the content of his soul, and this, more than anything, had not pleased him.

During the tedium of his days in Jerusalem, he had tried to dull this inner eye with wine and women and gambling. But the numbness occasioned by these diversions had not lasted, it had only served to make him feel more keenly the dishonour and shame of a man who lives a borrowed life, an undeserved life.

He grumbled, and took a glance behind him to the chariot carrying Claudia Procula. He could not see her face clearly, only the outlines and the general form of it, but his inner eye knew that she was beautiful, for her soul bespoke beauty.

Soon after Pontius Pilate had arrived in Judea he had given Cassius the charge of following his wilful wife and maintaining her safety. At first this assignment had made his temper disordered, for not only was it demeaning for a centurion of his calibre and experience to waste his time minding a stubborn woman, he also found it difficult to keep track of her with his worsening eyes. Not wishing to draw attention to the secret of his failing vision, however, he had made the best of it.

In truth, he had never understood women and their ways, having spent most of his life in the military. They were creatures wholly foreign to his experience, good for distracting a man from boredom, dulling the bitterness of defeat, or helping him to celebrate a victory. As a centurion, he was aware that it was good for his men to trade the glory of steel for the pleasure of skin and warmth from time to time, but he also knew that a woman was like wine; she could make a man forget the smell of blood and disappointment in the evening, but in the morning she was a headache and a bad taste in the mouth.

And yet, here was something new! As time passed, he began to welcome this diversion with the lady Claudia! He began to look forward to hearing from Susannah, her mistress, that Claudia was leaving the pr*ae*torium. At first all had gone smoothly, but Claudia Procula was an intelligent woman and soon came awake to his task.

Perhaps, even in those early days, she had already made a guess at his malady, for she was in the habit of losing him. He often wondered, as he floundered in the crowds like a fish looking for water, if her eyes were observing him from some corner with merriment. Yes, he had become a plaything, blown by a woman's will, like a feather in the wind.

In the end, though they never spoke of it, a quiet understanding developed between them; she would not venture to dangerous places and he would let loose his rope a little and give her a small semblance of the liberty she craved. All had gone well, and in time even his esteem grew for her. For he realised that when Claudia ventured out of the palace, it was not always for her own pleasure, but also for the good of others. Often times she would take hampers of food which she would deposit at the mouth of leper caves, or which she would distribute among the poor.

Despite himself, and beyond his true recognition of it, he had grown to love her. And as the years passed, with the lessening of his vision there grew a picture more vivid in his mind's eye of her beauty, whose characteristics he recalled each night with great care – as if the image of her were a precious blade in need of a careful polish at the end of each day.

Now, upon this road to Capernaum, he wondered if he had given her too much rope.

Some time ago she had sought him out on the pretext of discussing the security of the household. Instead, she had ordered him to take her along when next he set off to find the man Jesus of Nazareth. Having such an order put to him by her in person had made him quite unable to speak. She had taken from him the self-possession to say no, so that a strange covenant was then added to their other unspoken agreements by virtue of his silence, which he could not later undo without causing disrespect to her person.

Reason told him it was one thing to allow a woman some small indulgent freedoms, and quite another to take her on a stolen journey to Galilee, to hear Jesus of Nazareth speak, while the Governor was away, taking care of those duties pertaining to the running of his province. Where would such matters lead? He could not presage.

Such things were on his mind as they reached that place where Jesus was known to preach. When they found him, Cassius squinted to see. It was afternoon and the sky was like an ocean of red. He realised he could only make out the shape of a man standing among a great crowd on a hillside.

Claudia Procula, having come from her chariot, was now beside him, and they stood not far from the crowds facing east, behind a group of shading trees. The nearness of Claudia made him nervous. He had to curb a desire to lean into the smell of her body, scented as it was with roses. Perhaps it was this nervousness, or the heady scent, or the magic of the woman, or even his old eyes playing him for a fool, but whatever the case, he was not prepared for what he saw.

All these years, he had grown out of the habit of looking at the sun, since Mithras was no longer to be found in it. Nor did he feel the god in his heart, which seemed to him like a wasted vessel. And yet, as birds flew in the soft-coloured air to find their homes, and the frogs called, and the people full of plagues and infirmities came to Jesus to be healed, he let his old wasted eyes look on Jesus and he saw something grand; he saw that from him came a light as mighty as the sun! A night-sun was rising in his heart, even as the day-sun was setting.

This let loose in Cassius what had not moved since those years before, in that cave dedicated to the God Mithras. This movement unleashed from the locked places inside him his long-lost devotion and his reverence, and it seemed to him like the universe was a hollow space and that he was stood in that hollowness like a pillar of salt, about to be blown away.

'Do I live?' he asked himself then, 'Or am I in the heaven of the Greeks?'

When he looked again, it was over.

Cassius tried to tuck it away, and made up his mind not to think on it. For what madness had visited him, he did not know.

He turned away to Claudia Procula, and discerned that she was weeping.

'Mistress, you are in distress?' he asked, worried now.

She shook her head and told him with a small laugh of embarrassment, 'I am not distressed, my dear Cassius … tell me, did you see it too? It was only a moment, but did you see how the sun shone from out of him into the oncoming night? Oh Cassius!' she said to him, 'I cry for joy, because I am full of that sun! I am full of grace!'

Cassius did not know what to say.

CHAPTER 40

THE CALL

Lazarus walked the road from Endor among the seventy or so who followed in his master's train, but he did not feel himself to be one of them.

After all, he had not been baptised by John, nor had he followed Jesus directly. His destiny, like those of his sisters, had been a different one. It had been to wait.

John the Baptist had told him, during the months he had spent with him, that his baptism would be a new one, performed by Jesus himself, and that he would have to wait and see, for Christ Jesus would call him only if the other disciples failed him. Now, looking about him, John felt the imminence of this call, for among those chosen disciples there did not seem to be one who could hear the fullness of the word of God, which lived in his master's voice and in his gestures. If they had seen it, surely they would not complain constantly to him of their tired feet, or challenge him with their trivial thoughts, or ask him ignorant questions, or sit with him as if they were his equal!

Lazarus could see it and so he kept himself apart.

Sometimes his master's eyes would fall on him from a great distance and they would stir in him grand pictures, pictures that seemed to him to be more vivid than life. At other times those eyes would be full of promise for his call but he would sense in his heart – not yet.

Lazarus obeyed.

Such were his thoughts before they were interrupted. The group had come to the gates of the township of Nain and had met a great many people leaving the city. The great crowd striving to enter it, among which he stood, were met by a funeral procession emerging from the township, and because neither party could easily give way, both were made to stand still.

The funeral procession was led by a line of lamenting women accompanied in their wails by the chanting of rabbis and the sounds of flutes, cymbals and trumpets. The cacophony rose in frustrated pitch and injured the quiet of the end of day, causing even the birds to keep far off.

Lazarus looked for the body and saw that it was carried according to the tradition of his forefathers, on a bier made of wickerwork. The body was not yet wrapped in burial cloths, but lay with its hands folded over the chest and its face covered with a napkin. Lazarus discerned by its dimensions that it was the body of a youth.

His master moved through the crowds, unperturbed by the excited words and gesticulations of the two sides. He sought the woman who was weeping the most bitterly, knowing her to be the mother of the dead youth.

Lazarus picked his way through the people to get a better look.

'Was this your son?' his master asked the woman, whose face was creased with anguish and streaked with tears.

'My only treasure is gone!' the woman cried. 'My only son! Weep with us, rabbi, for our hearts are bitter!'

'No,' he gentled her, 'no ... do not weep, widow!'

She looked at him, puzzled then. 'How do you know I am a widow?'

Lazarus saw his master take himself to the wicker bier held by four men, and then saw him touch it with a hand.

'Young man,' he called, 'I say to you ... rise!'

All around, those who followed Jesus gasped, for it was not lawful for a rabbi to defile himself with the greatest of all defilements, contact with the dead. Some said that by overlooking this strict ordinance Jesus was demonstrating how great was the difference between him and the Pharisees and scribes. Others, those sent to keep a watch on his doings, spoke of arrogance and pride.

But Lazarus was not listening to these words, for he was hearing something else, something that had made his heart full; those words spoken by Jesus, words that had flowed out into space in rings and resonances and tones. They had drawn his attention to the youth, who having heard the command from beyond death, was now compelled to rise up from it.

When the young man sat up and the cloth fell from his face and he looked about, Lazarus was transfixed. At that moment, time ebbed. The world of space darkened and was vanished, leaving a pathway between Lazarus and the boy on the bier. This path was lit up by virtue of the effulgence that came from his master, and when his master looked at him, and at the same time pointed to the boy this is what he saw:

Lazarus saw molten fires and burnished metals, pyramids and ziggurats and wars fought. He saw great walls falling and the rebuilding of mighty temples. He saw the wisdom of kings and the love of queens. He saw the future, when he would be standing in a fortress on a great mountain, sequestered by the followers of this young man. This, he knew, would be an important life, and he understood how it would be prepared for him by this youth. Thus was made plain to him the web of destiny that was spun between them – and would last for all times.

All was noise and haze as the world returned.

And he knew in his heart this was his call.

‡

'Who is that young man of Nain, Lea?' I put down my quill and took up a new parchment.

'He was born again, *pairé,* as Mani, the founder of your faith. Soon you will see why, through Mani, you are united with Lazarus.'

'With Lazarus?' I looked up, surprised.

'Soon you will know it … do not be impatient! First, we must speak of his sister again, for Mary Magdalene has found a use for her mother's unguent …'

CHAPTER 41

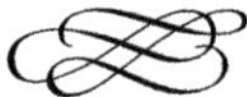

THE ALABASTER JAR

Since that experience in the field beneath the shading tree, Mary had carried her mother's jar with her wherever she travelled, and it was with her now as she snuck out of the rooming house and made her way to the residence of Simon the Pharisee.

Months ago, when Mary and her sister heard Lazarus' retelling of his experience at the Baptism of Jesus, they had felt a sense of destiny and had begged their brother to take them to Capernaum, to the place where Jesus taught and healed the people.

Mary's only fear had been what she might see hovering over him. But she had not seen anything but light, and love, and life. A life so abundant that she understood instantly that she must offer herself up as his disciple. And yet, she had hesitated, for her malady continued to plague her and the words of the rabbi at Magadala, even after all these years, still echoed in her ears.

The courage to go to Jesus had only come this night, when she heard him say these words to those who needed healing:

Come unto me all who are heavy laden, all of you who are burdened and I will give you rest.

She thought of these words now, and warmth entered into her

heart as she walked resolutely, clutching that jar, made from cool translucent stone, which held her mother's oil.

It seemed to her appropriate to use this oil in just *this* very jar to perform the most humbling act which she knew how to perform: to prostrate herself before him, to anoint his feet, and deliver her soul into his care. And it did not matter to her that her Lord was dining at a house that belonged to a well-known and respected Pharisee, among men of wealth and stature who might make fun of her and call her to account for her madness. She did not fear their opinion, nor indeed did she worry for her family's shame! Something beyond these trivial things moved her legs. A sense of the wonder working magic of destiny had taken a hold, and it worked deeper than her doubts and fears, to fire up her limbs and to guide her up the steps, through the antechamber and an open door that led to the sumptuous and well-appointed dining hall.

The reception room was grandly lit, music played and servants hurried past, backwards and forwards, carrying food and drink to be laid out on the long table. She was dressed simply and could seem like one of them, and so she slipped in unnoticed. She was not prevented from finding Jesus at the table and from going to him where he was seated on a couch. She saw that he was in deep conversation with the Pharisee Simon, and with the other rabbis who were scattered among the closest disciples of Christ Jesus.

Simon said to him, 'This evening John's disciples asked you if you were the awaited one. You said you were not a prophet, for the age of prophets is past, the age of Abraham is past. You said you were something more. What do you say that you are then? John the Baptist would not eat and drink with us, but fasted and lived in the wilderness. You, on the other hand, are here among us, drinking and eating. Is this the conduct of a Messiah?'

Magdalena came from behind Jesus to kneel at his feet. She set down the jar and took out the stopper. She bent reverently to pour the oil but paused, for he had begun to speak.

She heard him say, 'How shall I liken the sons of Abraham? They are like children who sit in the market place, and say to one another:

'We have played a happy tune, and yet you do not dance to it! We have played a mournful tune, but you have not wept!

'You have long expected quite another Elijah, and quite another Messiah. You have expected a prophet who was one of you, and a king who will not be among you for his high mightiness! You say that John the Baptist is no prophet, for he will not eat bread nor drink wine with you, and you say the Son of Man, who eats with you and drinks with you, is a gluttonous man, a wine bibber and therefore cannot be the Messiah! But your eyes see only outward forms, and so you do not recognise that what lives within John the Baptist makes him the greatest of the sons of Abraham, the greatest of those that are born of a woman. And you do not see that I am not a king, but that *I am the kingdom*, for I am not the son of a woman, I am the Son of God!'

At this point, he turned to Mary and in that moment the sun and the stars were his eyes! She saw a darkened chamber and moonlight and she was once more a bride, for recognised was the bridegroom of her dream. This was Christ!

Her heart fluttered with panic, like a bird caught in the confines of a house. And yet, in her heart's voice she heard these words,

When a bridegroom knows his bride, this knowing leads to love. So it is with a teacher and a pupil. I love you because I see the light in your heart. See these men, they are learned, but you possess in abundance what they do not have.

Stunned, trembling, her heart asked him, 'But I am a sinner ... I have a curse!'

You see many things, Mary. In the past those who had spirit sight, carried this power in the length and thickness of their hair; now you must let go of this power, if you are to gain a new knowledge through me.'

He had said this in silence, and she felt the warmth of his life entering into her.

'If you do so, I shall close your eyes to what is troubling you ...'

She began to cry, and her tears fell over his feet. Hastily, for she did not wish to defile him, she gathered her hair to wipe them away, and realised that in so doing, she was laying at his feet all of her old treasures. This affected her heart so dearly, that she found herself bending further and touching her lips to his feet in a kiss! And another! In a moment she was pouring her mother's oil over them, and while the tears continued to flow, she rubbed his skin and anointed his feet with her mother's very essence, and kissed them again and again, for he was now her comforter and her guide.

This is what I have done for you so that you will perform a task for me. One day, before my death, you will anoint me with this oil again and wipe my feet with your hair. You will be the tower that will bring the God in my soul closer to the man in my body so that I can accomplish my task. Until then you shall be the flooring of my soul.

She would give up her life, she said to him silently, to do this.

He touched her head with one hand, and a spark flew from it and entered into her spine. Of a sudden she was a child again and yet wise also. Rest, warmth, love, goodness had entered her to the marrow, and from the heights of this ecstatic ritual of forgiveness and acceptance, she heard the thoughts of the Pharisee and they pulled her down to earth:

If you are the prophet why do you not know what kind of woman this is that touches you? She is a sinner, and she defiles you!

She had heard it, but once again, not with her ears, with her heart-sense.

Taking his eyes from her, Jesus said to Simon the Pharisee, 'Why do you forsake this woman?'

The man was aghast. Christ Jesus had read his thoughts!

'Answer me this riddle,' Christ Jesus said to him. 'There was a certain creditor who had two debtors: the one owed five times more than the other. When they had no money to repay the debt, the creditor forgave them both. Tell me, therefore, which man loved the creditor the most?'

Simon did not need to think on it, for he spoke directly, 'I suppose it must be the man who was forgiven the most. He will love the most, who owes the most. Much for much … little for little.'

'Shall I apply your principles to this woman then …?' He looked down at Mary. 'See how she kneels! How she washes my feet with her tears and wipes them with her hair. When I entered into your house, you did not give me water for my feet, you did not anoint my head with oil. This woman has anointed my feet and kissed them, while you have not even given me a kiss of welcome. You, who have much, have given me little, yet she, who has little, has given me much. Why does she treat me so well, while you show me not even those polite attentions and tokens of respect that one should offer a guest at a feast? It is because in her heart, she has a light that sees who I am, and that is why she loves me! She does not love me because I forgive her the most. It is her abundant love, the light in her heart, which attracts my forgiveness. The little love you show me is a sign, that you do not know who I am, that is why I forgive you less.'

Then to Mary he said, 'Magdalena … your love is great, and in the same measure, so are your sins forgiven you … go in peace.'

She gathered up her alabaster jar and left the room. Behind her she could hear a great commotion, for those who were present were saying in their hearts, 'Who is this sinner who can see what others cannot? How can this Jesus of Nazareth think himself able to forgive sins, when he is only the son of a Carpenter … he is not even a rabbi?'

Magdalena came out into the night, leaving those words behind as if they were dirt on her shoes, and looked about at the trees and the air and the sky. She saw no devils, she heard no whispers, she saw only the light of those pinpointed stars above and she heard only the nudging of the sky onwards in its rounds. There was a solace in this quiet, in this peace, a solace that she could not describe even to herself!

The chill autumn air touched her skin only lightly, as she walked back to where she was staying with her brother Lazarus and her sister Martha. For within her there radiated a warmth like unto a midday sun.

CHAPTER 42

THE DANCER

Her mother had always told Salome that she was a creature conjured from a dream; created, essentially, not from blood, like a mere mortal, but from thin air shaped and moulded and sculpted into a pleasing likeness of Herodias.

The sorceress, the performer of miracles, the wonder-worker, said that Salome's father, Herod Philip, had contributed only a seed, while she had breathed life into a dead thing, and so without her, her mother assured her, nothing would have been made that was made. Salome therefore grew up thinking that her heart moved to the rhythm of her mother's blood, that her thoughts were begotten from impulses in her mother's will, and that her limbs were motivated by the tenor of her mother's thoughts, and while she believed this, harmony ruled the universe.

On the day Salome's body began to issue forth, from its own free will, that individual substance that marks a girl a woman, the spell was broken. The woman inside the girl saw that she was made from blood after all, and she understood that Herodias had kept this from her. Afterwards Salome began, little by little, to shed her mother's image, like a snake sheds its skin, and to dream herself a second birth. In so doing she discovered what her mother had not told her:

Salome was beautiful. This was her first awakening. For she was possessed of those seven sought after attributes: luxurious hair, well-shaped eyes, full bodied lips, breasts like moons, wide hips, rounded buttocks and shapely legs. And Herod Antipas, her stepfather, had been the one to confirm it.

From the first, Herod was the only man who dared to look at her. His fiery, lustful hunger had quickened a sense of womanliness, an urgency and a vitality that had seduced her. But an instinct told her that to be desired while remaining desire-less was a far more potent elixir. With such an elixir, a woman could bewitch her image so deep into a man's soul that it would be known beyond the annihilation of sleep ... perhaps even beyond the extinction of death, making her eternal, immortal!

This was her second awakening.

With a new vehemence did Salome set about growing her talents, cultivating the power of her endowments, and educating the efficacy of her seductions. She contrived with calm purpose to learn the seven pagan dances, the hardest of them being an artifice of seduction so exacting that it had not been mastered by many. Such a dance could make a woman's body a messenger of lust and delectable provocation, a labyrinth of secret potions and concoctions and magic spells – the instrument of an immortal goddess and the undoing of the Tetrarch of Galilee.

For sport, she had set out to seduce her mother's new husband, with the patient concentration of an artisan creating a box of tempting Jewels. Each gem was carefully shaped to attract the light and the eye and therefore the man. But that had been before John the Baptist.

That day at Ainon, she had felt a great attraction for the tall man browned by the sun, muscular, strong and serious. When her mind, despoiled of its devices and enchantments, had listened to the voice of this attraction, it had discerned that it came not from those places where pleasure pulls and tugs, but from her very heart! The joy of discovering this feeling of love was, however, soon traded for fury, when she realised that the man who had quickened it was himself rejecting her as if she were filth.

After that, Herod moved them to the odious fortress of Machareus and she had applied herself during those endless, tedious days, to driving her stepfather to madness. But when news reached her that his guards were bringing John to the dungeons of Machareus in chains, in her soul was ignited her love afresh, and she had waited for an opportunity to go to him.

Now, as she slipped out of the citadel and made a way across the compound to the dungeons, she was full of a strange anticipation.

She paid the guard handsomely and he allowed her passage to the cell, and left her alone with the man in chains. She took the ring of keys from a nail in the stone and went to a barrel of water and took a cup full. She would clean the sweat from his brow and the blood from the whippings on his arms and shoulders before releasing him.

After a moment of indecision, standing in the shadows, she dared to come to him. To her eye he seemed less than he had been and yet that strange sensation now came over her again, not a thrill of ardour, not a pounding of her heart for the passion of her loins, but something tender. She would be his selfless, willing disciple.

Later, she would wonder how she, a princess of Judea, could have bowed so low before such a man, but for now she was not thinking of herself, she was thinking only of the bond that existed between them, and how it had drawn her heart from its prison and changed its nature.

She set down the cup and contrived to kneel before him, to take the shackles from his hands and feet, but his eyes came suddenly open, arresting her movements. In them she saw no reflection of her warm-hearted thoughts, only confusion and exhaustion and what more?

He said to her, 'Who is this that looks upon me?'

She hesitated and stood then in the light from the torches, so that he might see more clearly how she had changed. 'I am the Hasmonean Princess, Salome. You met me at Ainon, but I am not as I was.'

Something moved the muscles of his face, something flickered in his eye – what was it?

'Why are you come, woman? Your presence profanes the chosen one of God! Do not touch me! Let me be!' he said quickly, moving to get away from her.

This struck her a blow and she was assailed by incertitude. Could he be rejecting her again, as an unsuitable, blemished and unworthy sacrifice? Surely the great prophet could see beyond what she had been to the creature of devotion that she had become? Her heart was numb. Her hands trembled. Her image of herself, having faded through selflessness, now floated away from her grasp. Soon she would disappear, having slipped through her own fingers!

She clung to the edges of her mind with the fingernails of hope, 'How can I, a princess, profane a filthy criminal lying in chains?'

He looked at her, 'Put on a veil and pour ashes over your head … seek forgiveness for your sins and offer up what you have made pure to God. Do not come to me, to tempt me with beauty of the flesh, Lilith! I am beyond temptation!'

'I did not come to tempt you!' she said, with a flicker of anger in those magnificent eyes. 'If I had come to tempt you, you would have already succumbed to my wiles! I have come to gloat, to see how low is made the great man, the great prophet who does not see what is before his eyes! Perhaps, now that I see you my heart feels sympathy for your wretchedness, and I am of a mind to take away the chains, and to set you free!'

'The freedom you offer is worse than these chains!' he said to her, 'It is a temptation to iniquity!' His eyes softened then and his voice grew gentle, but this gentleness cut more deep into her flesh than anger would have done, for he spoke like a priest, who, from a high place, looks down on a poor, simple creature,

'Oh, Lilith! You also tempted Eve, and Eve tempted Adam, and because he was weak and succumbed the world is now ravaged by sickness and death! I will not succumb to you! Leave me to my misery!'

He was discarding her in the same way she discarded trinkets that did not please her. She had made a mistake and had lost herself for a moment, but not for always. If he did not value her pure offering of love then he was no prophet. He was just a man in a dungeon. How dare such a man, such a common man, treat her with disdain?

Anger blazed in her eyes and furies howled for vengeance in her head and these combined with the spite, hate and revulsion she felt in her heart for herself. She spat her frustrated hopes at the ground and walked out of the stinking cell. Burning with abhorrence and shame for her stupidity she took herself to her bedchamber to scheme.

This was her third awakening – a man's desire for a woman might have the power to make her immortal, but a woman's love for a man had the power to make her extinct!

For days she did not come out of her bedchamber, taking all her meals in silence, searching in her mind for ways to redress the balance. Finally, the opportunity came, on the night of the Belshazzar-feast, the anniversary of the death of Herod the Great and her stepfather's ascension to the Tetrarchy.

That night she took long to ready herself: bathing and dressing, combing and primping until every inch of her was as polished smooth and inviting as silver. Herod's vanity had given her the opportunity she had desired but had not been expecting so soon. And so it was with the cold, cruel heart of a woman scorned that she honed her finest asset, the instrument of pleasurable torture and delicious torment, towards achieving one end and one end alone.

Revenge!

CHAPTER 43

DUNGEONS AND DRAGONS

In the dungeons of Machareus sat John the Baptist in a pool of filth and excrement and rat dung. His tortured body, chained to the wall of rock, was so contorted that every muscle and sinew screamed with pain and his mind, having held tight to it-self these months, now began a slow unravelling. He knew, therefore, that it was only a matter of time before those crawling things that lived in the corners of his cell would come to feed upon his carcass.

For a time, he had kept those dark things at bay, but recently Herod had come to him with news – John's followers had returned with an answer to the question put to Jesus of Nazareth:

Are you the coming one? Or are we to await another?

According to the Tetrarch of Galilee Jesus of Nazareth had said that he was not a prophet or a king. That among those born of woman there was no greater prophet than John the Baptist and that blessed was he who was not ashamed of Jesus!

These had been painful words to hear! No tortures devised by Herod and his adulterous wife could have made him suffer more. No pincers or knives, no fire could have caused his heart more sorrow, his mind more torment! And now those serpents and dragons, those malformed devils that lay hidden and hungry in the darkness came out, attracted to him by his doubt.

Herod's stepdaughter, Salome, had appeared in a dream and had stood before him with her emotions seething inside her. He knew the creature was not Salome but Lilith, an ancient feminine devil. Lilith had come dressed in fineries, with her heart on her sleeve, but he knew that she was a shape-shifter and a temptress and that her desire was to take a man from his destiny, and so he had sent her away and she had gone. But soon other devils had come in the guise of companions in the cold. In the black of night, they came into his mind. In the black of day, they stood before his eyes – those same eyes that had seen the Lamb of God in all His glory! How could these eyes have fallen so low and become so profane?

He could not remember if he had asked that question which had led to his madness –

Are you the coming one, the Olam Habba? Or shall we await another?

His mind, distorted and confused, unfed and tortured, could not recall the precise details, and yet, there it was, there it was the answer, with its dread-cold breath on his cheeks.

A voice came near his ear and hissed:

'Think of all those years in the wilderness, the fasting and meditation, the self-denials and sufferings … for what? Your scrap of a life has been marked by errors, and you have led others to error thereby, for where is the Kingdom you proclaimed? Where is the Messiah you promised?'

John knew that he had seen Him with his very eyes! He had seen the spirit dove!

'Ah … but was that not a fine dream? Was it not a fleeting reflection that, like a delusion in the desert, is uncaused by reality? Was it not a trick of the light, of the mind, of the soul that wallows in its own one-sided raptures? You are less than less, remember that! No more than a speck of a speck, and nothing you have done has meaning!'

What a traitorous thought this was!

And yet … did he not himself say aeons before, that he must decrease while that other increased? That he must be less than less, so as to make way for Christ, who would come after him and who would be more and more? For was He not greater for His outward meekness? Was He not more powerful for His outward powerlessness, more Godly for His outward manliness? What had Christ Jesus said? He searched in his arid mind until he found it:

Blessed is he who is not ashamed of the man Jesus.

He understood it!

For who could be ashamed, who had seen what lay above, and below, and within him? Those who were ashamed that he was not a prophet or a king in outward ways, were only so because they had no faith to see the inner Greatness, the inner Power, the inner Godliness!

The dragons and demons and serpents, fearful of these thoughts, began to writhe and to uncoil and slither away from his soul. Repelled, they moved into the dark corners of other cells. And so it was, that deep in the dungeons of Machareus, John the Baptist fell into peace, while not far away, from the Palace of Herod, there came the sound of shouts, of wild revelry and drunken merriment, wafting on the dark breezes that passed over the sea of death and into the valley of tribulation.

For it was the anniversary of the death of Herod the Great, and, at this late midnight hour, Herod had run short of amusements to offer to his satiated guests.

And it was at this very moment that he called on Salome … to dance!

CHAPTER 44

THE DANCE

The first time Herodias held the sword she was not taken by it because of the purity of its steel, or the ornate craftsmanship of its pommel, or the breadth of its tang, nor even the trueness of its edge. She was impressed by its history.

Tales spoke how the sword, made from a metal fallen from the sky, and tempered in the blood of a dragon, had been in the hands of Goliath when David slew him. David, having no weapon save a sling, had cut off the giant's head with it and had kept it for his own. Later, fearing its magic he had its hilt altered to depict not the dragon emblem of the Philistines, but his own star – the Star of David, which became the insignia of the Hebrew people. It was passed to his son, Solomon, who put a caveat on the sword so that it could not be used for evil. And that is how it had descended through the generations and came to rest in Herod's hands, who, in turn, gave it to Herodias as a gift on the eve of their commitment to marry.

Once Herodias was wise to these things, she set her heart to unlocking its occult powers with a mighty ambitious greed. But despite all her concentration on it, its secrets continued to elude her until a vision in the smoke told her that the sword would not work in her hands until Solomon's bewitchment was reversed, that is, until it shed blood again –not the blood of a Goliath, an evil man of great authority – but the blood of a pure man stripped of all power.

Such a man was John the Baptist!

She had waited a long time, but this night it seemed as if her plans might finally fall into place. After all, Venus was in Leo, and she felt it in her bones that the moment was chillingly near.

It was the anniversary of her husband's accession to the Tetrarchy, and his birthday. A great banquet had drawn Herod's Lords, his military authorities, and all his chiefs in Galilee and Perea to the fortress where they would drink and eat until they were drunk and satiated, bloated and replete.

Herod's insatiable need to be loved and honoured had driven him to excess: pearls and onyx and gold had been distributed in the food, and in the cups, sapphires and emeralds shimmered in the wine. One spectacle after another was performed – fire breathers, male dancers, magicians, and lion tamers. Even so, as the hours passed, the ignoble guests began calling for entertainment of a different kind. Entertainment that they knew only Herod could provide.

Now was time to cull some profit!

Herodias willed her thoughts into Herod's head, willed them as much as if they were beings flapping their wings at her disposal. Herod, thinking them his own creatures of madness, drank down his wine and leant his corpulence over the table towards that beauty, which he so sorely wished to empower and to possess. He said to her,

'I drink, therefore I am! I see your beauty, Salome, therefore I live!'

He raised his cup then, to that lithesome seductress, shaped and moulded and fashioned by Herodias for her own ends with incantations from smoke and air; that creation which she dangled always before Herod's eyes like a morsel to a starved dog, and which she astutely removed from his jaws when it took her fancy.

Salome gave him a sour eye.

'Don't be cold, Salome. Your father needs comfort this night!'

Herodias was fond of the fact that her daughter, too, thought herself a woman of her own mind. It made her smile to see the girl unleashing her seductions as if they were of her own invention. But the stupid girl was dull of mind, for Herodias had not woven intelligence into her birth-spell, and so she had no notion that her dances were only alluring and mesmerising because she danced to Herodias' tune!

Salome was still staring coldly at her stepfather. Herod had drunk too much, seeking to flee from the bat's wings, and he took to fondling her daughter's hair and saying, 'My beauty! Console your father, dance one dance to make him merry!'

The room now burst into agreement. Herod's chiefs and familiars had heard stories of Salome's dances, which were said to induce even eunuchs to torments of passion, and their eyes were full with those images that were called forth by wine and lust.

Salome, dressed in a sheer gown made from layers of silken fabrics adorned with pearls from Greece, opals from Rome, and Chrysolites, Beryls, and Topaz from lands beyond maps, gave Herodias a flash of daughterly disdain, and made her kohl-rimmed eyes bat their gilded lids at Herod.

'Dance?' she said, 'why should I dance?'

'The night is sad, Salome ... dance to please your father!'

'I do not wish to please you, for you are not my father!'

He turned to Herodias. 'Wife! Your daughter does not love me, again! Tell her she must love me!'

'Why should she love you?' Herodias said, 'your father was the son of a camel driver!'

Herod's vermilion face shone like a blooded moon. 'I order her to love me!' he said. 'Do you hear me, Salome, I order that you love me!'

The room broke out in uncertain laughter, and Herod laughed too, until the happiness of the audience was diminished, and he realised he must say something.

'Come, Salome ... dance your dance to amuse me, for I am not merry this night, my spirits are pale!'

'Your spirits are drunk!' she said to him.

'Yes, I am drunk on wine from Cyprus!' He staggered to his feet, and raised his empty glass. 'I am full of fish from the Euphrates, and peacocks fed on almond milk! I am a king and I am drunk, and being drunk I beg you ...' He doubled himself unsteadily, and brought his face close to Salome's. Indicating how small it should be with a thumb and forefinger, he said, 'One little dance?'

Before the girl could answer Herodias made time pause, and keeping herself inwardly still, imaged forth a thought from out of her very skeleton itself, which she breathed out into the air. This black thought remained wafting in the breeze until it was inspired by her daughter, into her soul, which had earlier been seeded with feelings of revenge.

The girl's eyes changed of a sudden and seemed to do battle for a moment with the birth of the ... *idea*. Her face fell sour, as if the taste of this new orphan child of her mind were not to her liking. Still, she could not prevent herself from saying, '... I can always be made to change my mind!'

A great silence fell. Even the musicians were paused waiting to hear what would come next.

Herodias felt Salome's delight as all eyes turned to her.

'If I dance, what will you give me?'

Herod was breathless now. 'What will you have? By my oath I shall give you whatever you wish for, if you will dance a dance! And I am a man of my oath, as all men know, I pride myself in this – that I do as I say. So, tell me, what shall it be?'

Salome stood and threw the veil from her hair, and called for a servant to remove her sandals. She clapped for music, drums, cymbals, flutes and as the song began, so did she begin to stir her body, moving her shoulders and her hips, contorting by degrees, more and more heatedly, agitating her rounded belly, contracting and gyrating all those warm, womanly muscles of pleasure, to the measure and cadence of the drums. Her eyes, big, black, liquid-some, promised to engulf the soul of her onlookers. Her hands caressed unseen lovers, her legs entwined around their thighs, her hips pressed against their insubstantial flesh, her lips kissed their airy form – until she was a dervish of silk and flesh and air and gesture.

A wave of yearning engulfed the room, hearts throbbed and

pounded and pulsed in a communal ritual of eroticism, and then, of a sudden, the unthinkable happened.

Salome fell to the marble floor and called for the music to halt.

From this position, crouching like a tigress waiting to pounce, breathless, watchful, with her colour high in her face and her alabaster breasts heaving, and those thighs, shapely calves and turned ankles, caressing the cold floor, she said to Herod, 'I will trade the dance of seven veils, for the head of John the Baptist … on a silver platter!'

Herodias smiled inwardly. Immersed in victory, she watched her husband's lecherous face, bloated and full of the blood of sexual tension, blanch.

'But my dear …' he stuttered, 'this is not possible!' He looked about him for encouragement from his chiefs and supporters, but it was too late, their faces were engorged with the heat of Salome's seductions and like wolves their jaws were ready to snap. 'He is a prophet! I cannot do it! I shall give you anything else, half my kingdom, anything at all! Name your pleasure … just do not ask me for the head of this man!'

'I will ask it, for it is what I want!'

Herod looked to his wife, and Herodias made a shrug.

He said to Salome, 'He is a holy man … I shall not do it! Notwithstanding my oath, I shall not do it … ask me for some other thing, my little one, anything at all, and it shall be yours!'

'You do not keep your oaths then! Here is a man that cannot be trusted,' Salome said to those in the room.

Herod said, 'All I am saying is that you may ask me for something else, if you like.'

'But I do not like anything else …!'

Herod grew fearful, and leant in to Herodias and said in a strangled whisper, 'This is your doing, you sorceress! You have enchanted the girl and now she wishes me to kill a prophet! I order you to put a stop to it!'

'I don't know what you mean, Herod.'

'Don't you see ... there is a terrible portent in such a doing, someone will suffer for it!'

'You seem to have become a prophet yourself!' she said aloud. 'Come husband, it is poor manners to keep our guests waiting for their entertainment!'

The room resounded in agreement.

She could read Herod's thoughts. He was stuck between a rock and a wall; cornered by his own oath and beleaguered by his conscience, facing dishonour on the one hand and, on the other, the ire of a God known for his disdain of aberrant kings.

His gaze fell on Herodias, and it said,

You are a witch and there is nothing to be done about it!'

He looked again at Salome. 'Let it never be said, that Herod Antipas does not keep his word!' It came out weak and lacked heart, 'And yet you may change your mind, my dear!'

Salome smiled whitely, clapped and began a new dance. She took her time and listened to her body's arousal, allowing it to titillate and to frustrate, to insinuate what it felt for itself. Amid a fever of rhythm and discordance, amid the shimmer of gold and silver, the ringing of the little bells and the pounding of drums, she dropped one veil after another, releasing, with her nakedness, the sexual force that she had enticed from the depths of her limbs, the hidden demons of lust in those inner wheels of pleasure embedded in her body. Their abundance made the room spin with an elemental force and caused a storm of passion to rise up into the hearts of men and women alike. And amid this spectacle of lust Herodias sat like a Titan, observing from the heights of her own cold Parnassus.

When it was over, a breathless Herod ordered his guards to bring John the Baptist to the hall, and Herodias arranged for her servant to bring the sword of David from its resting place.

When the man was brought forth, soiled, dirt encrusted, thin and emaciated, she was struck by his height, for great and awesome did he seem, despite his deprivations, like a powerless Goliath! He did not speak, but looked about, taking the room in with a guarded eye. Only when he was forced to kneel and his eye fell on Herodias, did he say something.

'Behold woman, the judgement of God shall come, and you shall be condemned for your iniquity! Lo, you shall never be at peace but shall wander the earth, bonded to your evil!'

She saw the gleaming of the burnished blade, and John the Baptist's head come free from his body.

It fell to the floor to a chorus of gasps.

It made a wet thud.

The guard kicked the blood-spewing body out of the way, and brought the head by the hair to a silver platter, which a servant hastened to Herod.

Her daughter, struck by some semblance of remorse, fled the room, her hand preventing the bile in her mouth from spilling out. Herod, ducking and weaving to avoid the devil's wings that flapped over his head, made a mournful gasp. All men sat shocked, brought back from the din of excess by the reality of death.

Herodias, however, was taken by the head upon the platter, for seeing it increased the magic in her bones, and made her feel so big as to engulf the earth with her jaws, and it was only when a servant removed the head from her sight that she awakened from this fascination. Now, from the night, came the hoot of an owl. But was it a portent of good fortune, or bad? It was too early to tell.

She gathered in the folds of her soul, and attentive, watchful, with her spine as cold as marble, she looked to the moment.

CHAPTER 45

EXCALIBUR

John the Baptist was dragged, whipped, pushed and prodded across the cold compound and into the citadel of the castle by Herod's guards. Upon entering the banquet hall he was blinded by light and stood a moment dazzled at the spectacle of debauchery before him. Demons fluttered before his gaze, having escaped from some foul source. Drunkenness, licentiousness and depravity were everywhere made plain to him.

Then he saw it – the blade of blue-burnished steel. It enticed him.

He was pushed to his knees and looked about until he found her, the witch and sorceress, that Jezebel reborn; Herodias. He saw it then, in her eyes, the kernel of many lives to come when she would bear the weight of the same message he had once proclaimed – that she would wander the earth with no peace. He told her so and waited.

The world pulsed.

He heard a whish past his ear and felt a sudden tug, a jolt.

The blade repulsed him and the world and its sufferings were taken away on the wings of the fine airs.

And this, after all, is bliss!

Lifted from the world, a crystalline clarity entered into him that near blinded his spirit eyes. This clarity was an angel, that great and mighty angel that had come to him in the cave came again to take him from the captivity of his body, and away towards the open spaces, towards the hills of Hebron and to the deep clefts of the Jordan Valley, to the oasis of Jericho and to the wilderness of Judea, to Bethlehem and Jerusalem. Along the way, the angel showed him all the scenes of his life, all of his labours, the sum of all his accomplishments, spread out like breeze-blown clouds over a wide expanse of sky. And he saw something else … the angel showed him what had not yet been.

‡

'What does he see, Lea?' I asked.

'He sees a room, *pairé,* and in it a painter.'

'Oh!'

'He is engaged in painting a picture of himself, so he is standing before a mirror. But there is a moment when he does not only see himself in the darkling reflection – he does not see the man with the heart-shaped face, with wide-spaced black eyes staring back at him. His self changes to another man.'

'To another man? Who is it?'

'In a far off future, men will ask the same question, *pairé.* They will wonder who it is that in so intimate a way, occupies a place in this painting, which he will call *Self-Portrait with a Friend*. They will not know that the painter sees not only his own image, as he is in that life, but also a likeness of himself when, in the past, he was John the Baptist. This is why he paints the two men together, for they are his two selves.'

I thought on this. 'What is the name of the painter?'

'He will be called Raphael, *pairé.*'

'Like the Archangel?'

'Like the Archangel, and he will paint many paintings of Mary with two children, he will even paint me, floating in the skies, holding a child in my arms … and yet it is unclear if he will come to paint the Transfiguration.'

'What do you mean, unclear?'

'You see, a part of the future must always remain inscrutable, *pairé*, even for the gods who order destiny, because a man's heart is free.'

I was about to ask her many questions, particularly concerning the creation of destiny itself, but she had already begun to tell of other things.

CHAPTER 46

BREAD OF LIFE

It was near Passover, *pairé,* when Jesus sat with his disciples on that mountainous fertile outcrop near the Sea of Galilee. He had brought them here, again, to teach them of those things that were hidden from others ...'

‡

... Simon was sat near his master, looking out at the moon that seemed like a splinter in the flesh of the black sky and the stars that were locked in conversation. Simon knew nothing of the moon, save that it enticed the waters, and he knew nothing of the stars, save that they pointed the way home, so he looked at the sky is if it were a silvered sea, and this calmed him.

It had been over a year since he and his fellow fishermen had left their boats to follow Jesus, and since then, Simon had seen the master turn water into wine and cause the lame to walk and the deaf to hear. He had watched, awed and fearful, as he admonished the Pharisees, as he cast out demons, and cure plagues. His wonderworking had not only brought a girl back from the brink of death, but also a dead youth back to life, and at those moments he seemed like a god known only to a man in his dreams – an awesome, powerful, terrible God, full of glory. At other times, when he slept and taught and walked with them, he seemed no more than a man.

In truth, when his master was not teaching or healing, he was often times quiet and withdrawn, walking ahead of them with his feet bloody from blisters and his head bent, like a ghostly shape that either melted into the heat-haze, or dissolved into the desert wind. Many times Simon found himself speaking like his master. His fellow disciples too, seemed inspired by his way of being, so that they also talked in his manner, with his voice.

These were strange goings on for a lowly fisherman, and whenever he thought on it he felt a dullness overtake him. He missed his sea and his boat, and asked God for a dream, a dream of his boat, limed and new and ready, with its lateen sails full of breeze.

And so he slept. And God granted him a dream.

He dreamt of crowds on the shores of the lake. They were hungry and were fed bread and fish by his master, who seemed happy. But then his dream took him out on his new boat but it was not a calm day, the water was raging and the lateen sails were torn and the great waves broke over the bow. His master was in the water, calling out to him to come. Simon was afraid, and yet he attempted it and found he could not stand on the water; he was sinking, and he knew it was because doubt had made his faith run out.

On waking, he remembered the dreams, and did not know what to make of them. Even at that hour, many were arriving at the shores of the lake to be healed, and after a hasty breakfast of bread soaked in honey, his master began to address the crowds.

He took some bread in his hand, and said to them. 'You eat bread to feed your hunger, but your souls need something else, your souls need what I teach, which is the bread of life. Unless you eat of my teachings, you have no life in you! Nothing everlasting, for the bread and water of ordinary life are not meat and drink for heaven!'

Murmurs came from the crowds and someone said to him, 'Are you not Jesus, the son of Joseph? Why should your teachings be like bread, and why should we eat of it?'

'Those who know me, also know that if they eat of my teachings they shall have life even after death!'

Simon saw red beard, Judas Iscariot, making a mocking face to a number of people who were shaking their heads. Thomas was frowning and so were others.

The crowds became restless.

A man, no doubt a scribe sent from the Pharisees, stepped forward.

'When you tell ordinary people these hidden things without preparing them, it is like letting them eat bread without washing their hands!'

Jesus did not speak, but waited. The crowds grew noisome and angered, and it was a long time before his calm voice caused a well of silence to form. 'Well did Isaiah prophecy of you hypocrites …' he said, 'for you concern yourselves more with who is listening and care nothing for the teaching that I give you. It is not what goes into your mouth that defiles you, but what comes out of it … for your teaching, Pharisee, is like putrid meat!' he said.

Offended and angry, the Pharisee and those who had come with him made to leave with much hatred in their hearts.

Later, when the master and his disciples walked on the shores of the lake again, trailing behind those few who had remained with him, Simon deigned to ask him a question.

'Those folks were offended at what you said. They did not know what to make of what goes into the mouth and what comes out of it. Come to think of it, I don't know what to make of it myself, but that is because I am ignorant and stupid!' He looked askance, 'But there are others … clever men, who do not love you as I do. They follow you with disdain upon their faces. What you say offends them.'

He looked at Simon without anger and raised one quizzical brow, 'Do you say this because it offends them, or because it offends you, my brother?'

Simon felt shame rise to his cheeks and he averted his eyes. 'My rabbi, all your followers will go if you keep with such talk, and you will be left with nothing but scraps …'

'I have you. Is this not true?' he said, looking at Simon and others who were gathered about.

Simon's face opened up. 'Yes, of course, rabbi, always shall you have me, a thousand times shall you have me, but how must the few of us who are true to you gather in the harvest?'

'Yes, rabbi,' Andrew added, catching up, 'how are we to do it? After all, we are a sorry lot!'

His master regarded Andrew. 'The blind cannot gather a harvest, this must be left to those who see ... if a blind person leads a blind person into a field, they will both fall into a hole. Let all those who are led by the Pharisees, who are blind, go after them ... they shall not reap much together, that is certain. They are not my concern.' Then, 'Andrew, tell me, what do you see?'

Andrew could not hold the master's eyes. 'I am only a fisherman, Lord. I understand about fish and nets and the sky and the sea. I know very little of these things you tell, but I believe in you.'

The master clapped him on the shoulder and gave it a shake. 'You have always asked me to speak plainly to you, and yet, is there one of you who hears my words? What shall you do when I am no longer with you, hmm? What shall you do, when you have no one who can tell you how to live?'

The day had turned hot as they walked along the lake's edge. His master brought up the cowl of the robe without a seam and put it over his head and sat down on the sand with his feet touching the cool water. The others all did likewise, except for the red beard, Judas.

'I have spoken plainly to you, but you don't listen. Listen ... the Pharisees give the people something they can take hold of, laws, traditions, but these are not eternal, they are only for the body, you see? What I give you is something that you can never take hold of, but once you have it, you can never lose it because it will have a life in your soul, it is eternal. Do you understand?'

He looked to Judas and to Thomas. 'I see that there are some of you who do not believe in my words. And I say to you that you are in this circle because it pleases God ... even those whose hearts are hardened against me.'

Judas shook his head, 'My heart hardens when you speak of the soul without telling us how we are to liberate our bodies! First, you must liberate us from our oppressors. Then, only then, we will eat of your teachings!'

'If you liberate your souls,' the master said, 'if you change your souls, then the world will also change, not the other way around. The world is as hard as it is, because in your hearts you are hard.'

'You are not in me, and you do not know how I feel.' Judas said.

'You say I do not know you, but you have no faith, Judas, and because of it you do not know yourself. Faith melts away hard hearts and wakes the mind so that it can know itself.'

Simon remembered his dream, the multitudes and the bread and the fish, and his faithlessness in the stormy seas, and now he understood! Yes! Of a sudden he saw his ordinary self, fall away from him, the self that was made up of country, of folk and family. In his heart a vision arose of another self, a higher, more clearly his – self. And this self was none other than his teacher, who sat among them.

Fish and Fisherman were one!

He realised then, that what his master had given them had many names, and yet had only one name. This bread, this food, these teachings, this kingdom brought down to earth, was an intimate thing – a light that pierced his soul. Suddenly, all that his master had said had come true! The river of the world roared in Simon's ears then, and he told himself,

This is that something you can never take hold and yet once you have it, you can never lose it – your own eternal selfhood, which is given to you by Christ!

‡

'What a riddle!' I said to Lea.

'Yes...but he understood it, *pairé*,'

'Well, are you going to elucidate it for me?'

'It just means, quite simply, that a man's word, his I AM, is the God in the man.'

'The God in the man is his Word! Oh! Yes … the fish and fisherman were one, pupil and teacher, lower self and higher self! I see, my child!'

'And that moment of grace, of exquisite, concentrated knowing, would never leave Simon. Even many years later, when Roman soldiers nailed his racked and tortured body to an upside down cross, he would recall it with joy; that once, amid life's dream he had caught a glimpse of his true self.'

'What every man would seek to see outside himself!' I said, 'Even though it is always looking at him, from within his own heart – Christ, the Son of the living God!'

Lea smiled once again, like a proud parent.

CHAPTER 47

THE BEARER

Joseph of Arimathea stood at the gate of his garden rubbing his beard. The people called this place 'the paradises' because it was not far from where stood the tomb of Adam and the shrine of Jeremiah. Its verdant lushness also separated Jerusalem from the harsh desert, and that hill of the gallows, used by the Romans for their crucifixions.

The day was not yet woken from sleep and in the cool airs Joseph bent to remove a weed. He was a wealthy and prominent member of the Sanhedrin, an Israelite deemed worthy to represent the people of Israel, but if the truth were told he was more at ease in his garden with his weeds than at the temple.

'Who would know him from an ordinary man?' his wife would say to her neighbours. 'He wears old clothes and old sandals, and when he's not digging in his garden he is visiting the Essenes! Anyone would think he has no family!'

Joseph sighed now to think on it. Over the years he had been designated a 'friend' of the order, which meant that he was given generous hospitality at any of their houses, whether they be monasteries in the desert or fraternal houses in the towns.

'He gives those ascetics everything, while his family must cope with crumbs!' his wife would say, 'even that house in Jerusalem he owned with Nicodemus has been given over to them! It's no small wonder they love him so!'

Joseph passed a hand over his brow. He knew the Essenes did not love him only for that house, which they had made their own, but also because he had entered into their teachings with energy and with vigour and had withstood many trials and passed many tests.

He paused to take in the aroma of his garden, the fragrant scent of dew and wet grass, and his mind turned from his wife's nagging, to that time not long ago on the banks of the Jordan when he had seen something remarkable. After witnessing the Baptism of Jesus he had gladly neglected all his duties at the Sanhedrin, and yes, he had left his family and friends to follow Jesus from place to place, town to town, in order to listen and to learn from him.

One evening, as he was near to falling asleep, Jesus came to him and said, 'Joseph of Arimathea, wake up, my brother! You should return to your home, for the time is near reached when you must prepare your grave.'

He must have seen the apprehension on his face for Jesus said, 'Don't be fearful, Joseph...death always comes, and when it comes, it is better if there is a grave. Go now, before it is too late!'

Remembering his sadness for his oncoming death, he paused at the threshold of the great walled vaults of his sepulchre and peered into the darkness of it. He knew his grave contained enough niches to house thirteen bodies, and so it was grand by normal standards, with even an anteroom, and two further rooms beyond it. The work was near finished and still he did not feel ready, God forgive him! To think on it made big tears fall from his eyes to the dirt at his feet. A gasp escaped his mouth and he fell then, with his knees on the wet, fragrant dirt outside the grave.

He kissed the dust and cried, and kissed it again, and cried again. 'Dust, dust! How stiff-necked and stubborn you are! How shameless you are that you consume all the light in the world and then grind it into nothing! How impertinent you are that you will take Joseph into your bosom to eat him up when he is not ready!'

But a bird flew overhead and his eyes were directed to the heavens, to the gold-gleaming of the waning moon making its slow descent towards the west. He saw something in the moon's dark shadow; in that great disc dimly visible above the shimmering vessel there was something so faint as to be only a whisper of the eye …

He remained upon that impertinent dust, looking up to the heavens long after the moon had set and the sun had risen and the day had begun. When his stonemason found him, he sent one man to Joseph's wife and another to the physician, for he thought that Joseph had collapsed from some strange malady. But no one knew what was wrong with him.

They did not understand that Joseph was not ill at all, but merely overwhelmed with a feeling of veneration, which had, for a moment, seized his limbs and made them like stone. For he understood what he had seen in that black disk within the gleaming gold sickle of the moon: it was a word written in the cosmic script … a name …

Joseph.

CHAPTER 48

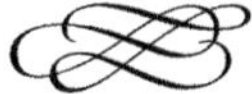

WHO AM I?

They were near the coasts of Caesarea Philippi, and Jesus walked ahead of the large group. Young John bar Zebedee walked beside his brother James, and Phillip and Simon, and they talked among themselves. These last weeks had been difficult. Many of those that in the beginning had followed the master willingly with love in their hearts, those that had been healed or saved from evil spirits, had been turned away from him by the sermonising of the Pharisees.

Numerous deputations had come from Jerusalem to lure Jesus with questions that worked like traps, seeking always for answers that transgressed the laws of Moses, or that spoke ill of the Romans, answers that could be used to brand his master either a blasphemer or an insurgent. But Jesus, time and again, saw beyond all their tricks and answered their questions eloquently and skilfully.

Others came to discourage him, telling their master that Herod Antipas was seeking to kill him. To these men he said,

'Tell that fox that a prophet does not die outside of Jerusalem. When I am ready to die, I will come to the city and offer myself up to be killed!'

As time passed, temple guards, as well as other soldiers at the behest of Herod, were sent to seize him and to take him away for questioning, but they did not know him from his disciples and were forced to turn back. Amid these vicissitudes his master led them over the land like hunted men, fleeing over the sea one moment, or to the farthest reaches of Palestine the next to escape the clutches of those who would do him harm.

Some days previously, a report had arrived of John the Baptist's beheading at Machareus, and this had caused great mourning and anger among the disciples. Afterwards, Jesus spent many a day deep in prayer. Young John and his fellows wondered what their master would do next, feeling afraid for their own safety, desolate and alone for the absence of the one whom they had followed even before Jesus.

Even so, John sensed the beneficent presence of John the Baptist, as if his spirit were paused over them in blessing. He tried to tell his brother and the others of it, but only Simon would acknowledge it. The others turned their grieving ears more and more to Judas.

This day, as the sun sat close to the margins of a sky scattered with cloud, John walked with the others across a great plain of reed and marsh. Judas was speaking to them and to the greater following that trailed behind, with his dark eyes and his soft rasping whispers.

His talk made John low in spirits since it began to shape the thoughts of his fellows and turn them against his Lord. As the sun descended, even his own mind turned to his sore and aching feet and to something to eat and a cool place to rest, and he too began to wonder if his master were considering their exhaustion and their need for comfort.

He was full with relief when, having come to a place where there were a number of Essene herders, his master made a sudden pause and gestured to a great tree atop a grassy knoll where they would spend the night. The air had been hot all day and now there was the rumble of thunder. John thought it a shame that it was not yet night, for he loved to see the lightning chase the skirts of the clouds. He ate their cheese and drank their milk, grateful for food, and was lost in his thoughts when Jesus' voice disturbed him,

'Compare me to something, and tell me what I am like.' His voice was light and in his eye the look spoke of a riddle. John liked riddles and he looked around the circle and the others were all looking at him. His smiled waned and he was full of uncertainty.

'You are …' he began.

But Phillip, who had been chewing on his cheeks, broke in. 'Some say you are inspired by what comes from Elijah or what lived in other prophets … they say you are a messenger!'

'Would you call Elijah a Son of Man?' he said to John again.

John felt his face flush. A long time he felt it, and then he harnessed his courage to say, 'You are …'

But his brother interrupted, 'We have learnt from you that John the Baptist was a Son of Man, as was Elijah, Jeremiah and the prophets. They were the elect of the Earth, for they had pure souls.'

Jesus nodded, 'Yes … that is what I have said of them, but what do you say of me?' He looked at John again.

'Some say you are a wise philosopher,' Matthew Levi broke in, looking at the others for support.

Jesus raised a brow, and looked about the circle, 'Do they? They say that I am a wise philosopher?'

Thomas, seized by enthusiasm, turned his crossed eyes to Jesus and said, 'Teacher! My mouth is unable to say what you are!'

Jesus let his benevolent regard fall upon him, 'That is because your mouth is full!'

All of them laughed.

'Have I not told you, Thomas, I am not a teacher, and yet you continue to call me rabbi? Can your eyes not see more than this body? From whence comes the power in me?' he said to them, 'Do any of you know?'

John faltered again under his vigilant eye. He wanted to say that he thought him like a priest, the highest priest of all, but he was uncertain again. His brother too did not speak; only Simon had the courage to say something.

He said to him, 'I have seen that your power comes from the light of the world! The priests call all those souls who are purified, Sons of Man. But in you, lives more than a purified soul. In you, lives the Son of the living God, who has come down from the cosmos! I have seen the light of Christ in you with the eye of my heart!' He looked to the others, 'I have seen it!'

Jesus seemed full with pleasure. 'You have seen it, Simon. Yes, I know that this is so, and blessed you are for it! One day you will help to carry my cross … you will be the rock that grinds the wheat into bread … the rock upon which my church shall be built, and so from now on I shall give you a new name, Petra – Peter! Peter, you will lead a community, faithful to my teachings, against whose truths even death shall not prevail.'

Peter, who was Simon, was flushed and happy with himself, but a moment later he seemed sick to the stomach with worry. 'A new community! And I shall be its leader? I am no leader, rabbi … I am only good at two things, catching fish and eating them.'

The others laughed again and Jesus laughed along with them, for Peter's child-hood. 'It will take time but you will find your footing, even in a storm. It shall not be smooth sailing but a toil and you will have to cast your net far and wide into the world, and like the good fisherman that you are, you will catch many men. Andrew, your brother, will also help you.'

Peter remained unsure, 'But, rabbi,'

Jesus raised a hand.

'I mean, master,' Peter corrected himself, 'all fish do not swim together, they swim only with their own kind … and they eat each other up, the big fish eat the little fish, and so on!'

Jesus leant his head towards him. 'Look around in our circle; many of you are not related, but are here because destiny has brought you together. There are big fish and little fish among you, but you do not eat one another. This is a new community. You see, Peter, it is not enough just to have the light in you. As fish swim together, so should you join with others who are the same as you, who also have the light. Such a community will be bound to me by destiny, on earth and in heaven … this you will tell men after I am gone.'

'You speak of the end of your life without concern,' Matthew Levi said, 'yet it concerns us all a great deal.'

'We worry for it,' said Andrew.

Jesus looked at them, grave-serious. 'In the same way they killed John, so will they kill me, but this is my destiny, and you must get used to it. The spirit of God that lives in me, shall be delivered up as has been foretold by the prophets. That is why I am preparing you, so that you can withstand the end when it comes, for I will need witnesses in the world, and you are the eyes and ears that shall see and hear and proclaim it.'

Peter said, with great emotion, 'God forbid this should happen to you, master!'

Jesus' eyes were full of disappointment, 'What now Peter? A moment ago you spoke so righteously, you understood! This is not the light in you that speaks, but only what is dark … this darkness inspires you to disdain suffering and death as something that must be shunned! This darkness is Satan, who tempts you and bends your soul to his delusion that only earthly life and comfort are of value. I say to this being that deludes you: get thee behind me Satan!' When he said it he spat at the ground.

John felt chastised, for he had thought the same. Above, the clouds gathered and a flash was seen, and a rumble shook the circle as if to put a seal on their master's words.

'What will we do when you are gone? How shall we manage when we are only poor fishermen and shepherds and day labourers …?' James said, because night was falling and he too seemed to be falling into his old melancholia.

'Love one another like brothers, love another life as if it were your own life,' Jesus told him.

'What did he say?' asked Andrew.

'He said, "Love one another!"' Peter shouted, annoyed.

'So that is all?' Judas said from his standing position, leaning on a tree. 'You have had us follow you these many months for this? So that when you are gone we shall know to love one another?' He left the tree now and came to stand nearer the circle. 'What of the trials of Israel? What of the salvation of her people? The storm gathers about her and yet you do not seek to find shelter for her!'

Jesus regarded Judas as if he were an aberrant child that must be brought into line. 'You think what I tell you is a simple thing, Judas, and yet I tell you there is nothing harder. To love another truly, selflessly, one needs to know oneself first. If Israel knew herself, she would realise how full of faults she is, and then she would not think herself so high and mighty. She would love even those who did not belong to her and she would not need to seek shelter.' Jesus said to him. To the others he said, 'When I am gone you must remember … learn to know yourselves, so that you can love others truly.'

'But why must you die? How can the world benefit from losing you? What shall your death accomplish?' John asked, because he was of a sudden full of sorrow.

'Yes …' James, his brother joined in, 'The Pharisees will be happy to kill you, and then they will continue to teach the old ways and to send men to their ruin!'

There was seen another flash and it was accompanied by the tearing up of heaven in a thunderclap.

Jesus looked at all of them. 'Courage, my brothers, courage! Do you see the thoughts of the gods in the heavens? This lightning is like the thoughts that flit about in your heads … but what of the thunder? Do you not hear the thunder in your hearts; listen to your hearts, my Sons of Thunder!' he said to John and to James, 'It resounds the truth for all who can hear it; it is only by dying that I can save the world from death!'

Philip scratched his head, 'But how can a dead man do anything, much less save the world from death?'

'Phillip, you soft head!' Simon-Peter said to him, exasperated. 'Didn't you just hear me say a moment ago that Jesus is not just a man? That he is also Christ, a God in a man!'

Phillip waved a hand at him in a sour mood.

'Listen,' Jesus called their attention to him. 'My death will be different from any other death before me. It will be different because no god has ever died an earthly death.'

'Well then … I shall die with you!' said John, overcome with love.

'And I!' said James his brother.

Andrew cocked his head, 'What did they say they would do?'

'For the love of Abraham, Andrew!' Peter said. 'They will die with the master ... that's what they said!'

'Oh! And so shall I then! I shall die with him also, and then I will truly know him!' Andrew said.

The men were arguing as to what martyrdom they would be prepared to suffer, when Judas spoke out.

'Listen to you lot! Trying to surpass each other in your martyrdoms! You are like children!'

Jesus raised a hand. 'You do not need to die to see who I am. I tell you, that if you become like children in your hearts, if you let go of your doubt, some of you shall know me, even before natural death itself!'

The others did not know his meaning, and they talked amongst themselves trying to fathom the depths of these words. John, however, was filled with a sudden peacefulness. He considered what it would be like, to be one of those who could see the Son of God. How this might come about he could not presage, but even so his soul was full of hope that he might one day be among them. In this mood he surrendered himself to his master and to God, and soon fell asleep.

CHAPTER 49

TRANSFIGURATION

It was night. All were asleep except for Christ in Jesus. He sat upon the mountain of stillness while the soul of humanity, the out-breath of villages and cities and towns and countries of the world lifted upwards, wafting towards the tangled stars.

Below, the earth breathed in its orchards and sandy wastes, its oceans and cobbled streets and trembling deserts and verdant forests, and while men slept it awakened from its daily dream and turned its mind to inner activities. He could feel its soul stir beneath him; he could hear its heartbeat quiver and he could smell its breath in the sweet scents borne on the breezes.

Since he had come into Jesus, he had grown accustomed to the increasing burden of the man's heart, to the organs speaking to him of pain and suffering, to the solidity under those feet, to the weight of that body, and to the sharp thoughts that pricked at his spirit. Now, the world no longer clawed at his senses or pierced into him like daggers. Outwardly, he was composed and quiet and sometimes he was that man of Nazareth whom all knew and spoke to; he was the man who seemed simple and kind and laughed at the childish ways of his disciples; the man who gave his friends riddles to solve and who sometimes listened politely to the insults of the rabbis and the doubts of the people. He was one with that man Jesus, yet inwardly he was also a god, an exalted being who had come down from beyond the stars to be poured out into an earthly mould, a god with a task that was never far from his mind.

To ponder it, he would take himself away from men, away from their questions, away from their grasping, their lack of understanding, and their stubborn ways. And he would receive solace then, not only for his spirit, but for his body also, since at the same time that his spirit communed with his Father in heaven, his body was rejuvenated by the angels on earth, as all human bodies are rejuvenated in sleep, and he was happy for it, while it lasted. But he knew that his body was unlike other human bodies. In the past, men had been overshone by those angels and gods who had inspired them, but no God had ever entered into the blood and bones of a man, no God had ever died an earthly death – but this was his task – and he did not know if the body of Jesus would be capable of withstanding the immense power of his spirit to the very end, or if it would be torn asunder prematurely before the performance of his duty.

Even now, things were altering. He could sense it. The deeper he entered into flesh and bones, the more those abilities that had so impressed the people began to fade, and he knew that a time was close by when his body would be seen outwardly as old, and wasted, and incapable of producing miracles of any kind, and he would be mocked as powerless and feeble. Would his chosen ones remain faithful to him then? Would Peter with his stubborn ways, and Andrew with his deaf ears, and James with his melancholic doubts, and John with his insecurities, remain steadfast? He did not know. He did not know if they understood that it was not his task to come as a great king, to wield power and to lead peoples, but to become ever more powerless.

The breathing of his men was woven into the night and became one with the chaotic thoughts, the despair of every human heart – the mute, expressionless longing of a multitude of human souls. Christ in Jesus breathed in the dreamers of Israel, the dreamers of Samaria and Syria and Greece and Rome. He breathed in the world and its desires and hopes and fears, and he breathed out solace, comfort and consolation. Even so, on setting aside their blankets in the morning, by small degrees, men's eyes would return to their blindness, and their ears to their deafness. They would forget that he had been with them, when in their beds they shook with fear or humiliation, or raged with hatred, or cried with sorrow into their pillows.

He looked to his disciples, wrapped in their dreams. When their wills were set free by sleep, he taught them. To one he gave this teaching, and to the other that, but in the waking day their minds fettered them, and they were prevented from remembering. Only three of the twelve had recognised him in the day enough to awaken to his splendour in the night; these were John, Peter and James.

And to them he said:

Awaken! And behold the spirit of creation!
Its beginning, its centre and its end.
I am the cause of east and west, of north and south,
I am the cause of all that is in the heights above
And in the depths below,
I am truth itself,
I am revelation,
I am knowledge,
Piety and the law.
I am almighty!

Among this brilliance, legions of spirits, a multitude of elemental beings of water, air, fire, and earth, awakened to see him and to answer his call. Moses and Elijah, too, came to stand beside his outspread arms, and thus it was, that between the Way and the Truth, between the stars, and the earth, He shone like a vermilion sun, a splendour that would not be seen again until his resurrection.

This was his gift to the world of the elements, and to his chosen ones. A vision of His true ethereal person, of the light, love and life that would not only renew nature itself, but would also sustain his disciples in the coming difficult months ahead, when his body outwardly aged, and his health inclined towards death. But unlike nature, Peter, John and James did not awaken fully to his call! No! Instead, they trembled in their dreams, and could bear to see his grand and celestial dimensions only darkly, and to hear his call only feebly.

He despaired, for if they were not able to awaken in their sleep with his help, how would they remain awake when he needed them? He watched them fall away from him, one by one, and like every other soul in the world, continue sleeping.

And he knew he must look for another man to take their place.

CHAPTER 50

THE RICH YOUTH

The world was sleeping. It sleeps darkly still, trembling with fear for the truth! I think on it as I continue to make my way down this mountain, singing my song. Those who accompany me on this downward journey are good souls, and although I share in their destiny, I no longer share their fears or their misconceptions. Lea's words, of the renewal of nature, and the gift given by Christ to his disciples, had awakened me to a knowledge that the world of soil, and water, and air, and fire is not a hell created by an evil God, as our church believes, but is a place wherein lives Christ! And so, there is nothing in nature that does not breathe with His love.

If I incline my ear, I can hear the stone heart of the mountains beating with love in its dark depths. I can hear the living juice of love that moves in the trees. I can hear the love in the buzz of this little bee, which leads the way down this mountain. I can even hear the love, however misplaced, that rises with the cadence of the song of inquisitors, the *Spirite Sancti*.

I want to tell them that, like streams, all religions of the world long to return to the one source. They have become estranged, they have wandered far, they have become muddy, and stagnant, and yet, a memory lingers of that clear source, from which they came – their faith in Christ!

I can tell them this because during those days of the siege I had begun to see. Yes! This is faith after all! Faith is revelation! When I climbed to the parapets I was no longer interested in the encampment below but instead looked to the blue expanses above, where the brightness of the previously unseen world of elements was becoming visible to me.

I wished then that I could show it to the inquisitors! I would say, 'Look up to the stars! Do you not see how they speak one to the other in a profound geometry? Look at the trees! Do you not see the halo glow of light around each one and how it breathes out to meet the glory coming from the heights? Look at the clouds and the sea! Do you not see in these, the ethereal bodies of the angels?' But, alas! The inquisitors, fearing that such things in the soul are the work of the devil, would not see them, for fear itself is what blinds a man and dissolves his faith, as Peter so well understood!

In my own infinitely small way, I can comprehend the sorrow of Christ for the blindness of his disciples. He had one alternative left to him, Lea told me that night, one man on whom to lay his hopes – Lazarus.

Lazarus, too, had once gazed out from his tower in Magdala, to see the word of love weaving in all things, and so when Lea began to tell of Bethany, with its sleep-locked houses shaded by almond, fig and olive trees, I could feel how different it was from Magdala. I know this even more so now, because I am descending from my tower, to a place where I will have to let everything I know die away. I know that only in such a place as Bethany could Lazarus answer his call, as I am answering mine in that field below.

‡

Situated on the northern face of a mount known for its olive trees, the castle, bequeathed to Lazarus, Martha and Mary by their father, was large. It had rooms and accommodation for many, and was surrounded by gardens and terraces and fountains. In one of these walled gardens there stood an ancient date palm, under which was erected a booth, made to commemorate Israel's pilgrim days and the holiday known as *The Feast of the Tabernacles*. Here Lazarus sat with his master, in this leafy booth constructed from the boughs of living trees.

He reclined his ailing body on cushions and closed his eyes to let the smells of fish and rosemary and the sounds of the women cooking in the house comfort him. His master sat on a rush mat, so quiet and still that it seemed to Lazarus as though only the body of his master was before him, while his true essence was very far away.

Lazarus closed his eyes again and his thoughts turned to arduous journeys, to rain and to sun, to being hunted and to fleeing. In his dream, he saw his master sending the followers away to the townships to proclaim him, and he saw himself journeying home with the women to Bethany.

For a moment the mislaid world returned, and he opened his eyes. He was in the booth. He heard the women arguing in the house. He saw his master. His eyes closed, and he dove down again, into half dreams where he heard his master's words:

'You must forsake not merely your worldly riches, which are easy to sacrifice, Lazarus, but those riches of your old soul, the riches of other lives,' he said to him. 'You must become like a poor man who has not even a loin cloth; like a little child that is not ashamed to stand naked before God. Only then will you enter the Kingdom!'

When Lazarus opened his eyes again he realised his master was returned, and was looking upon him with kind concern.

Jesus said to him, 'I have been in Jerusalem … in secret.'

Lazarus shivered. 'At this moment … as you sat in contemplation?'

'My spirit is still able to leave the body, and so I can speak in the Temple while I sit here with you … this ability will not last.'

At that moment Magdalena entered the booth to bring Lazarus a cool cloth. She was so beautiful to his eyes, his little sister, whom his master had saved from the madness of her visions.

His master looked upon her with love, for she was also his spirit pupil. He said to her, 'Stay a while … I must speak with both of you.'

She sat at his feet.

'Listen to me Magdalena, Lazarus … soon the time comes for my sacrifice, but first must come the sign.'

Magdalena fell to weeping, and Christ Jesus put a soothing hand on her head and said to her tenderly, 'Weep not, for you will be the first to see me when I am raised, so be strong. For now, we will speak of the last sign that must be performed before the Son of Man can go to his death. Your brother has near discarded the garment of his body, and soon he will pass into spiritual worlds. He will die, and you and your sister will have to prepare his body for the burial. You will sit with him and hold him in your heart, you will be the guardian of his soul, Magdalena, while Martha will be the guardian of his body. Do this until I return. Have faith, support your brother as you have supported me. For in every death there is a rebirth. Wait for my call when the last sign shall be accomplished. I will raise your brother from the world of the dead. I will do this to reveal to all that Christ lives in me.' He looked to Lazarus then; 'Remember Lazarus, my brother, this is only a preparation, for you will live long. Years from now you shall see the heavens part above you, and all those things which you shall witness, in your dying and becoming, will be made more clear to you. Your heart shall catch on fire and your soul shall be as a parchment on which God shall write his words. This is not the end for you, but it is only enacted to show the glory of God in me.'

Lazarus could barely hear these things. He felt a sudden peace overtake him. The world was still. Quiet was the sea and air, and the very heavens came to rest, and among this harmony did his acquiescent soul lift up from him.

And that is when he entered the Kingdom.

CHAPTER 51

THE SIXTH SIGN

It was the Feast of the Tabernacles, a time of great commemoration in the Hebrew Calendar, and Claudia Procula, having heard that Jesus was in Jerusalem and discoursing with the Pharisees at the temple, made hasty preparations to see him.

She took herself out into the streets dressed like a Jewess so as not to attract undue attention, and it was not long before she sensed, as she made her way through the crowds, the presence of Gaius Cassius, following some way behind her.

It was her custom in those days to alert him of her movements by way of a note sent with Susannah. She understood that he followed her not only because it was his charge but also because between them an understanding had formed, bound not by duty, but by a friendship grown over many months as they now and again travelled to see Jesus.

This understanding had made her feel strangely disloyal to her husband, and there were many times when she almost told him of her doings, of her soul's newfound joy, and the wide horizons that lay open to her heart's senses. She wanted to tell him that she considered herself a follower of Jesus, but each time something had prevented it, and the words had come into her mind – not yet.

She considered that these feelings of guilt may have been the cause of the frightful dream that had woken her in the night and left her drenched in perspiration.

In the dream, she had seen herself walking into a world that above and below was the colour of blood and storm cloud. Into this world, she walked towards a great gathering of people, dressed in white. In her arms she carried a ream of the finest white cotton, which was taken up by the gentle breezes and began to unspool behind her. Where it touched the ground, it became soaked in blood. The smell of blood was everywhere, and a terrifying sense of urgency. She sensed something of grand and frightening proportions awaited her beyond the crowds, but the crowds would not let her pass, and she knew the reason: within her lived the cursed blood of the Caesars! How could she cross the threshold to see the portent of her dream, when it was sure to send her mad, as it had sent her forebears before her?

When she woke she could taste blood and smell it on her hands, and the smell did not go, no matter how many times she washed them.

Distressed now to think on it, she made her way to the temple on the Octave of the feast. As she pushed past the worshippers and entered through the porches to the court of the Gentiles, she thought only of finding a way to Jesus to beg him to cleanse her blood of the sins of her forefathers.

When she saw him she was filled with hope. He stood in that grand court like a dream, for it seemed as if the day's light alone had collected itself into the form of his shape. He was speaking to the Pharisees and her heart swelled to hear his voice resounding with authority. But something caused her to pause, something not outwardly apparent, a fidget of the eye, a whispered word, she could not tell. She looked for Cassius but he was nowhere in sight. Of course! The man's eyes were not good and she was dressed like a Jewess! How could he tell her among so many? Her husband's words of warning rang in her ears now, and into her heart came Jesus' voice.

"I am the foundation of the very world! I am not only one with Abraham, but I was before Abraham was!'

The Pharisees seemed to have become incensed. A great commotion erupted all around her. She could not understand it for she only knew the language of the people, the simple and beautiful Aramaic. She knew nothing of the harsh language of the Pharisees, whose whipping words struck the crowds like blows, fomenting their anger and causing them to take up stones to throw at Jesus.

She felt herself pale. She thought of her dream – the blood, the crowds! Was this the meaning of it? Would they kill him now? Would they stone one of their own, in their very temple? She pressed through the crowds to find Cassius. Surely he would prevent it! But the people crushed forward, clamouring to get to Jesus. She slipped on her own skirts then, and fell into the tangled darkness of arms and legs.

She could not breathe.

She heard shouts in Latin, and the world of bodies above her parted, and a hand heaved her up and away.

Dazed, she felt herself taken through the throngs. Pilate's guards were around her and Cassius was hitting out at the people to make them give way. He yelled and spat and cursed as his strong hands helped to move her out of the court.

'Make way! Make way, you animals!' he shouted.

Trumpets sounded and soldiery on horses arrived and the people dispersed in fear. Beyond the crowds, through the confusion of voices and bodies, she looked and saw Jesus. This time he was stooping over a blind man. How he had escaped the madness she did not know.

When Jesus looked up again, his eyes found hers, and into her mind he said these words:

See this man born blind? His parents have not sinned, nor has he sinned in this life, but his blindness comes from a former life in which he had sinned. I can work with what passes from life to life; I can make null and void the consequences of your former lives, so that you can start anew.

She saw him spit on his hands and take up the clay-dirt at his feet. He made a paste with it and used it to anoint the man's eyes.

Now the words of the poet, Virgil, came to her lips:

What a sublime vision for the eye of the seer! A superman walks on earth again! A hero ... a new Dionysus ... a ruler over the hearts of men ... full of peace!

This was not Jesus alone she could see, for she could see something else, yes ... that Sun-like godhood ... the Christ in him!

‡

'What happened to her, Lea?'

'Claudia, who had once been Virgil, was born again, *pairé*, nine hundred years after Christ, as a blind child.'

'A blind child? But what had she done to deserve it ... is this compensation again?' I said, squinting and rubbing my own tired eyes.

'Listen, *pairé*, her father was the Duke of Eticho, and he wished to kill his own child because he did not want his vassals to say that her blindness was caused by some fault of his. But the mother spirited the baby away and later, when the child was baptised by a Bishop, her sight was restored and she was given a new name, Odile, which means Sun of God.'

'Saint Odile? Oh, my! Claudia Procula becomes Saint Odile! There is something in that!' I thought on it. 'Virgil loved that blind poet Homer! He was born as Claudia who befriended a near blind man, and she was then born blind in another life, because she remembered the healing of the blind man, is that what you are saying?'

'Blindness is the key to all her lives, as you say, *pairé*. In particular Jesus' healing. It lived so deeply in the soul of Claudia that it became a part of her body in the next life.'

I took a moment to ponder it. 'We are not meant to escape the endless wheel of incarnations, are we, Lea? We are meant to return again and again, as Buddha told Jesus. Perhaps we have been like the Essenes in our faith!' I fell into despondency to think this. 'We have kept ourselves pure by closing ourselves off from the world. Perhaps we too have become prideful? Have we not forsaken the earth as a place of the devil, and do we not see the incarnation of the soul again and again as a punishment? We even take the *consolamentum* so that we may never return!'

'But the Catholics too, have erred, *pairé,* since they do not see past one life, and have bound themselves to dogmas and laws like the rabbis. Your faith has grown too light, and the Catholic faith has grown too heavy. One sees only purgatory, while the other sees only heaven … the ideal lives between them, in the middle,' she said.

CHAPTER 52

SEVEN

In those days I wondered: Why must morning always come with such regularity? Why can I not remain a vassal of the everlasting dominion of the night? Only fools love the day more, for the night is like death to them!

It was not so to me. I lived for the night.

One such night, waiting for Lea to come, I had a moment to look out onto the world outside the fortress. A heavy rain was falling to entice the buds on the trees and to attract the wild flowers from their beds. It reminded me of standing at the gates of the fortress a year ago, when I had the sense that I would not live to see a new spring. It had been a true sense, to my reckoning, for despite my newborn love of life and youthfulness, despite my open eyes and light-filled heart, I knew the end was near and the sadness I felt was not for death itself, but for a wasted life.

I heard a humming in my ear then, a bee, crawling on the windowsill. Strange it was to see a bee out at night, with her little wings drenched from the rain. Guilhabert's words returned to me. He had told me that I must seek the rose like a bee, and my thoughts turned now to those songs sung by troubadours, songs of a love so chaste that it recalled the love of a bee for a flower.

If I were a bee, then surely Lea was the rose!

I did not tell her my musings when she came, finally. I was ashamed and confused, elated and forlorn as I listened to her voice tell about the Mother of God and her concerns for Jesus, who had just returned from his travels to Bethany.

‡

Jesus seemed weary and old, and his face, which had once shone so brightly with the majesty of youth now waned, pale and dry, as if the fire in his soul had all but consumed the wood of his body.

These long months she had gradually come to know in her heart the measure of her son's destiny, of the pain and suffering he would have to undergo, and it caused her a deep sorrow. Perhaps her son sensed her sadness, for he began to spend long moments with her. They walked in silence together or sat in each other's presence in prayerful meditation, each feeling the wave-like proportions of the future hurrying towards them. Sometimes he touched her arm as she walked past, and she was full of comfort. At other times it was a look or a word that filled her soul with warmth and strength.

In one sense, the pain of these dragging days made her almost unable to breathe, and in another, her heart wished to hold back the time forever, for she wondered how she would endure it when it came? How long would last her strength? How long could she bear to witness the violence and hatred and death that were to be visited upon him?

Recently, Lazarus, the young man who had provided so well for all of them these many months, had become unwell. His sickness had grown worse and he had lain consumed with fever in the cool of the booth for most of the feast. He did not rise even when Nicodemus and Joseph of Arimathea came to warn of the desire of the Pharisees to seize her son.

Soldiers had been dispatched to look for him in every place and they must be careful. To add to this, the disciples began to return again, two by two, from their apostleship in the villages and towns of

Judea and Galilee. They brought more followers in their train, and now the household was consumed with activity and the forward march of things - the feeding and housing of so many men and women. And yet in the quiet of the afternoons, beneath the date palm in the walled garden, she found time to sit among the other women to listen to his teachings

These past months the women had marched in her son's train with their skirts tied around their ankles and their sandaled feet bound in cloths. They did not sway like the women from the cities when they walked, for they had learnt that to travel long distances one had to conserve one's strength. Now he was speaking to them without the men, of things only appropriate for the ears of women.

He said, 'Listen to me…men will rule over you only for a small time, for it is the task of the male to make a way in the world of matter, since it is the task of the mind to tear the world apart. But a future will come when what lives in the heart, what lives in you, will take precedence over the mind. What lives in you will unify the world, not tear it apart. Into your souls will be born a new spirit of *good will*, and it will not be male or female. Then the world will rejoice when a child is not born from the womb of a woman, but when the spirit is born in the heart, in the soul like a sun. Then shall healing come to the earth, for my spirit shall unite with my mother in heaven, and the earth itself will give birth to a new sun. This is the mystery of the blood, which I did unveil to the men when I raised Jairus' daughter, but they could not yet understand it, for only women who bleed can know it – how the blood shall have a sacred task in future times, the sacred task of fashioning the heart into a sun.'

These things he taught them because they were seven, since every truth has seven meanings and that is why wisdom has built her temple on earth with seven pillars.

'I tell you that I will be with you always,' he continued, 'even unto the ends of the earth. For even though I shall not be among you in this body I will return in the beating of your hearts and in the pulsing of your blood … here shall you always find me. This is what I mean when I say that you abide in me and I in you, like a bride and groom abide together in the bridal chamber of the heart. Soon I will be beaten and killed and my blood will spill over the earth. Even so, take heart! When I was conceived in the Jordan I died to the spirit. Thus, my death in the world will be a spirit birth! You will soon behold me as a man of sorrows but remember, I will soon be joyful and among you again. I shall rise again. Remember these things which I have spoken to you, for I tell these things to no man, since women were the first to think, to imagine and to remember, and they will be the first to see!'

After these teachings, her son gathered to him his male disciples and left for a place beyond the Jordan where John had baptised his followers. In the meantime, Lazarus finally succumbed to his fever and Martha fell into an inconsolable grief. She could not help in the preparations so it was left to herself and Magdalena to wash and dress the young man's body in linen cloths for his burial.

Magdalena sent word to Jesus and together the women waited, knowing, awake, mournful and praying. For they understood that the time had come: ancient time, the devourer of its children, had moved forward, despite all their efforts to restrain it.

CHAPTER 53

SCORPION~EAGLE

They came into Bethany and Judas followed last of all, his mind full of strange thoughts. The sun began to drop its bruised body into the godforsaken hills as they neared the township and the men were weary, having travelled since yesterday.

It was now more than three days since word had reached them of Lazarus' worsening sickness and all feared that he was dead. But Judas was not concerned for it, something else made his brow dark and his eyes aflame. That spirit which had plagued him these many months had begun to make a way into his head and he could feel it, rearranging the rooms of his mind. It wrapped around his heart to combine his disappointments, his hate and his lust into a poisoned leaven for his limbs.

For months now he had waited for Jesus to bring back the glory days of the Maccabees, but benevolence and kindness, patience and love were all that he had offered. In Judas' mind all the deeds of salvation enacted so inconspicuously by Jesus, whatever they might be, were worthless. Words of compassion and tolerance were not enough to change the world, only the sword could change it. Blood for soil!

It had taken him time to see it but finally Judas had realised that Jesus was not the Messiah. For revolution and war were not accomplished by a man deliberate in his desire to change nothing, but to leave all men free.

The other disciples spoke of Jesus as the Son of Man. They spoke of how he had fed thousands, how he had quietened storms and produced otherworldly transfigurations of his being. Judas had seen nothing and yet he had been with them always. How could they have seen what he had not? He supposed that they had seen dreams ... only dreams ... and even now none of them could see what he could see: that even in his body, once so youthful and strong, Jesus was less vigorous and obviously headed for decay, like a wasted old man.

But something more had stirred his hate and made his rebellious spirit rip at his soul; a fire-laden desire had grown in Judas for the woman whom Jesus had named Magdalena.

From the first he had disliked her brother, the Hellenistic youth, Lazarus, whose life was lived in luxury and privilege and whose soul was the opposite of his. However, in Magdalena, Judas had sensed something akin to his own restlessness, a soul full of dammed up passions. But it was not only her soul that drew him, the woman's unparalleled beauty had also stirred his loins, a beauty that betrayed her attempts to mortify it or to conceal it. For no matter how many veils the woman wore, or how coarse was the garment draped over her shoulders, a fundamental note of allure was plucked from the instruments of his manhood each time he saw her, and he would have the song played in full!

Each night his daily thoughts rose up into the ecstasy of dreams full of the consummation of their mutual passion. In his dreams she had wanted him with a near crazed desperation, which had fired his virility and turned the seed inside him and churned the waters of his soul.

During those long months apart from her, when the women were sent to Bethany for their safety and the disciples were sent out, two by two, into the villages to announce the coming of the Kingdom, Judas' desire had matured and curdled in the darkness of his soul. So much so that by the time he had returned to the rich youth's house with the other disciples, it had sought, by any means, to find its satisfaction.

What dread force of hate had he felt then on finding that in his absence a love had grown between Magdalena and Jesus? A love that others said was warm and calm of heart, full of wide spheres and generous pastures – a love that cared nothing for itself but sought only the welfare of the other.

A love he did not understand!

He suffered when he saw how Magdalena's eyes were full of devotion for a man who would never take her in his arms and ignite her womanly passions.

Even Peter had seen it, and had asked Jesus, 'Why do you love her more than all of us?'

'Think of it like this, Peter,' Jesus had told him, 'I am the light of the world and your soul receives my light, my love, according to its capacity to see and to receive it. Magdalena's soul has more capacity than yours, and for this reason she receives more love than you.'

Judas, blinded by anger, schemed and schemed.

Many of the disciples were simple fishermen and they did not know that Jesus had, in the past months, revealed secrets of initiation to ordinary people. The betrayal of these secrets was punishable by death and it was for this reason that the Pharisees and Sadducees sought vehemently to find witness of it. Judas would use this to his advantage, an advantage that became clearer at Perea where Jesus finally unveiled his reason for leaving his ailing favourite, Lazarus, behind.

When Jesus told his worried disciples that Lazarus' sickness was not unto death, but only a sleep, that his sleep was for the glory of God, Judas had put two and two together. Lazarus was not dying but undergoing an initiation, and this was the reason why Jesus waited a day before returning to Bethany, since the initiation must last three days.

Jesus wanted to make a show of his power near to Jerusalem, not those powers that had made possible the raising of the dead boy at Nain, but something higher. Jesus would show to all men what lived only in the deepest recesses of the mystery temples: the raising of an initiate from the tomb, from the underworld of the dead!

Everything now made sense. Throughout their time in Perea when Jesus spoke of the good shepherd who gives life to his sheep he was pointing to himself as the priest who is the awakener of initiates. When he had spoken of other sheep which were not of the fold but which the shepherd must bring forth with a call he had been speaking of Lazarus. But when Jesus had said that he and the Father were one, Judas recognised these as mystery words. Words that meant a priest was ready to use the forces of the Father, that is, the forces of his will to awaken the body of an initiate and to raise him from his *temple sleep*.

No man came to the Father, that is, no man returned to the physical body from the three-day initiation sleep except through a priest!

Jesus was not a priest! This would be enough to destroy him.

Now, when they arrived some furlongs from the township of Bethany, they passed that desolate place of burial where tombs are set into the walls of the hills. Here, near what they called *The House of Rest*, many men stood mourning without their women, as was the custom. The sun was near gone over the land and made long shadows of those dry hills when the mourners turned to see Jesus and rushed to tell him of Lazarus. Soon Andrew was sent to fetch Martha and the woman came, in her drab attire of lament, with her face the colour of ashes.

She fell at Jesus' feet and told him that Lazarus was dead. She said that had Jesus had been here he could have prevented his death by performing a miracle. She said her sister Magdalena was full of grief and was sitting as still as death in the house waiting for him to come.

Judas watched Jesus carefully. His face showed pain for her sorrow and something else, which he could not discern. Jesus told Martha that Lazarus was not dead, for he was the resurrection and the life and all who believed in him though they were dead would live.

Lowering her head, she affirmed that he was Christ, the Son of God.

He said to her, 'Tell Magdalena I call her. That she must arise, for I need her by my side.'

Martha took herself away and many came to gather around, speculating as to what Jesus might do next, but Judas was taken by something else that emerged from out of the sun's vanishing luminance – the figure of Magdalena.

Judas saw only her tearful face gazing out from her mourning veil. And what a face it was! Arresting, inscrutable! His blood made skips in his veins. He was restless. He waited for her to glance his way. He beckoned her to look just once.

The women of the town, those who had followed Magdalena's steps, came upon the place where Jesus now stood with his disciples. They wept and pulled at their clothes while Magdalena bowed before Jesus – without so much as a fidget of a glance in Judas' direction.

He waited. Quiet fell over the day, save the groaning and moaning of the mourners.

'Had you been here my brother would not have died!' she said to him. But her words were spoken differently, for in them Judas noted a tone of thankfulness that Jesus had not come sooner! Could these be tears of joy?

Jesus raised Magdalena's chin with a finger and Judas saw then what passed between them, and this awakened in him a realisation. Rage and discontent surged through him and he could taste gall in his spit. He wanted to howl like an animal for the anguish of it – not only for its intimacy, which must be clear to all, but also for its complicity, since he now understood that Magdalena was in some way entangled in Lazarus' initiation.

His bowels were full of thorns.

'Where have you laid him?' Jesus asked her, his voice soft and tender, his eyes veiled with tears.

Judas knew that he was harnessing a force of love in his heart, a force that would raise his pupil from his death trance. Even those who were not his disciples sensed it, and said, 'Look how Jesus loves Lazarus!'

Magdalena showed Jesus a grave that was covered with a great round stone.

Would Jesus do it now? Judas leant his mind in his direction, daring him to do it.

Jesus walked to the grave and paused before it. Looking troubled he turned and his eyes fell on Judas. Judas felt a gasp come. Could Jesus have discerned the nature of his thoughts? But Jesus, for his part, was now telling those gathered around to take away the stone blocking the grave.

Martha was alarmed, 'But Lord! By this time there will be a smell, for he has been dead near four days.'

Jesus said to her, 'Martha, did I not just say to you that if you believed you would see God glorified in Lazarus?'

Martha lowered her eyes, 'Yes, Lord.'

When the men rolled away the heavy stone and returned to the crowds the people put the corners of their garments about their faces to fend off the smell. But there was no smell.

Jesus raised his eyes and said, 'Father, I thank you. That my word is one with you in spirit, and that you hear me always, but because of the people who stand by, I will say it out loud, that they too might hear how the Word, your Son, is in me, so that they might believe that you have sent Him to me and that through Him you and I are one!'

Judas knew that by saying this Jesus wished to reveal how in himself lived the Word, the Son of the Father, which he would make enter into Lazarus' soul to awaken him.

'Lazarus, come forth!' resounded the forbidden words.

Nature drew a breath. Above came the sound of a great eagle making its noises as it rose upwards over the mountains, circling the skies and falling away into the melting sun of day's end. The world followed it, and Judas also followed it as it soared aloft and died away. A thought, foreign to his experience, now crossed his mind: why could he not be like that bird, basking in the light of the sun with hopeful abandon? Why must he live always like a scorpion fearing the sun?

But this self-understanding was short-lived, for upon hearing a round of gasps his concentration was now returned to witness the beloved of Jesus, the initiate, coming from out of the black mouth of the cave bound with graveclothes.

'Loosen him and let him go!' Jesus told the women.

Martha, shocked, remained behind. Only Magdalena went to Lazarus to help. After that Jesus was thronged by all those who had come to the burial place, and was swept away to Bethany, but not before turning once more to look upon Judas.

That glance made a path clear from Judas' head to his heart. He understood now that he was standing upon the soil of freedom, between his hope and his fear. Here, it seemed to him, was a last occasion to love this man, to love him despite his urge to betray him, to recognise his greatness despite his impulse to follow his destiny.

But he could not.

The eyes, multi-coloured and endless-deep, held and held him until they held no more. Gasping, with his head turning in circles, Judas was let go and he sat upon a rock to get his breath back. It was a long moment before he could rise again and make his way to Bethany with his eyes tethered to the ground.

High above him the eagle scooped wind with its wings and circled him. Its eye ranged the sky … its gaze was upon him, unblinking, open, shut, perfect … but Judas did not see it.

Instead he told himself, 'The time for pruning has come!'

CHAPTER 54

ANOINTING

'What happened after that?' I asked Lea.

'Well, after his raising Lazarus did not follow his master to Ephraim with the other disciples but remained behind at Bethany with his sisters. He needed quiet, a time to recover. Don't forget, *pairé,* he had just returned from the realm of death and had to accustom himself to living in the world again.'

'What did he see in that realm of death, Lea, can you tell me?'

'In that realm he stood before Christ wearing only the loin-cloth of his soul and Christ baptised him with fire and He gave him a new name.'

'A new name?'

'Yes ... he named him John ...'

'Why another John, when there are so many?'

'Because the finest and most noble essence of John the Baptist would live with Lazarus from that time on, so that the two would be like one, and those who recognised this union called him Lazarus-John, or the apostle John.'

'The Apostle John! The writer of our Gospel?'

'Yes, *pairé.*'

I was astounded, speechless, overcome! I could not believe it! I took myself to the window to look out at the black night. 'But Lea, I had always thought that John was little John of Zebedee!'

'The difference between John the apostle and John the Evangelist,' she instructed me, 'will not be understood for a long time, *pairé*. But you will soon see how little John of Zebedee will allow Lazarus-John to replace him in the circle of followers. Even so, because of his selflessness, he will still maintain his place in the circle, through Lazarus-John.'

'So that is how the chain of love was bound between all Manicheans to John and his Gospel? John had once been Lazarus! Lazarus and the young man of Nain, who became Mani, had been united in common purpose by Christ!'

'Shall I go on?' Lea asked.

'Please …' I said coming back to the bench. I took the quill in one hand and put the other hand to my mouth, lest my heart leap out.

‡

Among these strange and awesome transformations, Lazarus-John felt as if a drop of divinity had fallen from out of Christ and had entered into his own being. The prophecy of Photismos, his teacher, had come true after all – the Word that had once overshone his soul from above, did indeed shine from inside him now and out to the world, so that he could say; not I, but the Christ in me.

It was six days before the Feast of Passover, and he was taken with this knowing as he helped his sisters prepare a supper for Christ Jesus and his disciples. They had only just returned to Bethany from Ephraim. On their arrival, his master had seemed full of exhaustion and had spent most of the day in meditation. Lazarus understood that he was preparing himself for his final entry into Jerusalem, and this would initiate all that would come after. And as Lazarus-John looked about him now at the faces of the other disciples, it was plain to see how fear had laid a grip on their souls because of it.

But he no longer felt fear, for he had died and had returned to life altered. In particular, his nights and days had lost their meaning. The hours passed unbroken by sleep, so that in the course of an unfolding day he could see, overlayed upon it, the fulfilment of the heavenly pattern he had seen in the night. This understanding of *above and below* made his vision threefold: he could see not only the present moment, but what had led to it from the past and what it would bring about in the future.

This peculiar knowledge cancelled out any notion of fear.

But Lazarus-John was never more aware that among his master's dearest disciples there were varying degrees of understanding. There were those who struggled to see beyond Jesus, the master who stood before them in a body that was crumbling and turning to dust. Then again there were those who had risen only to an imperfect understanding of Christ. In truth, he knew that in the future this would spawn great conflicts and men would argue as to the divinity of Jesus and the humanity of Christ and that many would die because of it. If only those who were closest to him could understand this perfect marriage of God and Man in its fullness, perhaps these conflicts might never come?

Lazarus-John knew that he had been raised for this very reason – because those around his master had failed to recognise the God in the Man. Lazarus would be the witness. He would be the only one capable of giving evidence of both the earthly Jesus and the heavenly Christ.

When the meal was over and the women had come into the room to listen a quiet fell over the evening. Lazarus-John observed how Judas' eye fell upon his sister Magdalena. She was kneeling before Christ Jesus preparing to anoint his feet with pure nard and to wipe them with her hair. The perfume filled the room with a sad blessing and made the air glow with warmth but it cast a shadow over Judas' face. His blood was boiling, and his anger was poorly hidden.

'Why does this wasteful woman not sell that ointment?' he blurted out. 'It would fetch more than three hundred silver coins for the poor, enough to feed a farmer for a year!'

Lazarus-John entered with his spirit into Judas and saw what was made plain by his words: his lustful heart.

Christ Jesus looked up. 'Why do you trouble her, Judas?' he said, gently. 'You have the poor with you always. Whenever you wish to serve them, you may do so. But you do not have me always! See how the heart of this woman is full of service? Death comes, my brothers, and when it comes I shall be anointed and ready because of this woman. She alone is capable of uniting me further with the God in me so that I may go to my death in the right way. That is why whenever this day is spoken of, this woman will be remembered for having loved me more than the worth of this costly ointment!'

Judas looked around at the other disciples, flying daggers from his eyes, but found no support for his outburst, not even from Peter, who did not like Magdalena. And so it was, Judas put a morsel in his mouth, and let it go. But Lazarus-John saw how crowded was the air around him with dark shadows, and he knew that in freedom Judas had chosen to hate.

CHAPTER 55

THE PUPIL

It was the afternoon of the 12th of Nissan, a time when Pilgrims and natives of Jerusalem were accustomed to come to the temple to mingle happily in the Court of the Gentiles, to partake of its cool airs and to listen to the discourses of the rabbis. Today was a restful day, for tomorrow throngs would gather here to purchase their paschal lambs. The next day they would return again for the slaying and the sacrifices, going home afterwards to make preparations for the Passover Feast.

Gamaliel was in the temple with Saul of Tarsus when Jesus and his disciples entered the court of the Gentiles through a porch.

Two days before, Jesus had made a triumphant entry into Jerusalem and had been welcomed with ecstasy, hope and joy by a people well acquainted with his healings and miracles. Yesterday however, he had overturned the tables of the vendors and money-changers in the temple, as he had done three years before, raising the ire of the Pharisees again. But the crowds continued, despite warnings against it, to throng to the temple each day to see Jesus when he came to teach.

These years he had followed Jesus' doings and had grown more and more concerned for him. He had come today to see for himself what had become of his pupil and friend.

Saul, who was beside him now, had also been his pupil in those early days. Soon he would be chosen by members of the Sanhedrin for ordination into the office of Rabbi, and Gamaliel could not prevent himself from pondering the parallels between the two men. However, among the similarities there were also great distinctions. Saul did not have the depth of feeling and understanding for the suffering of others that had been the guiding force of Jesus' life. Saul might have a brilliant mind, but it was full of stern impatience. He sensed that Saul's restless heart could either be guided towards the channels of wisdom, love and devotion, or become fired up by zeal into a blaze of wrath that was merciless in the judgement of others. And Gamaliel wondered how Saul would judge Jesus.

When Jesus began to speak the Pharisees entered the court enclosure. Having heard that he was returned to the Temple this day they had turned out in full force against him.

'You have no authority to teach, son of a carpenter!' said a scribe. 'You are no scholar, you are no rabbi, who has given you the right?'

From the sea of people one man called out, 'His plumb lines and saws have given him the right!'

Laughter rang out in the Temple and was reflected from its walls causing a great din.

Jesus waited for quiet. 'I will tell you by what authority I say these things,' he said, serenely. 'But only if you will answer me one question: Was the baptism of John inspired by a man or inspired by heaven?'

This threw the Pharisees and scribes into turmoil. Gamaliel knew the measure of his old pupil's wisdom. The Pharisees would be reckoning that if they said that John's baptism was from heaven, this in itself was an acknowledgement of Jesus' authority, for John had baptised him and recognised his mission; then again if they said that John's baptism was not inspired by heaven they would be disavowing John the Baptist, whom the people counted as a great prophet.

They shook their heads and shrugged their shoulders.

'You don't answer for fear of saying the wrong thing. You see how dishonest you are?' Jesus said to them.

The people nodded and smiled to themselves, for they too had seen it.

'For this reason I shall not discuss with you further by what authority I do these things!'

Jesus turned to the people now and told them a parable, which made plain to all how God would overlook the priests and seek out others who were more worthy.

The Pharisees, in their cunning, took another tack. They asked him if a Jew should give tribute to Caesar.

Gamaliel was breathless in anticipation for his answer, for if he answered yes he would be going against Judaic law, and if he answered no he would incur the wrath of Rome.

'Why do you tempt me with such questions, which are only snares? Give me a coin that I may see it.' Jesus said. When he had inspected it he returned it to the scribe. 'Whose image is it on this coin?' he asked him.

The man said, 'Caesar Tiberias.'

'Well then, give unto Caesar Tiberias the things that are his, and to God the things that are God's.'

There was a great murmur.

One Pharisee said, 'Jesus, son of a Carpenter, are you not from the line of Nathan? The Messiah is not destined to come out of the line of Nathan but from Solomon's line!'

Jesus said, 'The Messiah is the son of *which* man?'

The scribe replied, 'The Messiah is destined to be the son of David!'

Jesus looked at this a moment. 'Well then … if what you say is true, how can David call the Messiah his Lord, if the Messiah is also his son?' He waited for an answer and none came. 'You do not know how to answer because you do not see that the Messiah is not only a man born of a blood line, but that he is also a God born into a man through the spirit!' Then to the people he said, 'Beware of the Sadducees, the Scribes and the Pharisees who are hypocrites and liars and distort the scriptures to suit their means! They tell you to do as they say but not as they do, since they say much and do nothing themselves! They burden all of you with heavy oaths and vows but they do not live by them because they are not concerned with the goodness of their hearts, but only with how good they look in their rich fineries, and whether they are given the best seats in the synagogues, and the uppermost rooms at feasts! Woe unto you, Scribes and Pharisees, you hypocrites!' He pointed to them. 'You shut up the doors to the Kingdom of Heaven because you don't want to concern yourselves with it, and yet you bar the way for others so that they cannot enter! Woe unto you, Scribes and Pharisees! You beautify the outside of the cup, but within it is ugly and full of filth … don't you realise that God can see into your hearts?'

A Pharisee called out, thrusting his aged head at him, 'Who are you?'

He looked at the man, 'You read the face of the sky and of the earth, but you cannot recognise the Messiah, for whom you have so long prepared! You have prayed for deliverance, you have mourned and called out to God and you have beaten your breasts and ripped at your clothes for a Messiah and now that he stands before you, you do not know him! You do not know how to read this moment, which you have longed for, so how can you escape your own damnation?'

There was a thunder in the heavens. All looked up to see if the world would soon end.

Gamaliel's eyes were opened then, and for a moment he saw the sky part over Jesus. He saw wings and eyes and thrones and lights and he could taste honey on his lips, a sweetness in his soul. What a mighty thing was this?

He laughed, happy as a child.

'The Christ in me must die!' Jesus said then, 'But when I am lifted up from the earth I will draw all men with me!'

'How can you say that you are Christ and that you must die and be lifted up, when they say that the Messiah will live forever?' a man cried out.

Gamaliel, overwhelmed by his vision, now turned to look at the man who had said it. It was Saul.

Jesus regarded Saul with a grave face, 'Life on earth is but a passing moment to you, but life on earth for me shall be eternal and it will only come when I die. I have chosen to make the earth my heaven. I will light up the earth, for I am the light of the world!'

The people were hushed by these words.

'And while you have the light before you, believe in it, so that you can also one day have the light inside you!'

Gamaliel's eyes were full of light! He looked to Saul and realised that he was full of stern hatred. He was appalled and said to him, 'Saul, did you not hear it? Did you not see it and hear it and know it in your heart the voice of God?'

Saul let his dark eyes fall upon his teacher a moment, before he answered, 'I heard nothing except arrogance and blasphemy! Look at him! Boasting about being the Messiah! If he keeps up this show he will train the stupid people to forsake the faith of their fathers when they should be preparing for the true Messiah! If I had it my way I would have this pretender stoned!'

Gamaliel held those eyes full of rage and he remembered Jesus' words to him on that day of parting so many years ago. He had told him that the Messiah would not be recognised by the rabbis if they continued to create an image of him in their minds that did not fit the truth. Gamaliel could see now the veracity of those words, for Saul would never see the Messiah in Jesus, since Jesus did not fit the image of an awesome, angry God come to pronounce judgment on all those who did not follow the law!

The realisation of this warning, spoken so long ago by his old pupil, made Gamaliel full of despair, for it made him realise something else – what lived in the heart of Jesus, that light of lights, was the Kingdom that was promised! This was Christ, the hope of all Jews and the consolation of Israel!

Gamaliel remembered cautioning Jesus that the priests could unmake him with just one word, and his answer resounded now in his heart,

'The priests may unmake me and perhaps they will … that's true, but they can never unmake the truth … that, rabbi, is imperishable.'

Gamaliel fell to his knees.

CHAPTER 56

BETRAYAL

Caiaphas, the high priest and chairman of the Sanhedrin, sat among his priests and rabbis in the cold room lit by torches and bothered by draughts, trying to prevent himself from scratching the terrible itch, which like worms crawled under the skin of his back.

His physicians were all bent in the direction of the Pharisees, he was sure of it, for they all agreed his itch was due to transgressions of the law: he had either eaten honey not blessed separately, or crumbs from the table of a gentile, he had either kindled the incense before entering the sanctuary or, worst of all, spilt the water of libation upon the altar on the Feast of Tabernacles.

Incantations had not worked, nor had the poultice of onion, aniseed and saffron, which he had worn day and night for a year and whose smell, being combined with his natural perfume, caused revulsion in all those who came near him.

How he hated the Pharisees! He hated them because he was a Sadducee and it was only natural that a Priest of the line of Levi should hate such a mongrel breed; for they were a plague on the earth with their endless laws and their predilection for religious concerns. It was ill fortune indeed the Sanhedrin was composed of both Sadducees and Pharisees in somewhat equal parts, since it forced him to be conciliatory and amicable to these upstarts! Meaning he must live always with one eye keenly upon the Romans, to whom he owed his office and its privileges, and the other upon those Pharisees, who hated all things Roman, and would, by the by, subject even the light of the Sun itself to their laws!

In truth, he did not put them beyond causing his itch with their evil eye!

But it was not only his eyes that were made to stretch to unnatural performances. Caiaphas' ears, too, were also pulled in diverse directions. One ear was reserved for his father-in-law, the bilious Ananias, whose intrusions, disapproval and superior scorn he suffered day in and day out, while the other ear was reserved for his wife, the old man's daughter, whose only trace of womanliness was her constant nagging.

He surmised that his itch came, therefore, from a stretching of his soul in every direction at once! A stretch that his poor skin was forced to follow! Of course he prickled and broke out in sores!

Oh, the hour was late! And beyond his bodily distress his head was also full of inconvenience. Still, he could blame no one but himself, for he had called this council together at this hour so that it might be held in secret. For only this way could the exclusion of those members of the Sanhedrin known to be sympathisers of that annoying Jesus of Nazareth be guaranteed. Joseph of Arimathea, Gamaliel and Nicodemus had succumbed to Jesus' soft words and he knew they would have proved unhelpful to his plans.

For his part, Caiaphas had grown a special hate over the years for the arrogant Nazarene, a hatred that had fired up the festering wounds on his back whenever he thought of him. Two nights ago, quite alone, he betook himself to the sanctuary to consult his priestly oracle. He threw the sacred stones over the altar and in their patterns he had discerned death for Jesus of Nazareth at the hand of Jerusalem's enemy. He made a resolve, then and there, to side with power: he would sneak in first and make a present of the insurrectionist.

Afterwards, he had sent his guards to seize Jesus, but the stupid men had returned time and again saying that many spoke like Jesus and looked like Jesus, so they had not known whom to seize!

Now in the cold hall a sudden raised voice brought him to this testing moment.

'Caiaphas! This man does too many miracles! He raises the dead from the *temple sleep* in broad daylight and the people are in a frenzy over it! Something must be done!'

The council erupted in agreement:

'Blasphemer!' said an ungainly Pharisee.

'Devil!' said a Sadducee with sheep's eyes.

A crusty old rabbi shook his fist. 'Conjuror of magic tricks!'

'No, he is more ... he is the son of Beelzebub!'

The roar of their words was so fierce that Caiaphas thought their vehemence had seized the torches at that moment to make them flap.

'What will he do next?' said a pale priest with no teeth, 'If we let this man go on his way the people will believe in him and what will that mean for us?'

'I'll tell you what it shall mean, Jeroboam!' answered another. 'The Romans won't stand for it and our temple and nation will be taken from us!'

Supporters of this rang out their loud approval.

A Pharisee tried to rise above the din, 'All week he is at the temple! We've tried to trap him and make him speak blasphemy, but he twists our laws around his tongue!'

A Sadducee called Simon snarled, 'That's because you have so many laws, that loopholes can be found everywhere – loopholes big enough for thieves and murderers to crawl through!'

Rabbi Tolomei, said, 'Without laws, we are no better than animals! But you would not know it, being an animal yourself!'

'Listen to me, to rid ourselves of this animal, we have to forget laws!' The toothless priest countered.

The room broke out into a tirade of disagreement and insult. When a representative of the Pharisees spoke, a representative of the Sadducees countered it, and so the meeting degenerated into a free for all.

'He healed a blind man on the Sabbath! This is enough to convict him!' said one.

'But it is permissible to pour wine over the eyelids on a Sabbath!' said another. 'Since it's considered washing!'

'On the eyes, yes, you fool! But not *in* the eyes! And not with spit, since that constitutes a remedy and remedies are forbidden on the Sabbath from the neck upwards. Besides, he made clay with his spit and applied it to the eyes – this is work!'

'He has transgressed the Sabbath many times!'

'But the people love him!'

'Even the proselytes, those hateful Greeks, are spellbound! What shall we do?'

'Cut his throat!' said a priest.

'This is above the law!' said a rabbi. 'I will not stand for it!'

'Can we not appeal to Rome?' asked another priest.

'If we bring Rome into it, you idiots, what shall the people say – that we are licking the skirts of our enemies!' retorted a rabbi.

'This is no good! You are all fools, the people will revolt against us, for they love him!' snapped another.

Caiaphas was fed up. He stood, but no man noticed it. Finally, he yelled, 'Silence!' And there was quiet. 'We can pay men to hate him and those that love him shall not wish to do so when they learn that I shall impose the highest excommunication extending to all places and all persons on any man who comes forward in support of Jesus. Meaning that such a man must be considered dead by his relatives, for he shall never again have intercourse with his family and his people. He shall be shown the road out of the city and told never to return again to the temple. Who would risk such a fate to defend a blasphemer?'

There was a sudden silence.

'But how can you do this?' the toothless priest said, 'Since any accused man has the right to answer to accusations and to witnesses who can speak on his behalf without fear of excommunication!'

Caiaphas waved it away, 'Yes, yes ... we shall listen benevolently to our little heretic, and it is my guess that if the right questions are asked, he shall profane the name of God again. He must do so before the crowds, so that thereafter it is clear that *whoever* confesses that he is the Christ is likewise profaning the name of God and shall suffer the same fate he suffers!'

'What you speak of is unlawful to my ears!' cried the ugly rabbi. 'Such doings are evil!'

Caiaphas bore down his condescension over the Pharisee and said, quite plainly, 'Is it not fate that this man should die? Is not everything foreordained to the Pharisees?'

Another spoke out against it, 'If we do not follow the law this council shall be defiled!'

Caiaphas stamped his foot and brought down his crosier at the same time. 'Silence! In this Jesus is right ... you Pharisees *are* hypocrites! You say that pure water does not lose its purity, despite the vessel, and yet you cannot see how this council will not lose its purity for having dirtied its hands to cleanse itself of a defiler!'

A great commotion erupted, one side against the other, until Caiaphas, irritated and itchy, stood and raised his crosier.

An uneasy quiet fell again.

He felt a chill in his kidneys. 'No matter how you see it, that man will bring our nation to unrest and possibly to its ruin! Shall an entire nation perish because of one man? No! One man shall die for a nation! We will take him, trial him, and let him answer our questions. In this way our conduct will be lawful.'

The room broke out again.

'But how do you propose to take him, Caiaphas? No one knows which one he is, for he and all his followers look the same and they speak the same way, one moment one speaks and then another?'

'Kill any one member of his group and you will put fear into them all!' answered an old Sadducee.

At this point Ananias interjected with his thin voice, 'I disagree! If we take the wrong man Jesus will continue to foment the people. Even our guards are deceived by him!'

The elders consulted with one another and the room was again abuzz with conversation.

One man stood and said, 'How are we to know with certainty which is the right man?'

Caiaphas sat down full of satisfaction, since this man had asked the question he had been waiting for. 'Only one of the disciples, one close to him can say which one he is. And one of his disciples has come and is now among us!'

The gathering of elders looked to where Caiaphas was pointing, to the cold shadows of one of the yawning arches. From it emerged a man, dark of hair and eye and red of beard. He moved out of the inky hollow like a wild beast coming from a thicket, looking about him with the cold eye of suspicion, not knowing if a snare or an arrow awaited him.

A shiver of whispers was sent running through the small council at the sight of him.

Caiaphas grinned to his very ears, but something caught his eye then … something in the bearing of the man bespoke an exchange with death, something mildly disconcerting. It was as if to look at this man called Judas, was to look into the horrid depths of one's own soul and to find beasts hidden therein. His heart thumped. His fellows must have seen it for a chill silence was poured out over the room. A momentary thought came to Caiaphas and it caused him to hold his breath; was he making a bargain with a man, or was this the devil himself, which stood before him? And if a devil, what would befall Israel from such a bargain?

'He is a member of the Sicarri!' said one.

'What if the Romans hear of it!' said another.

Among these words Caiaphas continued holding his breath until he could hold it no more, and when he let it out, the thought went with it and was dispersed about the room, and he saw it for how it was – these days one could not choose one's instruments.

'His name is Judas of Cariot,' Caiaphas said, 'one of the disciples of Jesus and he is a friend of Pontius Pilate. He offers us a solution to all our problems. Come forward, Judas and tell us your proposal.'

Judas spoke with eyes shifting from this to that. His words in Hebrew were fine, very near scholarly, and his voice was an odd mixture of passion and practicality, 'There is no way for you to tell which of them is Jesus without me,' he said, 'the others all take his place and he speaks through them … their love for him prevents you from knowing who he is.'

'Yes, yes, get to the point!' Caiaphas said, desiring that all of it should move along. 'Have you come to tell us what we already know?'

'I can show you which one he is!' Judas let it out all in one go.

The room exploded with conversations and rumbles and utterances.

'And why would you do this, Judas of Cariot? For advantage … or … money?' Caiaphas said, looking askance at Ananias with a smile of satisfaction.

Judas hid behind his dark brows and said nothing.

'Money then!' Caiaphas cried merrily, 'Silver, the colour of the soul … in return for betrayal!'

The word betrayal seemed to sting Judas. 'It is Israel that is betrayed!' he burst out. 'He is not the Messiah that was promised!'

A ring of laughter circulated the room.

'Really? And I wonder if you are the *traitor* that was promised?' Caiaphas said, to a further chorus of laughter. He leant forward and threw a bag at Judas, like a bone to a dog, and watched him bend low to catch it.

When Judas straightened he did not draw the string to peer inside the bag.

'Thirty pieces,' Caiaphas informed the elders, 'You can count it if you like,' he said to Judas, 'that is the measure of your master's worth!'

'How should I point him out?' Judas said.

'Where does he spend the Passover feast?' Caiaphas asked.

'In the cenacle of the Essene house.'

Caiaphas pursed his lips in concentration. 'He cannot be seized there, it is a sanctuary erected over David's tomb. No. He will be protected there. You will have to wait until he goes out. Take the guards to him then, when the people are in their houses asleep, so that it is done quietly and with a minimum of fuss.'

Judas hesitated, and Caiaphas grew concerned that the man was developing a late pang for his wrongdoing.

'What will you do to him?' Judas said, finally.

'Do to him?' Caiaphas raised his brow, a little amused. He prepared to flick away this annoying insect called Judas. 'That is no longer your concern, for you are on different ground now, since you have sold your loyalty. Go earn your wages!' As he said it he made a gesture of dismissal and the man stood a moment looking about him, unsure of what to do, before giving them his back and running out of the chamber, like a phantom into the night.

Caiaphas was weary. He put his staff on the stone dais and, leaning on it for support, stood.

Glancing about with his mind already contemplating a good scratch against a rock wall, he said,

'We go!'

CHAPTER 57

LAST SUPPER

I look behind me now to see that the sky is near tinged with a soft promise of light. How different everything is from this place below the fortress!

I remember that terrible night, when the garrison tried to take back the barbican. A detachment of men had traversed the narrow space between it and the fortress, to come upon the French by surprise. All had gone well until one of them disturbed a rock and alerted the enemy. A terrible fighting had broken out on the steep slopes then and our men had tried to make a hasty retreat back to the fortress, but they found the narrow pass blocked from behind. The valiant knights of Pierre Roger de Mirepoix fought desperately to break through the barrier of knights and archers. Thankfully, they managed to make a way to the gates, dragging the wounded behind them before the French could storm the fortress, but not before countless knights and soldiers fell to their deaths.

I hope we do not find their bodies scattered along our path. What grief would we feel then? I do not wish to think on it.

Once inside the gates, our knights and archers fought to repel the Crusaders, some of whom had pushed their way in as far as the forecourt where a skirmish had broken out.

In that terrible commotion the wounded were set down in any place available. It was dark and only a few torches were lit, making it difficult to see, but the smell of blood and the cries of pain directed us to those who were dying. I went from man to man, each more wounded than the next by way of sword or arrow fire. All of them wanted the *convenenza*; the consoler, the Holy Spirit, which had been promised to every man in John's Gospel. At the time I was troubled about whether I should give it, though I knew the gesture would offer such a comfort that I could not, in all conscience, withhold it.

That was when the Marquésia de Lantar came to me, and I hardly recognised her due to my panic and the darkness. She was old and determined: she wanted the *consolamentum*.

'Why now, Marquésia? In this turmoil!'

'I will go to help, and I do not wish to die without it,' she said.

'Come, what can you do? There are younger persons who can do such tasks.'

'It was a woman who killed Simon de Montfort!' she said with some pride. 'In all that fighting in Toulouse, a woman threw a rock from the barricades and it hit that devil right between the eyes and killed him! I don't want to kill a man, *pairé*, but I will offer to help with the wounded; that, at least, I can do.'

I thought of that young boy wandering the fortress alone, the child who could not speak and whose eyes penetrated deep into the world. I asked her about her charge,

'Will you not think of him?'

'Come now, *pairé*, you and I both know I will not leave this place! Whether I die helping or I die on the pyre … it is all the same … the boy will be taken care of … he is not destined to die here. I have already arranged for my son-in-law to have the troubadour take him away.'

Screams tore the night in two then. I could barely see the Marquésia's determined face. I took her hastily aside.

'If you receive the *consolamentum* you will not be able to deny it, since to deny the Holy Spirit is the greatest sin … is that clear to you?'

'Yes, *pairé*,' she said, 'I know it.'

'You wish to embrace the faith?'

'Yes, *pairé*, bless me.'

'Then kneel, my dear.'

I asked her the ritual questions and she answered them, and then came time for the solemn promise.

'Firstly,' I said, 'you must dedicate yourself to God, and to John's Gospel. You must never lie, never take an oath, never have any contact with a man, nor kill an animal, nor eat meat …'

'I promise,' she said.

'And you must promise never to betray your faith, no matter what death awaits you.'

'I promise.'

I gave her the benediction and placed the Gospel of John near for her to kiss, now my hands found her head and I prayed for the Holy Spirit to descend upon her. I said the Lord's Prayer as I had done countless times, but now a peculiar thing happened. It seemed to me that I was not hearing my voice alone, but another voice, a higher voice, a voice weaving with mine. Recollection of the words of the Bath-Kol came to me, recollections of the transfiguration, and all of the words spoken by Christ Jesus. They welled inside me, I could feel the mighty power of their wisdom entering into me, and oh! What a love did I then feel to know it! A love more rapturous than words can tell! The light of the spirit flowed through my hands like fire, a flame of gleaming colours and lights that came pouring out from me into the Marquésia to make her glow. Between us, wisdom moved the soul to pictures and I saw how Christ lived in me and in the Marquésia. I saw how He lived in every man who came and went, both within the fortress and without. He was in every child and woman, He was even in the inquisitors and the French who fought us.

I don't know how long we stood there, the Marquésia and I, locked in the flow of heaven's grace, only a moment perhaps, and yet it seemed like hours. When the spirit finally let go of us I was left expanded, panting and shaken. I looked at the form of the Marquésia as she knelt and told her she was pure now, blameless like a rose. I touched her back with the Holy Book, and she stood and was paused a moment. I could sense that she had felt the strength of the spirit, as I had felt it.

'Thank you, *pairé*,' she said, wiping her face, perhaps wet with tears. 'I have always wondered how I would feel when I received the *consolamentum*. Now I know it does not matter how I feel ... but how Christ feels in me! That is what matters!' she said this, and walked away from me.

For my part I stood in that court with the sounds of battle fading to nothing and no other noise save the beating of my heart in my ears. And in that moment I knew without a doubt that among the errors of our faith we had managed to understand one truth, that it was possible for every person to receive the Holy Spirit. I also knew that despite our suffering, or perhaps because of our suffering, this understanding was destined to be our most important gift to the world.

When I fell out of this peaceful reverie and returned to the world of men I saw that the garrison had managed to repel the French assailants. They had retreated to the barbican and the gates were closed again. So many lay dying I could not walk without stepping over the mutilated bodies.

Two nights later Lea came again; she said she would tell of the crown of all earthly misunderstandings.

'I will show you how a God died an earthly death in the body of a man and how He raised this man to a God.' She said, and I opened my spirit's heart to her.

As she began to weave her wonders into my soul I imagined that I was walking a path lit by the light of an Easter moon; I imagined that ahead of me stood a diaphanous apparition, paused, with her hand outstretched. On her brow, the evening star spread its rays like wings, and made her gleam like a silver ghost in the moonlight.

She asked me, 'What comes before love?'

'Faith,' I told her.

'Then do not be tempted to sleep, *pairé*,' she said, 'For it is on the eve of Passover, upon the sun's decline into the bosom of the night that the end begins; when the first three stars become visible and the threefold blast of the trumpets from the Temple announce the commencement of the Feast. Now, more than ever … faith is needed.'

I opened my eyes and I realised that I was sitting at my table and that the quill, having fallen from my hand, had made a blot on the parchment. I realised too that I had been listening to Lea and dreaming her words to life.

‡

On the south side of Mount Zion, there stood a property owned by Nicodemus and Joseph of Arimathea, which they had given over to the Essenes of Jerusalem for their celebrations. Here, in an upper room called the cenacle, a room reached only from the outside by a staircase, Jesus gathered with his disciples for the celebration of the Passover feast.

The room glowed from the warmth of firelight, and from the windows there came only the scant light of the silver moon rising now in the ocean of black above. The tables, set like a horseshoe, followed the shape of the room and were surrounded by divans upon which the disciples reclined. On the middle divan sat his master, John sat to his left, and on the right sat Judas, with the rest dispersed here and there, according to their fellowship.

The tumultuous events of the past week had given way to a contemplative mood, and a renewed feeling of gloom and foreboding began to fall over those present, which the oncoming night made more real. They could hear the whispering of an unearthly wind that whistled around the walls of the houses, and made the trees shiver – made John shiver. This wind recalled to him the stories of that first Passover, and the sweeping destruction that had been visited on the people of Egypt by the angel of death. That destruction had passed over the houses whose doors were painted with the blood of the lamb. A thought now came to John:

A blood sacrifice had once saved the people.

He thought on this as the others ate and talked quietly among themselves, as the women came to refill the cups with wine and the baskets with the unleavened bread. When his eyes fell on Christ Jesus he was taken by his radiant presence and another thought came, like a fish glimmering below the surface of a stream:

He is that image handed down from generation to generation. Jesus is the true Passover lamb! He must die to save Israel!

Full with this realisation he looked about him, but realised that none of his fellows had seen it, they were hanging on his master's words.

'I have desired to eat this Passover with you,' he said to them, 'before I suffer my sacrifice ... for I say to you that I will not eat again until the Kingdom of God has fulfilled its task in my body.'

He took a basket full with unleavened bread and gave thanks for it and began breaking it into small pieces and handed it to those present.

'This bread is like my body, which I shall sacrifice for you. A time will come when you will not see me, though I am within your hearts. When you eat of the bread, which is made from wheat, remember what I am telling you, that you will be eating of my body, which will have become one with the earth.'

Taking the jug of wine then he gave thanks and filled a jasper cup and said, 'Drink this among yourselves.'

He lifted the cup high.

'When you drink wine made from grapes remember, you will be drinking of my blood, which I will have shed for you. Look at this cup. In times to come, when you shall not see me, take comfort, for I will be with you in your soul in the same way that the wine sits in this cup.' His countenance looked about the group. 'I will be in the hearts of all, even those who do not love me.'

'We all love you!' said Phillip.

'You may say that, Phillip, but even now one among you at this table will betray me.'

John saw anxiety scurry over his fellows, like a light disturbs mice in a dark room. Whispers and looks and wisps of glances were exchanged and all around men fell into disbelief, moving their hands this way and that way.

'Who is it, Lord? Is it I?' one man after another asked.

At this point John felt as though he were entering a dream. Quietly Lazarus-John, the beloved of his Lord, came into the room. To John's mind he carried a basin and a pitcher and on seeing him the others began to mumble and to argue among themselves, not as to the betrayer but as to who was closest to their master. In his heart John, son of Zebedee, felt no desire to be greater than the one who was raised from the dead. In fact, he had felt a certain kinship with the beloved of his master. His raising had meant that some strange mystery was affixed to Lazrus, which John did not fully comprehend, but which he knew in his soul to be of profound significance.

In this dream, he saw his master lay aside his garments and gird himself with a towel. He saw him pour water into a basin, which he brought to the table. No man knew what he was about to do until he knelt and started removing the sandals from Andrew's feet. Andrew seemed astonished when his master washed them. All were amazed as his master proceeded to the next disciple, and the next.

He continued to wash their feet, one by one, and while he did so he said to them, 'Who is greater, the one who sits at the table or the one who serves him? Is it not he who sits at the table? But I sit at the table and yet I also serve those whom I love. For you are like my feet and hands and arms,' he said to them, 'what would I do without you? Just as the head must bow down in loving, humble service to all that lives below it, so must I bow down before you who are a part of me ...'

He came to Peter, and he, aghast, fell to shaking his head. 'No! No! I shall never let you wash my feet!'

Jesus looked up with merry eyes, 'But Peter, my brother, if I do not wash your feet you cannot be a part of me!'

Peter changed his mind, 'Lord! Not my feet only, then ...' he said, and put both his feet into the bowl, '... but also my hands, and my head! My whole body!'

There was a quiet murmur of laughter among them.

'Your feet are the lowermost part of your body, they help you to stand on the earth,' he instructed, wiping them with the towel, 'When they are clean your body rejoices. But your soul defiles your body when it is bound by passions.'

John of Zebedee came awake now and saw that Jesus was sitting at the table as before and he was saying, 'For this reason your soul must not be your master, but you must rather be the master of your soul, or you will pollute your body. All of you who sit with me represent various degrees of perfection. You, I can lead to the Father, for you are clean and unpolluted, all except the one whose soul has mastery over him - whose passions have taken control of him.'

The disciples looked about them again, not knowing whom he meant.

'He is the one who shall betray me.'

'Whom do you speak of, Lord?' Peter asked anxiously.

Lazarus had taken a seat beside Jesus and was inclining his soul to his master's words and listening with his heart. It seemed to John that his master had answered Peter's question for he heard these words:

He is the one, whom I shall give a sop when I have dipped it.

His master dipped a portion of bread into his wine then and handed it to Judas, and this, being a most intimate and honoured act, made Judas hesitate.

Judas shook his head.

'You have been given your wages, do it quickly,' Jesus encouraged.

With eyes round and strange Judas took the sop and put it in his mouth, and in a flicker John saw the deathly vision of Satan reflected in his eyes. Judas took his bag then and was gone into the night.

The others thought that because Judas held a bag full of money, Jesus had either asked him to buy something for the feast or had sent him to give something to the poor. John knew the truth, however. In his heart he knew it, though he did not know how. Judas had already been paid for his betrayal!

When Judas left the upper room Jesus said, 'Now the circle is made pure, for all that is selfish and full of passion has left it.'

They knew now who it was.

After that, they ate the bread and wine without appetite and gave thanks by singing a Paschal hymn from the second portion of the Hallel. John's heart was low. He did not wish to think on how the betrayal would come, or when.

After the Hallel, Jesus stood, and having found his mother, said some words to her and kissed her on the cheek. John saw how his Lord's mother near lost her footing for it. When she was *consoled* he returned to his disciples and he said, 'We go.'

Taking some torches, they went out into the darkness of night. Above, the hiding moon gave scant light and they were afraid.

It was a strict observance of the Passover to remain inside the safety of the home, for in the open no man was protected from the avenging angel of death. But John loved his master and trusted him, and despite his fear he fell in with the others and followed him into the chilly air.

When they passed by the gate north of the Temple and descended into a desolate part of the valley of Kidron John realised how tired he was. The long week had made inroads into his body, and weariness now caused him to feel breathless. Even so, he followed the others as they walked on, until they crossed the swollen brook and took the road that led toward Olivet, to the garden of Gethsemane.

His master told them, 'Soon you will not see me … I will be delivered to the Levites and they will take me to the Gentiles, and I will be crucified.'

The wind sang in his ears and John felt wilted with terror for these words.

'I will follow you!' said Peter, stumbling in the darkness, 'I will fight cheek and jowl with your enemies. You see how I have brought my filleting knife? It is sharp too and no mistake! I am ready to go to prison and to march into death with you!'

Jesus observed him in the mysterious blue light of that spring moon. 'Put your knife away, brother … you say you will lay down your life for my sake and yet I say to you, you will all desert me.'

There were gasps.

'All,' he said, significantly.

'Not I!' Peter answered. 'This lot may, but not I!'

He stopped to fix Peter with his eyes. 'Before the cock crows you will have denied me three times.'

Peter howled then, like a wounded wolf. 'Not I! Tell me it is not so!'

Jesus was grim-faced and stern, 'Satan desires to have you and take the best of you for himself as he has taken Judas, but I know that in your heart you are full of faith and for this reason I have prayed that your faith will not fail ... I have prayed that you will stay with me, to help me carry my cross!'

'I will carry it!' said Andrew.

Looking to Andrew he said, 'Yours shall be a different cross, Andrew, and for this reason it shall be remembered by all men ... I tell all of you, this night, none of you will remain with me, you will scatter, every man to his own, and you will leave me alone for fear. But I will not be alone, because Christ is with me, and through Him I will overcome the world!'

Jesus walked on, breathing heavily, as if all things were now an effort for him.

Peter, who would have fallen to his knees after those words from his master, were it not for Philip and Andrew beside him, trailed behind, sorrowing, 'Why did you say that you would carry the cross, Andrew? Do you always have to better me ...? I will carry it, by God! I will not fail you, master! I will not fail you!'

Some of the disciples began to mourn. John's eyes filled with tears.

Jesus said, from his position ahead of them, 'You are sad now, I know it, and I tell you that you shall be even more sad later, but your distress will be turned into elation. Have courage! Do not let yourselves be afraid, for fear will make you sleep and I need you awake! Is it not true that when a woman labours she is full of sorrow because her hour is come, and then as soon as the child is born she is full of joy? I will die, that is certain, but what is death if not a spirit birth? Death, my brothers, is only semblance. I say to you, I was born from the spirit and again I shall leave the world, through death, and I shall return to the spirit and I will live again!'

John had known it all along, but only now did the others understand that their master was indeed going to his death. To this was added the understanding that his death would bring forth new life.

'What do you wish us to do?' asked Bartholomew, between tears. 'Tell us, and we will do it because we love you!'

'As I have told you, I am like a man taking a long journey. I leave my house and I command the porter to watch the gates until I return.' He paused now to say to them, 'You are my porters … if you love me keep watch! Do not let me find you sleeping … do not be tempted to sleep!' His voice seemed full of exhaustion.

Joseph of Arimathea had given them the key to his garden, which was full of olive trees and roses and fruit trees, and they had often come here for contemplation, rest, and prayer during the last week. His master used the key now to open the lock and they entered into the garden where all seemed strangely evil.

Peter said, 'Lock it again, Lord, it will buy us time.'

'Why should I buy time? The Wheel of destiny is set in motion and all will be as it will be, you cannot change it …' He took Peter's face gently into his hands and looked deep into his eyes. 'When will you understand, my little rock, why I have come to this earth? When will you see that I have not come to teach, or to heal, or to cause miracles? I have come to die!'

This last word took all of his breath, and he let go of Peter's face and continued walking. 'The hour of darkness is at hand, the people, the guards, the priests, they all have their parts.'

'Does no man have a choice?' Philip said to him, catching up. 'What of the freedom you have told us about ... are all things foreordained so that nothing can be changed? What of those who will persecute you, do they not stand a chance, or will they be condemned forever to pay for it?'

He said, 'Until now you have all been bound to necessity and you have not been free. You have not been free but you have believed that you are free because you are trapped in illusion. What is to befall me soon is still *necessary*, Philip, but after my death you will have freedom and the possibility of salvation.'

'Freedom from what?' Philip asked.

'Freedom from the illusion of death,' Jesus answered. 'I will die and overcome death to save the world from illusion, to show all of mankind that after death there is life. Then salvation may come for all, *not only* for those who love me, but also for those who are against me, those who raise their hands to strike me, and those who come this night to take me to my death. Rest assured, although these men do not know me, although they may spit upon me and call abuse and wound me, they shall remember me even after death, and this will prepare the way for them to come to me freely in their coming lives.'

'What did he say?' said Andrew.

Peter, stunned by his master's words, lost his composure entirely. 'Why don't you listen, Andrew! Must I always be your ears? He says that everything that happens to him is destined, but that after he dies his death will bring about freedom, so that even those who do not love him now may choose to love him in the future!'

When they reached a clearing bordered by trees their master said to them, 'John, Peter, James, come with me, the rest may remain here ... pray that you do not fall asleep, that you are not tempted to lose yourselves. Through you the world will know how I have fought to wrest men's souls from the clutches of death.'

John followed, full of gloom, as Christ Jesus took them to a different place, deeper into the garden.

Here he left them while he went to a copse not far off. John looked around to the shadowed corners, to the sky above and the moon that came and went behind clouds. A damp, frozen wind swept the trees and wound around the shivering group.

What would they do without him?

Where would they go?

They huddled together, those who had walked with him, broken bread with him and suffered with him all the deprivations of the last three years. They looked at one another with dread-filled faces for they understood with clarity that the hour had come. Had they not been warned of it time and again? And yet their eyes were matched in their un-readiness for it. Fear made a longing for the oblivion of sleep, a longing for the comfort of nothingness. Above, winged shadows menaced the moon and the wind was full of voices.

John's exhaustion was deep. He remembered that such a feeling had come over him before, upon the mountain of spirit, when he had not endured the vision of his master's glory. He would not sleep again. No. But his eyes were heavy. He could feel a dullness rise upwards to wipe away his thoughts, like a dreadful guardian who bars the mysteries from the undeserving. Perhaps his will was not equal to sleep's unstoppable force? He looked at the others. They were already asleep. He pinched his skin and rubbed his eyes, but the sounds of their regular breathing lulled him. He made a prayer in his heart for strength to withstand it, since he did not want to fail his master again. He told himself that he must 'watch' and yet, how blissful the others seemed to him in their numb peace! Perhaps he could close his eyes for a moment ... surely a moment would scarcely matter? How consoling it would be to rest, to forget the unpleasant and dreadful events that he knew would soon come. Time enough to worry about everything on the morrow.

He blinked. It was only one blink, and then came the sound of his brother calling through the darkness of the garden,

'Get up! They come!'

Standing among his fellows now, with his mind in a fog and his mouth dry, he rubbed his eyes and saw a great number of torches striking a path through the garden. He realised that with a blink fear had drawn a frozen hand over his eyes and he had failed his Lord.

CHAPTER 58

GARDEN OF GOOD AND EVIL

The shame of it would live with him many years, *pairé,* until a fateful day in Jerusalem, when those who opposed his preaching began to pelt him with stones. In that far off time, little John, now a full grown man, would stand erect, with his head held high, and he would remain wide-awake until the very last stone found its mark.'

'Oh my! Poor little John, I see now what you meant when you said that Lazarus-John took his place in the circle. But Lea, what happened to Christ Jesus in the garden?'

'When Christ Jesus left Peter, John and James, he sensed the footsteps of Satan and trembling from the weight of his body, he walked to a nearby clearing bordered by olive trees to pray.'

‡

His heart was full of woe, for he did not know if any of his followers, even his chosen ones, would be capable of remaining awake with him during his tempestuous struggle with death.

He looked to heaven; the wolf was biting at the moon and clouds were covering her face. He remembered that temptation in the wilderness those years ago and recognised the feeling of dread that was upon him.

The wind paused – a reprieve.

It was a moment stolen from out of the stream of time. Soon his agony would begin, but not yet. For now, the part of him that was a man took in the smells of the night and the aroma of wild roses. It recalled to his mind a tale spoken with his mother's voice of a Nightingale that loved a white rose and sang the most beautiful songs to it, but only from afar, for fear of its thorns. One night, beneath the swollen moon, having drunk her fill of song and emboldened by love, the Nightingale resolved to embrace the rose. Clasping it to her breast, she was pierced through by a thorn, and yet she sung the most beautiful song she had ever sung; a song of sacrifice and true love found, pressing the thorn closer and closer to her heart. When she died the rose mourned, and stained with her heart's blood, it forever bloomed red.

He thought on his mother, dead so many years and yet so alive in his stepmother. He thought of Yeshua, dead and yet hovering over him always. He reflected on the mystery of love and bent his heart toward Jerusalem, which stood deathly pale and shivering in the scant moonlight. He had embraced her and sung his love-song to her and still she did not love him. Soon, she would pierce him with her thorn and he would stain the world with his blood.

His sadness was a deep well and yet lofty was his love, which was higher than life. For what was the heart of a bird compared to the heart of a man? And what was the passion of a man compared to the passion of a god? He looked up. The cold moon died away and the man's thoughts became the thoughts of the God.

'The hour is come,' he said to himself, and prayed for strength.

The wind began its stirring. Time established its dominion over the world. His body resumed its work, dissolving in pain. He knelt on the ground in what he knew were death throws. He felt the cold breath of death near his cheek and he shivered.

'Father in heaven, help them to remain awake!'

But they were faltering. He knew this because the Holy Spirit was loosening from him. Soon he would be alone and he did not know if he would be strong enough to hold back the tide of his godhood beyond this hour.

'Peter!' he cried. 'Watch with me!'

There was no answer.

And yet ... he was not alone.

From the wind came a whisper. It was the blue Archangel, Satan.

'Greetings, Son of God! You have lasted longer than I expected in that wretched temple. But rejoice! I have come to unlock the door and to let you out!'

'You mean you have come to ensnare me in your prison!' he said to him.

The God of Death seized him tenderly by the head to peer into his eyes. 'Son of God, Alpha and Omega, Lamb of Lambs! You are deluded! Do you not see how much I love you? Look around you, where are your disciples? The moon herself hides her face and leaves you in darkness. Even the Holy Ghost is taking to its heels without so much as a god-speed! I alone have remained at your side in this dark hour, and I come to bring you sleep, rest and comfort!'

Satan's blue, claw-like wings made to enfold him but he prised them away. 'Leave me be! I will die in freedom!'

'Stop joking, for God's sake! There is no freedom in dying, only the necessity of the Father and I am his master craftsman! You might be His son by name, but you are a son to me by nature! You are stubborn and full of longing ... like I am! Come then, give your father a kiss ... now or later, what does it matter?'

His breath drew near.

'Get away! If this body is to pass from me before my task is accomplished then let it be God's will, not yours!'

The angel sighed, filling the whole world with shadows. 'You wanted earthly life, you stooped to drink from my fountain – and you have drunk it dry! Now your flesh is drunk and your soul is drunk and you must succumb to my will! Let me take you home before you hurt yourself. Forget those fools you love, they have already forgotten *you*, for they do not love you like I do. The truth is that when I come into a room, memory goes out the door. You see, memory is a whore, she loves the man who pays her the most, and my purse is always full!'

Christ Jesus took in a breath and Satan slipped into it, filling the span of his lungs. Satan would have him breathe out, but he would not. When he could stand it no more his out-breath gave wings to Satan's words,

'I die!'

At that moment, the moon's dark spectres floated away from her. Demons and ghosts and phantoms were drawn to him like vultures to dead meat. They came down in a gust of wind to encircle and enfold him in their shadows, called forth by Satan's words in him.

Stripped bare of the living forces of the Holy Spirit by that creature's power over his disciples, he could not prevent the mighty force of Christ from entering to the very bones. This was Satan's realm, the bones, and here death would seize him too soon, before the performance of his sacrifice.

An ice-like pain tore through him now. He could feel the heavenly power of divinity invade his organs, it began to macerate his liver and spleen, burning holes in his lungs, erupting into his heart and bladder and brain. It broke through the walls of those earthly veins with such power that it flooded the cup of his tissues, making blood seep through the pores of his skin and from his eyes.

He was knocked down by it and fell with his face in the dirt.

The world turned.

The wind dropped.

A sudden quiet fell over the grotto.

How could he die now?

Upon the midnight hour in the garden of good and evil, the struggle of life with death made a pause.

A sublime effulgence, a subtle warmth descended, melting away the coldness of death. This gold-giving radiance gathered into the sparkling, shimmer-glowing form of an angel, the angel of John the Baptist. He bent life's cup to Christ Jesus' lips and let him drink the nectar that would bring strength and life and vigour to his wasted body.

The moon's old forces were obliged to unwind from him and to scurry away. A shriek was heard in the bowels of the earth and the blue archangel of death fell back into the shadows. Satan had not succeeded. The moment had passed. Jesus had survived – for now.

Relief washed over him. He would go on to accomplish his deed.

CHAPTER 59

THE ARREST

'But I don't understand Lea, why was it necessary that the disciples stay awake? They were weary … why could they not sleep?'

'He told them that he needed them,' Lea said.

'Yes, but what could they do for him?'

'Well, *pairé*, it is like this: for three years the circle of disciples had been held together by the Holy Spirit which lived among them; this spirit had provided Jesus with the power to withstand the entrance of Christ's spirit into his Soul, his blood and his body. Now, when it was time for them to stay awake and keep the Holy Spirit within their circle to enable Jesus to withstand to the end, they could not do it, they were faithless.'

'But how, how were they faithless?'

'Their fear had dissolved their faith, *pairé*, in the same way that a breath blows out a flame. For this reason the Holy Spirit had to flee, and this left Jesus powerless. You see, the Holy Spirit can only linger in a circle which is faithful,' she said to me, and I was stunned by this.

The Marquésia and I had experienced the fullness of the Holy Spirit and we had been only two! But then, I remembered Christ Jesus' words in Matthew's Gospel,

Whenever two of three are gathered in my name, I am there among them!

Lea looked at me. She had discerned my thoughts. 'The power of faith lives in each soul, *pairé,* like a knife sits in its sheath, but the Holy Spirit lives in a circle *only* to the extent that each member is faithful to Christ.'

Tears fell over my face, so moved was I by sadness. 'And so … He was alone,' I said wiping my tears with my stained hand. 'Even the Holy Spirit had deserted Him!'

'But you are forgetting the women, *pairé*! They were always awake; he did not need to hold them, for they had always held His soul in their care, since a woman is like a vessel, as you know. Yes, he had the women, but he needed one other … he needed a witness; this could only be a man and there was one, one who was faithful, one who did not sleep.'

'Who was it?'

'Observe … listen … learn …'

‡

Christ Jesus was powerless for a time, until he could assemble to himself the fullness of his senses. When he finally stood he made an unsure way back to where his disciples lay sleeping. He saw that from beyond the garden there came the glow of moving torches and the sounds of men.

'Rise!' he told them, out of breath, 'The hour is at hand when I am betrayed!'

John, Peter and James stood. In a moment, the others came to warn him of impending doom.

'Quickly! You must flee, Lord! They come!' Matthew cried.

'No, Matthew, I deliver myself up without resistance.' he said, as the guards of the Sanhedrin, some twenty in total, entered the clearing.

The guards were made up of Jews, Syrians and other races and they were dressed for battle: armed with swords and spears and sticks, staves and clubs. They trampled their way to him, and ahead of them came Judas.

When the company entered the clearing, Judas, from a small distance, said an anxious, 'Hail, master!'

He came close then, and leaned in, allowing his breath to linger over the cheek of his master a moment before he kissed him. As he kissed him Christ Jesus remembered Satan's words, *Now or later, what does it matter?*

Jesus took Judas' face then into his hands and looked deep into the pit of his eyes, he discerned in them no recognition, no love, only Satan looking back at him. *I told you ... my purse is always full!*

He said to Judas, 'Friend! Is this why you have come, to betray me with a kiss?'

Judas did not answer. He freed himself and stepped aside to allow the guards to come forward, and then he ran away with his purse jingling.

Christ Jesus wished the guards to know that he was coming freely to them so he asked them for whom they sought.

The Jew leader of the band answered, 'Jesus of Nazareth!'

He nodded. 'I AM, he!'

These words possessed such a power that the guards fell back in awe, but in a moment they came to their senses and moved to seize him.

Of a sudden Peter came forward brandishing his filleting knife and smote the Jew commander's ear. A great confusion ensued then and among the chaos Peter ran away. A guard, seeing a youthful figure leaving the clearing, made to seize him, but he did not know that it was not Peter, it was the Holy Spirit, the Spirit of Christ, leaving him.

A wolf made a howl.

'This is the hour of the power of darkness!'

As he said it, he was set upon from all sides like a wild dog that must be tamed. He was bound with cords and belts around his middle and his neck and his hands were tied ahead of him. He saw his disciples take themselves out of the garden and away from him, scattering into the night, as he had foretold. He was struck a blow to the face and he fell to his knees. Blood flowed from his nose but he was paused only a moment for the rope around his neck soon tightened and he was jerked upwards to the balls of his feet and he staggered for balance. The rope strangled him. When it slacked he took a breath and heard laughter. A boot struck the small of his back and sent him hurtling forwards, whereupon he was again pulled from behind, so that without his arms to stop his fall, he fell on his back.

He was kicked and spat upon and in that moment before he was again jerked upwards to his feet he caught a glimpse of someone watching from the shadows. This one had remained. This one had not slept! Christ-Jesus remembered how thankful he had been at Bethany to know that one man had been found worthy to follow him – Lazarus-John was present in that hour with his far-seeing eyes.

He alone would be his witness.

CHAPTER 60

DREAMER

Days after the failed sortie, Raimon de Perella and Pierre-Roger de Mirepoix swallowed their pride and descended the pog to parley with the French. The garrison was much depleted from that fateful battle and it would not take long for disease to take hold, with so many dead and no place to bury them. On top of it, we were trapped, with no food and no help from the Count of Toulouse.

Our fate had been sealed.

A long night was spent in prayer over the dead and the dying and in the morning I was barely awake when the horn sounded on the ramparts marking the return of the *seigneurs* from the fields with the terms of surrender. The garrison would remain in the fortress fifteen days and the French would take hostages to prevent a night escape, *en mass*. The garrison would be pardoned, as would the killers of the inquisitors (this amazed us all), the men at arms could leave with their belongings but would have to appear before the Inquisition to confess their errors. All others would have only light penances provided they abjured their heretical beliefs and made confession before the Inquisitors. But those who remained stubborn and did not confess the errors of their faith and all its rituals, rights and beliefs, would be burnt to death. This was the terrible addendum that we had feared.

We had fifteen days to make our preparations, and to choose: death or life.

A cry of despair reached to the very heavens then, for those who had taken the *consolamentum* could not recant their faith, they could not deny the Holy Spirit. For this reason, the only alternative left to them was to choose the pyre, leaving their friends and family to watch as they burned. I knew that many believers would ask for the *consolamentum* in the coming days, for what life was there beyond the walls of Montségur without family and friends? What life was there in a country now foreign to their eye, a country full of inquisitors, danger and malice? What was there to return to? After all, their farms and castles had been seized, their animals stolen, and their vassals sent away. How must they live a life hounded by Rome? Better to die pure so as to be raised to the light of heaven. One moment of pain was small payment for an eternity of bliss!

Or so they believed.

Each man found his wife and children. Families gathered together to pray, weeping and talking and holding one to the other.

These fourteen days would bring peace and a chance for us to celebrate the *Bema* on behalf of our founder Mani. And it was on the eve of this festival, as the yellow moon illuminated the world outside the window with a silver incandescence, that Lea and I were together again. Quiet and solemn, we sat for a long time and I contemplated her loveliness, realising that my attitude towards her had changed over these months. It had moved from wonder to reverence to surrender and finally to a strong insatiable love. But it was not the love of a man for a woman. At least I did not think so. I would liken it to the love of a man for the beauty of the mountains and the wisdom of the seasons, a love for the personification of nature as a woman, the Demeter of the Greeks or the Diana of the Romans. For is it not nature herself that makes our ears and eyes more attentive? Is it not through nature that we can learn to grasp subtleties and fine distinctions? The wisdom in the heart of this elfin girl had grown in me a love for everything visible, and there is nothing more noble or sacred than a quiet, dispassionate love. This is the love I felt as I sat before Lea. That is when I started to worry for her safety.

'I still do not know who you are, Lea.' I told her, 'Whether you are a spirit or a person, an image or likeness, or just an old man's pleasant dream. I do not know! But when I begin to think you real, my dear, I am terrified for what will happen to you!'

She looked upon this as she looked upon everything, with equanimity and silent acknowledgement, and yet I did see that her spirit, beautiful and sincere as it was, had become completely absorbed by my words. She inclined her head in thought before she spoke. 'I am what man has made me and what I will be is also in the hands of men. This is my destiny. But my heart is certain of goodness because I have found it in your heart, *pairé,* and that is how I know that one day I will be released from my imprisonment.'

The poor naïve child! What did she know of the hate of men? I resolved to instruct her. 'Listen to me, Lea, I don't believe the inquisitors will stand by while the enemies of their faith walk away. As soon as we are off this pog they will make their arrests and despite the French assurances all those who do not die on the pyre will be thrown into prisons. Have you heard tell of them, my dear? No light, no food except bread and water, with your wrists shackled to the wall for days, months, years! Matteu comes soon, by way of the Porteil Chimney. He will take the treasures of our church over the wall with him. He is also taking the Marquésia's child and three perfects. It would not be difficult to convince him to take you as well; what do you say?'

'No, pairé, I cannot go, not yet. I must stay for my mother's sake,' she said, looking at me with those azure eyes.

'Your mother? Who is she? I promise that I will see to her if you go. Will you not consider it?'

She shook her head. 'But it is my mother who wishes me to stay, *pairé,* so that we can continue, for there is little time and much to tell. Shall I begin?'

I sighed, crestfallen and downhearted. I did not wish to face the pyre with Lea beside me, but I was defeated by her determination and the look in her eyes and so I said to her, 'as you wish, Lea, please, begin again.'

She smiled then, and so sad and noble and beautiful was it that I had to look away, afraid lest I dissolve her beauty with my clumsy observation.

'Pick up your quill now, *pairé*, for I will tell you about the Roman woman … Claudia Procula. She is sleeping when Christ Jesus is taken from the Garden to the palace of Ananias. Now her dream comes again and she sees herself walking among a great field of people. The world above and below is the colour of blood and storm cloud, and into this world she walks dressed in white. Her arms hold a ream of the finest cotton cloth, some of which is let loose behind her to be taken up by a gentle breeze. But this dream is different, now the crowds part before her like a great black sea and she sees what she has not seen before. Revealed by the crowd's mysterious gesture is the figure of Christ Jesus, lying on the ground, his body broken and battered and bloodied. She realises that the blood that has made red heaven and earth in her dream is not her defiled blood – it is *His* blood!'

‡

She woke with a start, and sat up in bed full with fear and covered in perspiration. Her first impulse was not to wake her husband but to gather an outer garment over her shoulders and to run barefoot through the meagre lit halls with her heart in her throat and the shadows of dread all around her.

She came to her maid's quarters. Susannah was also a follower of Christ Jesus. She said to her, 'Quickly! Go to the fortress of Antonia, to the Centurion Gaius Cassius. Tell him these words: Our master is in danger! Go … run …!'

She watched the girl dress and stood in the halls observing her shadow disappear into other shadows with the cold spring wind penetrating her to the very bones.

This night would see the unmasking of her faith and of her secret journeys with Gaius Cassius to see Jesus who was Christ. This night the world might end! For all things seemed to her to be standing upon a knife's edge. Fear for it made her unable to move. She could not yet will her legs to turn around and take her back to her rooms and so she stood, without a further thought on what she would tell her husband.

CHAPTER 61

WE ARE NOT ALONE!

Even before Lazarus-John had arrived to tell them the news, Mariam had known it. For she had heard the howling of the wolf and she had come awake and remembered! Dear God! This was her dream come to life! The dream she had dreamt over and over on her way to Egypt those many years ago. She did not open her eyes but lay there as the agony came into her heart, a longing to be with her son, and something more! A suffering that echoed a thousand times in the stillness, for it was not only her own suffering and grief that concerned her, but also the anguish felt through her by heaven itself!

When finally she opened her eyes she was in that room full of women in the house at Ophel owned by Veronica. In a moment came Lazarus-John's whisper in her ear.

'It begins!' he said.

Then it was into the night for all of them: Magdalena and her sister-in-law on either side, with Salome and the others, Joanna Chuza, Martha and Lea, trailing behind them.

On her mind were his last words to her after the Pascha, before he left to take his disciples to Olivet.

'Be consoled, the Holy Spirit is always with you ... I will go now, and when you see me again, you will sorrow exceedingly, but as the

Father is with me, so must my Mother be with me to the very end. Follow me, find me, stay with me. Be the eyes of heaven!'

Her benumbed and tired eyes filled now with tears to think on it, and she stumbled and was caught by Magdalena. She said to her from afar, as if she were not upon the ground but upon a mountain, 'Where is he, Magdalena? We must find him!'

With difficulty they made their way through the crowds, for all had come out into the streets of Ophel having heard the noise of the many guards and the uproar of the soldiers. Her son's disciples, Andrew and the sons of Zebedee, now joined them, and some way off she could see Philip and Bartholomew looking on. Soon Peter was at her side and falling at her feet.

'Mother! They have him! They have our Lord!'

She could only nod to Peter and continue walking amid the cries of grief and lamentation that rose up from the people who loved her son. When they came near the gates of the city she saw him. Those who came too near to him were struck by the soldiers and told to return to their houses.

'What will you do with our Lord!' they cried.

'Yes, what will you do to him?'

'You should mind the company you keep!' they told the people. 'This man is a blasphemer and a heretic, an inciter of rebellion! Go back to your hovels, lest you be tried with him and suffer his fate!'

These ignoble guards struck her son with cords, and kicked him and spat on him.

He fell.

The mother made to go to him but the crowd swelled and prevented it.

Lazarus-John said to her, 'I will go and alert Nicodemus, Joseph of Arimathea and Gamaliel ... go on ahead with the others, I will find you again!'

She followed the crowds as they passed through a door made in the wall and beyond the pool of Bethsaida to the forum, descending with the growing numbers of citizens down a steep street and turning south towards the whereabouts of the house of Ananias, father-in-law of the high priest. A number of Roman guards came then, and a centurion upon his horse.

The centurion interrogated the crowds concerning the commotion, but no man answered him. She struggled to move forward through the multitudes and called out in Latin, 'They have seized an innocent man, and they take him to Ananias without a Roman trial!'

The Centurion came closer and leant over the neck of his animal to bring a torch to her face.

'I recognise your voice!' he said.

And she too recognised his.

'What is his name?' the man pressed.

'Iesus Nazarenus!' she told him.

The man heard it and was gone into a memory, his horse whipping the air ahead of the crowds.

Magdalena, beside her, was overcome with grief and said to her, 'Mother … how shall we endure it?'

She let out a breath and the world grew still, as still as a light beam caught fast through a gap in trees. In this splinter of a pause floated sun-like stars, and she was directed to their seeming. In her mind came the face of her old friend Mary. The dead mother of Jesus stood before her with the sun in her eyes and a smile playing about her mouth. She gestured upwards to heaven's vault and when Mariam looked, she was lifted out of her soul to a place where there was nothing but love and light and life.

When it was over she realised the crowd had moved on through the gates and the other women were crowded around her. Her eyes moved over them, each face creased with pain and panic. A soothing calmness came into her voice now, 'Be consoled my little ones … we are not alone ...' she told them.

CHAPTER 62

TRIALS AND VISIONS

The stepbrother of Jesus was asleep in the sanctuary of the Temple. Before that, he had spent the hours since the Paschal feast on his knees communing with God and in contemplation of his destiny.

Years ago, after his baptism in the Jordan, Jacob son of Mariam, had let go of the power of his inherited birth right and had wandered the land like a fish without a sea, not belonging to any place. The corrupt priests and hypocritical rabbis of the temple could not draw him to their side and he did not feel at ease with the Essenes, though they welcomed him always in their outer circles. He did not even consider himself a Nazarite in the strictest sense, and so could not call himself a true follower of John the Baptist.

He was a man in search of a spirit home.

As the years passed conflicting words had reached him concerning his stepbrother. He had heard of John the Baptist's testimony and rumours had abounded of Jesus' healings and his exorcisms, his sermons and signs. Other rumours told that his stepbrother was a magician, a sorcerer ruled by devils, that he had broken the laws of their forefathers, that he had blasphemed and desecrated the Sabbath.

For his part Jacob had kept himself aloof from all of it, not wishing to know what truth there might be to one or other rumour. That is, until the Paschal week.

Of late Jacob had come to Jerusalem to celebrate the holy day and to unite with the heart of his people. He was tattered and thin after long months of wandering through the land, long months of punishing his body with fasting and prayer, and had sought a place to rest his head. But here, in Jerusalem, he could not avoid his stepbrother, who seemed to be everywhere, speaking out against the priests in one place, condemning the rituals of the temple in another. Making more and more enemies as each day came, not only in the Sanhedrin but also among the people.

He had not seen Jesus since that afternoon at Nazareth those years ago and on hearing him in Jerusalem these last days it had been hard to imagine him the same man, so strong and full of authority was his mien and so powerful were his words. Yes. His baptism and those years of wandering had made Jacob's ears sensitive and discerning, and he heard the ring of truth in his stepbrother's voice and over the holy days this had formed in him a question.

After all this time, and after all the wanderings and painful prayers ... do I now realise that I have been in search of something which I have always known?

On the eve of the Paschal feast he took himself to the house given over to the Essenes, where he knew his family would be celebrating the Pascha. He took the steps that led from the outside of the house up to the cenacle, the upper room lit by candles, but when he came to be standing beneath the lintel, not quite in view and yet at the threshold of the room, he was taken by incertitude. In his heart, something told him that the circle around his stepbrother was closed and that there was no room for him. He was overcome with a feeling of grief for it and had decided to go, when a man he recognised, one of his stepbrother's disciples, brushed past him making for the stairs. He had seen him at the temple, speaking to the priests. His name was Judas Iscariot; wild-eyed and taken by his thoughts he did not excuse himself but continued on into the darkness.

Disconcerted, Jacob had made his way to the temple where he

waited in the cold, awful wind for the gates to open to allow those who were in charge of preparing the morning offering of the *Chagigah* to enter. In the court of the Nazarites he kneeled, and alone and confused, fell asleep until he was disturbed by the sounds of the bleating of the animals and a great commotion.

As he came out into the streets to see what had caused it, he realised that he had slept long, for the night was near given over to the green light of morning. A great crowd had gathered at the palace of Caiaphas. Many stood beneath lamps and torches and he went to them.

The pregnant moon hung in the west as he made his way through the outer court and into the inner court of the palace. He looked about for anyone he knew.

'What has passed?' he asked a man.

'The heretic Jesus of Nazareth is seized and stands trial,' the man answered.

With a vacant nod Jacob glanced about at a number of men huddled around a coal fire in the middle of the court. The glow of the fire's blue flame threw shadows over a face he recognised, another of his stepbrother's disciples. Jacob went to him, but when he came near he heard a Levite say to the man, 'Are you not Peter, one of those who followed Jesus, the heretic?'

The disciple buried his face in his wool robe and said, 'No … I am not!'

'Yes, I saw you at the Garden!' another Temple guard added.

'No! I tell you, you are wrong!'

'He lies!' said a woman nearby. 'I have seen him with the Nazarene!'

He turned on the woman, 'I do not know what you are saying, addled woman! For I know not the man! Leave me be!'

A cock crowed then and perturbed by it, the disciple hunched his shoulders and ran off into the crowds.

Jacob did not go after him; he continued on to the palace where he was recognised and allowed passage. Once inside the great rectangular hall surrounded by columns he searched among the many faces. The torches flapped in the breeze and in that cold light he saw no face he recognised. A great uproar was heard coming from the front of the hall, where on the raised platform sat the high priest, Caiaphas, among members of the Sanhedrin. From what Jacob could see there were only just enough men present to make a quorum, that is, twenty-three priests and rabbis, in a half circle formed by seats. As he made a way through the crowds he realised that the man who stood before these elders, surrounded by his accusers, was his stepbrother.

What had become of him since the supper in the cenacle made Jacob take a deep breath. Nothing could have prepared him for what now met his eyes. His stepbrother was a battered man, leaning to one side, with one eye bruised and the other squinting away at the blood that oozed from cuts to his scalp and his forehead. His nose was broken, his lips were swollen and he shook from his head to his bare feet, for his garments had been torn from his body and his hands were trussed up before him like an animal ready for the slaughterhouse.

A rising up of indignation was caught in his throat and his eyes filled with tears. He looked about for a support and found a column and leaning against it, transfixed, he watched and listened while the room erupted in screams for his brother's blood.

Caiaphas was speaking to Jesus from his grand position on the dais, 'Witnesses have heard your words, which make of you a defiler, a seducer and a heretic!'

Jesus did not answer.

One by one came the accusers and their opponents to shout out their charges and claims.

'He said he would destroy the Temple, and rebuild it in three days!'

'But he did not say he would build it with his hands!'

'He calls himself the Son of Man!'

'No! He says he is the Son of God!'

'But he heals the sick, and he casts out demons! Is this not a holy man, who can do this?'

'He might cure the sick but he does it on a Sabbath!'

'He casts out demons because he is a demon himself and he is in league with them!'

'He teaches false doctrines!'

'He does not wash his hands before he breaks bread!'

'But he speaks of peace and love and breaks bread with the poor!'

'Yet he has members of the *Sicarri* as his disciples!'

These contradictions fell into a confused rabble of voices.

Jacob saw a well-respected member of the Sanhedrin, Nicodemus. He entered the fray, followed by Gamaliel and Joseph of Arimathea.

Nicodemus came up to the horseshoe of gathered men and said, 'Why have you called this council without us? This meeting is not lawful! There has not been proper notice and an attendance of all the members of the council!'

The people grew quiet.

Gamaliel pointed to Caiaphas and added his own words, 'You have tried to prevent those of us who do not agree with you from being here! Such a trial, conducted in haste while many of the council are preparing this morning for the ceremony, is not legal!'

Joseph was angry. 'Where is the passage in the law that approves trying a cause at night and so close to a feast day?'

Caiaphas stood and came forward with a scornful eye. 'My colleagues, it was not our intention to exclude you but we had to act quickly. If we had not seized this heretic and stopped him from inciting the people to rebellion the Romans would have done so and caused grief to the temple and to Israel!'

'But these accusations only show the confusion of your witnesses, for they bear no proof of his wrongdoing!' Nicodemus said to him.

'Well then!' said Caiaphas, coming up to Jesus. 'Let the man say something himself!'

But there was only silence from Jesus.

'Why do you not give answer to these accusations?' Caiaphas taunted, 'I adjure you to tell us if you are Christ, the Messiah, the son of the living God!'

When the voice came Jacob recognised no authority in it, it was the voice of a man, not the voice of a god, 'If I tell you that I am he, you will not believe me … and if I ask you who you think that I am you will not answer me, nor let me go … no matter what I say, I am condemned.'

'Are you the Son of God?' the high priest asked.

'This is a question which only you can answer,' Jesus said. 'For it only has value if you, yourself, can see the God in me. But I tell you, one day all will see the Son of Man, sitting on the right hand of the power of God coming in the ether-cloud realms of heaven. Then, you will know that I am He!'

He knew in his heart that Jesus was speaking the truth! But he was torn from the vision by terrible words:

'*Giddupha!* Blasphemy!'

He realised that Caiaphas had a blade in his hand. 'Blasphemy and sedition!!!' the man said, and took up the corner of his outer and his inner garment, and made a tear from top to bottom rending both. 'What further need have we of witnesses! Now all of you have heard it for yourselves – with your own ears! What say you to this,' he said to the crowds, 'for life or for death?'

The hall resounded with such fierceness, that it near reached heaven.

'Death! Death! Death!' was the chant.

'No!' Gamaliel cried, outraged. 'A capital sentence is not legal unless it is pronounced at a regular meeting of the Sanhedrin!'

But no one heard him. The priests were already coming off their dais. Each man took his turn to spit into Jesus' face or to hit him with a staff or to slap him with a hand before leaving the court.

Jacob's soul welled up with anger and he spoke out,

'The golden band on your mitre has the graven words, "Holiness unto Jehovah"! It means you have the power to atone for those who blaspheme!'

There was a breathless pause.

The cold, fierce gaze of the high priest moved over the crowd until it fell on him.

'I will not atone for a man who profanes the name of God, again and again!' Caiaphas raised his staff and looked to the vaults of the hall. 'I–will–not!'

A terrible draft, unearthly and cruel, washed over the room, and Jacob saw shadows, and shadows of shadows, sweep over all gathered there. Like malignant birds borne by an unfelt wind they fluttered and he saw with his own eyes how these shades were inspired into the very souls of those present to entice them to rise up in a high pitch of hate and rage, so that snarling, like one great rabid animal, the throng moved on Jesus.

Caiaphas shouted out over the din, 'Put this king in the dungeon until he is delivered to Rome, for only Rome can render him what he is due!'

By the time the members of the council had left the tribunal the crowds had descended upon Jesus and were revelling in trampling upon the fallen greatness of the man they had welcomed to Jerusalem like a king only a few days before. He was clubbed and beaten with fists and insulted and hit with staves, and in the midst of this brutality, this coarseness and ferocity and profanity, he fell, and was swallowed up by the crowds and Jacob saw him no more.

Jacob was aghast. The representatives of the highest human knowledge in Jerusalem had failed to see the Messiah of their people! But he was soon reminded of that peaceful morning when, looking into Joseph's workshop, the image of his brother had surfaced on the face of Jesus, and he had not wished to see that Jesus was really one with his brother.

Was he any better than these men?

And so it was. On that terror-full night, when all hell was let loose on the world, Jacob finally found the purpose of his life and his spirit home …

And it had come too late.

CHAPTER 63

WAGES OF SIN

Judas was present during the trial in the palace of Caiaphas. Among the crowds he watched and listened and clasped that bag of silver tight to his chest, talking to himself and making strange gestures in the air. Divergent thoughts flitted like phantoms across his mind and fought for dominion over his reason. He considered them his unruly companions.

He looked for Magdalena and found her with her brother and the stepmother of Jesus. Her sorrowing face told him that she was in that agony he had prepared for her, and he was glad for it. He was glad for it all, for the screaming of the masses and the abuses of his master and the hooting of laughter and derision.

Glad.

And yet not glad!

For a small voice now began to take from him his gladness.

Look scorpizein! Look at what you have made! You will long be remembered! Yes ... your name will be a curse on every man's lips!

He shooed the thought away – a dirty insect of a thought it was.

Betrayer!

He took a swipe at it.

Lover of demons.

He cowered.

All faces seemed now to bear down on him, their countenances full of strangely distorted grimaces and frowns.

They accused him with their stares and pointed at him with grimaces.

This is the one! Look at him!

He felt disordered, broken into a thousand pieces, all of them ugly and disfigured, rotten, despoiled and shrivelled up. His soul was eaten to the nub. He could smell the stench of his own decay, the putrid manure of his being. He looked at his hands and the skin began to split apart to reveal maggots; maggots and flies were everywhere around him. He swatted them. His breathing grew quick but he could not catch air for the flies trying to enter into his mouth. Round and round was his head turned by voices. Too many people, too many fingers pointing, too much whispering, too many maggots and flies!

He stumbled out of the palace, through the courts and out to the streets where the wind pursued him like furies. It caught his garments and pulled at his hair and poked at his eyes. The wind entered into his head and moved about in his mind. The wind was a woman, as cold as the Pascha moon, as cold as death. It was a dead hag looking for living things to kill. It was a pale virgin trembling with wrath. It was a demon with sharp talons and long teeth and yet, with skin as soft as a lover's bare breast! It was a phantom, come to devour his soul and if it so desired it he would freely give it! For the wind was Magdalena! Beautiful, cruel Magdalena! And when she shrieked her vengeance upon him he heard the sound of a thousand birds and there came a vision of them feasting on the carrion meat on his bones.

He ran out of the city and found a cave in which to hide. With his head between his knees and his hands to his ears he fell into a fitful sleep.

When he woke the sun was up and the streets were quiet. He betook himself to the temple, to where he knew the priests would be preparing for the morning ritual. He ran, slipping and falling on the smooth marble steps. He saw some members of the council conferring in the court of the Gentiles and went to them. Frantic, he tore the bag of silver from his belt. He was a child, weeping for the breast, weeping for a father's approving glance.

'Take it back!' he pleaded, 'Take back your dirty silver … release him! I have sold innocent blood!'

But the faces of the priests were turned into the faces of hellish imps, frowning through the folds of flesh at him.

They seemed both annoyed and amused, both fascinated and revolted.

'What have we to do with your sin? If you think you have sold innocent blood that is your own affair! You have earned your wages this night for Jesus is already judged guilty and today will be crucified. Now go on your way, before you defile us!'

Horror struck a note of discord in his spine, and clutching the bag close he turned his dismal mind to what he should do. It came then, the thought, and he took to his heels. He went through the courts of the Gentiles, over the steps and through the Beautiful Gates to the Court of the Women and onwards to the Courts of Israel making for the sanctuary, where was situated the altar and the Holy of Holies.

'Stop!' he heard voices echo behind him.

But he did not stop. He ran past the incensed Levites, escaping their clutches until he came to the boundary that separated the Court of Israel from the pavement of the sanctuary. Here he flung the bag with all his might and it burst open and the coins toppled onto the marble flags.

He took the thirty pieces of silver, and cast them to the potter, in the house of the Lord!

After that he ran with heaven and earth slipping from his grasp.

May the devil stand at his right hand; when he is judged may he go out condemned!

There was no escape, no help, no counsel and no hope!

Where should he go? There was a moment of incertitude and then a voice told him,

Go to the valley of Hinnon.

He turned and ran, gulping for air, over the bridge that crossed the torrents of the Kidron, across the valley and up the steep sides of the mountain to the potter's field.

Run Judah, betrayer of your brother! Run Judas Maccabeus, betrayer of your people! Run Judas Iscariot, betrayer of God! Run to the field of blood, dead man, old man! Run to the potter's field, the field of blood, and be broken!

Where the two valleys merged he slipped on the cold clay, cutting himself on the jagged stones. He looked for a place and saw a gnarled tree growing from out of the rock. It was surrounded by rubbish and death. He could smell it. Turning he saw the origin of the smell, it was the carcass of an ass, bloated and swarming with flies and maggots. Death, yes death! Death to the ass! Death to the old ways! The old ways were at an end. Israel was like that ass! He climbed to the top of the rock, unwound the long girdle that held his garment and fastened it over a limb. He heard a voice:

Put an end to it ... put an end to your misery! The wages of sin is death!

He tied the girdle around his neck.

Jump! Let yourself be saved from this miserable life!!

He went to the lip of the rise.

No mother will ever desert you!

He looked down to the jagged rocks below.

No woman will ever turn away from you!

He took a breath.

No disappointments will ever again assail you!

He let his foot slip ...

Jump!

He fell!

But he did not fall far enough and was hung in the air, a heavy dying lump, grasping for the girdle.

His throat was cut off sharp, and his eyes bulged with blood.

He choked.

Pain! Horror!

No!

Not yet!

He struggled.

His tongue grew as big as the world in his mouth.

Above, the knot unloosened, and for a moment time lay suspended. In that arrested flow he saw Satan leave his soul, expelled with his out-breath. All the demons that had possessed him, in swarms were gone from him. All things were now different to his dying eye. He saw his entire life pass: the betrayals, his wanderings with Jesus, his baptism, his time with the Sicarri, his failed initiation, his birth and then …

Behold!

He saw a vision of Christ.

Now, for the first time, he saw Him! He was not an initiate, He was not a priest, He was not a king, He had not come to save Israel. He had come to save Judas' soul!

He was a living God!

Only now could the future become manifest before his dying eyes.

‡

I was afraid and put my hands to my ears. 'No! Tell me no more!'

'What do you fear, *pairé?*'

'I fear, I fear that I am him, that I am this man Judas!'

'Oh! Many men fear this, *pairé,* but they would not if they knew of his redemption.'

'Redemption? How can he be redeemed? He is the betrayer of betrayers! Does he not go to hell where every day is Good Friday?'

She laughed a little. 'No, *pairé.*'

I was full of wonder, 'Tell me then, what happens to him, what does he see before his dying eyes?'

'He sees a solitary man writing his confessions in a quiet peaceful cell. This man is a good man. His name is Augustine.'

'Augustine?'

'Yes, he is born again as Augustine.'

'Well that makes sense! I can see how a betrayer could become Augustine, one of the Fathers of the Roman Church!'

'Now, now, *pairé*, don't forget that Augustine was a Manichean before he took up the Catholic faith.'

I was nodding, for it was true. Augustine of Hippo had been a Manichean. I had forgotten that!

'Judas' failed initiation and the betrayal of his people lived deeply hidden in Augustin's will, and drove him to betray his people again. You see, he turned his back on the Manicheans when he was converted to Catholicism and wrote his polemics against them.'

'Augustine is the father of those men who sit below this fortress in judgement of our faith,' I told her, 'since the Dominicans took up his rule!'

'Yes, that is true.'

'What happens to him after that?'

'He will have another life in which these memories will be transformed into pictures.'

'Another painter ...?'

'Yes ... this man is yet to come. Many returned as painters, *pairé*, to tell what they had seen. If all goes well, the man who was Judas and Augustine will create wondrous works of art in which he will often depict Magdalena and her brother Lazarus-John over and again. Sometimes he will confuse them, one with the other, and people will say that his John is really Magdalena, but this is only because he could not prise them apart himself. His greatest achievement, though, will be his hardest task; he will paint the last supper, but he will struggle to paint the dark face of Judas, his own face.'

'Oh!' My sense of wonderment increased. 'Will he paint his own face?'

'That remains to be seen. One day you will know how close he came to his own ideal. He will also see me, as you do, and I will tell him many things of the past, and the future, and he will paint my portrait. Many will think he has painted the face of a wealthy woman, but in this woman's face he will portray the soul of all women! He will take that portrait with him everywhere as a memory of our meeting, and will loathe to let it go. One day you will look at it carefully, *pairé*, and you will see that in the background he has painted that place in which he died, the valley of Hinnon.'

'So he does not go to hell!' I said, 'He is given the chance to redeem himself as Augustine and then as this painter!'

'You see, *pairé,* the wages of sin might be death, but from death comes new life … that is the gift Christ gave to mankind, that is what the church of Rome has hidden from men, for their Christ is like the God of the Sadducees and Pharisees – a God of death.'

'What happens now to Judas?'

'At the very moment he sees who he will become, the girdle around his neck lets go, and he falls onto the rocks. His last thought is of Magdalena and of the rocks … something he will also paint. But at that moment, as he falls, he hopes for nothing and he fears nothing. He is free in his spirit, *pairé,* for the first time in all his lives.'

CHAPTER 64

WHAT IS TRUTH?

Before I could take these things into my heart, Lea had begun again to tell of Pontius Pilate who was standing, stone-faced and weary, upon the court outside his palace.

‡

Some called this court the *Pavement,* because it was inlaid with mosaics, and others called it the *Gabbatha,* or the high place, because from it one could glimpse the township of that name. Whatever the case these days Pilate had made it a raised tribunal, erecting at one end of it that marble seat from which he always pronounced his sentences and judgements.

A wide sweeping staircase, usually a-swarm with guards at these times, led from the Pavement down to a great square, bounded by stone walls and lined with columns and seats, where the people could gather. He stood stiffly looking down upon it. It was near the *hora secunda,* the second hour of the day, and even at this early time it was already hot. Above, the smoke from the sacrifices made columns rise towards the heavens, while below in the temple the Levites pierced the valley with their woeful songs. These ordinary things on such a day as this made him full of discomfort – for this was no ordinary day. Pilate wiped his brow and thought things through.

Last night around the midnight hour his wife had woken him, fearful for a dream in which Jesus of Nazareth was covered in blood. It had taken him long to console her. The sentinels, he had told her, were doubled and the cohorts drawn up, as was customary during the feast. Nothing could happen without his knowledge. Still she had wept and among her weepings had confessed her belief in the man, how often she had seen him and heard his words, and how much she feared for his safety.

Later, reports reached the pr*ae*torium of a commotion in the city and he understood the accuracy of his wife's augury. His Centurion, Gaius Cassius, had returned from the palace of Ananias with news that the Jew had been arrested on made up charges and was being taken to face trial by the council at the Palace of Caiaphas.

Cassius had told him that the followers of Jesus would not oppose it for they were peaceable, but Pilate considered that the Sicarri might use the unrest to play upon the different factions for their own ends. All these years he had feared another uprising of great proportions and now that it was near he felt ill prepared for it. He had ordered Cassius to gather the men and to use force if necessary, but had cautioned restraint. If the entire population of Jerusalem decided this day to rise up against Rome, his meagre soldiery would not suffice to hold them back and there was no time to send for reinforcements.

After that he had not returned to bed but had paced the halls, waiting on further reports, thinking on his wife's dream and on her sudden confession of faith. It was clear to him now why she had so often urged him to be lenient with the man, why she had advised him to allow Jesus to come and go freely and to speak as he saw fit in the city.

These last days his men had reported to him that Jesus seemed peaceable, a man who spoke of a heavenly kingdom, not an earthly one. But Pilate had sensed ferment in the people –why he had not listened to his reason, he did not know.

Before the sun rose pale and cheerless over Jerusalem he had washed, anointed himself and waited for word. The message had come as the sounds of horn blasts announced the break of day. The message was from Caiaphas. The priests would bring Jesus of Nazareth to him for sentencing when the city had quieted down. Pilate knew the Jews would not be coming to him for a light sentence, since they were given the sanction to punish any crime against their religious laws as they saw fit. They were coming to him for a civil judgement and had no doubt already found him guilty.

He stood now upon his court thinking on Claudia's warning to him of the terrible reprisals he would suffer should he condemn a living God, and at the same time feeling keenly how tight was Rome's leash around his neck. The Governor of Syria would not look kindly upon him if he defended a Jew at the expense of the peace of an entire province.

Now, as the members of the Sanhedrin and scribes came flowing like a malignant smell into the forum, he looked to the moment and prepared to exercise his mind's best guidance.

The forum was a large area that stood opposite the pr*ae*torium. It was used as both a market place on ordinary days and also a public place of punishment. It was usually crowded with people and merchants but since this day was a holiday it stood empty. An archway connected the forum to the square outside the pr*ae*torium and it was here that the party of priests stood paused at the threshold of his square, and he knew why. This day marked the commencement of their *Feast of Unleavened Bread* and the priests could not risk contact with a gentile.

He squinted away the sun whose light edged a green-grey cloud to see Jesus being led in chains to the foot of the steps leading to the pavement. The Jew had been beaten to a pulp and walked with a limp.

Pilate made a sigh of distaste. 'Why do you bring this man here?' he said to Caiaphas in Latin, forcing the man to speak the tongue he despised.

'For sentencing,' Caiaphas told him.

'At this early hour?'

'It is urgent, procurator.'

'What has he done? Look at him! Will you tear the man to pieces and execute him before he is judged by me?'

Caiaphas spoke with a ring of apology in his voice, 'We would not have disturbed the Roman Governor if this man were not already judged a malefactor. Take him to you and listen to our accusations.'

'Bring him to me then ... hurry up!' Pilate told the Jew guards with an impatient hand.

The temple guards moved at once to deliver Jesus to his men and they contrived to bring him up the steps but it was slow work since the man's chains prevented him from moving freely and he near fell from the obvious exhaustion, and perhaps from the pain of those wounds. Once on the Pavement he was left to stand midway between Pilate and his centurion.

Pilate moved an eye over him.

The nearness of the man he had seen only from a distance made Pilate feel overtaken with conflict. Though he was made small and ravaged from his beatings, something in the man spoke to him of eloquence and some hidden, inner power affixed to that frail and sorry form.

'What is the accusation?' Pilate said to the priests.

'He is a blasphemer!' Caiaphas told him.

'Why do you bother me, then? If he has transgressed your religious laws it is not for me to judge him but for you to sentence him according to the dictate of your laws! I will have nothing to do with it!' he said, and made a turn to go.

Caiaphas forestalled him.

'You know well, Governor, that we cannot condemn a man to death!'

Pilate turned around again. His head ached.

'What has he done that you judge him so harshly?'

'He has violated the Sabbath by curing the sick.' Caiaphas gave back.

Pilate made his voice laconic, 'It seems to me that compassion should make no distinction between one day and another. Surely if you were sick you would not care if you were healed on a Sabbath! This is not a good cause, you waste my time!'

'It is our law!' Caiaphas shrieked.

'Then you should look to change it,' Pilate answered.

The old priest, Ananias, shuffled forward. 'Governor, he is a magician, he turns water into wine and bread into flesh and tells that if one eats of his flesh and drinks of his blood they will have eternal life!'

Pilate considered this, recalling the Mithraic rituals of the military. 'Are you one of his disciples then? For you seem to be following his doctrines very well. I see with what eagerness you seek his flesh and his blood!'

'We have not told you all,' Ananias added, 'he incites rebellion by telling the people to deny Caesar his tribute!'

'If he had done so I would have heard of it ... I have good spies. I have heard only that when you tried to ensnare him with that question he answered that you must give to Caesar what is his!'

Ananias was not to be put off, 'And yet he calls himself a king and says that his followers wish to take from Caesar the kingdom of Israel! Two of his disciples are members of the Sicarri!'

Pilate turned an eye to Jesus of Nazareth before ordering Cassius to bring him to an adjoining apartment.

Here, away from the priests, the man stood before him in his much-abused state, with spit and blood mingled in his hair.

Pilate took a moment to formulate his thoughts. 'Well then ...' he said to him in Latin, 'they say you call yourself the King of the Jews. Is that true?'

Jesus lifted his good eye to look at Pilate. The other was bruised and closed shut. In that open eye's many coloured profundity Pilate saw something.

'Do you say this of me because you believe it? Or do you say it because others have said it to you?' Jesus asked.

Pilate was taken back for the man spoke in perfect, learned Latin. His voice was full of certainty and calm and it seemed to be challenging him to see for himself who Jesus truly was.

'Why should I believe you to be the King of Israel?' he told him, disconcerted, put off balance. 'I am not a Jew! Your own priests have delivered you to me and they seek from me a sentence of death. I only mean to ascertain for myself what it is that you have done. Are you a pretender to the Kingdom of David?'

'My kingdom is not of this world, for if it were, my servants would have fought for me and prevented me from being delivered to you.'

Pilate felt something in his heart and he was amazed to feel it! A *feeling* for the truth of his words!

He did not think before he said, 'You *are* a king!'

'You recognise what I am,' Jesus said to him, a little breathless, 'And I tell you, for this reason was I born, for this reason did I come into the world, that men might see what lives in me. That I should come and be among them, that with their own eyes they might see the truth as it stands before them.'

Words were caught in Pilate's throat now and he held them, scarcely knowing how to formulate them, for here was that very question on the tip of his tongue!

'What is truth?' he blurted out.

Jesus swayed and steadied himself, and it was a moment before he could speak, 'It lives beyond this world, beyond your *reason,*' he said. 'With reason, you know only what you see of this world, and with faith you believe what you cannot see ... which is higher than this world. But reason and blind faith will last only until you can make eyes that can see the *truth* of the spirit in all its glory – then you shall know it because you can see it, that I am the truth embodied in a human being. Every man that sees what lives in me, sees the *truth,* and will also hear its voice when I speak.'

Pilate was astounded at the sense this made to his mind! The quandary between his wife's feeling and his reason now seemed perfectly resolved. This man must truly be a prophet, a holy man! His wife was right. How could he sentence a holy man to death? He paced up and down, trying to think on what to do. He took himself out of the arch to the portico then, and told Caiaphas, 'I find no cause in him!'

Caiaphas was sent into turmoil and in his poor version of Latin said, 'If you do not … revile him … his followers will rise up!'

Pilate called for Cassius to bring Jesus of Nazareth out, 'Do you say nothing to this? Look how they accuse you!'

Jesus of Nazareth remained obdurate.

Pilate steeled himself. 'I'm not a fool, Caiaphas; it is plain that what you allege is false!'

Ananias stepped in. 'If you let him go, he will continue to incite the people to revolt, not only here, but also in his home of Galilee … do not think he will stop at Jerusalem! The entire province will fall under his power! It shall be said of Pontius Pilatus that you are no friend of Tiberias!"

Pilate curbed his anger and took a moment to think. 'Of course, this man is a Galilean! I had forgotten it. I say to you, he is not my concern … he belongs to Herod!'

He said this and without waiting for an answer walked off through the marble columns into the pr*ae*torium, leaving the priests behind him.

It was not over.

Herod was weak willed and would not make a judgement, and the man would return to his hands. What would he do then? Once more he felt himself standing like two pillars on either side of a raging sea: one pillar was the Roman statesman and the other was the man. How must he marry his mind's reason to that soft voice that had begun, only now, to speak of that strange thing called truth?

He did not know. And so he walked away, and tried to think no more on it.

‡

'Reason and faith … polarities that are ever at war, one with the other,' I said with a sigh, massaging my cramped hand.

'Mind and heart, *pairé*.'

'Yes, yes … I know … the middle way.'

'You see, if Pilate could only have seen beyond that life, his gaze would have fallen on an old man in Rome many centuries from that time – an old pontiff called Nicholas.'

'Nicholas?' I sat up, full of attention, 'Which Nicholas? Not the Pope in the ninth century? Tell me, does Pontius Pilate become Nicholas I?'

'Yes, *pairé* ... imagine him sitting before a great fire holding an ancient codex, asking himself if he will throw it into the flames.'

'What was this codex?'

'*The Isidoric Decretals*. They were forgeries, which gave a pope power over unruly and immoral kings. He wanted to marry faith with reason once again. He was a good pope, the last pope who was inspired by the Holy Spirit.'

My mind was searching through the annals of knowledge in my head. 'I remember ... after his death, there was a great council of the church in Constantinople. It used the power of these Isidoric Decretals to make it an anathema to say that a man was possessed of body, soul, and spirit! It was the cause of the schism between the Greeks and the Romans ... Oh, Lea! A Roman Procurator becomes a Roman Pope! His name was Pontius, and it becomes, *Pontifex Maximus* ... Pontiff ... Pope!'

'Yes, *pairé* ... he was still a bridge ... Ponti.'

'So *he* is responsible for us being upon this mountain then, responsible for the arguments between our church and the Romans concerning the Holy Spirit!'

'In many ways, you are united with Pilate through that one deed which began it all, long before, in Jerusalem.'

'Me?' I said, shocked, my heart drained of blood. Now came the question that had lived silent and wary in my heart, 'What do you mean, Lea? What deed? Who have I been in past lives and what shall I become?'

The light of the stars was in her eyes; she looked queenly then and full of knowledge. 'That is why I am here ... patience, *pairé*, soon you will come to know the world, and in the world, you will recognise yourself.

CHAPTER 65

SHOW AND TELL

When Pilate's man arrived with the message that Jesus was on his way to his palace, Herod was flattered but not surprised. The night before he had been informed of the judgement by the hasty gathering of the Sanhedrin and this morning from his rooms, built on the north side of the forum, he could hear the commotion at the Gabbatha and had sent his own men to see to it.

Now he was full with anticipation as he sat upon his large dais set at the end of the great hall, anxious for it all to begin.

Gathered around him were those members of his court who were called to observe the spectacle and Herodias his wife, wearing an incongruous white robe that made her countenance grey-grim.

Since the death of John the Baptist she had fallen into strange ways, shutting herself up in her rooms with the man's decaying head and that sword of hers. She had hoped to extract from them something to her gain, but her disappointments had reverberated through the halls and courts of Machareus for weeks, foaming over the walls and catapulting onto the expanses of the Dead Sea. In truth, her screams and strange bouts of laughter had been enough to make even the ghosts of the old Hasmoneans shiver!

The poor woman has lost her magic!

Yes! This was his lot! To have his ugly wife lose what had been her only talent in itself was bad enough, but why must it come at a time when he was beset by so many concerns?

No, nothing had gone well for him since the death of John the Baptist! For one thing, Salome had been thrown into despondency and kept herself shut up in her rooms, and for another, war threatened to break out at any time with King Aretas, his former father-in-law. On top of everything else that ominous shadow with its flapping wings kept him awake night after night, threatening to tear away his soul and to take it to hell.

So disturbed had he been by these night terrors that he had finally succumbed to his doctor's ministrations. They had given him a malodorous concoction to drink, made from mushrooms and other heinous substances – a potion which brought him oblivion in the night, yes, but made him dull-headed in the day. To counter this they gave him stimulating herbs to chew, which made his muscles twitch and his eyes bulge and caused him to jump at the slightest noise. Soon he found himself afflicted with every degree of symptom known to mankind: itches, pustules, lack of feeling in his feet, pains in his muscles, headaches, sore teeth, bad breath, colic and poor digestion. His nerves were ruined, his mind was ravaged, his temper frayed. He was certain that John the Baptist had added a further curse to cause his ailment, and he had but one hope.

Jesus of Nazareth.

Months ago he had sent his soldiers in search of the man but the fools had returned empty handed every time. Frustration and anger had filled his days and nights until now. Now Herod could hardly believe his luck. He was still in a good mood when the dreadful-thin Ananias and the short fat Caiaphas entered his hall.

These men were opposite characters that had long ago found a common purpose and had made a marriage of their priesthood. Like mismatched twins they came into his presence without waiting to be announced, which annoyed him. Behind them came their prisoner in chains, dragged by a horde of brutal temple guards, which delighted him.

A second glance made him take a gasp of surprise for the condition of the man that was brought before him.

Without waiting for Herod to speak, the tiresome priests began their accusations, which he hardly heard, for he was already on his feet making a close examination of Jesus.

'In the name of God!' he exclaimed. These words inspired a chorus of giggles from his audience and loud audible gasps from the priests. 'What have your animals done to him?'

He walked around Jesus with a hand to his face, for the smell of blood was decidedly high.

'The animal is bruised and battered!' he told them. 'Look at him! His eyes are near shut, his head is covered in mud and spittle and garbage, his nose is broken and he is full of cuts and bloodied all over! All of this before breakfast!'

Hoots of laughter echoed in the hall.

Ananias, looking as if he had not slept all his life, moved an indolent eye over Herod and said, 'He is a blasphemer, he desecrates the Sabbath and causes unrest in the people, he – '

Herod raised a cautionary hand. 'Did I tell you to speak, old man?'

Ananias was caught with his mouth open.

'He calls you a fox!' Caiaphas slipped in.

'Really? A fox?' Herod turned around to his adoring audience, 'Better a fox than a dog like my father!' He gave them a splendid smile.

In the midst of this splendour Caiaphas was a black hole. 'He has defiled Temple secrets! Who knows what else he'll do? Moreover, he says that he wishes to take away your kingdom! For this alone you must condemn him!'

Herod arched one plucked eyebrow very high. 'Must I? *Must* I? Well, well, what would I do without your counsel? But my dear priests, if Pontius Pilate did not feel compelled to find cause in him … why should I?'

Ananias came towards him, breathing his malodorous breath into the space between them, 'The governor is not a Jew and does not know our laws!'

Herod shrugged his shoulders and said pointedly, 'Some say that I am not a Jew ...' he let it hang in the air like that, and then made a laugh of it. 'And as far as our laws go ... well ...' he looked at Herodias, 'they did not help us did they, my dear, when we petitioned the law for our marriage?'

Herodias stared hatred and loathing from under that low brow at the priests but the rest of her was stock-still, like a dog that has lost its bite.

'You should not have married a woman who is your sister-in-law and also your niece!' Ananias spat out his reason. 'The finger of God will find you as it found your father before you!'

Herod paled.

'Snake!' Herodias hissed.

'She is wicked, my niece,' Herod said to cover up his anxiety and looked at his people. 'Perhaps I shall have her reverse the miracle of Moses and turn these snakes into sticks!'

All broke out into required chuckles.

Herodias did not laugh.

Caiaphas, from behind his father-in-law, said, 'What did you expect us to do? Flaunting your depravities in the open. Now you are facing a war with Aretas – all for that harlot!'

'Tell them to shut up!' his wife's voice cut through the air like broken glass.

'Yes, shut up!' Herod reiterated without passion, 'Both of you – get out!' he clapped his hands, 'We wish to interview the man alone.'

The two priests were shocked to the roots of their long greying beards, but they stood their ground and did not make a move.

'Out! Out!' Herod shooed them like chickens, 'Are you deaf as well as stupid?'

More chuckles and hoots, and they were gone with their sour looks.

Herod let his eye fall on Jesus.

He considered the man, and a sudden and inexplicable terror came over him. He was glad he was not alone with him. Perhaps, he considered, this was John the Baptist, come again to curse him further?

He held his breath and controlled his fear and brought calmness to bear upon his soul. 'I have long desired to speak with you, Jesus ...' he said, mincing his words. 'I have wished to ask you of your doings for I have heard much of your wisdom and this Kingdom of Heaven of which you teach ... I would like you to tell me about it.'

He waited, but there was no response.

'They say you can perform miracles ... that you can turn stones to bread, or perhaps it is that you turn bread to flesh? I have heard that you like to divulge priestly secrets to the multitudes. Will you not divulge something now to us? We have heard, for instance, that you can raise the dead and cause the blind to see. How comes this talent to you? Will you not show us one of your tricks? Come! Perform a miracle to amuse us. Can you cure nightmares? Can you take away the stains of the blood, the madness of souls? Can you take the ache from bones? No? Perhaps you need a greater challenge to impress us ... we give you permission to destroy the armies of Aretas!'

Jesus did not look up but stood, leaning and silent, with blood dripping from his wounds.

Herod put his sandal to the blood to rub it into the stone tile and it smudged and made a red mess, which vexed him. He sensed restlessness in the air; by now he must seem a fool. He proposed to himself alternatives.

'I have long wondered if your powers come from the spirit of John the Baptist. They say he lives inside you, is this true?' He encircled Jesus. 'Like two peas in a pod? And while we are on the matter, I will tell you that it was not my wish to kill the baptiser. We had many conversations together and I was beginning to feel a certain ... friendship growing between us. It was, well, it was an unfortunate oath, which I could not undo, you see, and before I knew it, his head was on a platter! I am sorely unhappy for it and I wish there were a way for him to know that I meant him no harm ... perhaps you can speak with him on my behalf? If you can raise the dead surely you can speak with them? Tell me, how is it for them, do they suffer much? Is there such a place as hell? Is it, as they say, separated from heaven by a hand's breath? Is it full of burning coals and sparks of fire to punish the wicked? Tell us ... can you wipe away the sins of men? Can you take away the shadows of wrongdoing that like a bird's wing flaps over the wicked?'

He paused, sensing their nearness. This sensing filled him with vexation. 'For the love of God!' he shouted, stamping a bloody sandal. 'Why don't you answer? I have the power to release you from these chains, and this humiliation! I can ensure your freedom if you tell me something marvellous, if you show me some … some small miracle! If you do, I will keep the priests from tearing out your throat like blooded dogs!'

But the man was obdurate, as pale as a statue beneath the butchering.

'Make him speak, Herod!' his wife shouted, and his court broke out in agreement.

Crossly, Herod gathered his soul in, for he wanted to splutter and spit out his wrath, but instead he took another tack, 'Kings from the East visited my father, looking for a child …' he narrowed his eyes and came very near Jesus, 'they called him a king! Is it true that you are this child who escaped from my father's clutches? If so, how did you manage it? Did you make yourself disappear? Come … do you think yourself the King of Israel?'

Not a word escaped the wounded man.

Herod, full of frustration, lashed out, 'Answer me!!!!'

A curdled silence fell in the great hall as Herod walked away from Jesus to sit upon his cushions. He wanted to rip out the man's tongue for his insolent silence, but outwardly he made light of it before it was too late.

'He is a fool!' he said, making a merry laugh.

'Then he is a fool that has made a fool of you!' Herodias said, quite taken with her own wit, 'I think him smarter than John the Baptist!'

'No!' Herod said to her, 'Even I can see it … he is nothing like that great man!' He looked at the feeble figure, standing in chains. 'He is not a king or a Messiah! The people may have sung Hosannas when you rode into the city on an ass,' he said to him, 'but now they call for your blood; if I let you go, they will surely get it!'

Jesus of Nazareth looked at him a moment and Herod grew hopeful. The moment was long and in that stare lived a form of heavenly wrath, which took away Herod's breath and planted in him a feeling he had never before experienced.

He sat up. His face grew warm.

Shame!

He did not like this new-felt sensation and broke the stare. The burning feeling died down. It was plain now, that he could not coax the man to converse on level terms. Feeling querulous, with his brain pulsing against his skull for this quiet ridicule, he called for the priests. He told them, with no small satisfaction, that he could not condemn a man whom Pontius Pilate had pronounced innocent for the sake of good relations with an old enemy – Pilate. Besides, the man Jesus did not seem guilty of anything, he was simply mad.

'He is as mad as they come!' he said.

Herodias and his entire court found this touchingly funny, and they laughed and laughed until they near burst.

Herod watched the priests leave and ordered the Levites to return Jesus to Pilate, urging them to have some merriment with him along the way.

'Amuse yourselves! Pay homage to the king of Israel.'

'Here …' said Herodias, flinging her robe across the room. 'Use this as a symbol of his purity, that all may see it and laugh as we have laughed!'

The Levites placed the white robe over the man's shoulders and they did laugh, all of them, except Herod, who did not feel merry at all, for he heard the flapping and saw those shadows come again to drive him mad.

CHAPTER 66

DECISION

The same moment that Claudia Procula woke from her dream, Gaius Cassius too sat up in his bed covered in sweat with his heart pounding the drum of his chest.

He had dreamt of a cold day and a sun, obscured by cloud, whose light was thrown over a man standing before a bull. The man, his heart bursting with fear and love, was held by a force, which travelled, pulsated and dissolved in pools and streams towards him. In his hand he held an ancient weapon, a weapon forged from the fires of heaven.

'You are born from fire!' he heard a voice in the dream say. 'Use the lance of fire!'

But when he made to plunge the lance into the bull, it became Mithras before his eyes, and being unable to forestall the lance he realised with horror that he had killed Mithras, the God, and that his blood was falling to the ground.

In the dream the man shouted, 'No!'

But it was Cassius shouting himself awake. With his mouth dry and his mind disordered he sat up in his litter and realised that he could hear a commotion coming from the streets outside the fortress. By the time the servant arrived with Claudia's message he was already dressed and gathering a number of his men to make a way out into the streets into the mayhem of people and torches and flares, with the wind howling into his bad eyes.

Much had happened since, and now, full of misgivings, he stood in the broad day upon the Pavement for the second time that morning, gazing down upon the great throng that now filled the square to the very corners.

Claudia's portent had been accurate, for Jesus was in peril.

Herod had not condemned him, and the priests, having got wind of it, had gathered up the population and no doubt paid a good sum to a score of malcontents to add weight to their cause. He was glad that he had doubled the soldiery on the steps to the palace and that he had also placed archers on the parapets that ran on all sides with their weapons aimed and ready. For now the noise-some and riotous rabble, coarse and fierce, cried out abuse and jostled, vying for the best view of Jesus, as he was pushed and pulled and dragged by his chains into the square.

But the man he had shadowed in Galilee and in other places was not this man who came into the square wearing a bloodied white robe. Jesus was almost unrecognisable to his diseased sight.

As he was brought forward those paid crowds mocked him and kicked and spat at him until he came to the wall of men guarding the stairs. They parted to let him through and he made a slow way over the steps and came to stand upon the *Pavement* nearby to Cassius.

The sun was high and it was hot. The cross that had been branded on Cassius' chest those years ago, after his third degree, worried him. Moreover, an intoxicating scent, a pungent perfume of roses came from some place, and made his nose twitch. Cassius knew it was a scent used by the lady Claudia. She would be watching the proceedings from one of the windows that gazed out into the court. She loved this man and thought him a living god and because she loved him, his heart was sorely affected for her part.

The court grew silent. Cassius squinted and saw that Pilate had returned and now stood on the other side of the Nazarene. He tried to wipe away the brown film over his eyes but could not.

'Where is Caiaphas?' shouted Pilate.

The priest's mitre was seen even before the man was, so engulfed was he by people crowding the archway to the square.

'Make a way for the priest!' Cassius barked at the people.

Caiaphas, with Ananias as his shadow, came out into the lime coloured light.

Pilate said, 'This man, which you say has perverted the people, I have examined. I have found no cause in him for your accusations. Herod has also questioned him and finds him innocent. I will chastise him and release him.'

'No!' Caiaphas yelled out, 'Rome must answer to the needs of Israel! If he is judged guilty by the Sanhedrin he must be condemned by Rome!'

A great clamour rose upwards to the clouding sky.

'The way you speak, Caiaphas, one would think that Rome was the servant of Israel and not the other way around.' Pilate sighed. 'Is there any man who will speak for this man's part?'

Caiaphas looked around him and Cassius could only guess that his look was a warning to those who might dare to say a good thing.

'I will speak!' said a man. 'My name is Nicodemus. I am an elder of the Temple. I told the priests, why do you contend with this man? He shows many wondrous signs, which no man has shown before. I have told them to leave him alone and to contrive not any evil against him! But their minds are set, for they held a meeting secretly, desiring that those who would speak on his behalf might not be present. They have also threatened any man that might come forward to defend him with excommunication, and they have paid most of the ragamuffins who are now in this square to speak out against him and to intimidate the rest!'

'Is this true?' Pontius Pilate frowned. 'Have you paid these people?'

Caiaphas drew a half smile from his face, 'Why should we do such a thing, Governor?'

'Liar!' Nicodemus said.

'Have you threatened the people?' Pilate asked again.

'Excommunication is a well-known punishment for those who defend blasphemers and those who profane the name of God! This man Nicodemus takes his part because he is a disciple of Jesus and cannot be trusted, governor.'

'Has the governor become his disciple also?' Nicodemus said, 'For I hear him speak on Jesus' behalf?'

Caiaphas near snarled, 'Shut up!'

Nicodemus countered, 'You do not like Jesus because he speaks the truth!'

Caiaphas pushed forward, 'Shut up again! If Jesus speaks the truth, then may you receive his truth, and his portion!'

Nicodemus retorted, 'Amen, Amen! May I receive his truth and I know you will make sure that I receive his portion!'

Emboldened by Nicodemus, other Jews came now from the forum and pushed forward into the square to speak out on behalf of Jesus. A great dispute then arose among the supporters and detractors – enough to deafen the ear.

In the midst of this an attendant came to the Pavement to whisper something into Pilate's ear. After that Pilate went to the pr*ae*torium and Gaius Cassius wondered if Claudia Procula had sent for him. When he returned he took Cassius aside and said to him, 'Glance your eye about and tell me, you know the Sicarri, do you recognise any among the crowds? Are these the men the priests have paid to brew this foment?'

Cassius looked at the sea of faces, each melting into the other. He could not tell who was who. They all looked alike to him, a rabble. But to admit it would be the same as buying a place on a long boat to a sedentary position in Rome. He wiped away the sweat from his brow. He had not heard anything from his spies about Sicarri, only that one of the man's own disciples had betrayed him.

'No,' he said, 'there is no love lost between the Sicarri and the priests and so in my estimation these are not the men they would have harnessed for their purpose.'

'Who is here, then?' Pilate's tone was full of annoyance.

He gave Pilate his best assessment. 'It is likely these are Jews from the city, men already known to the priests.'

'And those who love Jesus?' Pilate rasped.

'They are not from Jerusalem itself, but from other places. The priests have made certain that most could not find a place in this square.'

'I see.' Pontius pondered it, while the world fell into a clamour.

Pontius finally raised an arm and there was silence. He paused, looking at the crowds.

'According to custom,' he shouted, 'Rome entitles the people to a privilege during the feast – the deliverance of one prisoner. I have a man in my dungeon, a murderer, a member of the Sicarri, the son of Abbas, one of those responsible for the massacre of your own citizens in these very streets some years ago. We caught this Bar Abbas only two days ago, planning another insurrection with two others, one called Gesmas and another, Dismas. These men are all sentenced to die, murderers and dissenters and thieves. Remember, this man Bar Abbas was responsible for the blood that ran in these streets, the blood of your kin, and after that he deserted even his own dying brothers to seek his own safety. I will let you choose to release one man this day, either this murderous coward, or the man called Jesus of Nazareth, whom you yourself have called *the Christ*, a man whom you have seen heal and preach and console the people.'

The crowd seemed paralysed with uncertainty; a small group of his supporters called out, 'Free Jesus! Free him!'

But Caiaphas shrieked his odium over the noise in the court, 'No! Free Bar Abbas! Free Bar Abbas!'

A few people caught the contagion and more followed.

'Bar Abbas!' they cried with lustful passion, raising their fists. 'Bar Abbas!'

More and more joined in and drowned out the voices of Jesus' supporters until the din was unbearable.

Cassius realised the reason for Pilate's questions on the Sicarri now and the significance of it made the blood drain from his head.

Having first ascertained that there were no Sicarri present Pilate had made a gamble. He had gambled that the coins that were paid to this rabble would lose their lustre the moment the people were given the choice between freeing Jesus or the infamously despised creature responsible for the bloodshed of their kin. What Pilate could not have known was that he had gambled on the word of a blind man.

Pilate's voice spoke plainly of his amazement, and his annoyance, 'Which man?'

'Bar Abbas!'

'You wish to release a filthy criminal, a murderer who killed your own people?'

'Bar Abbas!'

'What then shall you have me do with the prisoner, Jesus of Nazareth?'

Ananias now provided guidance to the throngs, 'Crucify him!'

A chorus of yells and screams and vociferations now rang out and echoed in the court. The crowd swelled forward with excitement and vengeance, forcing the guards on the steps to pull up their shields and use them as weapons.

'No!' Pilate said, and it sounded impetuous, 'No! I will have him scourged ... then we shall see what you think of it!'

He made a gesture to Septimus, the man who had been Cassius' *optio* years ago, but was now advanced. Pilate leant into him to whisper in his ear and after that he told his men to take Jesus of Nazareth to the forum where he would suffer his sentence.

Cassius came to Pilate. 'I will go down with them to moderate the men.'

'No.' Pilate told him. 'There will be no moderation. He must be sufficiently punished or they will seek his crucifixion. I want you to go to the fortress instead, gather all the soldiery at our disposal and return immediately, I sense that this day shall not end well!'

'But who will control the executioners? They are blooded animals and when they are encouraged they will not easily give a moment's pause for your orders.'

'Septimus will do it.'

Cassius said under his breath, 'That man loves blood more than all of them combined!'

'That is why I have chosen him,' Pilate said, 'when they see what

Septimus can make of Jesus of Nazareth this miserable crowd will surely not seek more!'

Pilate left, and Gaius Cassius stood upon an uncertain moment. He looked out to the crowds through the broken haze of his eyes and watched the form of the Nazarene make his abused way through the archway to the forum. There, surrounded by the lustful crowd the guards prepared to chain him naked to a pillar.

Public and terrible was this punishment.

The scourges were made of leather thongs and armed with nails and spikes and bones. They tore strips of flesh from the back, the chest, the groin and the face until the prisoner was left an unrecognisable mass of blood and torn flesh.

Gaius Cassius was weary. He was too old for this. In his heart there was no thrill, no anticipation, no rush of excitement at the prospect of such a spectacle of blood. He felt a particle of discomfort settle in his bones.

All was dust and shadow he told himself.

But it did not suffice.

He looked at the young soldiers, eager for the show to begin. They would see it for themselves in time how the years passed before their eyes until one day they would find themselves standing upon the Pavement of Rome. They would find themselves sour in the belly and weary of this god-forsaken outpost at the end of the world and yet incapable of living elsewhere.

He let the thought of it sink into his mettle and sensing the eye of Claudia Procula on the back of his head he made a grunt and took himself through the court and onward to his duty.

But not before he found Abenader and told him what he must do.

CHAPTER 67

WATER OF LIFE

Magdalena had been with the Mother of her Lord throughout the ordeal of the morning. The various proceedings, the noise and hatred of the crowds, the humiliation and the mockery had wrung from her soul so many woes that she did not think herself capable of feeling more. She recalled to her mind the Mother's words, that they must remain awake and that they must endure all that he was enduring. But was it possible to do so? Had he asked too much? How could she bear to hear the imprecations and curses of those executioners when she could feel each blow of those instruments of torture as if they were tearing her own flesh?

She looked at the short, burly men, blunt of head and broad of shoulders. They wore a mix of hatred and pleasure on their faces as they struck her Lord. They tired easily, due to the ferocity of their blows, and were soon replaced by others who were no less like animals.

Roman soldiers were stationed at the perimeter of the forum to keep the crowds from advancing on the broken pillar at the centre to which her Lord was strapped. Others called out their encouragement from the guardhouse to those doing their bloody job. The more her

Lord's blood fell on the forum flags the more the world turned inward and she had to dig her nails into the flesh of her arm to stop her soul from seeking solace out of her body.

When finally a centurion made the men pause in their butchering and her Lord was dragged away all that was left were pools of his blood, which flowed now into those channels between the stones. The Mother of her Lord ventured out to the centre of the forum now and knelt on the ground to put her hands to the blood, so red and life-full, sinless and divine. She began then to wipe it with her skirts, and trembling at the knees, Magdalena joined her.

All around them the dulled sounds of the crowds dimmed to nothing. Magdalena was numb, parched of lips and drained of tears, and yet here, with her knees on the killing floor, tears came again from some undisclosed wellspring. She looked up to forestall them. The sky was streaked with clouds the colour of blood, blood all around, on her hands and on her skirts. She remembered her master's words to those Pharisees,

'You read the face of the sky and of the earth, but you have not recognised that the one who is before you is the Messiah ... you do not know how to read this moment!'

She wondered how many could read it now?

Something caught her eye – an angel? No! A woman! A Roman woman dressed in white was carrying a bolt of white cotton cloth. Some of it had come loose and was picked up by a breeze. Having unwound, the cloth floated now behind her as through the crowds the woman came. In the middle of the blood-soaked forum she knelt and her eyes found Magdalena's eyes, and the moment was stood still.

Magdalena recognised her. She was Pilate's wife, the people talked of her as a kind woman. Without speaking she held out the bolt of cotton and offered it to the Mother, who seemed not to understand what to do with it. By way of instruction the woman set it down upon the blood-soaked ground, letting the cloth take up the precious red pools.

Full of sorrow she wiped the abundant tears that tracked over her face with her bloodied hand, and the three women, kneeling together, understood – differences lived only in the world of men. They were women woven into the same moment and spun together by the thoughts of angels and so they knew:

This world is old ... but His blood is the Water of Life that will make all things new again.

CHAPTER 68

ECCE HOMO

Even before Cassius had reached the guardhouse adjacent to the pr*ae*torium, he could hear the chants of the guards.

'Hail Jesus, hail the King of the Jews!'

This was accompanied by much laughter. When he came closer he saw with his poor eyes the tortures to which the man had been subjected and the result of the abuses that the soldiers had inflicted.

The animals had made Jesus put on his muddied loincloth over his nakedness and had thrown over his shoulders a scarlet military cloak, a *Sagum,* as a gesture of mockery. On his head they had placed a platted crown made from thorny acacia; this they had pushed down hard on his head, so that its thorns had dug deep holes into the skin to make channels of blood run over his face. All of him was a mass of blood and mangled flesh from what he could see.

Cassius was struck by this spectacle for it recalled to his mind the mysteries of Mithras, in which an initiate was required to withstand not only pain, but also humiliation. It recalled to his mind his failed initiation and the cloak and crown that he had received, though he had not deserved them. To this was added what he had heard before from the Jews, that Jesus had told them to drink of his blood and to eat of his flesh. The mingling of these seemingly disparate things came together in his head and it was disturbing!

Was this an initiation made public? For this man Jesus seemed to be manifesting the mysteries of Mithras outwardly for everyone to see!

Cassius flew into a rage and yelled and kicked and pulled those drunken tormentors from the man. Picking out a number of the more sober archers he ordered Jesus taken out and escorted to the pr*ae*torium.

When they arrived, the square was now so crowded that his guards had to push the people away from the steps with shields and staves to keep them at bay. Here, on the portico of the pavement, half leaning, half standing, dripping blood and fettered with chains, dressed in the colours of royal majesty, Jesus waited, looking as if at any moment he would fall.

When Pilate came out, he said in Latin, 'Who was it that put that robe on him?'

'The guards,' Cassius answered.

'He looks like an initiate of Mithras, take it off!'

Cassius did as he was ordered, and the sight of the man disrobed caused even the crowds to gasp.

'What man could want more vengeance than this?' Pilate said, and turning to the crowds, yelled out, '*Ecce Homo*!' Then in Aramaic, so that all the people might hear it, not only the priests, 'Behold! The man! Here is his body and his blood transformed for you!' he said, 'Now are you satisfied?'

Ananias shouted, 'NO! He has made himself a Son of God and must be condemned!'

Cassius frowned. What strange day was this? A Son of God! To claim openly the title of Son of God, a God incarnate, was to rival Tiberias, who also claimed this title.

Pilate went through the arch and gestured for Cassius to bring Jesus to him. Pilate paced the floors, pausing before the figure of the broken, bloodied man.

'Iesus Nazarenus, tell me this … from whence do you come? Is it true that you say you are the Son of God?'

The prisoner was silent.

'Why do you not answer? Don't you understand that those filthy priests are accusing you of rivalling Tiberias?'

Jesus of Nazareth, leaning as he was and clinging to his life, said nothing.

'I have the power to crucify you or to set you free … but you must first deny it!'

When Jesus finally spoke, it seemed to Cassius that the voice was not the voice of a man torn and battered. It was a voice strong and full of authority, 'You can have no power over me unless that power is given to you from above. Those outside … those who delivered me to you, they have said that I am the Son of God; they say it because they know from whence comes the power in me and to Whom they are responsible. Because of this they have a greater sin than you.'

Pilate made a gesture of the hand, which Cassius could see meant they should go.

When they were once more upon the Pavement, the cries for crucifixion rose upwards with greater fierceness.

The day was low hung and that oppressive heat made breathing difficult under the darkening sky.

Pilate took himself to the raised throne, the official marble seat. Cassius knew he would now make a judgement, *ex cathedra,* that is, he would judge as a representative of Caesar. Whatever judgment was made, it would be as if Caesar had made it. The people knew it also and they grew silent, so excited were they at the prospect of what he would say.

'See this, your king! He is the Son of God, your Messiah!' he said to them.

Now the court broke out into a great clamour.

Pilate had made a royal proclamation! Had the infernal heat caused him to lose a wit?

'This man is the enemy of Caesar!' Caiaphas shrieked, outraged, 'We renounce him!'

'Rome has no quarrel with *this* Messiah!' Pilate gave back, 'His kingdom, he freely admits, is not of this world, and we are not concerned with him as long as he gives dignity to the name of Caesar!

'We renounce him!' echoed the people.

'Does this mean you will never demand liberation from Rome?' he sat forward on his seat. 'Does this mean that you will renounce all those who call for a Messiah, a King of Israel in future times? Think carefully!'

Gloom fell over the court.

Caiaphas yelled out, 'We have no king but Caesar!'

Uncertainty moved over the faces of the people. Cassius himself could not believe that a Jew, let alone a high priest, had spoken these words. This was indeed the strangest of days!

'And so you have spoken!' shouted Pilate. 'This means, therefore, that I am not responsible for your madness!'

Ananias answered it, 'No ... let the responsibility lie with us, let the blood of this man be on our own heads, and on the heads of our children!'

Pilate called to an attendant. 'So it shall be!' he said, 'You have spoken not only for your own sorry selves, but also for those Jews who love him and have no part in this, and are outside this square only because they would not take your money! Well then! I wash my hands of it ... bring me water!'

The attendant brought water in a pitcher, which was poured over the Governor's hands, as was his custom. When he had wiped them clean with a towel he stood and said to the crowds, 'I pronounce myself innocent of the blood of this just man!' Then to his scribes, 'Write this down ... *having been compelled, for fear of an insurrection, to yield to the wishes of the high priest of the Sanhedrin and the people who demanded the death of Jesus of Nazareth, I have handed him over to the guards for crucifixion; and upon his titulus will be written, in all three languages of the land, in Latin, Greek and Hebrew, his crime*: INRI ... *Iesus Nazarenus Rex Iudaerum* – Jesus of Nazareth, King of the Jews!'

A great shouting now came from the priests.

'You cannot name him thus! You have no right to give him that title!'

'What is written is written!' Pilate dismissed, and ordered Cassius to take Jesus away.

Cassius felt dreariness in his soul as he took the man through the crowds, but he had not a moment to dwell on it, since a great clamour and uproar now broke out over the titulus and all his thoughts turned to keeping the peace.

CHAPTER 69

VIA DOLOROSA

Wearing the seamless robe she had made him those years ago, her son, bounded by four soldiers and led by a centurion, was taken to his death through the streets of Jerusalem carrying the *patibulum*, or crosspiece, to which his arms were tied. It rested on his shoulders and the weight of it combined with his wounds, his thirst and his exhaustion, made him lose his balance.

People lined the narrow streets, shouting obscenities and jeering, and beyond these shadows of evil she stood with Magdalena, Lazarus-John, and her sister-in-law Mary of Cleophas. The procession headed north from the pr*ae*torium to the place of execution outside the city walls and so it descended through the streets until it came through the gate of the first wall.

Here, she did not hear the people taunting him, she did not hear the lament of the women, she did not see the Romans whipping his body and making all his wounds deeper, she saw only her son, and her God, and they saw her. His eyes asked:

Where is Peter? Why has he not come to help me carry my cross? Where are my disciples? Where are my followers? Are they still asleep?

She could not answer him, for she knew not where they were. Instead she took upon herself his suffering, so that she knew how heavy was the wood that tore at the ligaments of his lacerated shoulders, how hard was the way over the stones with his bare feet full of cuts and sores and gashes, she felt how his head throbbed from the thorns that continued to pierce it, how great was his thirst, which made his tongue cleave to the roof of his mouth, how the chills of fever shook him to his very centre, and how his entire being screamed with hurts because his wounds, both physical and spiritual, made inroads into his heart.

She understood now that this passion had begun the moment the God had entered into Jesus at his baptism, and that it was culminating in this dolorous way to his voluntary sacrifice.

His petition to her at the cenacle had never seemed more difficult than now. How was she to rise above her suffering in order to transform it into love? Love even for those Romans who called out abuse and dragged him by his weeping arms, scraping his skinless knees to raise him, love for the centurion who carried the *titulus* which would be nailed to his cross, love for his judges and executioners, love for those who were full of hate, who abused him for his alleged profanity from the rooftops and threw stones and rubbish at him.

The last gate out of the city was situated in the busy suburb of Akra and it opened onto the road that led to the place of execution. Here he fell and could not get up, no matter how many times he was whipped. This forced a halt in the cohort of Romans headed by Pilate that came from behind, escorting two more malefactors also destined for crucifixion.

Outside the first gate, in this suburb, those who loved her son outnumbered those who were swayed by the hate of the Sanhedrin and those who were paid to taunt him. They begged the Romans to stop beating and kicking him. But the Romans returned the supplications of the people with blows from their staves and whips. This commotion diverted the soldiers long enough to allow her a space in which to come near to him. Leaving the others behind her she went down on her knees and crawled to where he lay on the cobbles with his arms pinned down by the cross piece. She put her face to the ground so that he might see her and put a hand to his hair, matted and bloodied, to remove it from his disfigured eyes.

From somewhere came the smell of roses.

He looked at her and her heart trembled. She gasped for breath, and in that gasp a window in time was opened and held still. This was the last moment between them, and when this meeting flew away she would not come so close again until he was dead.

'I thirst!' he said, and there was the trace of a smile in his misshapen face.

'You are always thirsty!' she answered, smiling through the tears, 'But I have no water that tastes of wine to give you, my son!'

She could say nothing more for there were no wise and useful words left to her, only sorrow-filled ones, and these were held back for fear of breaking the enchantment of the moment.

'Get up, woman!' a voice said, and she felt herself dragged away from him, away from those eyes.

'Leave her be, Abenader! That is the mother!' she recognised this voice, 'See to him, or he will die before he gets to his execution! It will not do to lose him now after he has come so far! Find someone to help him!' It was the same centurion from the night before, the one upon his horse, his voice and words recalled to her mind that moment at the gates of Jerusalem those many years ago. He ordered a guard to take a pagan Greek from the crowd.

'Tu! Imbecile! Adiuvo! Sic! Tu! Imbecile! Adi-u-vo!' Then he shouted in Greek, *'Arêxis!* You're not a Jew, I know who you are, you're the Greek stonemason ... lift him up, you Greek bag of dung!'

He pushed him towards her son and after some further coaxing the man took him by an arm and lifted him to his feet.

Her son gave her one last look before the man helped him onwards.

She was taken with dizziness then, and Lazarus-John held her as the procession moved on.

And for a small time she did not see him.

CHAPTER 70

DESTINY

By the time the procession arrived at the topmost aspect of the rocky plateau they called Golgotha, the preparations for the crucifixion were near finished. It was almost the *seventh hour* and the Romans were resting, half dressed, drinking wine and rolling dice. When they saw that Pilate was among the cohort of soldiers they stood and put away their drink and made a small effort to look like soldiers.

Claudia Procula looked upwards to a sky drowned in cloud. The wind was stronger and the world was lulled by it into movement and when the cold air crossed her face after the heat of day it caused her to shiver. She pushed ahead of the crowds to come closer to the cross. She saw that Jesus had slipped and had fallen upon a rock. His moans made inroads into the hearts of the women nearby, and moved her to her very sinews with compassion.

She saw her husband inspecting his men. He did not look like the man she loved, like the father of her child. He seemed a stranger to her, and yet so confused was her heart that even as he prepared to leave the hillock, with that look of a man who has no floor on which to stand, a desire rose up in her to go to him. But she did not go to him and he did not see her, for she was once again dressed as a Jew and among the women relatives of Jesus.

The centurion called Abenader took a cup to where lay Christ Jesus and offered it to him. She knew it was wine blended with wormwood – to stupefy those who would suffer the coming punishment. Christ Jesus refused it. No. He would not yield to ordinary weakness. He was destined to suffer without quarter and to surrender himself only when all was done.

The guards tore off the garments from that aching, bleeding, weeping body full of lacerations, welts and swellings, dividing amongst themselves their spoils – all except his robe. They threw dice for it and laughed among themselves.

She looked away, for naked was he made to lie on the ground so that the guards could nail his wrists to the crosspiece. Blow after blow was struck until the tapered nail, having pierced deep into the flesh, was finally sunk into the wood.

She near fainted, for she felt his moans as hers, and his burning pain moved over her own arms and it seemed unbearable to her, this burning, a mighty conflagration!

Blood gushed over the archers and they cursed it.

Gaius Cassius looked about but with his bad eyes failed to see her. He cursed the archers and told them to hurry.

The two criminals were also nailed to their cross pieces and the sounds of their constant, woeful screaming reached the darkening vaults of heaven and made the world seem like a place full of torment. She looked to the woman called Magdalena. She had fallen on the ground and was taking up dirt into her hands to rub into her hair and her face. She wept and wept.

The archers had begun dragging Jesus to his feet and were now pulling him to the post wedged into a hole in the ground. Two men on ladders lifted his body until the post found the slot in the cross piece, and then he was let go. The crosspiece came down with the full force of Jesus' weight on his wounds, causing a great tearing and bleeding. All around her the sound of moans continued as the guards came off their ladders and took up their nails to hammer in the feet, but it took long, many blows of the hammer were struck before the bones were shattered.

After that came the convulsing of the entire body, which moved of its own accord. She could not bear it.

Claudia fell. She heard crickets in her ears and all went to black before the world was returned again, and with it a thought. She realised that ill did not attract ill after all! Only a great light, a great goodness could raise the hackles of evil in such a way and cause it to cast a dark shadow such as this!

At that very moment, Gaius Cassius, by some instinct, turned away from his work of overseeing the butchery and let his clouded eyes roam the crowds until they fell on her. His face bespoke bewilderment and surprise and his mouth came open slightly, as if he would speak. But he said nothing.

Of a sudden open to her heart was the thread of destiny that bound them and would continue to bind them from life to life. But in the same breath it slipped away from her, leaving only a faint trace of a memory, like a taste in the mouth of something sweet.

He returned to his work then, and she realised with relief that again he had not seen her.

CHAPTER 71

SOPHIA

At the foot of her son's cross, amid the dark-full outburst of elements Mariam's soul fell open. Now, all the waking dreams of worlds, all the wisdom that unites their intelligences and weaves them together, all that came from the sphere of the Virgin, the virginal selfhood of heaven, entered her fully. It was as though the Great Mother in heaven had lent her clothes to the smaller mother below to adorn her with her glory! She was made new!

Her son's words spoke in her soul,

'Mother! Behold Lazarus-John, he is now your son!'

She looked to the young man and knew that his soul was ready for wisdom.

Her son now told the young man, 'Lazarus-John, behold my Mother. See in her the Sophia, the wisdom that lives in me, this you must henceforth recognise as yours! Take this wisdom into the housing of your soul and dedicate yourself to it!'

Two worlds came together then, above and below, for the wisdom that was hers was bestowed upon Lazarus-John, as a gift.

The sky stooped over and made a tumble of the wind.

She heard her son say, once again, that he was thirsty.

The centurion, battered by the gusts, soaked a sponge in wine vinegar and put it through the end of a stick to lift it to her son's lips.

The wind railed against it.

The soldiers took up their weapons and began to flee the storm.

Only the two centurions remained.

From the cross Jesus said to the Christ in him, '*Eli, Eli, lama sabachthani.* My God, my God, how you have elevated me!' and Christ spoke then to the Holy Spirit above him, 'Why have you forsaken me?' And then He said, 'Father ... into your hands I commend my spirit ...'

She felt death come as he said, 'It ... is ... accomplished!'

With these words, she felt a great release, and she would have fallen, if not for Lazarus-John.

These words had fired in the east a spirit-light that could be seen far away in the west by the Druid priests in their stone circles. They saw it in the quality of the fine upper airs and in the colour of the auras around the shadow of the stones that a healing force was entering the world to save it from death.

But in the east, from whence came the light, a great rumble was heard. For the powers of death, frustrated and furious, began now to assail the world and the wind stirred dust made a cloud rise that blotted out the sun, and darkened the day, seeking to eclipse the day-radiant light of Christ as it entered the ethereal round.

Fear and fury was felt by the evil ones, those darknesses that had held sway on earth until now. These beings, wedded to the shadows, shrieked with pain and with anger when He came before them in all His power! For the spirit of Christ had overcome death, their master, and was now descending into the centre of the earth, that place which they call Hell, to imprison and to fetter all that was evil for a thousand years.

And it was from Golgotha that a crack was made in the earth, and it tore its way over the ground to that other Mount on which stood the Temple of the Jews – the Mount of Zion.

CHAPTER 72

FOUR VEILS

Caiaphas was in the Temple with Ananias preparing for the evening ritual when two Pharisees burst into the court with their eyes wide in their pale faces. He knew they were afraid, they were all afraid. The events of these last hours had all men jumping out of their skins.

But not Caiaphas.

He sighed and scratched his back absently. Would this day never end?

'What do you want?'

One man said, 'We've come to ask why you have not dispatched the Levites to Golgotha? They have to break the bones of those men before the beginning of the Sabbath so that they can be taken down!'

Caiaphas did not like being told what to do. He said, 'Impossible! It is too late, soon it is sunset; besides, I have to go and kindle the incense.' He began to ascend the steps.

But those dreadful Pharisees would not be put off.

'Listen, Caiaphas, there is time. If not, the families will have to wait until after the feast to bury them.'

'So what?' he said looking at the fools. 'Let them rot for a few days on their crosses … what harm can it do? It may be a good thing to let the birds have their fill of Jesus' pitiful carcass. Let all men see it as they come and go! That way whoever passes will be reminded that Jesus of Nazareth was not a god, just a liar full of his own importance!'

He turned to go but was prevented by the other man.

'No!' the stubborn Pharisee countered. 'The Sanhedrin must comply with the law. This Sabbath is a High day, Caiaphas, and you know as well as we that when the Sabbath falls on the second Paschal day the law is even more strict! How can the people celebrate the Feast of the Unleavened Bread with the smell and sight of carrion meat outside the gates!'

Caiaphas sighed a weary and bored sigh and waved a hand as if he were shooing a fly. 'Very well, you may send three guards.'

'But the Romans won't allow it unless you go, Caiaphas!' said the other annoying Pharisee, 'for without you the soldiers have no authority.'

Caiaphas turned an indolent eye upon the man, a look that could wither a plant, but it did nothing to change the resolve on that stubborn face. 'The lot, dear Solomon, has fallen to me, I must kindle the incense ... do you see how impossible it is?'

'If you send the captain of the guards with the lance of Phineas,' Ananias offered from behind them, 'the Romans will know that a mandate has been given and they must demur before it.'

Caiaphas was full of pleasure for this suggestion, since the lance of Phineas had been that lance used to kill those idolaters and adulterers who had also not complied with the laws of Moses. There was a species of poetic eloquence in using it against Jesus. He wished that he had thought of it himself!

After he gave the orders that it be done he ascended the three steps to commence the ritual burning of the incense. At this point a speck of a feeling announced itself, a feeling against all logic. He pushed it back into the dull corners of his ill-used heart and tried to preoccupy himself with his task, but it would not go away, it would have his ear until finally, it spread apart the curtains of his mind and announced itself loudly:

Could he have been the Messiah?

This petition rang out from his soul before he could snatch it. It fell over the heavy four-coloured veil that hung taut before the Holy of Holies. It fell over the golden altar of incense that glowed red with coals.

Oh no! He had unwittingly petitioned the ancient oracle!

Behind him the Levites were kneeled and he was full of relief – it had seemed to him that he had said it out loud, but he had not.

He gathered his wits to him, kindled the incense and took the golden censer from the fire, but at that moment a wind had entered the city, an ancient wind called Ruach. It moved over the colossal bridge and swept through the archways, forcing its way through the gates of the Temple, curving its back around the sanctuary of shining marble and glittering gold, sweeping through the court of the women, the court of Israel and the court of the Priests and entering the chambers so strongly as to fan the sacred fires into flames.

Ruach … Elohim … Aur! Breath … Elohim … Light!

It moved from behind the columns and the walls and reached out its hands to grasp at Caiaphas' vestments and to tear at his robes. He drew his hands to dampen its voice and dropped the sacred incense to the marble floor.

Dismay and confusion swirled around the sanctuary now, but Caiaphas heard only these words:

HE IS!

At this point day turned to night and the earth began to move of its own accord, sending the golden candlestick with its seven lit lamps crashing to the floor. Caiaphas lost his balance and followed it, hitting his head on the altar. The priests dissolved into panic as the wind, full of sand and dust, made them choke, and the shaking of the earth tore through the ground like the hand of a furious god.

Caiaphas struggled to stand but his vestments were lifted up to his face like devil's wings. And as the earth exchanged places with the air he was gripped by terror and tried to make a way out of the Temple, but there was a great commotion and confusion among those who had come for the service. The crowds, coming together of a sudden, made a crush through the porches and many fell and were trampled underfoot. At this point a crack in the earth was heard and those veils guarding the holy place, those veils long and wide and thick and wrought in seventy-two squares joined together, gathered the wind into themselves like sails and were made pregnant. In their convulsions and birth throws there began a rip, and a loud rent sounded as the four veils were torn from top to bottom, laying bare the most Holy Place to the eyes of all.

The storm and the earthquake swallowed up the cries of terror and shock. God Himself, in His wrath, had rent the four veils with His own hands and was gone from that place where he had dwelt in mysterious gloom. What portent was this? the priests asked themselves.

Only Caiaphas knew the answer, for he had heard the voice of the oracle. God had forsaken their Temple because they had killed His only Begotten Son.

CHAPTER 73

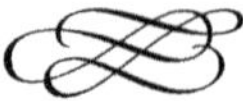

GRAIL SPEAR

The strange day was now near over. Each hour had caused Gaius Cassius to grow more anxious for what he was seeing and hearing, for in all of it he felt the acknowledgement of a peculiar truth.

Since his failed initiation he had held onto the only sure thing in his life – duty. But now this duty was pulling away and leaving him no firm foundation. For the deepest duty of an initiate was to keep the secrecy of the mysteries, and these had been violated and revealed before the eyes of all through this man Jesus.

This made him ask himself over and over:

What kind of man is this?

The more he asked it the further did he seem from his duty.

How many had he seen crucified? Hundreds in his time, and yet he had never heard those words – 'My God, how you have elevated me!' – a phrase uttered by every initiate who is raised!

This was an initiate. He had no doubt!

And yet …

What kind of initiate is this?

The more he grew meek and frail, the more he was beaten and tortured, the more abundant was his compassion and love for all who tormented him. And what kind of influence did he have over the elements when the greater his compassion the more the yellow storm clouds grew in the sky?

By observing these portents and signs, by these slow means, there began in Cassius' soul a certain change and a species of knowledge rose to his mind.

This crucified man is more than an initiate!

Did he not speak of the glory of God in him? Of *Exousia,* which meant that his body was enlightened by Mithras?

This was the ancient mystery wisdom:

Through God we are born!

He recalled that afternoon in Galilee when, beside Claudia Procula, he had seen the light of the sun spill out of Jesus. Now he wondered how he could have put such a vision from his mind?

'This man is surely the Son of God!' he said aloud.

The Centurion Abenader was hard-hearted, and yet even he was stopped with a look of amazement, for he too could see it.

In the midst of the tempest of air and light and earth, Cassius observed foot soldiers coming up the incline. By the time they reached the hillock, the daystar had grown cold and lifeless and was hidden so deep in the clouds that it seemed to Cassius to be a manifestation of the portents of those sibyls who had long ago foretold the end of the world.

The Temple guards, led by a captain, approached the crosses in haste and shouted for those Jews who had remained, the three women and one youth, to move out of the way.

Cassius knew what they had come to do, and yet he went to them and in the confusion of wind and dust and storm shouted in Aramaic,

'Halt!'

The captain shouted back, so as to be heard, 'Rome recognises our custom!'

'You may break the legs of those two,' he pointed to the malefactors. 'for they are yet alive; the other in their midst is by now dead!'

The captain of the guards, no doubt desiring to have it over with, did not argue but sent two guards to fight through the moving air to the crosses. They did not climb the ladders, but took their iron staves and broke only the legs of the men, who in turn uttered terrible cries as they struggled for breath.

These abuses made the storm-tossed women below moan and hold onto each other. The swirling world tore bites from their robes and beat into their faces but they did not move.

'I need to be certain this one is dead!' shouted the captain and moved forward to his task, but at that moment Gaius Cassius saw before his eyes his dream made real.

This was that cold day forsaken by sun, and obscured by cloud in the penumbral light! He saw that he was standing before the God Mithras! Mithras was upon that illuminated cross, defying the darkness! Overpowering was the memory of a child now, a child with stars over his head who had become a man and whose eyes were like suns! When had he seen this child? Was it at Bethlehem aeons ago?

An impulse came through him:

I am a Son of Fire and I will use the lance of fire!

He intercepted the captain of the Jew guard and shouted into his face, 'In the name of Caesar Tiberias I order you to give me your lance!'

The man, confused by wind and this strange command, did not know what to do.

'NOW!'

The man acquiesced.

Cassius went to the body of Jesus and, with a hand to shield his eyes from the sand-dust, lifted the weapon to the dead man's chest and made a thrust upwards, plunging the Jew spear deep into the light body of the God.

He shouted, 'He is dead, do you see!'

From the world we enter the spirit!

He said the ancient mystery words to himself.

‡

'Blood and water, rose-warm life, now sprayed over him, *pairé*, and fell into his eyes. A tremble came from the heart of the earth and tore at the very foundations of the world and the sky let loose a great crack of thunder, rending the skies, and among these tempers he saw Christ in all of His fullness and truth, in all of His majesty and splendour. Christ now showed Gaius Cassius Longinus a distant future.

'Tell me Lea ... what did he see?'

'He saw a man upon a great mountain fortress, gazing backwards in time at him. In that moment, the two places were woven into the same space in life's evolving stream, and those two souls could look upon one another knowing the other as himself.

'It was only an instant, but to Cassius it was an eternity, gazing with wonder and awe at all that would pass in between: sorrows and battles, births and deaths, lifetimes.

'And what of Cassius?'

'He never again said, *all is dust and shadows, pairé.* He never again saw life darkly, for the scales had been torn from his eyes by that light, which illuminates memory to dispel the blindness of death.

The light of Christ which is the fount of eternal life.'

CHAPTER 74

HOLY GRAIL

During those fourteen days we said our goodbyes and celebrated our love. Those who had chosen the pyre gave away their belongings: the other perfects gave Pierre-Roger a coverlet full of deniers, I gave him a small present of oil, some salt, and a piece of green cloth for his devotion, and the Marquésia de Lantar gave all her possessions to her grand-daughter Philippa, who was Pierre-Roger's wife. Others gave whatever they had, some small memento, a favourite hat, a purse, a little wax, even their shoes.

I gave the *consolamentum* to those of our people who desired it, and even two knights and a great number from the garrison. These men could have walked away from death but they chose to die with us.

So began the days of preparation for our martyrdom.

In the meantime, Matteu the troubadour arrived stealthily in the night. He spent some days with us telling stories and amusing the children and the adults alike. Soon he would leave us to take away the Gospel of John, the Book of Seven Seals, and that speechless child, the charge of the Marquésia. But we would only know if they had reached safety by the sign – a fire on the summit of Bidorta.

One day I came across Matteu while walking the courts. He was nearing fifty-four springs and yet he was hale and strong, his brow full of things seen and done and his eyes reflecting a youthful spirit.

He fell to his knees before me but I asked him to rise. I told him I was not worthy of his adoration.

'But you are a *parfait*, my friend!' he said.

'Who in the world can call himself perfect?' I said to him and took him aside to the gate now open to the expanse of the mountains. We both sat quietly together for a time, staring out, until I told him I wanted to speak to him about his songs.

He looked at me then with that intrepid eye, no doubt bracing himself for one of my invectives.

'No ... no,' I said, with a laugh, 'I am not going to rebuke you. I wanted to say that I have grown some sense of this song of the Grail that you sing.'

His face opened up in a smile, 'You? What do you think it is then, a stone or a cup?'

I said that I thought it to mean many things. I said that it was Jesus who came to earth to be the vessel for the Lord, that it was the soul of every man, the soul full of faith in Christ, and also that it was the earth and all its creatures, for it had taken up the body and the blood of Christ.

Matteu fell silent and thoughtful with his face to the dying sun.

He said finally, 'Do you know, old friend, I dream that it is a woman, a woman holding her dead son ... sometimes I think I see it when the moon is only a sickle ... sometimes it looks like that to me, like a vessel.'

I nodded with a smile to myself. 'Yes, that is a good likeness.'

'You know,' his voice changed, suddenly full of enthusiasm, 'I think after this I shall sing a new song ... I shall sing how once upon a time a castle of the Grail was threatened by the Devil's armies and that at the time of the greatest danger a dove flew down from the heavens to split open the summit of Bidorta over there ... with its beak. I will sing how Esclarmonde de Foix, the angel keeper of the Grail, threw the cup into the heart of that mountain to keep it safe. Do you think they will look for it a long time, thinking that it is in the mountains, *pairé,* because of my song?'

I smiled. 'Yes, I think they will.'

'They may burn all the pure ones, you know, but I will sing how Esclarmonde did not die, I will sing that she turned into a dove and flew off from the very top of the keep to the mountains of the land of Prester John, and that is why her grave will never be found because she never died!'

Prester John? There was something in that!

I looked at him. 'But Esclarmonde has been dead many years.'

'Yes, of course,' he said, 'but just between you and me, Bertrand, I feel her presence every now and again, in the night. She whispers songs into my ears … she is so beautiful!' He seemed to remember something then. 'When you came out of that hiding spot in Beziers, with fire all around, you told me that a beautiful woman had woken you in the night and told you to hide in the woods, I just remembered it!'

I paused, struck by his words, for something was now making perfect sense to me. I clapped him on the back. 'Yes, she saved my life and I don't think I have ever properly thanked her for it!'

We sat then for a time with our memories until he stood to leave.

I told him to go with God.

His face broke out in a wrinkled smile. 'And you!'

When he left my heart grew weary and sad and I sat upon that rock looking out long after the sun had set. I had said goodbye to a dear friend that I hardly knew! For in all the years I had seen him barely a dozen times. This strange, paradoxical friendship would only be made clear to me in the upper room when Lea came again to spin her words. For it was then that I would begin to see who Matteu had been in lives gone past, though I know that in this life our bond is that he is destined to carry this Gospel to its resting place.

‡

At any rate, Lea told me that Joseph had remained awake all night after the trials. He had watched the scourging and had followed the dismal procession to Golgotha. He was now on his way back again to the gallows, after receiving Pilate's authority to remove the body of his Lord to the place of burial.

As he walked beside his friend Nicodemus he realised what a fool he was to have thought himself near death all these months. For when his master had asked him to go home to prepare his grave he had meant that he must build a sepulchre in which His body could be laid. And as Joseph toiled the road to Golgotha he held this goal firmly in mind.

Behind him his servants carried the articles necessary for the burial, vases of water, bottles of unctions, bundles of linen and a litter. Nicodemus carried costly spices in barrels of bark strapped around his neck, while Joseph himself carried a lantern in one hand and in the other a flask of wine and the cup of Jasper used by Christ Jesus at the Passover feast to fortify those who had remained at the cross.

The sun had been dark all afternoon but now it began to hide itself altogether and the wind came up like a living thing, playing with their robes, fluttering the flame in the lanterns and taking the cloths from out of the hands of the servants. A sudden, sonorous rumble was heard and a number of hastening temple guards passed their group, taking themselves to the place of execution. By the time the little party reached Golgotha Joseph caught a glimpse through the mayhem of windblown rubble and chaos, of a spectacle – a man was piercing the side of his master with a lance!

For the first time in his long life Joseph moved without a thought. Thrown away was his prudence and let go was the lantern and the flask. He ran through the storm of dust to the cross. How could he allow his master's blood to fall on the ground? In a moment he was kneeling beneath the stream of blood, holding the cup to catch its flow.

Afterwards he looked at the centurion and a feeling passed over his heart that one day he would see that spear which the man held in his hands, and it would give him a vision of this moment as he stood beneath the cross.

He stammered when he told the centurion that he had a dispensation from Pilate to take the body down from the cross in order to bury it in his own tomb. And he was surprised to find both the centurion with the spear and the other man strangely full of tenderness for the body of his master. They tied it with cords and drew the nails out one by one, lowering it slowly from ladders, one rung at a time, and gave it into the hands of Nicodemus. Together the three men took it to the mother, who sat upon the ground with the woman, Magdalena.

The wind paused and the rumble grew quiet. In this sudden, otherworldly silence, Joseph was taken by a vision.

Clouds parted to allow a soft light to console the mother, who held her dead son. The world lay in hushed adoration of it. Even the moans and sobs of the women who had come to join them in their doings were now paused. Standing before this vision, holding the cup in his hand, a second realisation came. Joseph fell to his knees. Here was that image that he had seen in the heavens standing in his garden those months ago, but then it had taken the form of a slice of moon holding the dark disc of the sun! He looked to the cup and he looked to the mother in that light-radiance. He understood – mother and cup were one. For a mother's soul held her Son like the cup in Joseph's hands held His blood!

The light faded and night was drawing near. Joseph had to quiet his thought to lead the others to his tomb, for soon would commence the Sabbath.

‡

'It was later, after Jesus had been laid in the tomb and near the hind of morning, *pairé*, that Joseph, replete with sadness, was making his way home again. Through the dark and windy streets he walked, contemplating all that had come before, when not far from his house he was arrested by armed soldiers and taken by force to a tower, a deserted turret that formed a part of the city wall. There he was locked in a cell.

'Legend tells that it was among the rats and the dampness that

Joseph would experience the full teachings of the risen Christ, even as the other disciples experienced it, and so nourishing was it for his soul that though he was given no food and no water he did not die. All were astonished when they set him free, especially those high priests of the Sanhedrin who had ordered his arrest. But Joseph knew, *pairé*, what they did not know, that a man does not live by bread alone.

'And so, as the moon had shown Joseph that morning in his garden, he was destined to become the first guardian of this sacred knowledge, which he took westward to the island of Glastonbury, to that land of Druid priests. They would come to call this knowledge, The Mystery of the Holy Grail.'

CHAPTER 75

DO NOT TOUCH ME!

In the early hours before day rise, the mother of the Lord and the other women went to the rock-hewn tomb in Joseph's garden to see to the proper anointing of their master's body. Magdalena was late in following and she had not yet reached the garden when she was met by the mother and the others returning again from the tomb. They told her that on arriving they had found the tomb open and empty. In and around the tomb they had seen a vision of angels who said their lord had already risen and to look for him among the living.

Magdalena, full of concern, returned with the others to the cenacle to tell the men and found only Lazarus-John with Peter in the upper room.

Upon seeing them Peter came directly to the mother to beg her forgiveness. He recounted how on the night of Passover he had denied his Lord three times for fear of his life. Because of this, full of shame, he had gone to Olivet where he found a cave. In it he had slept fitfully until awakened by an overwhelming effulgence. It was the brilliant form of his master illuminating the gloom of his cave. His master told him to go and tell the others what he had seen.

The Mother of the Lord recounted what the women had seen:

angels, rolled away stones and an empty grave. Full of wonder the men resolved to see it and took themselves out of the city with Magdalena following in their train.

By the time the three of them arrived at the tomb a red-gold promise of sunrise lay on the margins of the horizon. Lazarus-John was carrying the lamp and he was first through the low door of the sepulchre. He told them what he saw: a great gash in the earth, a deep cleft had opened up and now the linen cloths were lying on one side of it and the head napkin on the other.

Peter, having by now entered the sepulchre himself, confirmed that the grave was empty. There followed some discussion between them and, not knowing what they should do, they left to find the other disciples.

Magdalena remained behind.

Alone at the entrance to the sepulchre a deep sense of loss beckoned tears from her eyes. Her master was gone, his body was not found and she did not know how he could return again without it. Not having seen the angels like the others she wanted to know it for herself but she had lost her spirit sight! She watched the sun rise over the hills and when it cast its benevolent rays on the mouth of the tomb she braced herself and dared to look inside.

She gasped.

Lit up by the birthing light were two angels, one at the head of the great stone bier and the other at the foot of it. She had regained her sight!

Woman, why do you weep?

She harnessed her mind to answer. 'Because they have taken away my Lord and I know not where they have taken him!'

Fearful she turned around but there was a man standing before her, haloed by sun. She did not know him but he seemed full of the power of burgeoning and sprouting life, as if he were a gardener, a planter or a cultivator. To see him made her hope that he might know where her master's body would be.

He took the words from out of the mouths of the angels,

'Woman, why do you weep?'

'Sir, if you have borne his body from here, tell me where you have laid it and I will take him away.'

The man now called her by her old name, 'Mary!'

The memory of her master's words rose through her feeling to her thinking:

Unite with the bridegroom in the bridal chamber of your heart, and from this union will arise in you a knowledge of Who I Am!

Her eyes saw Him now! The youthful body of Jesus, in all its flawless fullness!

'Master!' She moved to go to him, but he forestalled her.

'Touch me not, dear Magdalena, for it will pollute me; the mystery is not yet consumed. Christ must yet unite fully with me. Go, tell the others to wait, tell them not to be sorrowful for I will soon come to them!'

Joyful and obedient, she ran all the way back to the cenacle.

CHAPTER 76

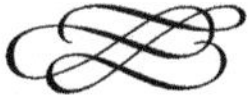

LEAVE-TAKING

That evening, when his followers were gathered in the cenacle, Christ Jesus returned to bestow peace upon them. He brought them the comfort of the Holy Spirit and they witnessed the nascent forces, the creative power, of his resurrected body of light.

Forty days passed in His presence and He taught them sacred things. When they listened to his teachings they imagined themselves in those far off places they had frequented with Him. Sometimes they saw themselves in a boat floating on the glittering Sea of Galilee with the sun shimmering in their eyes and their ears resounding with his words:

'Become fishers of men!'

But the vision of Christ Jesus walking and talking among them began to fade. He seemed to be ascending to a place beyond their ken and they began to fear they would never again see Him. Finally, they lost sight of him. Only Lazarus-John, Magdalena, and the Mother of God could sense how he hovered over them in blessing.

Full with despair, Jacob, stepbrother of Jesus, knelt in prayer from dawn to dusk. So intensely did he beseech with his questing heart to know the One whom he had not recognised until the very end, that Christ Jesus appeared to him in the fullness of his glory.

He said to him, 'Remember the bread and the wine, my brother? You who did not eat and drink of it must do so now in memory of me. I entrust this sacrament to your care – remember, where two or three are gathered in my name, I will be in the midst of them.'

‡

'And so it was, *pairé,* that in that cenacle, Jacob celebrated the first sacrament with the disciples, and it affected him so deeply that in lives to come he would find the strength to suffer martyrdom time and time again to protect Jerusalem – that sacred place where he had celebrated the sacrament.'

'So is this is why Crusaders go to the east and feel so much kinship with Jerusalem, Lea?' I asked.

'Yes, for every Crusader senses in the depths of his soul that in the soil and air and water of Jerusalem there remains a memory of Christ Jesus, and for this reason to them it is the centre of the world.'

All things were making sense.

'And the Pentecost?' I asked.

'Well, *pairé,* as you know, on the tenth day after the Lord's ascension His disciples were assembled again at the cenacle to observe the ancient festival of Pentecost. The celebrations had lasted all night and it was near sunrise when a wind entered the city. This was that ancient wind called Ruach and it moved again over the colossal bridge, sweeping through archways and forcing its way through the streets until it made a rise to the upper room where they were gathered.

'*Ruach, Elohim, Aur*! Breath, Elohim, Light!

'This is the Holy Spirit!' I said.

'Yes, *pairé,* and the disciples had heard the roar of it before, on the night of their Lord's sacrifice. Now it entered the room and swept over the mother of the Lord and she became a pillar of fire before their eyes; a fire whose cool flames swathed them in good will.

'Yes Lea! This is like our *consolamentum,* this is the consoler!'

'It came through the mother because it was her task to unite even those who were not kin by blood … this is the community of the future, *pairé,* which Christ Jesus had said Peter would lead.'

'I remember now! How the water had tasted of wine at the marriage of Cana where the husband and wife were not kin! I remember now what He said about the fish swimming together as one!'

'You remember well, *pairé,* but do you know what it means? It means, that it does not matter what blood a man possesses, what nation or race he belongs to, if his soul has married the spirit then he can unite with others who have done the same.'

I took a moment to understand it. 'Why does the church of Peter not recognise this spirit of the Pentecost, then? Why do they persecute us? Is it because we have a reckoning of it?'

'Because they fear it, *pairé.*'

'Why do they fear it?'

'Because if all men believed they could come close to God without a priest or a church they would fall into error.'

'Perhaps this is the same reason the church of Rome does not allow the translation of the bible into the vernacular; why only priests can own a bible without incurring punishment?'

'But listen now, *pairé,*' she continued, 'for I will tell how a mighty awakening was experienced by the disciples after Pentecost, and they realised how they had been like sleep walkers for three years. Looking back, they now understood they had never seen clearly what had lived in Jesus. They had only glimpses.

'Christ, the resurrected one,' they said to themselves, 'was with us in Jesus. He took us into his kingdom without our knowing it; we wandered with Him and He revealed to us His secrets! Only now, after the Pentecost, are we awake to what we experienced in a dream!'

And so it was that the disciples went out into the world to proclaim the *good news* to those who would hear it.

They were not welcomed by Rome or by Israel and many of them suffered horrible martyrdom, and yet knowledge of Christ Jesus survived despite Roman and rabbinic hate. It survived because of their suffering, which engendered love.'

'And what of the women?'

'They lived on. Some of them grew old and died far from Jerusalem. But they all returned, whether in body or in spirit, to be at the side of the mother of their Lord and to see her taken by the spirit of Mary to the bosom of the great mother in the heavens.'

'Oh my, Lea! This is a beautiful picture!'

'Yes, that is how each, in their own way, drank from their master's cup and surrendered their lives for the One who had always been worshipped by men and had been called by different names; the God who lived and died like a man – Christ Jesus.

Lea fell quiet. Her words were spent.

I went to the window to watch the sun throw its gold mantle on the world. For a moment the entire Gospel stood before my eyes in the awakening clouds that were spread over the skies above the valleys and mountains, rivers and streams of the world.

'Yes … it is magnificent!' I said.

She pointed to the dawn and she seemed to grow tall, white and fair before my eyes. I trembled, for her voice was grave, 'Look there! Do you see a world full of wonders and marvels?

I looked and I saw a twilight land of strange buildings and contraptions.

'That is the future. Do you see, *pairé*, how there are castles that fly, carriages that go at great speeds without horses and torches that have no flame? In this future, *pairé*, the thoughts of men will travel like lightning from one end of the earth to the other and a man will be able to hold all the books in the world in the palm of one hand.'

'All the books in the world!' I smiled to think on it. 'This is truly remarkable!'

'Yes, but every light casts a shadow.' She looked at me, cold and solemn. 'The greater the light of goodness, the darker the shadow of evil. Wars will continue again and again and lead to dark times. In the past men fought over their misunderstandings of Jesus and Christ, now they battle because they no longer understand the Spirit, but in the future the battle will be for the human Soul itself. It shall be more heinous and violent than any other battle that has come before! In those far flung days what is written in John's Apocalypse shall come to pass: the woman with the sun in her belly and the moon at her feet shall come to give birth to the spirit of Christ in the clouds; the soul of humanity will give birth to the spirit and the dragon will try to kill it as soon as it is born in the same way that Herod tried to kill Yeshua. That is when this gospel shall be needed, *pairé*; before the end of the fifth age.'

I was breathless, caught in the swirl of images, which she had shown in the sky before my eyes. Fear and dread entered into my heart and a sudden thought came. 'Soon I will descend this pog, Lea, and what you have had me write down on those parchments,' I pointed to them, 'will turn to dust. It has all been for nothing! No man will know the Fifth Gospel!'

'There is no accident in the universe pairé, nothing is ever lost. What you have written will come to you again, though differently, and you will remember.'

'What must I remember?'

'Look at me, pairé, what do you see?'

Before my open gaze her face seemed to change: one moment I saw the evening star, the next she was Demeter the mother of nature, again she was Solomon's bride and after that the lady who steals into the heart of every troubadour, the ideal woman, the good and beautiful and true in the soul of every poet. When her face paused in its transformations I realised with a sense of wonder and awe that I was gazing at a countenance that I had only seen in my imaginations; it was the face of Mary, the Galilean mother of Jesus. I realised that I had been in the company of wisdom all along, night after night! As I suspected, she was the rose which by another name was Evangelea, the angel that carries the Fifth Gospel into the souls of men to make them evangelists, and she was directing my gaze not to the future this time but to the past again. When I looked back I saw a hillock overhung by dark clouds on which stood three crosses. There was a man standing beneath them holding a spear in his hands and staring at me. In that fragment of a moment the two places were woven into the same space in life's evolving stream and our souls could look upon one another, knowing the other as himself. Ah!

It was only an instant, but to me it was an eternity of gazing with wonder and awe at all that would pass in between: sorrows and battles, births and deaths, lifetimes. Just as she had said.

After that Lea lifted a further veil to show me other things, things that had passed and things that would come to pass, things I am not permitted to tell; suffice to say that I understood now how this very moment was the culmination of what had begun long ago on that hillock called Golgotha, and that many who were here at Montsegur had been with me before.

And so it was that when I had looked into myself, I had found Lea, and now, miraculously in Lea, I had found myself.

CHAPTER 77

THE BEE AND I

I am not a troubadour and yet I sing. I am a bishop and yet I do not belong to any church. I have come to what I know by way of ignorance and what I possess is mine because I am dispossessed. I am only here because I have sacrificed all certainty and yet, that is how I am certain that the end of my song is only a beginning.

It has taken me long to descend this pog and all the while you have listened to my song. I think you and I have always known how it would end, haven't we? I am not sad for it and neither should you be. I must atone for all the lives which I have taken and all the mistakes that I have made. Those that have suffered at my hand are now waiting to pronounce judgement on me on that field below; this is the Wisdom of God and I bow down to it in freedom and choose to love even those whose task it is to carry it out.

And yet all is not lost. I look now to the summit of Bidorta like that centurion who long ago sat upon a horse waiting for the sun to creep over the rim rock of the mountains. This dawn, however, I am not looking for Mithras, I am looking for the sign that our treasure is safe, for only then can we go to our deaths in peace. My eyes are fixed to that summit as I walk into the palisades built to contain us on this field, a field which one day you will know as *The Field of Fires*. Holding the hand of the Marquésia de Lantar on one side and the hand of Saissa de Congost on the other I step onto the logs constructed into one great pyre and I think of Guilhabert.

Poor Guilhabert had seen the future those moments before he died. He had seen where his promise might lead and had been desperate for my forgiveness. How strange and yet how natural it is to know that he was once that stubborn woman, Claudia Procula! In Guilhabert her independence had been transformed into service, her love into his joy, her devotion into his understanding. The woman I revered in one life became my dearest friend in the next, and so it will go on, from life to life.

But the soldiers of France are setting fire to the straw and the fagots that have been dipped in pitch. The air is damp and the smoke rises black at the perimeter and we, two hundred men and women, all Friends of God, huddle in the middle, watching the plumes stain the air around us. The black friars, the inquisitors and the Clergy move away, singing their songs and so they do not see what I see.

There is the sign! High above on the snowy summit of Bidorta a light is kindled, a blaze of yellow fire as bright as the sun illuminates the dawn and causes us all to smile! I am full of peace, for the child is safe! You see, amongst those many things that Lea showed me was the identity of the charge of the Marquésia de Lantar. That beautiful boy who is Lazarus-John born again. *He* is our greatest treasure, a child destined to be the founder of a great school of knowledge whose members will be called Rosicrucians, those who can add the living wisdom of the rose to the cross of death, for Lazarus John was baptised with fire by Christ Himself. Perhaps in those far off times I shall meet him again? Perhaps I shall be one of his followers?

Matteu will also safeguard books of John and those writings I have called The Fifth Gospel which are interpolated among them. Yes, before he left I gave them to him. So for now they are safe! Lea showed me how in future times Matteu will return to find these treasures again as a young Grail historian, a German. He will save them from the grasp of unworthy souls.

But the bee's buzzing takes me from my ruminations. It circles over my head one last time before flying upwards to that saffron dawn. And as the flames rise higher and come nearer and the heat begins to prick my skin – in that moment before the pain consumes me and my own screams fill my ears – I imagine that I follow the bee out of this momentary terror and waste. I imagine that I float over the Fields of Fires a moment before flying away with her to a rose hedge to wait for the future.

In that far off time the sun will continue to rise in the east and to set in the west, Raphael and Leonardo da Vinci will have come and gone, thoughts will travel from one end of the earth to the other in the blink of an eye and a man will be able to hold all the books in the world in the palm of one hand. And if you are holding *this* book in your hand, then perhaps it is because The Fifth Gospel has not been forgotten?

Only you can know this with certainty, my friend, for although it is true that no accident rules the universe, it is also true that the heart of a man has a will and something of his future must remain a mystery, even to God.

ACKNOWLEDGMENTS

Over the centuries many have foretold the coming of a new Gospel. In the twelfth century Joachim of Fiora spoke of an Immortal Gospel. Novalis, the great poet also presaged it. In Revelations, St John speaks of an Everlasting Gospel, a fifth gospel that would be given to humanity by an angel at a time of great tribulation.

Just before the First World War, the Austrian philosopher and Spiritual Scientist Rudolf Steiner gave the world The Fifth Gospel. But before doing so he had to make appropriate preparations. In 1911 Rudolf Steiner touched on a very controversial subject – the mystery of the two Jesus Children. In a series of lectures he answered age old questions concerning the differences in the canonical gospel accounts of the birth of Jesus, particularly the differences found in Matthew and Luke.

It is hard to imagine today the impact of such lectures on the minds of the people of those times, particularly because the mystery involved two Children. The first child, whom I call Yeshua, was born at the time of Herod the Great and the other child, whom I call Jesus, was born around two years later at the time of Quirenius and the Census. According to the Matthew Gospel, Magi visited the first child. Conversely, in Luke's account, Shepherds visited the second child. Rudolf Steiner resolves these discrepancies by explaining how both children were destined to unite as one to become the man known as Jesus of Nazareth.

It was not until later, in October 1913, that Rudolf Steiner gave his lectures on The Fifth Gospel, a gospel that can only be read in the Akasha. In these lectures he illuminates for the first time those 'missing' years in the life of Jesus of Nazareth between his 18th year and his 30th year, and his ultimate unification with Christ. I would highly recommend a reading of his lectures if you would like to continue exploring the many mysteries found in this novel.

As you can see, I could not have written this book without Rudolf Steiner. But I also owe a great debt to Alfred Edersheim, a biblical scholar and converted Rabbi who combined his knowledge of both Judaism and Christianity in *The Life and times of Jesus the Messiah,* printed in 1883. These volumes were a godsend! They were a rich resource of detailed information not only on the history of those times but also on the intricate economic, religious and cultural details of day-to-day life. Edersheim gave me the tools I needed to carve out an authentic milieu replete with smells, colours and sounds.

I must also acknowledge those who are nearest and dearest to me. I would not have written this book if not for my mother's encouragement, as it seemed to be such a daunting task. She listened to endless readings of my work and gave me many valuable suggestions, and I am forever indebted to her. I would also like to thank my husband Jim, who gave me practical and moral support and read countless drafts, helping me to sensitively edit a very long book (yes, longer!) and to cut it down in size without losing its essence. I am always truly grateful for his pragmatic and systematic approach to difficult problems. I am grateful to Simone Selby for providing valuable input from a Judaic perspective and to Jennefer Zacarias and Brigitta Gallaher, who gave the book their attention and support. Lastly, thanks must also go to Danica Wolkiser and Richard Distasi, for their help with editing.

When Rudolf Steiner gave his lectures on the Fifth Gospel he said that, 'some time in the future it will be put into definite form'. This novel is one attempt; no doubt there will be others. For my part, I have endeavoured to breathe life into the more important elements found in Rudolf Steiner's Fifth Gospel and his lectures on the other four gospels, as far as this is possible within the framework of a single novel.

As this is a work of fiction, I have used artistic license to paint a vast picture with broad strokes, adding texture and context by interpolating into the main narrative a time in history when humanity's struggle to understand the manifold and complex mystery of Christ Jesus resulted in intolerance, persecution, suffering and war.

Palestine in 33 AD was not so different from France in 1244.

Today the struggle continues ... will it ever end? Perhaps not, but in struggle there is suffering and in suffering compassion, and in compassion true brotherhood.

ALSO BY ADRIANA KOULIAS

Book 1 TEMPLE OF THE GRAIL

Book 2 THE SEAL

Book 3 THE SIXTH KEY

Links to books

Printed in Great Britain
by Amazon